NEW YORK TIMES BESTSELLING AUTHOR

NICHOLAS SANSBURY SMITH

GREAT WAVE INK
PUBLISHING

Books by New York Times Bestselling Author
Nicholas Sansbury Smith

The Sons of War Series
(Offered by Blackstone Publishing)

Sons of War
Sons of War 2: Saints (Coming Fall 2020)
Sons of War 3: Sinners (Coming early 2021)

The Hell Divers Series
(Offered by Blackstone Publishing)

Hell Divers
Hell Divers II: Ghosts
Hell Divers III: Deliverance
Hell Divers IV: Wolves
Hell Divers V: Captives
Hell Divers VI: Allegiance
Hell Divers VII: Warriors

The Extinction Cycle (Season One)
(Offered by Orbit Books)

Extinction Horizon
Extinction Edge
Extinction Age
Extinction Evolution
Extinction End
Extinction Aftermath
Extinction Lost (A Team Ghost short story)
Extinction War

The Extinction Cycle: Dark Age
(Season Two)

Extinction Shadow
Extinction Inferno
Extinction Ashes
Extinction Darkness

The Trackers Series

Trackers
Trackers 2: The Hunted
Trackers 3: The Storm
Trackers 4: The Damned

The Orbs Series

Solar Storms (An Orbs Prequel)
White Sands (An Orbs Prequel)
Red Sands (An Orbs Prequel)
Orbs
Orbs II: Stranded
Orbs III: Redemption
Orbs IV: Exodus

NicholasSansburySmith.com

For my twin brother Zachary Angaran Smith.
Thank you for all that you do for at-risk youth.
We need more men like you in this world.

"Hell is empty and all the devils are here."

—William Shakespeare

Note from the Author

Dear Reader,

In Spring of 2020 I updated this section to reflect the current international medical crisis. As you all know, we are in the middle of a pandemic with extreme damage being done to the global economy. Trade has come to almost a standstill and the major gears of the supply chain have ground to a halt. We have an overwhelmed medical industry focused on COVID-19 and a shortage of personal protective equipment (PPE). The meat and poultry industry has been hit hard, slowing production, and resulting in shortages. Over thirty million people have filed for unemployment in the United States.

And that isn't even the full picture of just how much has changed in the past five months. An EMP attack now could cripple the United States to the point of no return.

If this attack were to occur, I believe North Korea is the country that would be the most likely to carry it out. Despite international efforts to stop them, they are still advancing their nuclear weapons and ballistic missile programs in defiance of the United Nations Security Council resolutions and sanctions.

At the end of April 2020, there was another twist to this explosive situation, with reports coming out of the Korean peninsula and Japan that North Korean leader Kim Jung Un was either dead or in a vegetative state. If this is true, it adds a new element to the fragile international conflict.

Whoever replaces Kim Jung Un could be worse, furthering the risk of war. On the contrary, they could help bring unification to the peninsula. I've updated this note again in May to reflect reports of Kim Jung Un being spotted in public. Some analysts are saying it's a body double, others say it is indeed the leader. Only time will tell if he is still alive, but either way, the situation remains a powder keg.

And that is exactly what this story is about.

Before you dive in, I've included some background on how this story came to be. In 2016 I was finishing up book five of the Extinction Cycle, and at that time, I thought Extinction End would be the "end" of the series. I decided to write a new type of story—a story without monsters, zombies, or aliens—about a different type of threat.

Rewind ten years. I'm a planner with the State of Iowa sitting in a meeting with other agencies and utility companies talking about solar flares and a weapon called an electromagnetic pulse (EMP). It was there that I realized just how devastating an EMP could be to the United States if it were strategically detonated in the atmosphere. The longer I heard about the effects, the more I started to wonder—why would our enemies poison our soil and destroy our cities with nuclear weapons or waste their troops in a battle they probably couldn't win, when all they had to do is turn off our power and sit back and watch the chaos and death that would ensue?

During this meeting with other agencies, I was shocked to learn there wasn't much being done to harden our utilities and critical facilities to protect against such a threat.

A few years later, I started working for Iowa Homeland Security and Emergency Management. I had several duties as a disaster mitigation project officer, but my primary focus was on protecting infrastructure and working on the state hazard mitigation plan. Near the end of my time at HSEMD, I was also assigned the duty of overseeing the hardening of power lines in rural communities.

After several years of working in the disaster mitigation field, I learned of countless threats from natural disasters to manmade weapons, but the EMP, in my opinion, was still the greatest of them all.

That brings us to today. We're living in tumultuous times, and our enemies are constantly looking for ways to harm us, both domestically and abroad. We already know that cyber security is a major concern for the United States. North Korea, China, and Russia have all been caught tampering with our elections and our systems. We also know other countries are experimenting with cyber technology that can shut down portions of our grid. But imagine a weapon that could shut down our entire grid. The perfectly strategized EMP attack gives our enemies an opportunity to do just that. And that is the premise of the Trackers series.

Before you start reading, I would like to take time to thank everyone who helped make this book a reality. Many people had a hand in the creation of this story. I'm grateful for all their help, criticism, and time. I'd like to start with the people that I wrote this book for—the readers. You are the reason I always try to write something fresh, and the reason I strive to always make each story better than—and different from—its predecessors.

Secondly, I'd like to thank the Estes Park Police Department.

In the spring of 2016, my wife and I spent a few weeks in Estes Park, Colorado, a place I had visited many times growing up. I wanted to show her this gorgeous tourist town that borders Rocky Mountain National Park, and I decided it would also make a good setting for some of the scenes in Trackers.

The police department very graciously allowed me to tour their facilities and ride along with Officer Corey Richards. Department officers and staff explained police procedure for tracking lost people, and their operations and response to natural disasters. Captain Eric Rose, who is in charge of the Emergency Operations Center, described what they went through in the flood of 2013, when Estes Park was quite literally cut off from surrounding communities.

I've spent time with many law enforcement departments over my career in government, and I can tell you Estes Park has one of the finest and most professional staffs I've ever had the pleasure of meeting. Thank you to every officer for serving Estes Park and assisting with Trackers. I hope you find I did your community justice.

I'd also like to thank my literary agent, David Fugate, who has provided valuable feedback on each of my novels. The version you are reading today is much different than the manuscript I submitted, partly because of David's excellent feedback.

I also had a great group of beta readers that helped bring this story to life. You all know who you are. Thanks again for your assistance.

Trackers is more than just a post-apocalyptic thriller about the aftermath of an attack on American soil. It's meant to be a mystery as much as it is a thriller. There are a lot of EMP stories out there, but I wanted to write one that included new themes and incorporated elements of Cherokee and Sioux folk stories. I spent years researching and reading Native American history at the University of Iowa where I received a certificate in American Indian studies.

This story, like many works of fiction, will require some suspension of belief, but hopefully not as much as my other science fiction stories. Any errors in this book rest solely with me, as the author is always the gatekeeper of the work.

In an interview several years ago, I was asked why I write. My response was that while my stories are meant to entertain, they are also meant to be a warning. Trackers could be a true story, and I hope our government continues to prepare and protect us from such a threat.

Captain Eric Rose of the Estes Park Police Department told me that he wasn't sure he was ready for a post-apocalyptic Estes Park. I'm not either. Let's all hope this story remains fiction.

With that said, I hope you enjoy the read, and as always, feel free to reach out to me on social media if you have questions or comments.

Best wishes,
Nicholas Sansbury Smith

Foreword

Dr. Arthur Bradley

Author of

Disaster Preparedness for EMP Attacks and Solar Storms
and The Survivalist.

When used conventionally, a nuclear warhead could destroy a city and cover the surrounding region in deadly radiation. Horrible to be sure, but at least it would be localized. When detonated in the atmosphere at the right altitude, however, that same warhead could generate an electromagnetic pulse (EMP) that would cause almost unimaginable harm to our nation.

The most significant effect of such an attack would be damage to the nation's electrical grid. Due to the interdependency of systems, the loss of electricity would result in a cascade of failures promulgating through every major infrastructure, including telecommunications, financial, petroleum and natural gas, transportation, food, water, emergency services, space operations, and government. Businesses, including banks, grocery stores, restaurants, and gas stations, would all close. Critical services such as the distribution of water, fuel, and food would fail. Emergency services, including hospitals, police, and fire departments, would perhaps remain operable a little longer using generators and backup systems, but they too would collapse due to limited fuel distribution, as well as the loss of key personnel abandoning their posts.

In addition to the collapse of national infrastructures, an EMP could cause widespread damage to transportation systems, such as aircraft, automobiles, trucks, and boats, as well as supervisory control and data acquisition hardware used in telecommunications, fuel processing, and water purification systems. Such an attack could also damage in-space satellites and significantly hamper the government's ability to provide a unified emergency response or even maintain civil order. Finally, many personal electronics could also be damaged, including our beloved computers and cell phones, as well as important health monitoring devices.

With the collapse of infrastructures, loss of commerce, and widespread damage to property, an EMP attack would introduce terrible financial ruin on the nation. Consider that it is estimated that even a modest 1-2 megaton warhead detonated over the Eastern Seaboard could cause in excess of a trillion ($1,000,000,000,000) dollars in damage.

Testing done in the 1960s, such as Starfish Prime and the Soviet's Test 184, provided some idea of the potential damage, but weapons have become even more powerful and our world more technologically susceptible. No one really knows with certainty the extent of the damage that would be felt, but expert predictions range from catastrophic to apocalyptic. What is universally agreed upon is that the EMP attack allows for an almost unimaginable amount of damage to be done with nothing more than a single nuclear warhead and a missile capable of deploying it to the right altitude. Given that there are more than 128,000 such warheads and 10,000 such missiles in existence, it seems prudent to better understand and prepare for this very real and present danger.

What many do not know is that the U.S. has been

openly threatened with an EMP strike by Russia, Iran, and North Korea. Leaderships of these countries have come to appreciate the truly asymmetric nature of such an attack. Consider that an EMP strike would be largely independent of weather, result in long-lasting infrastructure damage, and inflict a damage-to-cost ratio far greater than any conventional weapon, including a nuclear "dirty bomb." Worse yet is that our enemies would not limit themselves to a single EMP strike. Rather, they would detonate several warheads, carefully timed and positioned across the nation to achieve maximum damage.

Author Nicholas Sansbury Smith understands how an attack could cripple the United States. I first spoke with him when he was working for Iowa Homeland Security and Emergency Management in the disaster preparedness field. He reached out when he was writing a science fiction story about solar storms with some questions about my book, Disaster Preparedness for EMP Attacks and Solar Storms. Since then, Nicholas has also spent a great deal of time researching EMPs.

Trackers is a work of fiction, but many of the places in the story are real. Utilizing his background in emergency management and disaster mitigation, Nicholas has done an excellent job of describing a realistic geopolitical crisis that sets the stage for an EMP attack. The following story is a terrifying scenario in which brave men and women must adapt to a challenging new world—a world that we could see ourselves being thrust into. Part of me wishes Nicholas had continued writing purely science fiction stories about aliens and government designed bio-weapons because Trackers is a novel that could become non-fiction.

— 1 —

Sam "Raven" Spears watched the refugees in Bond Park huddle around the fire. A cold rain fell from the sky, threatening the flames, but it was still better than snow.

He put a hand on his head, as if that would help the migraine. His shredded ear pulsated with pain, and his entire body felt like someone had taken a hammer to it. He remembered the old Marine Corps saying about pain being weakness leaving your body.

Yeah, that's bullshit.

Pain was one of the rawest feelings a human could experience—the body's way of ordering someone to stop doing stupid things that could kill them. Raven had never been great at following orders.

But he was still alive, and so was his family.

Now he had to figure out how to keep it that way.

He walked over to Bond Park, searching the crowd for Detective Lindsey Plymouth. Only two days had passed since Chief Colton had been taken hostage, which left them only one more day to deliver their prisoner, Jason Cole, and the first supply drop to Highway 34.

Time was running out, and he needed to find Lindsey to go over their plan. A voice stopped him halfway across the street.

"Sam, we got a situation at the roadblock on 34."

Raven turned to see the police dispatcher, Margaret, holding the door to town hall open. He jogged over to her.

"What kind of situation?"

Lindsey came running around the corner of the station. Dressed in a coat and stocking cap, with her duty belt around her waist and a Bushmaster AR-15 slung over her back, she looked ready for a battle.

"We're about to have company," she said.

"I'll get the horses," Raven said when he saw the look on her face.

A flare shot up from the Crow's Nest. He followed it into the sky.

"No time. We need to take the Volkswagen," Lindsey said. "I've already grabbed you a rifle."

Raven bolted toward the parking lot around the side of the building, where the Volkswagen Beetle was already loaded with gear and weapons. He grabbed the AR-15 in the passenger seat and palmed a magazine into the gun. It wasn't his crossbow, but times had changed. He needed bullets to deal with the enemies closing in on all sides.

The small car tore out of the parking lot, tires squealing. The streets were mostly empty on the way out to Highway 34, aside from several kids riding bicycles on the side of the road. They stopped to wave at the car, but Raven didn't return the gesture. Every parent here knew the threats outside the town. It blew his mind that they would let their teenaged kids out.

Raven rolled down his window and yelled, "Go home!" Then he chambered a round and looked over at Lindsey.

"You got any idea what's going on?"

She shook her head. "All I know is that Dale Jackson

reported a vehicle stopped near the turn-off for Storm Mountain."

"Shit," Raven muttered.

They sped down the open road, the old bug purring like a cat with a smoking habit. The chassis rattled at the high speed.

"You get any sleep last night?" Raven asked, making a stab at small talk.

She shook her head. "Did you?"

Raven shrugged. "I've been trying to keep Creek comfortable, but his eye is really bothering him. Damn cone around his head isn't helping either."

"I'm sorry," Lindsey said quietly.

They were both still rattled from the attack on Storm Mountain. Don Aragon and Officer Hines had paid the price for their betrayal. Their bodies were still rotting in the woods, but that didn't make Raven feel any better. If a man like Officer Hines could try to kill Lindsey, then the world was in major trouble.

Raven clutched his rifle, gritting his teeth, and prepared for another fight.

They rounded another corner and the roadblock came into view. Dale Jackson and three other men had their rifles shouldered at a pickup truck that had stopped about a quarter mile from the barriers. Raven could vaguely make out two men sitting in the cab and a third in the bed.

"Looks like we got some observers," he said.

Lindsey parked the car behind the concrete barriers and killed the engine. Raven opened the door and kept low on his way to the two trucks backed against one another on the bridge over the Big Thompson River.

"What you got?" Raven asked Dale.

Dale kept his gaze on the truck. "Three males. All heavily armed. Said they wanted to talk to someone in charge."

"That's me," Lindsey said. "I'll see what they want. Watch my six."

"Hold up," Raven said, grabbing her arm. "Could be a trap."

He let go of her sleeve and did a quick scan of the spindly trees framing the gorge, dividing the area horizontally into thirds and scanning the canvas from left to right, right to left. Nothing stirred in the hills to either side of the road, but that didn't mean there wasn't a sniper out there.

"I'll go," Raven said.

"No way." Lindsey started to move again, but Raven grabbed her by the arm a second time. She whirled around and glared at him.

"Let *go*," she growled.

Dale raised a brow. "You two gonna dance, or you gonna go talk to those guys?"

"Fine," Raven replied as Lindsey squeezed between the barrier.

"She means business," Dale said. "Better not to argue with her, man."

"No shit." Raven kept one eye on her as she made her way down the street.

"Detective Lindsey Plymouth with the Estes Park Police Department," she shouted. "Identify yourselves."

The two doors on the pickup opened, disgorging men dressed in military fatigues and wearing ski masks. The guy in the pickup bed unslung his rifle and pointed it at her. Raven lined up his sights on the center of the man's Colorado Rockies hat.

"Try it, you piece of shit, and I'll give you a third eye," Raven grumbled.

Dale glanced over, but then turned back to his own scope.

The driver of the pickup strode toward Lindsey, carrying a duffel bag in one hand. He stopped about twenty feet from her and threw the bag at her feet.

"Sheriff Thompson has a message for you about his request," he said.

"We have another day to fulfill his request," Lindsey said.

"Right," the man said with a shrug. He walked back to the truck while his buddies covered him with their rifles.

Raven kept his crosshairs centered on the man in the bed, his finger on the trigger, ready to squeeze off a shot.

"What the hell do you think is in the bag?" Dale whispered.

"Not sure I want to know." Raven's gaze flitted to Lindsey. When she picked up the bag, it left a trail of red behind on the road.

Raven cursed. Thompson had threatened to send Colton back in pieces if they didn't comply with his demands. Lindsey hurried back to the roadblock with the bag. The driver and passenger got back into the pickup truck and slowly turned around. The muffler fired like a gunshot, making Lindsey hit the ground as the truck peeled away.

The man in the bed hollered, "See you soon, bitch!"

Raven hopped over the barricade and ran to her. Lindsey remained on her knees, looking down at pavement. The contents of the bag had rolled out when she dropped. A severed head lay face down in a puddle of water.

Dale and the other men made their way over. "Is it Colton?" one of them asked.

Lindsey slowly reached toward the head, but Raven placed his hand on her shoulder before she could turn it over.

"Let me," he said, helping her to her feet.

The volunteer deputies and Lindsey all watched as Raven took a knee, held in a breath, and slowly turned the head over.

Cold brown eyes looked up at Raven.

He let out a breath. It wasn't Colton after all.

Raven plucked a note from the man's mouth. Standing, he smoothed out the paper and read it aloud.

"See you tomorrow with the first drop and my man, or Colton's next."

***

Police Chief Marcus Colton took a drink of the watered-down soup. He wasn't all that hungry, especially after seeing Clint Bailey dragged out of his cell at sunrise. The screams had continued into the morning, and ended in a guttural choking.

He knew he would never see the farmer again. And if he didn't find a way out of here, he would suffer the same fate. But Clint had been his best hope of escape, and even if Colton did manage to find a way out, there was nowhere to run.

He looked out the barred windows as the sun went down over the hills. Snowflakes fluttered past the glass. Several men armed with rifles and shotguns patrolled the walkway around the compound. Sheriff Thompson was using this place as a hub to terrorize the surrounding communities. According to the chatter Colton had overheard, Estes Park was the next stage of his expanding operation.

A Jeep pulled up outside the building, and Colton clenched his jaw when he saw it was Raven's. They had taken the vehicle, his gear, his guns. And soon, he feared, they would take his life.

He stalked away from the window and turned back to the cell door. Being on the wrong side of the bars in this place made for one of the worst moments in his life. The combination of fear and loneliness threatened to send him over the edge. Sitting in the darkness, having no way of knowing what time it was, how his family was doing, or if he would ever see them again, brought him to the dark edge of post traumatic stress.

You have to be strong. You can't give up.

Colton finished the bowl of soup, downed the glass of warm water, and moved back to the bench. The food and water was a good sign, he decided. They wouldn't waste resources on someone they wanted to kill.

Now that he had nutrition, he needed rest. Several minutes after settling into his bunk and closing his eyes, the door at the entrance to the jail clanked open and footfalls clicked on the concrete.

Colton sat up, alert and ready. He balled his hands into fists, just like before a boxing match, prepared to fight if he had to defend himself.

The light from several candles warmed the hallway. Next came the glow of a torch. Three men walked in front of his cell door and stopped. In the glow of the flames, he saw the rough face of Sheriff Mike Thompson.

"Marcus, good to see you," Thompson said, like Colton was an old friend. His eyes flitted to Colton's fists.

"Now that's no way to greet me, is it?"

Colton ignored him and scanned the two goons alongside Thompson. They were both carrying rifles, and had machetes sheathed on their duty belts.

"What did you do with Clint?" Colton asked.

A crooked smile from Thompson. "Didn't you hear?"

Colton tried not to react, but he wanted to throw a punch so badly he had to count to ten in his mind to calm his rage.

Thompson stepped up to the barred door and squinted at him. "Clint told me you two were planning to escape. Is that true?"

Colton kept his lips sealed.

Thompson slammed the bars in front of Colton's face with the speed of a boxer. When Colton didn't so much as flinch, Thompson smiled again.

"I'm going to give you the benefit of the doubt, Marcus. I'm going to assume Clint was lying about your little escape plan."

"I say we kill 'em," said the man on the left, in a Russian accent.

Thompson frowned and looked over at the man. "Ivan, we can't kill everyone, or we lose our leverage. Maybe they didn't teach you that in the motherland." Thompson directed a finger at the cell. "Marcus is leverage."

Colton had noticed several of Thompson's men were Russian. Years ago, Colton had worked several cases involving the Russian Mafia, who had come to Fort Collins for the marijuana business. They brought other drugs. Harder drugs that destroyed families. The mobsters themselves were ruthless, brutal men who murdered their adversaries and dumped the bodies in ditches like trash.

Colton added the Russian mafia to the growing list of threats that included Nazis, organized crimes bosses like Nile Redford, and desperate civilians.

Thompson turned back to Colton. "Your people have one more day to deliver my man, Jason Cole. You better hope they do, Marcus. You better hope they also bring those supplies and don't short me. I really don't like to be shorted."

Colton wanted to tell Thompson to go fuck himself, but he said nothing.

"You're a quiet son of a bitch today," Thompson said. "I figured the great Marcus Colton would have more to say. Maybe that little redheaded detective will be more entertaining."

Colton grabbed the bars and squeezed. "Don't you touch Lindsey, you piece of shit, or I'll stomp your face in!"

Thompson grinned in the torchlight. "Ah," he said. "The dog still can bite. That's good. I got plans for you."

Colton cursed himself for losing his cool.

"Don't worry, I won't hurt her. As long as your people come through." Thompson wagged a finger and added, "But if they don't, I'm going to have some fun with her."

Colton clamped his jaw shut and watched Thompson lead the two men away from the cell. He knew he shouldn't call after them, but the anger was too much to hold back.

"Hey Thompson, why don't we finish this the old-fashioned way? Like men. You and me. One on one in a cage match."

That got Thompson's attention. He halted, and then slowly walked back to look at Colton.

"I heard you're a boxer, but you're nothing more than a washed-up old man now, Marcus. You wouldn't be able to last a minute with me." Thompson laughed, but there was no real humor in his stony expression. "Maybe I'll take you up on that, actually. When I'm done beating your eyes in, I'll piss in your hollow sockets. But not tonight."

Thompson left with his men. Colton took a seat on the bench, his heart stuttering and his breathing labored. He knew his chances of getting out of here alive were slim to none. There was only one man he could count on now to help him get back to Estes Park and his family.

— 2 —

The white corridors of Constellation were quiet. The underwater bunker was usually much more active, but tonight only a few staffers walked through the halls of the underwater facility.

The calm before the storm, thought Secretary of Defense Charlize Montgomery. She had just come out of a meeting with the new vice president, Tom Walter. He and Secretary of Health and Human Services Ellen Price were leading the effort to combat the spread of cholera in the survival centers. Several had already been abandoned due to the outbreak. All across the country, people were dying from diseases that had been mostly eradicated in the twenty-first century. The conditions, both at the FEMA camps and in the cities were terrible.

But there wasn't much they could do.

They were lucky here at Constellation, where they still had access to plenty of food, clean water, and state-of-the-art medicine. She was heading to the medical ward now to visit Albert Randall. Charlize wanted to check in on him before hitting the sack for a few hours. Big Al was fighting for his life. He was in a critical condition from the round he took to the abdomen while rescuing his sister in Charlotte, North Carolina. The doctors were doing everything they could to save him, but internal bleeding and complications from the first surgery had left him in a coma.

Her breath caught in her chest when she considered that they might lose him. She tried not to show how worried she was, but Ty heard it anyway.

"You okay, Mom?" he asked, turning slightly in his wheelchair.

"Yes, sweetie. Everything's okay." It was a lie. She wasn't okay. She'd lost her chief of staff, Clint Johnson. She'd lost her brother. She'd almost lost Ty. And now she was close to losing her trusted bodyguard and closest friend.

After checking to make sure no one was coming down the hallway, she stopped pushing Ty and, kneeling down in front of his chair, wrapped her arms around him. "I just want you to know how much I love you," she said.

Ty's voice was muffled by her tight embrace. "I knew something was wrong."

Charlize struggled to find the words to express what she was feeling. "You can never tell someone you love them too many times," she said at last, letting him go.

"Everything's going to be okay," Ty said.

Charlize smiled, but her heart was breaking. She was supposed to be the one comforting him, not the other way around. "I know. You're such a brave boy."

She stood and returned to the back of the wheelchair. "I got it," he said, taking over.

They continued down the passage, with Ty wheeling himself faster than she could walk.

"So, it sounds like you and Dave are getting along pretty well," she said, trying to keep up. "He's about your age, isn't he?"

An enthusiastic nod from Ty. "He's funny. I'm happy Albert was able to rescue him from the bad people in Charlotte." He slowed down and waited for her. "Mom, are the bad people everywhere now?"

In the past, she'd been careful what she told her son, but he was old enough and had experienced enough to understand now. It was also important that she didn't keep things from him. She wasn't sure how long they would be living down here, and the last thing she wanted was for Ty to grow up sheltered from the real world.

"Yes, sweetie. But there are also good people too, and good will always outweigh the bad," she said. "People like Big Al."

"Yeah," Ty said. "But the bad ones keep getting away. When are you going to find Fenix?"

The question stung. "We will find him," Charlize said. "You have to trust me."

When they got to the medical ward, she placed aside her anger at the man who had killed her brother. This was a place for healing, not thoughts of revenge. The thirty-bed facility was filled to the max, with patients ranging from an injured congressman to Albert's twin sister, Jacqueline.

The empty lobby was outfitted with cream-colored chairs and a rack of magazines. The engineers who designed this place had made it look damn close to the waiting area of a real hospital. Charlize could almost forget they were deep underwater.

"I'll be right back," she said. "Can you stay here for a minute?"

Ty reached over to grab a magazine off the rack. His fingers couldn't quite reach, and Charlize plucked the magazine for him. It was yet another reminder that he was limited by his disability—and limitations would kill most people in the new, brutal world they lived in.

Doctor Parish was typing at her station around the

next corner. She looked up when Charlize approached.

"Ah, Madame Secretary, good evening," Parish said with a tired smile.

The doctor's dark features sagged with fatigue. Chances were she'd been working for over twenty-four hours; that was normal for many people at Constellation lately, including Charlize.

"How is he?" Charlize asked.

"He's made some improvement in the past two hours," Parish said. She gestured for Charlize to follow her. "Come see, I think you will be surprised."

"Can I bring Ty?"

Parish shrugged. "I don't see why not."

Charlize returned to the lobby. "She said we can see Big Al!"

He wheeled after Charlize and Parish down another hallway, past a nurse leaving one of the rooms. The young woman nodded at Charlize and smiled at Ty.

Charlize glimpsed the room where Albert's sister was resting. She was sitting up in bed and staring blankly at the opposite wall. The sight chilled Charlize to the core. The flow of drugs across the Mexican border hadn't stopped after America's lights went out. Things were only going to get even worse.

Parish stopped outside of the fifth door on the right, and opened it to allow Ty and Charlize inside. Albert lay in the hospital bed with a white sheet up to his chest. Charlize hadn't thought it was possible for him to look like anything less than a giant, but the former football player seemed almost fragile. He gritted his teeth as he tried to sit up.

"Easy there, sir," Parish said.

"Good evening, ma'am," Albert said when he saw

Charlize. His voice was strained, but his tone was as polite as ever. He smiled as Ty wheeled into the room. "How are you doing, buddy?"

"I'm good," Ty beamed. "How are you, Big Al?"

Albert managed to shrug a shoulder, which appeared to hurt, judging from his reaction. "I feel like I got shot," he said.

Charlize walked over to his bedside. "How long have you been awake?"

He looked to Parish.

"A little over two hours," she said.

"How's Jacqueline?" Albert asked.

"She's going to be okay," Parish said. "In twenty-four hours, she should have most of that poison out of her system."

Albert relaxed against his pillow. "And Dave?"

"He's my new friend," Ty said. "We're gonna play racecars later."

"He's a good kid." Albert slowly shook his head again. "He saved my life."

Charlize narrowed her gaze at him. This was the first she'd heard about Dave saving anyone's life.

"He told me that he slayed one of the Orcs, but I thought he was kidding," Ty said. "Is it true?"

Albert looked up to Charlize and then back to Ty. "He stabbed a man who would have killed me."

A nurse knocked on the door and opened it. "Sorry to interrupt, but Colonel Raymond is here," the young woman said.

Charlize nodded. "Let him in."

Colonel Mark Raymond moved into the open doorway. "Good to see you're awake, Officer Randall," he said.

15

"Thank you, sir."

Raymond's gaze flitted to Charlize, and she could see he wanted to talk to her alone. After excusing herself, she stepped into the hallway, leaving the door slightly ajar.

"Sorry to bother you, ma'am, but I have an update on the Chinese fleet," he said. "The first ships will be here in the next twenty-four hours, and are landing at twelve different ports on the east coast."

"Good," she said. "Are the ports prepared?"

"Our troops are deployed and ready to accompany the Chinese as soon as they arrive. General Thor just set up our first meeting with General Ken Lin, who will be leading the Chinese recovery efforts. I'm headed to Fort Lauderdale tomorrow to meet with the general and the Chinese delegation."

"Let's hope they can get those supplies and equipment moving," she said. The FEMA administrator seemed up to the task, but there were still a million things that could go wrong. "I'll stop by Command when I'm done here to discuss it in more detail."

"Sounds good, ma'am."

Charlize returned to Albert's bedside. Ty looked up at her, his curious gaze signaling an imminent question.

"Are the Chinese the good people or the bad people?" he asked.

For a second, Charlize wasn't sure how to respond. She still wasn't convinced the Chinese had nothing to do with the initial attack, but there was no doubt they could have done more to stop North Korea from developing their nuclear program over the years. She didn't exactly blame them for the war, but she also didn't trust them.

"We're going to find out soon," she said. What she didn't say was that she would be going with Colonel

Raymond tomorrow to meet with General Lin.

***

Engines roared, mufflers choked, and metal frames rattled over the asphalt as the armada of vehicles moved out. The scent of gasoline and exhaust filled the air. General Dan Fenix loved it. It was American, and he would continue fighting for this great nation until the day he died. Fortunately, he had just found a way to prolong his life.

All he had to do was kill Raven Spears and capture the town of Estes Park, and hand over a shit-ton of guns and gold.

Fenix wasn't going to do it alone. In just under an hour, he was going to meet up with the Sons of Liberty. Sergeant Zach Horton had taken charge of the other divisions, and was on his way, with the rest of their brothers, to the rally point.

But Fenix understood Nile Redford wasn't an idiot. He probably knew the rendezvous could be a setup, which is why he had ordered Fenix to remain in cuffs and have a gun pointed at his head for the meeting.

The Sons of Liberty were the best of the best. Experienced men. Hard men. Many of them with time in the suck. Men with shaved heads and cold hearts. Not wannabee neo-Nazis. Real neo-Nazis. The fucking SS would have been proud to fight with these men.

Sitting next to Fenix was Nile Redford's version of a hard man. Hacker, the guy with the duty belt full of fancy torture devices. The cliché made Fenix want to laugh, but he held it in. He would have plenty of time for laughing later.

"Your men better come through," Hacker said, shooting a glance at Fenix. "And the loot you claim to have better be real, or I'm going to cut your balls off."

"I'm a man of my word," Fenix said.

Hacker shifted his linebacker shoulders back and pulled his duty belt up over his gut. "Yeah, we'll see."

"The rendezvous is just ahead," the driver of the Jeep said. Fenix had heard Hacker call him Jade. A red bandana held back the American Indian man's thick black hair. He looked in the rearview mirror and scowled at Fenix.

Redford's cousin Theo turned from the passenger seat. He wore a black pinstripe suit and cowboy hat. For some reason, both Theo and Redford wanted to look like old-school mobsters, but Fenix just thought they looked silly.

"Your men better be here, and they better be unarmed," Theo said. His eyes flitted to Hacker. "If this Nazi prick makes any sudden moves, you put a round between his eyes, got it?"

"With pleasure, man."

Fenix didn't feel much like grinning anymore. Now he was just mad.

"Maybe I'll take care of him," Theo said, pulling out a shiny .357 Magnum with a long barrel.

Deliberately ignoring the wannabe mobster, Fenix turned to watch the snow-brushed pines pass alongside the road as the small fleet of trucks climbed up a narrow pass. They were somewhere on the western side of the Rocky Mountains, but he didn't know the exact location.

"We're here," Theo said a few minutes later. He pointed at the roofs of several cabins protruding from the trees on the right side of the road.

Hacker opened his door and came around to let Fenix

out of the Jeep. Theo had the barrel of the .357 Magnum pointed at Fenix's face the moment his boots hit the gravel.

"Don't think I won't blow your backward-thinking brains out," Theo said. "I don't care what Nile says. You're nothing but a dumb Nazi prick."

Fenix started walking up the trail, breathing in the crisp cold air. Not exactly the taste of freedom, but it was better than the cell back at Redford's underground gambling compound.

The hunting camp was comprised of five cabins with boarded-up windows, crooked gutters, and rotting decks. It looked like it hadn't gotten any use for a while. He didn't see any sign of his brothers, but he trusted the Sons of Liberty to be here.

"Horton!" Fenix yelled. "You out there?"

Behind him, twenty of Redford's men fanned out with automatic rifles. Jade slipped into the woods, no doubt to search the area for an ambush, his red bandana vanishing among the trees.

"Where is everyone?" Hacker asked.

Theo pulled the hammer back on the revolver. "Call out again," he said. "Horton!" Fenix repeated, his voice echoing through the woods. A bird cried in the distance, and a small animal moved in the foliage.

The door of the second cabin to the right swung open, and a man walked out carrying two duffel bags. Every gun angled at the figure.

"General," the man called in a rough voice.

Fenix grinned. It was Horton. No one else he knew sounded like a sixty-year-old chain smoker at the age of forty-five. "You're a sight for sore eyes, you old bastard," Fenix said.

"Good to see you're well, sir," Horton continued. He walked out of the shade from the pine trees and scanned the men pointing guns at him.

"Put the bags down," Theo said.

"No need for hostility," Horton said, setting the duffel bags down gently and raising his hands. "I'm unarmed, as instructed. I'm just here to talk to General Fenix and deliver the first batch of gold. The weapons are a mile away."

Theo dug the barrel of the .357 Magnum into the back of Fenix's head. "Watch it," Fenix growled.

"All clear out here," Jade called as he returned from the woods. "No sign of an ambush, snipers, or anything else."

"It's just me, like I said," Horton replied.

Well, that's unfortunate, Fenix thought. He had hoped this was an ambush, but maybe Horton had taken his orders over the radio literally.

Theo gestured toward the bags. Hacker grabbed them and began digging through the contents.

"Looks like the half we were promised," Hacker said.

"Excellent," Theo said.

Fenix took a few steps toward his second in command, Theo following him with the gun. Horton lowered his hands and clapped Fenix on the shoulder.

"Watch it," Theo said.

"Easy, man," Horton said. As he brought his hand away from Fenix's shoulder, he dropped something into Fenix's coat pocket.

Maybe Fenix was wrong—maybe Horton did have a plan that didn't end up with him back in the prison cell. He wasn't sure what the hell was in his pocket, and he couldn't look right now.

"As you know, the Sons of Liberty have entered into an agreement with Redford—" Fenix began to say.

"Mr. Nile Redford," Theo corrected.

"Right," Fenix said. He focused on Horton. "Have you finished the recon of Estes Park?"

"Yes, sir. Our men have identified nine roadblocks with at least fifty men and women holding them. Another thirty or so people are armed within the city limits. They've got a surprising amount of firepower, and are well organized."

"So they have a militia…smart. Really smart."

"I'm confident we can take the town. The question is, at what cost?"

"Far as I'm concerned, the more dead Nazis the better," Theo said.

Horton's eyes flitted to the redskin, but Fenix subtly shook his head.

"If you just want us to get this Raven Spears, that's another story," Horton continued.

"That's not the deal," Theo said. "Mr. Redford wants you to secure the supplies the government dropped off there after our first raid. In order to do that, you're going to need to take out their soldiers."

"Should I run this by Mr. Redford?" Hacker asked. Theo hesitated, then nodded. Hacker turned on a radio, static crackling. "Mr. Redford, do you copy? Over."

A few seconds later, the man's voice rang from the speakers. "Go ahead."

"We have the first half of the gold, but Estes Park is much better defended than when we raided them last."

"Let me talk to Fenix," Redford replied.

Hacker walked over and pushed the radio up so Fenix could speak into it.

"I'm here," he said.

"It's your lucky day," Redford said. "I just got word from an old friend that the Sheriff of Fort Collins has claimed Estes Park as part of their expanding territory. For now, tell your men to stand down. Just bring me the gold and weapons."

Horton clenched his jaw, a mannerism that told Fenix he was considering making a move.

Theo pushed the gun back to Fenix's skull. "Back to the Jeep," he said.

"Where are you taking him?" Horton asked.

"None of your business," Theo said.

Horton snorted. "You better watch it, mother—"

"Everyone stay calm," Fenix said. "Sergeant, I'll be in touch."

Horton's eyes shifted from Theo to Fenix. "Yes, sir," he finally said.

Theo snorted. "That's what I fucking thought." He jerked his chin at Fenix. "Let's go, you old dog."

"Some of the refugees spotted men in camouflage on the southern border of town, near the cabins where we put them up," Lindsey said. "I sent out our scouts, but they didn't find anyone."

Raven looked up from the map of the valley. "Men in camo? Could they have been refugees scoping us out?"

She shook her head. "I don't think so. I was told these guys looked like soldiers."

"Not American military. They wouldn't be scoping us out. They'd just walk into town and tell us what they want," Raven said. "Who told you this?"

"Jennie."

"Who?"

"The lady who came in with the last round of refugees. We put her and a bunch of other people up in those old run-down cabins south of Beaver Meadows. She's been watching the area like a hawk."

Raven ran a hand over his five o'clock shadow, trying to make his tired brain work.

"It could be a false alarm, but I think we should shift some of our guns to Highway 7 just in case." Lindsey pointed to the roadblocks on the map.

Raven handed her the red marker. "Take over for me, I need a smoke."

She grabbed the pen and took a seat at the table. Raven left the conference room. The Estes Park police station was jam-packed with militia members and newly deputized officers who had just come off their shift. Most of them were filling out paperwork, but a few eyes flitted toward him as he made his way through the halls.

Chaos had reigned for the first few days after Colton didn't return from Fort Collins, but Lindsey now had the place operating like a well-oiled machine. Everyone had a duty, and a gun. The location of every weapon and every bullet was kept in a ledger that was updated daily. Just like the food and medicine supplies. Everything was accounted for and rationed in Estes Park. It was the only way they were going to last the winter.

Only a few people knew where they had stored the majority of their supplies, and Raven planned on keeping it that way. No one would find it unless there was an internal leak. After what happened with Sergeant Aragon and Officer Hines, he didn't trust anyone except Lindsey. She was running a tightly-managed ship, and Raven was helping her do it.

He just wished Creek was here to help too. The dog was back at the Medical Center, resting and healing. Hopefully, in a few days, his furry best friend would be back on his feet, but for now the dog needed to remain under the watchful eye of his sister.

"Evenin'," Raven said to Margaret on the way out of the building. The dispatcher sat at the front desk, watching the radio like a soldier on nuclear missile duty waiting for the fateful order. She raised a hand in an informal salute.

Raven shouldered the door open and rolled a cigarette. Stepping into the chilly afternoon, he jammed it between his lips and struck a match. He twirled his buck knife while he smoked, an old habit from his days in the Corps.

It kept his hands busy so his mind could work. If the report of people watching the town was true, then there were more enemies encroaching on Estes Park.

Several citizens were walking down Elkhorn Avenue. The once-bright shops selling coffee, t-shirts, pizza, and cookies were all dark. Several of the windows were even boarded up.

"That's pretty neat, mister."

Raven stopped spinning his knife and looked down at a girl standing nearby. A colorful stocking cap was pulled over her braided hair.

"Jeez, kid. You scared me," Raven said. "Shouldn't sneak up on people like that."

She stepped forward, a grin on her face. "Will you teach me to do that?"

Raven lowered the cigarette. He studied her for a second, seeing the determination in her posture—arms folded across her chest, hardened features.

"Smoking's bad for you," he said.

"Not smoke," she clarified. "I mean the thing with your knife."

"Oh, and no." Raven put the knife back into the sheath. "Shouldn't you be at home?"

"I'm here to help." She gave him a stern look. "I'm here to *fight*."

Raven raised a brow. "Where are your parents?"

"Dead." Her words were unemotional. But Raven could tell she was just suppressing the pain. He used to do the same thing when he was her age.

"I'm sorry." Raven remembered her now. She had come in with the last group of refugees.

"So you going to teach me to do that, or what?" she said, still determined.

"The knife is too big for you, sorry. Bet you've never even used one."

A cocky grin cracked her face. She was probably only ten years old, not much older than Allie or Colton's little girl.

"Of course I have. But I want to know how to twirl one like you." She reached out and gestured with her fingers.

Raven smiled, and then took another hit on his cigarette and moved toward the door. "Find me later and maybe I'll teach you, okay?"

"Okay." She pulled her stocking cap down over her eyebrows and took a step forward, clearly trying to follow him inside.

Was this what it was coming down to? Children joining the ranks of the militia. A little over a month had passed since the bombs fell, but it already felt like the past was a whole different world.

Raven swallowed hard. He was one of the last barriers standing between the innocent people of Estes Park— and the wolves that were coming. It was just a matter of time.

"You can't come with me," he said firmly. He took a final drag of his cigarette, and then stomped it under his boot.

The girl remained in the lobby of town hall while he continued to the conference room. Lindsey was drawing circles on the map at the table. Officer Tom Matthew, Detective Tim Ryburn, and ten other members of the militia were gathered around her. They looked in his direction but remained silent.

These were the best Estes Park had to offer, men and women that Raven and Lindsey had personally vetted when gathering the force needed to save their small town. Some were retired soldiers, like Dale Jackson and Todd Sanders. There were also a few cops, including Todd's wife, Susan.

"You ready now, Sam?" Lindsey asked, not even looking up.

"I thought Kirkus and his men were coming," Raven replied. "They here yet?"

"Nope. He's late."

Raven checked his watch. It was easy to lose track of time with the power off, and he saw she was right. Kirkus was half an hour late.

"You know who that girl is with the hat?" he asked.

"What girl?" Lindsey asked, finally looking up.

"The refugee kid with a rainbow stocking cap. Asks a whole bunch of questions."

"Oh, Sarah? She's a firebrand."

"She's also ten years old!" Raven shook his head. "We can't just have kids running around town like that. We could have another hundred Melissa Stones if we don't do a better job protecting our children."

Lindsey let out a sigh. "Raven, I totally agree with you, but I can't exactly keep tabs on everyone. Hell, I can hardly keep tabs on you."

"I'm not ten years old, and that ain't funny."

There were several chuckles from around the room, but Raven shook them off.

"I'll have my sister look after her, then," he said.

Dale Jackson spoke up. "I can put her and some of those other refugee kids to work at my place. Keep 'em out of trouble. Need help with my livestock. They'd be safe there."

Lindsey and Raven exchanged a look. "I'm fine with

it," she said. "Long as you got the time."

Dale shrugged. "Nothin' better to do now that the cable's out. Man, I miss TV."

The door creaked open, and Mayor Gail Andrews stepped inside with Administrator Tom Feagen.

"Detective Plymouth," she said.

Lindsey gave the mayor a tight nod. Tensions had been high since the night Aragon and Hines tried to kill Raven and Lindsey. Now that Colton was gone, Lindsey and the mayor had been at major odds. Still, they needed to work with the elected officials, or they would lose the trust of the town. Raven could live with Gail breathing down his neck, but Feagen was beyond annoying. The guy had lived a sheltered life, and knew nothing about protecting people or infrastructure.

"Kirkus and his men are here," Margaret said from the doorway.

"Let 'em in," Lindsey said.

The sound of boots slapping on tile echoed from the hallway. John Kirkus stepped into the room and took off his fancy white cowboy hat.

"Afternoon," he said politely. Two bulky men followed him inside, both of them dressed in winter coats and jeans. Raven had expected the survivalists to be wearing tactical gear, but maybe they were trying to blend in.

"Welcome, and thanks for coming," Lindsey said. "We have very little time before tomorrow's drop-off, so I'm going to get started right away." She looked to Raven.

"She means I'm going to get started," he said, cracking half a smile to lessen the tension. His stomach growled, but not from hunger. His nerves were tight. He still wasn't used to leading. "I'll start with explaining our updated defenses."

Raven picked up the red marker and pointed at the map. "I've added militia to our roadblocks on Highway 34 and Highway 36. Both are areas we could see an attack if things don't go to plan. Or if Thompson decides to attack us anyways."

Raven looked up to make sure everyone was paying attention. "Knowing what I do about Thompson, my guess is that he will try to sneak into town, which is why I've also assigned extra people to the two roadblocks on Highway 7. We have two people posted at the Crow's Nest at all times as an early warning system. On top of that, patrols will be combing the boundaries of the town constantly."

He placed the marker down and walked around the table to the dry-erase board, which was covered with shift schedules and other non-classified info.

"We currently have over a hundred men and women capable of putting up a fight if it comes down to it. We've spread them out the best we can," Raven continued.

"That's a lot of boots on the ground," Kirkus said. "Impressive."

"It's a start, but it's nowhere near enough to keep us safe on all sides. That's why I recently started a first response team. Think Special Forces or SWAT. The ten men and women in this room are part of that team. We've distributed the few two-way radios we have to them, and they all have access to some sort of a vehicle."

Kirkus stroked his thick white mustache. "We have a similar force. Consists of me, my friend Jack, and my brother, Lane." He jerked his chin at the two men standing next to him.

Raven grinned. "Good to have you here, Jack and

Lane." He had been wary of the survivalists at first, but after they'd helped save Creek, he was ready to go to war with these men.

You might end up doing just that.

"All right, so you're probably all wondering how we're going to deal with Sheriff Thompson tomorrow," Raven said.

The room went dead quiet, and he breathed in through his nose, still wondering if his plan was going to get him chewed out. The last thing he wanted was for these people to lose their trust in him after how hard he'd fought to gain it.

But he had to trust himself, too. *This will work*, Raven thought. *It has to work.*

"We're going to bring them Jason Cole tomorrow, like Thompson wants, and we're going to bring them the first shipment of food and supplies," he said.

"What?" Lindsey cried, shooting him a serious side-eye. "I thought you said we *weren't* going to do that."

"No way," said the mayor. "We can't give Thompson what he's asking for. Doing so will result in countless deaths in Estes Park. We need our medicine and every pound of food."

Detective Ryburn lowered his head and sighed. "She's right. I love Chief Colton, but we have mouths to feed. And Jason Cole can't go free after what he did."

Raven nodded at them in turn. "I understand—but if we don't do this drop tomorrow, we won't just lose Colton. We will end up going to war, which will result in far more death and suffering. That's why we need to gain Thompson's trust first. Make him think we're already beaten. Once he lowers his guard, I plan to strike him where it counts and get our food and supplies back."

A few of the militia exchanged glances, and the mayor looked over at Lindsey, checking her reaction. The detective's expression was closed off, and Raven worried that she might not back his play.

"Don't worry, we're going to get everything we give them back, plus some. You'll see," Raven said. "You just have to trust me."

***

Sandra Spears wasn't sure what the hell her brother was up to, but she trusted he was going to do the right thing with Sheriff Thompson. For now, her focus was on keeping her patients alive—including Creek. Neither Raven nor Allie would forgive her if she didn't ensure the dog's full recovery.

She walked through the hospital with a lantern to check on Creek, Teddy, and Allie before the next surgery. She was tired.

No. *Exhausted.*

The last time she had slept a full night through had been over a week ago. And that wasn't going to change anytime soon. Especially not tonight. After she finished her rounds, she was headed back into the operating room, which seemed to be a revolving door.

They had put Creek into Teddy's room, since they were running out of space. Teddy's parents were fine with it, and it helped Sandra focus on her work knowing Allie, Creek, and Teddy were all in the same place. When she got to the room, she slowly opened the door and roved the light over the space. Creek was sleeping peacefully in the small bed they had made for him in the corner, his face protected by the cone. Allie was on the floor beside him, curled up in a sleeping bag and holding the dog's front right paw in her hand.

The sight melted her heart.

"Nurse Spears?" Teddy called out.

Sandra quietly made her way over to his bedside and whispered, "How are you feeling?"

"I'm fine," he said, matching her whisper. "How are you?"

She smiled. "I'm good. Just checking on you guys."

"When can I get out of here? I really want to go home. I miss my dog."

"Soon. I promise. We just need to make sure you're healed, and it looks like you pretty much are."

Teddy smiled, but his hand went instinctively to the stump of his arm. "Thank you for being so nice to me."

She leaned in to hug the boy.

"Mom, is that you?"

Sandra pulled away to see that Allie was now awake. Creek sat up too. He tried to paw at his face, but the cone stopped him.

"Go back to sleep, sweetie," Sandra said. Her eyes flitted to motion outside the open doorway. Doctor Newton stood there, already dressed in scrubs and gown for the surgery.

"We're almost ready," he said.

"I'll be right there," Sandra said.

She bent down to kiss Allie and pat Creek on his head.

"I'll be back in a couple of hours," she said. "Sleep well."

Allie placed her head back on the pillow and watched Sandra leave. After closing the door, Sandra made her way down the hallway. Inside the first room was Martha Kohler, the doctor who had been rescued from the road to Estes Park. She was still recovering from the nearly fatal attack on the road, but she was doing much better.

In the operating room, Doctor Duffy was fully suited up and ready to begin. The other nurse on duty and Doctor Newton were preparing in the clean room. On the operating table was John Palmer, the firefighter and volunteer officer who had been shot at a roadblock. They had already amputated his left arm at his elbow, and now they were preparing to cut off his right arm up to his shoulder.

Infection had set in, even with the medical supplies dropped off by the federal government. Sandra eyed the plastic buckets on the floor next to the table, and the hacksaw on the metal stand. This had once been a modern hospital, but now it looked like something from World War I.

"Turn on the generator," Newton said.

Sandra flipped the switch, and the lights inside the operating room flickered on. They were running low on fuel, but they had no choice but to use it in this situation. She swallowed as she approached Palmer. He was awake and watching the medical staff, his eyes anxious.

"There's no other option?" he asked.

Newton shook his head. "I'm sorry, but if we don't do this now, you're not going to survive."

Palmer sucked in a deep breath and looked up at the ceiling.

"It's going to be okay," Sandra said.

His eyes shifted to her. "No. No it's not."

She wanted to say something reassuring, but he was right. How the hell was he going to get by even if the surgery saved his life? A man without arms was practically helpless to defend himself and his family. She wasn't even sure Raven could protect her and Allie now, with the threats coming at Estes Park from nearly every direction.

***

Colton knew he was dreaming, but he was unable to wake from the nightmare. Like always, the dream was so vivid that he could swear it was real. This time, it was a memory of his time in Kandahar, Afghanistan. It had been June of 2009, seven days after they'd touched down at the airfield. He and three other soldiers had been stationed at Checkpoint 14.

"Contacts!" shouted PFC Jay Reddker.

Colton wiped the sweat from his forehead and grabbed a pair of binoculars from the private. "Four contacts," he said, zooming in on a black Toyota pickup.

PFC Jacob Smith roved the M40 slightly to the right, the muzzle locking on the rusted hood of the truck. He spat on the ground and looked up for orders.

"Hold your fire," Colton said.

He centered the binoculars on the driver. A middle-aged man with tanned skin and a full beard. In the passenger side sat an elderly woman with a scarf covering most of her face. There were two figures in the back seat, small enough to be children.

Goddammit, *Colton thought.* Were they Taliban? *Sometimes the insurgents brought civilians along with them on suicide runs. Locals rarely ended up on this road unless they were lost, and this guy didn't look lost at all. He looked determined.*

Colton snagged the bullhorn from the pile of sandbags and signaled the driver of a Humvee parked outside the gate. The soldier in the turret nodded and readied the M240.

Bringing the bullhorn to his mouth, Colton said, "Stop and shut off your engine!" Speaking in Dari was difficult, but after repeating the same phrase hundreds of times, it had gotten easier.

The truck continued to race down the frontage road, dust swirling behind in the trail of their exhaust. Colton put their distance at a little over one thousand meters. Every weapon at Checkpoint 14 was centered on the truck. If the driver hadn't seen the firepower yet, he couldn't miss it now. There were also half a dozen signs in various languages along the dual fences. There was no way his presence here was an accident.

Colton checked the man again with his binoculars. Cold eyes stared back.

Those eyes were desperate—and filled with rage.

"Stop and shut off your engine!" Colton repeated when the truck was at five hundred meters. He'd hoped the show of firepower would deter the driver, but instead of slowing or turning around, the truck picked up speed.

Colton spoke in Pashto just to make sure. "Stop your truck!"

"Not listening, Sarge," Reddker said. "Want us to light 'em up?" There was a gleam of excitement in his eyes that disgusted Colton. He held up a hand and said, "Hold your goddamn fire."

Reddker and half of the men in Colton's unit were too young to understand death. They didn't get that once you pulled the trigger, you couldn't take it back.

Squinting into the blazing sunlight, Colton confirmed the pickup wasn't going to stop. The truck had passed the three-hundred-meter mark. On the other side of the fence were four F-16s waiting to be fueled by a tanker on the tarmac. The driver swerved toward them, and it was then Colton realized the pickup wasn't heading for their checkpoint after all.

"Open fire!" Colton yelled. "Raptor 2, get after 'em!"

The Humvee squealed onto the road, tires burning rubber as Reddker's M240 barked to life. Tracer rounds tore into the sand on the left side of the road, blanketing the truck with grit. Sweat poured down Colton's head as he watched the driver spin the wheel *and veer off the road toward the jets.*

A siren screamed in the distance, and the airfield came alive with movement. Humvees, armored vehicles, and fire trucks scrambled across the tarmac. But they were too far away. The only people who could stop the truck were Colton and his men.

Reddker continued firing, shells ejecting from the big gun and smoke swirling from the red-hot muzzle. He was hitting everything but the truck, rounds slamming into concrete and punching through dirt.

Colton pushed his M4 to his eyes and zoomed in with the advanced combat optical gun sight. A tiny face was pressed against the back window of the cab. Dark eyes, wide and innocent, stared back at him.

My God, Colton thought. The girl couldn't be older than six or seven. Nearly choking on adrenaline, he aimed for the tires.

A barrage of 7.62 mm rounds battered the bed of the truck as Reddker finally found his target. The Toyota jerked to the right, breaking through the first barricade and dragging a fence panel under the carriage.

Raptor 2, the Humvee Colton had ordered into the fight, pulled off the road and smashed through the fence one hundred meters to the west. Colton focused his crosshairs on the pickup that bobbed up and down in his gun sights. He saw the young girl's face again just before it vanished from sight as another salvo of rounds punched through the passenger door of the truck.

Somehow, the pickup was still moving. It slammed through the second fence and made a run for the F-16s. Reddker held his fire, out of range now, but Raptor 2 was unloading with everything they had. Three other Humvees were closing in behind the jets, a fire truck on their six.

Colton hurried over to his own Humvee. "Reddker, on me. Everyone else stay here!"

The private hopped into the passenger seat, breathing heavily, a grin on his face.

"I think I got one of 'em, Sarge!"

"There are kids in that truck," Colton growled.

Reddker looked at the truck, the grin fading. "Oh, shit. I didn't see…"

The clatter of metal snapped Colton awake. He sat up in his bed, forgetting where he was for a moment. The bars of his cell reminded him he was still in the jail in Fort Collins. A wave of anxiety tore through him when he also remembered that, in a few hours, his friends in Estes Park were due to barter with Thompson's people in exchange for his life.

The door at the end of the hallway opened, and a strangled voice called out. "Please…please let me go."

Colton moved over to the bars. In the glow of a torch, he saw three figures moving down the hallway to his right. Two guards carried a man under his armpits, his legs dragging across the ground. He was hurt, and hurt bad.

They pulled him past Colton's cell before he could get a look at the man's face. They stopped at the next cell, unlocked the door, and tossed the man inside.

The guards paused in front of Colton's bars. The man with the torch held it up, revealing the bearded faces of Thompson's men. These weren't the hard Russians that Thompson usually brought out. These were just grunts.

The one on the left had his hair neatly parted on the side, an odd look for a man with an AR-15 slung over a shoulder. The guy on the right wore a black baseball cap and glasses. Both of them smelled like they hadn't showered since the bombs dropped.

"Tomorrow's a big day for you, Chief," the man with the cap said.

Side-Part pulled out his knife and clicked the blade against the metal bar several times. "Hear that, Drew?" he said, looking at his buddy with a grin.

"That's the tick-tock of the clock, Chief," Drew said, taking over. "In the morning we'll find out if you get to live, or if I get to carve you up."

The men both laughed and walked away, but Colton remained standing, his heart still pounding from his dream and the fate that awaited him.

Down the hall, the guards opened the door. It clicked shut behind them. Colton gritted his teeth and squeezed the bars until his knuckles popped. He stood there, staring into the darkness, the anger eating at his insides.

In the past, his wife or his best friend would have been able to talk him out of the darkness, but tonight Colton was alone. Jake was dead, and Kelly might as well have been a million miles away. If he fell back asleep in this state of mind, he would just dream again of the girl he couldn't save in Afghanistan, or Melissa Stone, or...

"Marcus?" called a voice.

Colton loosened his grip on the bars. Was he hearing things?

The voice came again, but it was so muffled he could barely make it out.

"Marcus, it's me. Clint."

Colton let go of the bars. It couldn't be. Clint Bailey was dead. They had dragged him out of here and killed him.

This had to be one of Thompson's tricks.

Clint spoke again, clearer this time.

"They're going to kill you tomorrow," he rasped. "If you have a chance to run, do it."

— 4 —

Charlize boarded the Sikorsky UH-60 Black Hawk helicopter at dawn. There hadn't been much time, but she had put on light makeup and brushed her short hair into a style that looked somewhat respectable. Her outfit—black slacks and blazer with a white blouse—was clean and neatly pressed.

She took a seat next to Colonel Mark Raymond as the pilots prepared to take off. Today was one of the most important days in the history of the United States—it was the day the Chinese landed on American soil. The Founding Fathers would be rolling in their graves. But what choice did they have? The help from China would save countless American lives.

Charlize still had her doubts, and the decision to welcome an occupying military force weighed heavily on her mind. If there had been a conspiracy between China and North Korea, she would find out and deal with those responsible. For now, her duty was to help the country recover.

Over the comms channel, Raymond explained they would be meeting with General Ken Lin, the man the Chinese had entrusted with the recovery efforts. Charlize had never heard of him, but he was apparently well respected throughout the Chinese military.

The thump of the rotor blades sounded as the pilots fired up the bird. A dozen Green Berets jumped inside the chopper. Charlize had been through too much since the bombs fell to ever feel fully safe again, but having a special operations team along for the ride was reassuring.

Sergeant Andrew Fugate, a thin man with short-cropped red hair and a thick mustache, was in charge of the team. He took a seat across from Charlize, and handed her a flak jacket.

"Put this on, Madame Secretary," he said.

She did as ordered, and Colonel Raymond followed suit with his own vest. It was only a fifteen-minute flight to Fort Lauderdale, but they weren't taking any chances with security. Charlize looked out over the ocean to the east, watching the golden glow of the sun sparkle over the waves. She couldn't see them from her vantage point, but she knew the Chinese ships were out there. All across the Eastern Seaboard, the massive boats were beginning to arrive, and more would be hitting ports on the West Coast.

Initially, the plan had been for General Thor to meet with General Lin, but Charlize had decided it was her responsibility as Secretary of Defense to personally welcome the Chinese General—and assess the situation.

"Five minutes," one of the pilots said over the comms channel.

Charlize focused on the traffic moving on a road below. Vehicles drove on the highway at the edge of the beach, just like they would have a month earlier. Out on the water, several boats cut through the waves. From up here, it didn't look like anything had happened at all. Southern Florida had been spared from the devastating effects of the EMP attack. The cities here still had power, but north of Orlando, the United States was still dark. The only vehicles moving there were hardened military units or old cars and trucks built before modern electronics.

A train snaked along the terrain below, heading north, with a long line of cars packed full of supplies. Across the country, other trains like this one were arriving at their destinations with generators, food, and medicine, while convoys on the highways continued to get hit by raiders. It had been her idea to transport goods the old-fashioned way, by rail. But no matter how hard Charlize worked, it wasn't enough. They'd still had to turn to foreign governments for help.

The chopper came in on the eastern edge of Fort Lauderdale, passing over the beaches and the million-dollar mansions built in coves along the harbors. The Stranahan River came into focus, and Charlize got her first view of the Chinese ships.

Where cruise ships had once docked along the piers of Fort Lauderdale Harbor, there were now a dozen foreign aid ships. Equipment, vehicles, and troops were already being unloaded from the massive ships.

A month ago, there would have been happy tourists here, waving at departing cruise ships. Not today. Instead, thousands of American citizens were impatiently waiting in the streets for supplies to be distributed, all under the watchful eyes of Chinese soldiers wearing blue camouflage and carrying standard QBZ-95 automatic rifles.

"We need to keep those civilians back," she said.

Raymond agreed with a nod. "They aren't supposed to be here. The distribution point is another mile to the west. They must have seen the ships and come running."

Charlize lost sight of the view as the pilots descended over the US Coast Guard facility on the east side of the river. As soon as they landed, the Green Berets jumped out. Sergeant Fugate led the group, barking orders and gesturing for his men to take up position.

Raymond went next, then reached up to help Charlize out. She followed the men away from the bird, keeping low, what was left of her black hair whipping in the rotor drafts.

Thirty-plus American soldiers were already waiting with their rifles cradled. They surrounded her and Raymond on the way to the warehouse that served as a command center. Several Humvees with turrets were waiting outside, guarding the road that led to the beach.

"Captain Harris," Charlize said, recognizing a familiar face.

Captain Zach Harris turned from a conversation with several FEMA staffers. He threw up a salute and said, "Welcome to Fort Lauderdale, Secretary Montgomery."

They met in the center of the room. "Glad to see you again, ma'am," he said, light blue eyes crinkling behind the heavy black frames of his glasses. "I wanted to thank you personally for reassigning me after what happened at the survival center in Charlotte."

She stole a quick glance over her shoulder to make sure no one was listening. Most of the operations center staff were busy working at laptop computers or talking on radios, but she wanted to have this conversation in private.

"Is there some place we can chat?" she asked.

Harris led her to a small office. Stacks of boxes marked *Coast Guard* surrounded a metal desk covered in dust. Raymond waited for them outside the door.

"I'll only be a moment," she said. "Let me know if General Lin arrives."

As soon as the door shut, Charlize cut to the chase. "I had you transferred here for a reason," she said. "What happened in Charlotte was not your fault. In fact, I believe it was inevitable. Gangs have overrun every major city, which is part of the reason we accepted China's terms."

She pulled at the bottom of her blazer to straighten it under her bulletproof vest. "FEMA, first responders, the American military—they are simply not enough, as you know. We need the foreign aid to get the grid back up and running. And we need men like you."

Harris stiffened and held her gaze. "Thank you, ma'am."

"I was impressed with the way you ran the survival center, and despite the fact it fell, you remained behind with your staff to give others a chance to escape. Even in the chaos, you made sure the men and women under your command did not slaughter the desperate civilians. I respect that."

"I was just doing my duty. I'm grateful for the opportunity to run the command center here."

Charlize smiled and shook her head. "That's not your mission now, Captain."

He raised his brows over the rims of his glasses. "Ma'am?"

"I'm assigning you a different role. The most important of your career." After a short pause, she added, "I want you to work with General Ken Lin, and report everything directly to me. I trust you to be my eyes and ears in this matter."

Harris didn't reply, and she said, "Captain, do you understand what I'm asking you to do?"

He nodded firmly. "Yes, Secretary Montgomery."

A rap on the door told Charlize they were out of time. She opened the door and Raymond confirmed she was correct.

"The Chinese are here," he said.

The room quieted as she approached the front warehouse doors. Growling engines sounded outside. Five Chinese trucks and two black Honggi L5 limousines with tinted windows had pulled up.

Soldiers poured out of the trucks. One of them opened the side door to the second limo, and a short man with wide shoulders stepped out onto the concrete. He shielded his eyes from the morning sun with a pair of aviator glasses before making his way toward the warehouse. Charlize, Raymond, and Harris walked out to meet him.

"Good morning, General Lin," she said.

"Secretary Montgomery," Lin said with a thick Chinese accent. "It is a pleasure to meet you."

"And you, sir."

He turned and gestured toward the piers across the river, where the ships were still unloading.

"On behalf of the People's Republic of China, I humbly thank you for accepting our offer to help our American friends rebuild. You have our deepest condolences for the loss of life you have suffered in this outrageous and unprovoked North Korean attack. I assure you that we will do everything we can to help the United States recover as quickly as possible."

He smiled warmly. *The smile of a politician*, she thought to herself. She returned it with one of her own.

She was good at reading people, and she trusted her instincts more than his words. Nothing Lin said meant anything beyond a well-rehearsed soundbite. She glanced over at Captain Harris, who nodded back with understanding of just how important his mission was to the future of their country.

***

Fenix remained silent in the back seat of a Jeep, the blindfold back over his eyes to make sure he didn't see where Theo and Hacker were taking him.

They should have been back at Redford's compound hours ago, so they were taking him somewhere else. That made sense. They were playing things safe, just in case his Sons of Liberty soldiers were up to something. At least, that's what Fenix would have done if he were in Redford's expensive Italian shoes.

He kept his suspicions to himself, not daring to give Theo or Hacker a reason to search him. He tried to sneak a glance in his pocket for whatever it was that Sergeant Horton had dropped in it back at the cabin, but he couldn't see. If he had to guess, it was something to help him out of these cuffs.

The vehicle turned and began accelerating, which told Fenix they were back on a highway. Driving out here in the middle of the day had become increasingly dangerous, but he wasn't too worried about an ambush. Redford had over a dozen men and automatic rifles in the convoy. The only thing that could stand a chance of stopping them was an armored convoy of American soldiers.

"You know, I'm kinda surprised your boy Horton didn't pull any bullshit back there," Theo said, breaking the silence. "I'm also kind of disappointed."

"I told you, I'm a man of my word," Fenix replied.

"So am I."

45

Fenix waited for Theo to follow up the comment, but nothing came. He couldn't tell if Redford's cousin was an idiot or a wily bastard, and that made him uneasy.

"Where are we going?" Fenix finally asked.

Theo chuckled.

A rustling sounded, like someone moving in a seat, and suddenly the blindfold over Fenix's eyes lifted. He blinked at the gray light.

"Take a look for yourself," Theo said.

Fenix stared out the window at a highway dotted with stranded vehicles. A light snow was falling, dusting the ground with a layer of white. The mountains formed a fence on the horizon. Everything else was burnt to a crisp. Miles and miles of trees had been reduced to charcoaled logs and blackened sticks protruding out of the dirt. A FEMA sign warned of potential radiation contamination, but that didn't seem to bother Theo or the driver. The convoy powered forward into the burned wasteland.

It was a test, Fenix realized. They were taking him somewhere where his men wouldn't be able to follow easily.

"Don't worry, Dan," Theo said. "Those are our signs. It's perfectly safe out here." He grinned, a shit-eating expression that made Fenix want to punch him in the jaw. But he also felt a grudging respect. Redford was a smart man. Putting up signs to keep people off this road was genius. Even if his soldiers could find him, the radiation warnings would likely keep them back.

The lead truck, a gunmetal Toyota with a rusted-out bed, suddenly jerked to the left. Jade cursed and pushed down on the brakes. Theo turned back to the windshield, reaching for the AR-15 propped up next to the door.

The Toyota pulled to the side of the road, and the occupants jumped out, rifles shouldered. They moved toward a cluster of stalled cars, shouting at someone ahead.

"Hold us here, Jade," Theo said to the driver.

Hacker pulled out an M9 and chambered a round with a click. "Anyone got eyes on what's going on?" he asked.

"I see something," Theo said, straining to get a look.

The men from the pickup truck returned a few seconds later with a man holding onto a mountain bike. He was dressed in a white coat, white pants, and a white facemask to match. A gray stocking cap topped his head. The only exposed part of his body were his eyes.

"Stay here," Theo said. He got out of the truck, leaving the door open and letting in the cold wind.

Fenix scooted across the seat for a better look. The guy with the bike stopped about ten feet in front of their Jeep. Theo and his men surrounded him, rifles all pointed at his head. The biker gently sat his bicycle in the snow and raised his hands into the air.

"Please, please hold your fire," he said, shielding his head from the guns. Fenix could tell by his posture he wasn't a soldier. This was just a guy out on his bike, trying to get somewhere in a hurry.

"What are you doing out here?" Theo asked.

"I'm trying to deliver a message," he said. "That's it, I swear."

Theo took a step forward, lowering his rifle. "What message?"

"A message about the Chinese," the man said.

"What about 'em?"

"They are here," the man said, hands shaking.

Theo stepped forward again. "Dude, calm down and

tell me what the hell you're talking about."

"Chinese boats have arrived carrying thousands of soldiers. They're working with the federal government. I'm supposed to deliver the message to the next town, so we can prepare."

Fenix felt his blood boiling. There was no way this could be true. No way the United States government would agree to allow the Chinese army into the country. But the more he thought about it, the more it made sense. Someone in the United States government must have been involved with the North Korean attack—and the Chinese had to have played a role also.

He suddenly felt the urge to get out of the Jeep and run. He had to get back to his men. If China was invading, then the fight he had been preparing for his entire life had arrived.

"That's bullshit," Theo said. "We haven't heard anything about that on the radio."

The man lowered a hand, reaching for his pocket. Before Theo could say a word, a gunshot cracked, followed by a second and third.

The man screamed and stumbled forward, then dropped to his knees. He gripped his chest where one of the bullets had exited. A flower of blood blossomed on his white coat. The facemask fell away, revealing the youthful face of a teenager. Blood bubbled out of his mouth as he tried to speak. In seconds, it was over. He crashed to the ground, dead.

"You fucking idiot!" Theo yelled at the man who had fired the shots.

"I'm sorry," he said. "I thought he was reaching for a gun."

Theo shook his head.

The dead kid reminded Fenix a bit of Tommy, the pimpled-faced SOL soldier he had tossed out of the Castle for trying to help Ty Montgomery escape.

Theo moved the kid to his back, and then pulled a bloodstained envelope from his hand. He stood to read it.

"Holy shit," Theo said. "The kid wasn't lying."

— 5 —

Colton was dreaming again. He was back at the Kandahar
Air Force Base with PFC Reddker, pursuing the pickup
truck.

*The tire track peeled away like the skin of an orange, and the
rim screeched across the pavement. Raptor 2 continued firing, rounds
peppering the cab of the truck as the driver tried to maintain control.
Blood and dust caked the windshield.*

*Colton punched the pedal harder. The diesel engine hummed,
straining, as they gained speed.*

"They're toast," Reddker said.

*The Toyota fishtailed, lost control, and flipped onto its side,
tumbling over and over. The back door broke open mid-flip, and a
small body flew out.*

*Colton almost closed his eyes, but that felt like a cowardly thing
to do.*

*Fire suddenly exploded from the truck. It rolled to a stop as the
underbelly burst into flames. Two of the tires streaked away in a
cloud of smoke and shrapnel. Colton slammed on his brakes and
stopped the Humvee a few feet away from the tiny, broken figure
face down on the tarmac. He put the truck in park and jumped out,
the scent of fuel burning his nostrils. Sirens wailed from all
directions. The shouts of soldiers and support crew were barely
audible over the piercing shrieks.*

*A fire truck sprayed the wreckage of the Toyota as Colton
rushed over to the Afghani girl.*

"Someone get me a medic!" he shouted.

With deliberate care, he scooped the child up in his arms and carried her away from the burning pickup truck. The heat burned the back of his fatigues, but the physical pain was nothing compared to the mental pain of seeing the child's injuries. She had the same dark eyes as his own baby girl. They stared up at him, pleading and terrified.

"It's okay," Colton said in English. Then he changed to Dari. "It's okay. You're going to be okay."

It was a lie. Blood blossomed around what appeared to be a bullet wound. Her chest slowly moved up and down, breath rattling.

"Hold on," Colton said in Dari. He ran as fast as he could toward an ambulance. Reddker was still screaming behind him, "Sarge, LT wants you!"

Colton didn't care about orders right now. He had to save her. An explosion rocked the tarmac. He shielded the girl from the wave of heat as best as he could. When he looked down, tears were streaking away from her eyes. She tried to say something. Instead, she took in a long, final gasp, and died in his arms, five feet away from the ambulance.

He awoke in a cold sweat, sitting up so fast his head hurt. No matter what he tried to tell himself, it wasn't just a bad dream. It had happened, and he would never forgive himself for that girl's death. He hadn't saved her, just like he hadn't saved little Melissa Stone. In his mind's eye, he saw Kelly and Risa lying in the street, their bodies riddled with bullets.

In a fit of anger, he grabbed the bars and screamed, "Let me out of here!"

His voice rang against the walls, but no one answered.

Colton went to sit back on his bench when the door at the end of the hallway creaked open. Footfalls pounded the concrete. Multiple pairs of boots. He listened to the approaching men, knowing that this was it. They had finally come to shut him up.

To his shock, Sheriff Thompson appeared in front of Colton's cell with a grin from cauliflower ear to cauliflower ear.

"Mornin', Chief." He scratched at the back of his neck. "I thought about your suggestion, and I figured I'd take you up on it."

Thompson jerked his head at Ivan, the massive Russian man with thick black eyebrows and chest hair that crept out of his collar. He pulled out a key and unlocked Colton's cell.

"Hands behind your back," he said in his Russian drawl.

Colton did as ordered, and Ivan snapped a pair of handcuffs onto his wrists.

"Come on," Thompson said, jerking his chin.

Colton stepped out after a second of hesitation, and followed Ivan and Thompson down the hallway. They passed several other cells with more prisoners. He kept his gaze ahead, trying his best not to dwell on the fact there was a ten-year-old boy in the final cell. The kid was sitting up in his bunk, arms folded across his chest like he was hugging himself, teeth chattering from the cold.

They continued into the departmental offices. It was far different from the Estes Park police station. This was more like a barracks, with sleeping bags spread out throughout the workstations. But all of the beds and the desks were empty.

So where was everyone?

Thompson rounded the next corner, and pushed open a door into the lobby. Glass doors leading outside were propped open with bricks. The sun edged over the horizon, revealing a light dusting of snow over the parking lot and two dozen people standing in a circle. Several of them wore coats adorned with the Larimer County Sheriff's logo.

Ivan nudged Colton in the back when he stopped. They continued outside onto the landing, down the steps, and into the parking lot, where Ivan unlocked Colton's cuffs.

"Let's see how tough you really are, Marcus," Thompson said. He took off his coat and dropped it on the ground. Dressed in only a t-shirt and black tactical pants, he raised his fists, muscular arms flexing. His boots moved back and forth as he prepared to fight.

Colton couldn't believe his eyes. The sheriff had actually taken him up on his offer of a brawl.

"Beat his ass, Sheriff!" shouted one man.

"Kill 'em," yelled another.

Within seconds the crowd, gripped by bloodlust, broke into a frenzy; shouting profanities and threats.

A rock hit Colton in the side. He glared at the crowd, bending over in pain. Thompson also turned to look for the culprit.

"Who the fuck threw that?" the sheriff shouted.

That quieted his people down.

By the time Thompson turned back to Colton, he was ready to fight. He strode forward in a boxer's pose, leading with his left foot, his balled hands up to protect his face. It was something a fighter never forgot, like driving a stick shift vehicle.

Colton knew he couldn't let Thompson get him on the ground. The sheriff was a UFC fighter, which meant he knew mixed martial arts. Colton had to keep this fight on both feet, or he was screwed.

Thompson regarded the stance with a wide grin.

"You beat me, and I let you go today. If you don't, then you better hope to God your people—"

Before Thompson could finish, Colton jabbed at him with his right fist, shutting the cocky sheriff up with knuckles to the mouth.

Thompson took a step backward and reached up with a finger to feel the blood streaming from the cut on his lip. He pulled his fingers away and laughed. "You're fast, old man."

Thompson threw a fake right hook and ended up kicking Colton in the left thigh. Pain lanced up his hip and side. He fell back on his left foot, hunched down slightly, fists up. Then he stepped forward, planting his right foot, and threw a punch.

Thompson easily moved away from the blow with the speed of a man ten years younger. Before Colton could defend himself, Thompson kicked him again, hitting Colton in his right thigh this time. He did everything he could to stay standing, but lack of proper nutrition, fatigue, and the cold had taken their toll.

Colton let out a grunt and dropped to one knee, looking up just as Thompson slammed a fist down into his right eyebrow, with a crack so loud that the crowd screamed with approval.

The pain was sharp, but Colton ignored it. He got back up and focused on Thompson, who had his arms up in V-shape while his people chanted his name.

Colton just needed to clip the bastard once, really good, and this would be over. Blood dripped from his eyebrow, and Colton wiped it away with his sleeve.

He waited for Thompson to come to him. Colton watched his boots and hands, trying to predict which he would use first. Thompson swung as he approached him.

Once, twice, then a third time. Colton deflected the blows with his arms. He threw a jab after the volley of shots, and nicked Thompson's left ear.

"Shit!" Thompson yelled. He reached up and clutched his cauliflower ear.

"That had to sting," Colton said with a grin. He let out an icy breath and followed up the punch with another right hook, but this time Thompson hunched low, moving beneath the jab and coming up with one of his own, which hit Colton in the side of his jaw.

The blow stunned him, giving Thompson another opportunity. The sheriff seized it with a punch that impacted Colton above his left eyebrow. He felt knuckles open up his flesh.

Colton stumbled backward, stars floating before his vision. Blood streamed down both eyes now, and his jaw pulsed from the pain.

Get it together. You're fine. You're…

He took in a deep breath and brought his hands back up, watching Thompson move, his eyes flitting from shoulders and hands to legs and boots.

The next move came as a kick to Colton's shins, not that hard, but the steel-toed boots still hurt enough to send a shockwave of pain up his leg.

Colton swung wide with his right hand, and then came in for a left jab that was meant for Thompson's face. It hit him in the neck instead. This time Thompson staggered backward, reaching up to grip his neck. He sucked in breath through his nose.

Colton moved forward, using the stolen moment while the sheriff was trying to catch his breath. But just as he went to throw another barrage of punches, Thompson hunched down, dropped his hands, and used his legs to propel him forward.

Bringing his elbow down, Colton hit Thompson in the back as the sheriff plowed into him like a linebacker. There wasn't anything Colton could do now. He hit the ground hard, with Thompson on top.

The stars returned as his skull hit the pavement with a clank. Blood flowed from his forehead and down his temples, but at least it wasn't going into his eyes.

Thompson swung at Colton's unprotected head, hitting him multiple times in the cheek, jaw, and nose. It would all be over soon if Colton didn't do something drastic.

He tried to buck the sheriff off, but the man had him wrapped up tight.

"You're a..." Colton spat blood and pushed harder. "You're a fucking disgrace."

Thompson brought his elbow down on the bridge of Colton's nose with a crack. Several cries of excitement rang out from the crowd.

In that moment, everything came crashing over Colton. The violence, the fear, the atrocities of the past month. He summoned every bit of strength he had left and brought his skull up to hit Thompson in the center of his face, flattening his nose and breaking the cartilage.

Thompson rolled off, gripping his gushing nose, while Colton crawled away until he could push himself up. Blood flowed from his own nostrils, covering the snow with carmine. He pushed himself up, fell to his stomach, and tried again.

"Sheriff!" someone shouted.

Colton rolled to his back, gasping for air. He watched through blurred vision as Drew, the prison guard, came bounding down the stairs of the station and out onto the ground, his hand holding his cap on his head.

Thompson was already on his feet. "What the hell is it, Drew?" he grumbled.

"The Chinese, Sheriff. The Chinese are landing!"

The crowd went silent.

"It's not just a rumor, Sheriff," Drew said. "There are thousands of soldiers arriving across the country."

Thompson kept his hand on his nose, blood flowing from between his fingers. He strode past Colton, not bothering to look at him.

"We'll finish this later, Marcus," he said.

***

Raven zoomed in with his rifle's scope on a man walking down the highway wearing a parka and a hood. It was difficult to see his features with the hood shadowing much of his face, but what Raven could see was bruised and bloody. He roved the sights to bound hands and then pulled the scope away.

It had to be Colton, and Sheriff Thompson sure had done a number on the Chief of Police. A dozen of Thompson's deputies followed him down the road. They were followed by a pickup truck with a figure standing in the bed gripping a mounted machine gun. Metal sheets provided armor around the gunner.

Raven bit down on the toothpick in his mouth when he recognized it as the same pickup Thompson had used to attack the town several days earlier. The same gun Jason Cole had used to gun down officers and innocent civilians.

It was a slap in the face, but Raven wasn't going to take the bait. He moved his scope back to the team of horses pulling a trailer along Highway 34. Jason Cole was there, surrounded by the Estes Park militia, walking slowly with guns at his back.

It took every ounce of his willpower to not center the crosshairs on Cole's head and pull the trigger. But if Raven did that, he might as well shoot Colton himself. The only way the chief came home was if they played this by Thompson's rules. The plan was set in motion, and there was nothing he could do to stop it now. All he could do was hope both parties remained calm and civil. A single shot could spark a slaughter.

Raven settled behind the rocky outcropping with his MK11 semi-automatic sniper rifle. It was the same type of rifle he had used in the Marines. This one had killed a dozen Sons of Liberty soldiers back at the Castle. If things did go wrong, he would be ready to cover his friends below.

The caravan continued toward the drop point, where Lindsey and the members of the militia would hand over Jason Cole and the food in exchange for Chief Colton's life and the truce that would prevent a war.

For now.

At least, that's what Thompson and his men thought. Little did they know Raven was going to kill them all. Just not at this moment. John Kirkus and his men were watching too, ready to join the fight if needed.

Raven brought the scope up to his eye and zoomed in on the road again. Taking into consideration the chilly wind, distance, and lighting, he made some mental calculations and then adjusted his aim.

The caravan slowly crossed the crosshairs. Five militia soldiers up front, led by Dale Jackson, all of them armed with semi-automatic rifles and a secondary weapon. Then came the horses, pulling the trailer with crates of food and medical supplies. Behind that were five more militia soldiers surrounding Jason Cole. Raven focused on the man's bruised face, taking satisfaction in the fact that he'd given the man the bruises and cuts.

"Soon, you son of a bitch," Raven whispered. He had to force himself to look away. The temptation to end the murderous bastard's life was too strong.

The road barrier was just ahead, and several Estes Park civilians were positioned there. Raven cursed when he saw that one of them was Sarah, the young girl who had asked him to teach her how to twirl a knife.

He had told Lindsey to pull the women off the barrier today. But given how pushy Sarah could be, maybe this wasn't Lindsey's fault. He had a feeling the kid went wherever she wanted.

Raven continued chewing on his toothpick. He would have preferred a cigarette to calm his nerves, but didn't want to give up his position. With Creek in the hospital, he was on his own up here. Just him, his rifle, and a whole hell of a lot of problems. The slow burn of the coming winter, and the threats closing in, had him more anxious than ever. General Fenix was still out there, and Nile Redford too. Justice for Nathan was still on his radar, but his focus right now was on Estes Park and Colton.

Raven flicked the safety off the rifle and spat the toothpick into the dirt.

He looked for Lindsey on the road, and found her walking alongside the horses. She patted her favorite mare, Willow, on the head, trying to calm the horse. Even the beasts could sense the tension as they approached the roadblock.

The men there moved the barriers to let the horses and trailer through. They stopped ten feet from the bridge across Big Thompson River, and Lindsey unlatched the horses, leaving the trailer on the road.

Thompson's men stopped on the other side of the bridge. Raven centered his sights on the men, scanning each face to look for the sheriff, but as Raven suspected, he wasn't here.

There goes Plan B.

He knew it had been unlikely, but if the sheriff had shown up, Raven had intended to blow his head off and end this right here. Some of their people would die, but it was better than a lot of their people dying from disease and starvation over the winter.

It was the one plan Lindsey had agreed to without hesitation.

So it was now back to Plan A. Bait the sheriff, but don't take his bait.

Three of Thompson's men led Colton out onto the bridge. Raven zoomed in. The man's face looked like Rocky Balboa after his fight with Apollo Creed. It could be the chief under all those bruises, but between the injuries and the hood of the parka, Raven couldn't be a hundred percent sure.

Lindsey and Dale Jackson brought Jason Cole over next. They pushed him toward the bridge. The murderer jogged over to Thompson's men while their truck backed up to the trailer. Several of the soldiers used chains to hook it up while the man in the back angled the machine gun at the barrier.

Their duty done, Lindsey and Dale were herding Sarah away from the concrete blocks and stranded vehicles. With Sarah safely out of the way, Lindsey shouted something Raven couldn't make out to the man in the back of the pickup truck. He watched them exchanging words, straining to listen. All he could hear was Lindsey saying, "Chief Colton".

The pickup truck pulled the trailer away, and the men on the bridge standing guard left Colton alone on the bridge.

Everything continued to go to plan. So why was Raven's gut twisted into knots?

He focused the sights on Colton as he staggered across the bridge. His hands were bound by a rope. He paused in the center of the bridge and turned to look at the pickup truck. The driver stopped as the men on the road all piled inside.

"What are you doing, Chief?" Raven whispered.

Colton continued to look at the truck. One of the men in the bed yelled something, and Colton reached up to pull down his hood.

That's when Raven saw it *wasn't* Colton at all. It was a man Raven had never even seen before.

Son of a bitch tricked us!

Raven brought his walkie-talkie up to his lips to relay the information.

"Lindsey, do you copy?" he said.

"I'm here," she said.

"That's not Colton. I repeat, that's not Colton."

"I know," she said. "These fuckers said they would give Colton back on the next drop, long as all of them get home in one piece."

Raven cursed again. The sheriff hadn't lived up to his end of the bargain. He lowered the walkie-talkie and went to push his eye back into the scope when the crack of gunfire pulled his head away.

Three men in the back of the truck had opened fire on the bridge. The fusillade cut through the man who was not Colton, jerking him back and forth as the bullets shredded his body. A severed arm rolled across the road, and blood spurted from the riven stump of the man's shoulder.

Raven centered his sights on the shooters in the pickup truck, his finger hovering over the trigger. He held a breath in his lungs, trying his best to fight the anger. If they fired a single shot at the barrier, he would waste them all.

But doing so wasn't going to get Colton back. Patience was the only thing that would save the chief now, and he needed time for his plan to work. Especially against these animals. He didn't know who the prisoner on the bridge had been, but the message was clear. Thompson and his men were in charge, and there was little Raven could do about it.

The gunshots faded away, and a new sound emerged in the distance, a low rumbling that quickly grew into a roar. The men in the pickup truck stopped firing, and everyone on the road looked to the sky. Raven shifted his gaze to the clouds just as three fighter jets burst from the cover, emerging long enough for him to identify them as F-35 Lightning II jets. He swiveled his head to watch another squadron of fighters moving right behind them.

"What in the name of…?" he whispered when he realized these weren't American aircraft, but a trio of Chinese L-15/JL-10 fighter jets. For a fleeting moment he thought they were pursuing the F-35s, but the jets merely continued flying to the east, away from the Rocky Mountains.

Together.

The shock of being tricked by Thompson's men wasn't anything like the shock he felt when he realized what the sight meant.

The rumors of the Chinese armed forces arriving in the States were true.

What the hell was happening to his country?

— 6 —

"I agreed to authorize troops, but not fighter jets," Charlize said, frustration rising in her voice. She stood inside an office in the Coast Guard building with Captain Harris and Colonel Raymond, all of them looking at the satellite phone on the dusty desk.

The other line was connected to a room full of some of the most important people in the United States. President Ron Diego, Vice President Tom Walter, Doctor Peter Lundy, National Security Advisor Duane Ibsen, and General Justin Thor. They were safely located at Central Command in Constellation, monitoring the situation from the bunker.

She didn't blame them for staying at Constellation, but at the same time, she was increasingly frustrated at being out on the frontlines without the intel she needed to lead.

The report of the Chinese fighters had struck her especially hard. It was one thing to see troops on the ground, but fighter jets? A soldier could only do so much damage. A fighter jet could level a city.

"I authorized them," Diego said after a few moments of silence.

Raymond looked over at Charlize, apparently just as surprised as she was. At least she wasn't the only one who'd been kept in the dark.

"Without consulting with me?" Charlize asked. She

picked the phone off the desk and brought it to her lips. "How am I supposed to do my job if you don't tell me everything I need to know?"

"I knew what you would say, Charlize, being a pilot and all, but this was part of the deal," Diego replied. "I don't like it either, but the Chinese want to be able to protect their assets on the ground."

"Against Americans," Raymond said quietly.

Charlize's shoulders were a stiff line as she clutched the phone. "If one of those fighter jets fires on Americans, we're going to have a shit show on our hands. Our citizens may not have access to social media anymore, but stories will spread like wildfire. You do realize that, sir?"

"I understand your frustration, and I understand the risks, but this mission will save countless American lives if all goes to plan."

"And if it doesn't go to plan?"

"Then we deal with it accordingly, Charlize."

Vice President Walter chimed in with some thoughts, but Charlize was hardly listening. She wasn't all that impressed with the man Diego had picked to be his second in command. He was the former CEO of a major energy company with ties to China, which Charlize found all too convenient, considering he'd helped jam the Chinese deal down the president's throat.

Now wasn't the time to raise those questions, though. There was no use talking further with Diego about the fighter jets, either. He had made up his mind. Her job— her duty—was to make sure not a single missile, bomb, or bullet was fired by the Chinese. Although she knew that was going to be near impossible.

"Charlize, I want you to know that I've had multiple

conversations with the Chinese president, and he has assured me his pilots and troops will exhaust every possible solution before utilizing force," said Walter.

"Do you know how that sounds, Mr. Vice President?" Charlize asked, squinting in disbelief.

There was a pause, then Diego's voice spoke again. "Just do your job and we will do ours, Secretary Montgomery."

At least he called me by my title, she thought.

"Roger that, sir," she said as respectfully as possible. "In the meantime, I'm going to meet with FEMA and the Army Corps of Engineers."

"Madame Secretary?" said Peter Lundy.

Charlize sighed. She had had a feeling the chief scientist at Constellation was on the line for a reason.

"Please get me an updated count of the large power transformers the Chinese have brought. Those are the biggest hurdle we're facing right now," he continued.

"You got it," she said. "Anything else? I really need to get going."

"I'd also like an update on delivery dates for each power grid section."

"Understood."

"Good luck," Diego added.

Charlize hung up the phone and handed it back to Raymond.

"Chinese fighter jets?" Harris asked. "Did I hear that right?"

A nod from Raymond and a snort from Charlize.

"Another reason your mission is so important, Captain," she said.

They walked back into the command center that had been set up inside the Coast Guard building. She studied the maps of the power grid sections Lundy had referred to on the call. The United States had been divided into ten different regions. It was going to be a hell of a job to get them all functional again.

Horns sounded outside, the cry of more ships coming in to harbor.

She passed a group of FEMA workers talking about moving water trucks. The American Red Cross, along with several local and state government officials, were huddled around a map of northern Florida. Chinese representatives were crowded in with them, an interpreter translating the conversation.

Charlize slowed on her way out of the warehouse to listen to the multiple discussions. Judging by what she observed, the American and Chinese officials were working well together. Feeling more optimistic, she stepped outside and approached the waiting convoy of five armored Humvees. Her work here was done. Captain Harris would accompany the Chinese delegation, led by General Lin, as soon as they moved out of the city.

Her next task today was to see how things were being managed on the front lines. And she was already late.

The Green Berets were waiting for her. Colonel Raymond walked over to talk to Sergeant Fugate. He glanced over his shoulder at Charlize, then dipped his helmet.

"Okay, we're good to go," Raymond said when he rejoined Charlize.

"Good luck, and keep me apprised," she said to Harris.

"Yes, ma'am. I will do my utmost."

She watched him walk away. So much was resting in his hands, but she was glad she had someone on the ground. The young captain was going to be her ears and eyes out here over the next few months, possibly even years. The scope of the work ahead was staggering, but Charlize had to focus on one piece at a time. She boarded her Humvee and buckled in.

"Let's go," Fugate said from the passenger seat. The trucks rolled out, moving in combat intervals down Seabreeze Boulevard. More soldiers were posted along the road, holding sentry to protect access to the survival center headquarters they were leaving behind. They had moved the SC operations out to near the shoreline, in order to separate the headquarters from the distribution of food and supplies. It was a smart move; if something happened, the command center wouldn't fall, like it had in Charlotte.

Unfortunately, that meant the people she needed to see were also spread out. Both the FEMA regional administrator and the Army Corps of Engineers administration were at a forward operating base set up near the piers, which was where she was headed now.

They stopped at three more roadblocks before hitting the bridge over Stranahan River. To the north was the harbor, where the Chinese ships were continuing to dock and offload equipment. A crane lowered a bucket truck onto the pier. Forklifts, bulldozers, heavy haulers, and every type of truck imaginable, were being moved onto the platforms. This had been one of the busiest cruise ports in the world, which was one reason they had opted to bring part of the Chinese fleet here.

"This isn't looking good," Sergeant Fugate said, gesturing to the people gathered around the operation. "There's no telling what that crowd is going to do."

Hundreds of American and Chinese soldiers held the

surging civilians back, but Charlize could see they had their work cut out for them. It was pure chaos near the docks. Thousands of people, all of them looking for food and other supplies. She could hear their shouts rising into a discord that reminded her of a music festival.

"If it's like this here, I can't imagine what it's like north of Orlando, where the grid is down," Raymond said.

"Exactly what I was thinking." Charlize continued to watch while the convoy continued across the bridge. Yachts and fishing boats were docked in the canals below, and million-dollar homes lined the harbor. Most of that money was worthless now. In the blink of an eye, the wealthy one percent had lost everything, and many of them were out on the streets, just like the rest of the surviving Americans.

Palm trees whipped in the salty breeze, and Charlize prepared for her final meeting of the day by looking through the folder Raymond had given her.

The FEMA administrator was a man named Josh Howard who had worked on the recovery efforts during Katrina, where he'd made a name for himself after going in to clean up the mess. She would also be meeting with the Army Corps of Engineer regional administrator, Major General Troy Brock.

The Humvees took a left toward the piers and down another road guarded by American soldiers. After passing a small guard booth that had once monitored traffic coming into the cruise terminals, they arrived at their destination—Terminal 4, a large building with white pillars and a domed roof.

Metal fences held back the hundreds of civilians waiting in line outside. Soldiers motioned for the crowd to get back as the Humvees came to a stop. Fugate and his men fanned out, setting up a perimeter along the flower beds with their weapons lowered. Several of them accompanied Charlize and Raymond to the front steps.

Inside, the building was alive with activity. FEMA staff, Army Corps of Engineers workers, city officials, soldiers, and dozens of others hurried back and forth.

"Secretary Montgomery," called a voice.

Charlize turned toward a man sporting a salt-and-pepper crew cut. He filled out his Army uniform with a broad chest. A pair of aviator glasses were tucked into a front pocket.

"Major General Troy Brock," he said.

"Pleased to meet you," Charlize replied. "This is Colonel Mark Raymond."

"It's an honor, Secretary Montgomery, and good to meet you, Colonel. If you'd both follow me, Josh Howard is waiting for us upstairs."

The group continued to a large office overlooking the port. Sitting behind a desk was Josh Howard, a fifty-year-old man with a graying red beard, freckles, and receding hairline.

"Welcome to Terminal 4, Secretary Montgomery," he said, standing. "Colonel, welcome."

"Good to be here," she said.

"Thank you for meeting with us," Raymond said.

"As you can see, the ships have just arrived and are unloading. Others are still on their way." Howard pointed toward a round table with six chairs. "Let's have a seat to discuss what I know now, and what the plan is moving forward."

Major General Brock sat to his right, and Colonel Raymond sat next to Charlize.

"I'm told you were instrumental in the recovery efforts

after Katrina," she said to Howard.

He nodded. "We worked very hard in a very difficult situation. But this situation is a thousand times worse, and more complicated. I'm using lessons learned to help, but we have an uphill battle."

"There are 160,000 miles of transmission lines in the US," Brock said. "The EMP surge did not damage all of them, but hundreds of miles will need to be replaced, especially in the region hit by the ground explosion."

"Like Washington D.C.," Charlize said.

She was heading back to D.C. soon. She wasn't sure when, but the thought of returning to the crater that was once the symbol for democracy sent a chill up her back.

"We're also faced with repairing and rebuilding power plants, substations, and other facilities that were fried," Brock said. "I've talked to Doctor Lundy numerous times, and as I've told him, it's a mess out there. Frankly, I'm glad we have the Chinese help."

"I couldn't agree more," Howard said. "During the last hurricane in Texas, we had eighteen thousand boots on the ground. We're going to need fifty times that, plus protection for the crews while they work."

Howard let out a short sigh. "In a normal disaster, we're faced with replacing transmission lines and poles. However, in this case we have to replace large power transformers. Half of the total cost for these is electrical steel, and China just happens to make thirty-five percent of the world's supply. We're lucky they offered to help."

"LPTs are extremely expensive and time-consuming to make, but the Chinese have plenty for us to get started," Brock added. "With the help of their crews, we should be able to replace most of the LPTs in a year, instead of two. Assuming all goes to plan, of course. And only for easily-accessed areas. Other places won't be so fortunate."

Charlize nodded as she wrote down a few notes for Lundy. There was a moment of silence, in which she thought of the places that would suffer the most. Rural areas, like Estes Park, Colorado. The isolated mountain community her brother had crash-landed near during the night of the attack was a prime example of a town that was both low on the government's priority list, and difficult to access.

The quiet was broken by Raymond, who pointed at the window. "Is that one of the LPTs being unloaded right now?

Charlize stood and made her way over to the windows facing the port. Brock, Howard, and Raymond joined her there. The FEMA administrator handed her a pair of binoculars.

"Yup, that's one of 'em," he said, directing his finger at the machinery being unloaded by a crane.

After glancing at the power transformer, she pivoted and focused the binos on the crowd of civilians surrounding the piers. Food, water, and other goods were being distributed to the desperate civilians by Chinese workers, while American and Chinese soldiers stood guard.

"Look at that," said Sergeant Fugate. He was staring at a Chinese ship sailing into the harbor. She moved the binos toward the vessel, noticing the sleek stern and the guns on deck. This wasn't one of the vessels packed full of aid and equipment. It was a Chinese aircraft carrier, with dozens of L-15/JL-10 Chinese fighters on the deck.

All of a sudden, this didn't look like a major aid operation to Charlize. It looked more and more like an invasion.

***

Fenix sat in the dining room of a lodge that overlooked the Rocky Mountains. The restaurant had once served the upper tiers of society—the rich, who came here on weekend getaways to ski, drink champagne, and eat tiny plates of expensive food.

He had always hated those people, especially the political elite. They were the worst. The people who didn't think the law applied to them.

The tables around him were empty now, the people who had once sat here either in private bunkers or dying on the streets for a can of beans. He hoped it was the latter of the two.

But what boiled his blood even more than the thought of crooked politicians, was the idea of a bunch of damned Chinamen flooding his country.

Fenix looked down at his soup, his appetite gone. He hadn't believed the reports at first. How could the government have been so stupid as to let them in? This had to be the result of a conspiracy even deeper than he had ever imagined. Someone at the top levels of the United States government had conspired to bring the country to its knees.

The mission of the Sons of Liberty was more important now than ever. They couldn't let the Chinese take over the country. The thought made him sick.

"Not hungry?" asked Theo. "If it were up to me, I wouldn't have given you anything in the first place. I would have made you eat it out of a dog bowl, which is what you are, Dan. A dog with fleas."

The redskin sat at a nearby table, watching Fenix with rage-filled eyes. He knew what hate looked like, and this was something even deeper.

Fenix stared right back. He placed his spoon back on the table and turned to look outside, his heart stuttering in his chest, adrenaline rushing through his veins. He would have liked to pop his fist into Theo's face, but the truth was, he was more worried about the Chinese than the damned injuns.

The Americans had dealt with them before, and it hadn't ended up too good for Theo's people. But China? That was a different story. The cheeky bastards could crush what was left of America through sheer numbers.

The serene view of the mountains outside helped calm him. The moonlight spread over the terrain and illuminated the main lodge and surrounding buildings. Most of them had burned, along with the trees on the perimeter. It really made a great place to ride out the apocalypse. Redford was a real genius to come here—at least, Redford probably thought so.

"If you're not going to eat that, I'll give it to my men," Theo growled.

Fenix picked up the spoon and forced the soup to his lips.

"You really need to lighten up, you know that? Take a lesson from Nile… I mean, Mr. Redford," Fenix said, correcting himself. "We survived the apocalypse, and now it's time to take over the country. We can't let these Chinese fucks come in and take what's ours."

Theo set his spoon down gently on the table and then brought up a napkin to dab at the sides of his mouth. He stood and gave his suit cuffs a quick tug.

"I don't think working with a Nazi is something to take lightly," he said. "My cousin and I have never agreed on much, but if he knew your heart, I think he would agree that you deserve to die."

Fenix tightened his grip on the spoon and glanced at the .357 Magnum on the table in front of Theo. He was no more than ten feet away, but by the time Fenix got to the table, he would have at least two gaping holes in his body.

No, he couldn't try anything right now. He needed to be patient, and wait for his chance. But at some point, they were going to fight. It was just a matter of time.

Theo followed his gaze to the gun. He grinned.

"You want this?" he asked, tilting the gun from side to side.

Fenix shrugged and slurped another spoonful of soup. He went back to looking out the window. The moon peeked through the clouds, illuminating the landscape. Two deer, a buck with a nice set of antlers, and a fawn walked through the courtyard below, searching for a meal in the burned grass.

Theo walked around the tables, gun still in hand. The door opened across the room and Hacker walked in, pulling up his duty belt with one hand and carrying a plate of food in his other.

"Shit is boring up here, man," he said to Theo. "How long until we can get back to the compound? I want that poker rematch."

Theo didn't respond. Fenix figured it was because he didn't want him to know the answer, or perhaps because he didn't *have* an answer.

"You're supposed to be on watch," Theo said.

"Jade is on it." Hacker took a seat and shoveled several bites into his mouth. Theo silently watched him eat. He was clearly pissed off.

"Fine," Hacker finally said. "But I'm taking this with

me. I'm freaking starving."

Theo returned to his seat, and Fenix went back to watching the deer outside. The moon had slipped back into the gray clouds, shrouding the ground in darkness. Shadows moved in the weak light near the burned-out building to the east. They vanished before he could get a look at what was creating them.

"You know, I've been wonderin'," Theo said.

Fenix rolled his eyes. This guy just didn't shut up.

"How do you become a Nazi?" Theo asked. "Do you just wake up one day and think, 'Oh shit, I'm a racist asshole and I want to oppress anyone that's not white'?"

Theo waited for him to respond, but Fenix wasn't going to give him the satisfaction. At this point, the redskin was just annoying.

"Not going to answer? You don't want to give me some insight on what fills someone with so much hate for other races? Because I assume it's fear. Fear turns men into cowards like yourself."

Fenix still didn't take the bait.

Theo remained seated at his table, but reached for the .357 Magnum next to his soup bowl. He picked it up and pulled back the hammer, closing one eye and aiming it at Fenix.

"All that gold and weapons you promised are the only things keeping me from blowing your dumb head off, you know that?"

Fenix couldn't help himself any longer. "You sure are judgmental for someone that works for a criminal. Don't act like your shit don't stink, man."

He looked away, not worried about Theo pulling the trigger. Outside, the moon had returned. Another flurry of shadows moved across the landscape, and Fenix spotted a deer bolting away from the courtyard. Something had spooked it.

"Do you think I won't kill you?" Theo asked. He got up from his chair, still pointing the gun. Fenix watched the small man in the reflection of the windows as he approached.

The glass in the central pane shattered, and Theo jerked as a bullet punched through his expensive suit. He dropped to the ground, losing his pistol on the floor, and cried out in pain.

Fenix smiled at the sight and muttered, "Who's the dog now?"

The other windows to the right exploded, raining glass on the carpet. Rounds punched into the tables, floor, and walls. Shouting for help, Theo scrambled for the cover of the table he'd been sitting at earlier. He propped it up to shield his body.

Fenix remained where he was, his appetite slowly returning. He brought up another spoonful to his lips as bullets peppered the room.

Theo covered his head with his hands and shouted, "Hacker, Jade!"

He glanced over at Fenix, who was in the process of bringing the final spoonful of cold soup to his lips. He swallowed, set the spoon down gently, and stood, heedless of the gunfire.

The Sons of Liberty didn't miss.

Fenix walked toward the .357 Magnum. Theo reached out to grab it first, but gunfire lanced into the ground, forcing his hand back.

He picked up the pistol and aimed it at Theo. He was on his back now, hands on his gut, legs and feet squirming as he bled out.

The automatic gunfire continued for several seconds before waning into sporadic shots. Fenix brought the gun up and aimed it at the door as footsteps sounded in the stairwell outside.

The door swung open and Jade stumbled inside, three rosy spots on the front of his coat. He dropped to his knees, and Fenix fired a shot that hit him in the top of the head, blowing off his red bandana and splattering his brains over the wall.

Three more men emerged in the open doorway, carrying M4 rifles and dressed in all-black. The leader pulled down his facemask and smiled when he saw Fenix.

"General," Horton said in his gruff voice.

"About time, Sergeant," Fenix said. He moved over to Theo, who was looking up, eyes wide and fancy Italian shoes kicking at the ground.

Reaching into his coat pocket, Fenix pulled out the tracking device Horton had dropped inside back at the cabin earlier that day. He bent down next to Theo.

"You thought some stupid radiation signs were going to keep my men from coming for me?" Fenix asked. He tilted his head to one side. "That plan was almost as dumb as you talking to me the way you did earlier."

"Nazi pig…" Blood bubbled out of Theo's mouth. "Rot in hell."

"Maybe, but not for this," Fenix said. He stood and pointed the .357 Magnum at Theo's face just as more SOL soldiers moved into the room.

"Well, this is a pleasant surprise," Fenix said when he saw they had captured Hacker. The man stumbled through the open doorway, his hands bound behind his back.

"There's a few other prisoners downstairs," Horton said. "Figured I'd let you decide what to do with 'em."

Hacker glanced over his shoulder and growled at the SOL soldier who'd pushed him into the room.

"Hey, pencil dick," Fenix said, his smile returning. He waited for Hacker to look him in the eye, and then said, "Seems to me like you're out of a job. You want a new one?"

Hacker hesitated, then shrugged. "Never really did care for Nile that much, to be honest."

Theo spat blood in Hacker's direction. "Fucking traitor."

Fenix laughed, and aimed the barrel at Theo with one hand and motioned for Hacker to join them with his other.

"Tell you what," he said when Hacker got there. "You can join the Sons of Liberty if you perform one simple task."

Fenix pointed with his other hand at the pliers on Hacker's duty belt. "You pluck out Theo's eyes for me so I can send them to his cousin. The treaty between SOL and these redskins ends tonight."

79

— 7 —

The ancient pickup truck climbed a hill, chassis groaning like an old man walking down stairs. Another old man was sitting in the bed of the truck, blindfolded and hands bound in front of him. Like the truck, Colton's body had seen better days. His eyelids were both swollen and obstructing his view. The right eyelid was completely closed. His lip had been split in two, and he was pretty sure he had a stress fracture in both of his shins.

But the physical and mental pain would all be over soon.

This was it. He was going to die today. Clint Bailey's words emerged in his mind.

They are going to kill you tomorrow. If you have a chance to run, do it.

Clint was already dead. His body had been left on the road just outside Estes Park, according to Sheriff Thompson. He had ordered Colton to get into the back of the truck, and then had placed the blindfold over his eyes. The food drop must have gone awry, and he was going to pay the price.

They had been driving for about ten minutes, and were now climbing, which told him they were heading into the mountains. He considered jumping out of the bed, but even if the fall didn't kill him, it would break his legs, and then what would he do?

You are a dumb son of a bitch, Colton thought. *Coming out here thinking you could make a deal.*

He should have stayed in Estes Park. He should have never left his family behind. Everything had changed the night he found Melissa Stone and the fighter jets fell from the sky. The world had changed, and the wolves that had been hiding among the sheep were now in charge.

Colton shielded his swollen face from a gust of chilly wind as the driver took a right and accelerated down a new road. He wasn't sure who was in the back of the bed with him, but he had heard two other people climbing in. He guessed one of them was Thompson.

He wanted to be angry, but it quickly changed to despair. He had fought, and he had lost. Colton never thought he would plead for his life, but desperation set in. He wanted to see Kelly and Risa, to hold his girls again and never leave them.

"You don't have to kill me, Sheriff. Please let me go. I can help you. We can help each other," he said.

There was a chuckle over the noise of the wind, but it faded away, leaving Colton alone in the darkness and the cold.

"You're a brave man," Thompson replied. "But you lack what it takes to survive in this new world. You're a decent fighter, but you're not a killer. That's the difference between you and me."

The truck stopped a few minutes later, and the lift gate clanked open. Someone grabbed Colton under the arm and helped him down.

Then his blindfold came off.

He blinked into the cold wind, looking at the rolling hills east of Fort Collins instead of the Rocky Mountains to the west.

Sheriff Thompson and his Russian henchman stood

next to him, both of them focused on the burned-out FEMA Survival Center camp in the distance. A mile of debris spread across fields now covered in a sheet of snow.

"I own this land," Thompson said. He turned to Colton, a cocky grin under his broken nose and bruised eyes. "I'm the king."

"Not for long," Colton said. "The government will be here soon. They will stop you."

"What government?" Thompson said, his smile fading. "The only thing I'm worried about is the fucking Chinese."

Colton couldn't resist asking. "What about them?"

"Those bastards are streaming across our borders to 'help' with rebuilding efforts, from what we're hearing over the radio."

"Invading," Ivan said.

"I'll kill any of them that step into these parts. Like I said. I'm the king." Thompson shrugged. "Besides, I don't need the government's help, and never did. We have dozens of warehouses packed full of supplies, food, medicine, and other shit we took from the FEMA camp. Soon we will have the weapons to hold back the Chinese, and anyone stupid enough to try and take Fort Collins by force."

Colton could tell by the crazed look in Thompson's eyes that he already had a plan to deal with the so-called invaders, but his concern now was the sheriff's plan for Colton. Would he crucify Colton on one of the poles down the road like he had Sheriff Gerrard? Would he cut up Colton and send him back in pieces, like he'd threatened?

The questions swarmed his mind as they walked down

the road. Why would Thompson show him all this just to kill him? Maybe he just wanted to talk. He was a narcissistic sociopath, and those people were near impossible to understand or profile. They were the worst type of criminal, feeding off power. No remorse. No morals.

"Anyone who challenges me will end up like them," Thompson said. He didn't elaborate, but Colton knew who he was talking about. Almost every pole on the side of the road had a dead body nailed to it.

"You won't win," Colton said. "Evil never wins in the long term. It's always conquered by good men."

"Evil?" Thompson asked, sounding genuinely surprised. "Good men? You think you're a good man? Please, spare me the bullshit, Marcus."

Colton turned to get a better look out of his left eye. Judging by the confused look on Thompson's face, the man really believed he was doing the right thing. There wasn't anything else Colton could say. Thompson was batshit crazy.

"Let's go," he said. "Get back into the truck."

Colton hesitated to look out at the corpses one last time. This was what Thompson's kingdom would look like if Colton didn't find a way to stop him. But what could he do?

Ivan turned back to the truck with Thompson, and Colton saw a sudden opportunity. Maybe there was something he could do, and if he was going to die anyways, why not go down fighting?

He grabbed the Glock in Ivan's hip holster, and drew it with his bound hands before the big Russian could react.

Thompson spun to face Colton, but found himself

staring down the barrel of the gun instead.

"Don't move, or Thompson takes one to the heart!" Colton yelled at the two men who hopped out of the truck. They both shouldered rifles at him, but Colton kept his pistol aimed at the sheriff.

"Think about what you're doing," Thompson said. "This is a big mistake, Marcus."

"Tell your men to drop their weapons or I swear to *God* I'll put a bullet in your head and another in your black heart," Colton said.

Thompson held Colton's gaze, reading him for a bluff. The sheriff must have seen he was serious.

"Do it," Thompson said after a short hesitation.

"But boss?" Ivan protested.

"I said drop your fucking guns."

The driver and passenger slowly lowered their rifles.

"No, throw them in the truck," Colton said.

Thompson nodded.

Both guns went inside the pickup. The truck was still running, the muffler coughing in the chilly weather.

"Leave me a knife too," Colton said. "Then get over to the side of the road."

"You're making a *really* big mistake," Thompson said. He chuckled, and looked at Ivan. "It's actually really funny that he got the drop on you."

"You made the mistake, asshole," Colton said. "Now get moving or I'll shoot you right now."

"Feel free to shoot Ivan," Thompson said.

"I said move!" Colton said.

Thompson drew in a deep breath and nodded. The driver pulled a knife out of a sheath and placed it on the seat of the truck. Then he raised his gloved hands and walked over to the shoulder of the road with the passenger. They lined up next to Ivan and Thompson, while Colton retreated to the truck.

"You fought well against me," Thompson said. "I respected that. I was going to let you go. I was preparing to take you back to Estes Park and drop your dumb ass off, but now you're a dead man."

"We'll see about that," Colton said. He backed up to the front seat of the truck with the gun still aimed at the men. He could easily jump in and speed off, leaving them here. That would make him a better man than Thompson.

You lack what it takes to survive in this new world.

"Never let a rabid dog have a chance to bite you again," Colton muttered.

"What was that, Marcus?" Thompson asked.

Colton hesitated, knowing that what happened next would stick with him forever. This could very well be the defining moment of his entire life. Specters of those he hadn't been able to save formed in his mind, followed by the images of his wife and daughter. He couldn't let them die. He couldn't let a man like Thompson survive.

Thompson's eyes widened with realization just as Colton pulled the trigger, twice. Both bullets hit the sheriff in the chest. He spun away, hitting the dirt, and then rolling into the ditch.

Colton roved the gun to Ivan.

"*Nyet!*" screamed the Russian.

He ate a bullet that exited the back of his head. The other two men took off running. Colton aimed the barrel at the fat man on the right, but he had never shot a man in the back before, and hesitated again.

You can't afford to have mercy.

With the sights lined up, he shot the man in the back

three times. The second man turned and shielded his head, knocking off his baseball cap in the process.

"Please," he said. "Please don't shoot me. I have a family."

Colton looked over to Thompson, who lay in the dirt at the bottom of the ditch, his sightless eyes staring up at the sky.

"Please!" the man entreated.

Colton slowly lowered the Glock. "Tell your friends that Estes Park is off limits. If anyone shows their face there, they will meet the same fate as Thompson."

The man nodded rapidly. "Yes, sir. I promise."

Colton scanned his handiwork as he backpedaled to the truck; the fat man lay sprawled on the pavement with blood ballooning around the holes in the back of his coat; Ivan was face down, snow flurries falling into the gory exit wound where his skull had been moments earlier; and finally, Thompson.

A month ago, executing three men in cold blood would have made Colton throw up. But he was no longer that man. This was no longer that world.

After Afghanistan, he'd thought he had seen the worst humanity could do to each other, but atrocities like the burned-out FEMA camp in the distance, and the dead civilians hanging from poles on the side of the road, had taught him how cruel humans could be. Witnessing the things Thompson had done was sickening, but it had been necessary in teaching him what he needed to do to protect those he loved.

He was no longer a lawman.

He was one of the damned now.

***

Raven patted Willow on the neck. The mare snorted and continued up the trail. The sun was starting to go down over the mountains, leaving an orange streak across the iceberg-shaped clouds.

Chilly wind whipped Raven's long hair across his face. He pulled the curtain back and redid his ponytail. His ear was really hurting from the cold. The stocking cap helped a little, but he was really starting to worry. An infection could cost him his ear, or worse.

"It's cold as balls out here," Dale Jackson said. He rode Colton's horse, Obsidian. Saddlebags packed full of elk, deer, rabbit, and even squirrel meat hung over both horses.

"You think this is cold? Man, you white people don't know cold," Raven said.

Dale heaved a laugh, his breath coming out in a cloud of white. "You know, I didn't like you much at first, but you're a good guy, Sam. Funny, too. I didn't realize you had a sense of humor."

"I don't," Raven replied. He thought of the night of the North Korean attack, when Dale had nearly shot him on the road, and added, "For the record, I didn't like you much, either."

Dale hung his head ruefully. "I'm sorry. I wasn't thinkin' straight when I said those things to you. Went a bit crazy that night. Reminded me too much of…"

"No need to explain," Raven said. "I'm a combat vet too, you know."

"Right, and that makes us brothers."

"Yes it does."

He gave Willow a nudge, and continued down the road in silence, save for the sound of hooves clicking, as the sun retreated behind the mountains. They were headed for the new supply bunker on the eastern edge of town to store the meat. Raven had his crossbow strapped over his shoulder, wary of wild animals like coyotes and anyone that might be watching. He cradled an AR-15 and searched the woods framing the road for movement, but all was quiet.

After thirty minutes of trotting down the frontage road, they came upon the soccer field in the middle of the forest. It was a very odd place for it, but the perfect place to hide their supplies. Only two trails led to the area, and it was surrounded by forestland. The field was owned by a private school a mile away, and Lindsey had worked with the administrator to secure the land.

A pair of guards stood at the gate at the end of the dirt road. Dale dismounted and walked alongside Obsidian on the approach.

"Who goes there?" shouted one of the sentries silhouetted in the shadows of the pine trees.

"Raven Spears and Dale Jackson," Dale said.

"Ah, good evenin' gentlemen," replied the guard. They both lowered their rifles and opened the gate.

Raven saw the face of the first guard in the waning light. Rex Stone, the father of Melissa, nodded at him. Standing on his right was Jim Meyers, the former manager of the Stanley Inn.

"Todd and Susan Sanders brought home quite the prize today," Raven said. "They took down a buck with a couple of bows. We're dropping it off, along with a few other fresh kills, and then taking a tally before heading back out on patrol."

"Good news," Rex said. He finished opening the gate and gave Willow a pat on her neck.

"Pretty quiet tonight," said Meyers.

"Just the way we like it," Raven said.

"Heard things weren't so quiet on the highway today, though," Rex said.

"You heard right," Dale said. "But don't worry. We've got the situation under control. Right, Raven?"

"Yeah." Raven wasn't sure if he believed his own words, but the last thing he wanted was to scare people. Rex looked up as Raven and Willow passed, with the sad eyes of a grieving father. At least he had something to do. Being out here was better than sitting at home thinking about his little girl. Lilly, his wife, was working inside the bunker beneath the field tonight.

Raven and Dale guided their horses around the edge of the grass, and finally stopped when they got to a metal shed. After tying up the horses, they grabbed the satchels of fresh meat and lugged them inside the building while Rex and Jim stood guard.

The building looked like a machine shed, with racks of tools hanging on the walls and several tables in the center of the room. But under those tables was a trap door. Raven put the satchels down and then, with Dale's help, moved the table covering the industrial carpet. They pulled the carpet back and then opened the door, revealing a stairwell that led into a basement lit with an orange glow.

During the Cold War, the bunker had been built to shield the private school kids from a nuclear explosion. Now it was the best-guarded secret in Estes Park. And it was protected by a woman who wouldn't hesitate to blast an intruder in the face with her shotgun.

"Who goes there?" said Lilly Stone. She angled the gun up the stairs. Raven moved his head back and announced himself.

Lilly lowered the barrel. "Oh, okay. Come on down."

Raven and Dale brought the meat down in several trips. The chilly basement was a large open space with tables and racks full of canned food, massive barrels of water, medical supplies, and countless other goods. They had even turned a storage room into a refrigerator that doubled as the meat locker.

All told, it made up sixty percent of the town's supplies. The meat stored on Trail Ridge Road had also been transferred here.

Lilly handed Raven a clipboard, and he signed off on the new shipment. Then he went through the ledger, noting the supplies they had handed over to Thompson.

"That really hurt us," Lilly said. "Over five percent of our stock."

Raven scratched at the back of his neck. "I know, but like I said, we're going to get it all back, plus some. Trust me."

He didn't blame Lilly for her dirty look. After all, he hadn't been able to save her daughter. Even though it wasn't Raven's fault directly, he was sure Rex and Lilly hated him for his failure to bring their little girl home.

"You ready, Raven?" Dale asked.

"Yeah."

Raven handed Lilly the clipboard and followed Dale out to their horses. A few minutes later, they were on their way through the Beaver Meadows. Raven wanted to start the patrol off with a quick check of the area where Jennie and some of the other refugees had seen the figures they described as soldiers.

They only made it halfway when the walkie-talkie on Raven's duty belt crackled.

"Raven, this is Lindsey. What's your current location? Over."

"I'm just about back to town hall," Raven replied.

"We need you at the roadblock on 34. There's a vehicle. Meet me out front of the station. You can ride with me."

"We're on our way."

Raven clipped the radio back on his belt and gave Willow a gentle kick. "Let's go, girl," he said.

The two horses took off, breaking into a full-blown gallop along the side of the road. Lindsey was waiting with Detective Ryburn in the Volkswagen Beetle outside the station when they arrived. They started the car as soon as Raven and Dale rounded the corner. Saving gasoline was a huge part of their effort, which was part of the reason Raven and Dale were patrolling on horses, but this was an emergency. It would take thirty minutes to get to the roadblock on Willow.

Lindsey sped away as soon as they were all inside. They passed the first roadblock without even slowing, the car zipping through the open barriers at almost full speed. Another message came over Lindsey's radio as they approached the second roadblock, but she stayed focused on the road, flipping on the beams as the final glow of the sun receded.

"Get ready," she said.

Raven flicked the safety on his AR-15 off as Dale whispered a prayer. Lindsey slowed on the approach to the barrier. Raven squinted, unable to make out much. What he could see was several of the militia guards posted there with rifles lowered. They had someone surrounded.

"A refugee?" Lindsey said as she killed the engine. She

hopped out, and the men quickly followed her.

"What the hell is going on out here?" Lindsey asked.

Raven hurried over with his rifle at the ready, but paused in his tracks when he saw the battered face of the man the militia soldiers had surrounded.

"Chief Colton?" Lindsey gasped.

Raven took a step forward, confusion setting in. Was this some sort of a trap?

Colton moved out into the moonlight. His entire face was marked with a patchwork of cuts and bruises, and his right eye completely swollen shut. A gash divided his lips.

"Chief, what the hell happened to you?" Lindsey asked.

Colton wiped his mouth with a sleeve. "I killed 'em," he grumbled. "I killed Sheriff Thompson and his men."

Everyone went quiet, waiting for the chief to continue. But Colton just shook his head. He looked over at Raven, their eyes locking for a moment. Raven could see something had changed—something bad had happened to Colton out there.

"Get ready," Colton said to Raven, his voice raspy.

"For what?" Dale asked.

Colton shot him a glare. "For war."

— 8 —

Albert Randall sat up in bed. The pain was bad tonight. The worst yet. But that's what happened when you took a 5.56 mm round to the gut and refused most of the painkillers. He didn't want to end up like his sister—all doped up to the point he couldn't think or move.

After finally managing to prop his back up with the pillows, Albert watched Dave and Ty, who were sitting in chairs across the small room.

"Don't they have any movies in this joint?" Dave asked.

The boy Albert had discovered hiding in an abandoned apartment in Charlotte hadn't shut up for the past hour. Ty, on the other hand, had remained mostly quiet, waiting anxiously for his mother to come back from her trip. And, despite the doctor's orders, Albert was playing babysitter to them both.

"This place is boring. I want to go fishing. I thought they said we were gonna live at the ocean. I don't see no water." He tapped his tennis shoes on the ground, the noise grating on Albert's already frayed nerves.

"There are some movies in the lounge," Ty said. "But I don't think they have anything cool. Just sappy drama stuff."

"They got *Lord of the Rings*?" Dave asked.

Albert chuckled despite himself, and then gritted his

teeth to fend off the pulsating pain.

"Yo, Mr. Big Al! When are we going to get out of this place and get back to our quest?" Dave asked. "We haven't completed our mission to Mordor yet."

Albert couldn't tell if the boy was being serious or not.

Neither could Ty, apparently. "You're joking, right?" he asked.

Dave grinned from ear to ear. "Kinda. I've slayed enough Orcs for now. There shall come a day when men fail, but that day is not today."

Albert shook his head. The kid had slaughtered the movie quote.

"That's not how it goes. Besides, you're not a man. You're just a kid," Ty said.

Dave stood with his hands on his hips. "How dare you talk to Frodo like that."

"You're not Frodo either," Ty said with a heavy sigh.

"And you're not gonna join the Fellowship. You can't walk anyways."

Ty quickly furrowed his brows, and then looked at the ground. Seeing the boy's pain almost hurt Albert worse than the gunshot wound. It was a different type of pain that made his heart ache.

"Knock it off, Dave," Albert growled. "Ty is more than capable of keeping up with us when we head back out on our mission to Mordor."

Dave ran his sweatshirt sleeve across his nose, dragging a strand of snot.

"I'm sorry. I didn't mean you can't come. You can be a Hobbit too," Dave said. He waited a moment for Ty to respond, but Ty just shrugged a shoulder.

"Really, I'm sorry," Dave entreated.

"It's okay. I'm used to it."

Albert's heart continued to hurt for the boy. This wasn't the first time he had been put down for his disability, and Albert knew it wouldn't be the last.

"For real, though. When the Fellowship heads back out, you're coming with," Dave said.

Ty cracked a half smile. "Okay."

"I'm coming with, too," Albert said. "Keep you stinkers out of trouble."

The kids both chuckled, but Albert had to force a laugh. Ty and Dave had both seen the horrors out there. Hopefully, neither of them would have to face it again. Not if Albert could help it. That's why he had to get better. As soon as he was on his feet again, he had a feeling he would be heading back out into the fray.

A heart rate monitor chirped next to Albert's bed.

"What's that?" Dave asked. "Does that mean the Orcs are coming?"

"Yes," Albert said, trying to keep a straight face. He gritted his teeth again at another wave of pain through his gut. It felt like a hot knife jabbing his insides.

Both of the boys watched Albert anxiously, concern painted on their faces.

"Are you okay, Mr. Big Al?" Dave asked, his nasally voice cracking.

"Yeah, I'm..." Albert groaned. "I'm fine."

"I think Officer Randall needs to rest, boys," came a voice from the open doorway. Doctor Parish stood there, her arms folded across her white coat.

"Aw, man," Dave said.

"Let's go see if we can find a good movie," Ty said. He wheeled his chair toward the door, but Dave walked over and put his hand on Albert's.

"Feel better, Mr. Big Al. I miss hanging out with you."

Albert patted Dave's hand. "Thanks, kid."

Dave flashed a toothy grin and then followed Ty out of the room, pushing past a skinny figure standing in the doorway beside the doctor.

"Jacqueline," Parish said. "I didn't realize you were up."

Albert hardly recognized his sister. She was gaunt as a scarecrow, and her wrinkled face appeared ten years older than he remembered. The drugs had nearly destroyed his twin sister. But there was hope for her now. She was finally safe.

"Mind if I talk to my brother for a few minutes?" Jacqueline asked.

Parish looked at Albert, and he gave her an approving nod.

"Make it fast, ma'am. He really does need to rest."

Jacqueline dragged a chair over to Albert's bedside and took a seat. This was the first time she had visited him since he had woken up from surgery. She still hadn't looked him in the eye, her gaze constantly flitting from side to side, focused on anything but him.

"Hey, sis," he said.

"Hi."

"I'm glad I found you." He struggled to find the right words. "I'm... I'm sorry it took me so long to try and make up for the..."

He didn't even finish his sentence before she started crying. The tears streamed away from the crow's feet framing her dark brown eyes.

"Hey," Albert said, reaching out. "Don't cry, Jackie. It's going to be okay. You're safe now. You're going to get the help you need."

"I don't deserve it." She finally met his gaze. "That's

what you don't understand, Al. I wasn't just getting high when you found me. I was trying to end the nightmare."

Albert swallowed hard, unsure what to say. It was difficult for him to fathom just how dark a place she had been in. How could his own sister, his twin, want to end her life? But then again, the world had gone mad, and she was addicted to heroin. The combination could drive anyone over the edge.

He reached out, and she huddled closer so he could wrap his arms around her. The embrace hurt, but he didn't care about the pain.

"I love you, Jackie."

"You too."

Albert looked up to see another figure standing in the doorway. This time it was Charlize. She backed away to give the siblings some privacy, but Albert held up a free hand to tell her to wait.

As soon as Jackie pulled away, Albert said, "Secretary Montgomery, how was your trip?"

The hard look on her face told Albert there was trouble. She hadn't just come to see how he was feeling. It looked like he might be headed back into the field even sooner than he thought.

***

Sandra Spears put on a new pair of surgical gloves. It was the one item they weren't running low on, which was a good thing considering the number of patients going in and out of the operating room. The most important thing at this point was making sure everything remained sanitary. A cut could turn into an infection, and an infection could lead to sepsis, or staph, or Necrotizing

Fasciitis, the flesh-eating bacteria that had nearly killed Teddy.

Her next patient had plenty of deep cuts that could easily become infected. He was also the last person Sandra had expected to be treating during her shift tonight.

"Chief Colton," she said. "It's good to see you."

Colton acknowledged her with a dip of his head, but didn't reply. He sat on the table, stripped down to his briefs. Bruises and cuts marked much of his bare skin, including two nasty purple spots on both his shins.

Doctor Duffy asked Colton several questions, but the chief didn't reply to any of them with more than a shrug or a one-word response.

It was a product of shock, or perhaps post-traumatic stress. Sandra could only imagine what had occurred during Colton's captivity, but from the looks of it, he had been tortured. His right eyelid was swollen shut, and his lip had been split down the middle like a worm cut in half. She had only seen a few men beaten this badly in her life.

"Just patch me up. I need to get back to the station," Colton said.

"You're in shock, Chief," Duffy replied. "You need to rest and heal."

Colton looked up, his left eye homing in on the doctor. "There's no time to rest. Not with what's coming."

Sandra and Duffy exchanged a glance.

"Just patch me up," Colton said.

"Okay, Chief," Duffy replied. He nodded at Sandra. She grabbed the sanitizing supplies while Duffy prepared the sutures. She pulled out the antibiotic ointment and saturated a cotton ball with the liquid.

"This is going to sting," she said.

Colton remained quiet while she worked with the doctor to clean his wounds. By the time Sandra and Doctor Duffy were finished, they had given him twenty stitches in three locations.

"Thanks," Colton said. He stood and began putting his clothes back on.

"You're really not going to tell us anything?" Duffy asked. "I know you probably don't want to talk, but there's a lot of rumors floating around, and it would be good to—"

Colton cut the doctor off. "What kind of rumors?"

There was a short pause as Sandra turned away to put the supplies back into a cabinet.

"About what happened to you, and with Sergeant Aragon and Officer Hines…" Duffy said, his words trailing off.

Colton bent down to lace up his boots, gritting his teeth in pain. "Listen, I really got to get back to the station, and I don't want to tell this story more than once. If you can spare Sandra for a few hours, she can brief everyone here when she comes back."

Duffy shrugged his approval. "That's fine, I suppose."

"But Allie," Sandra began to say.

"She will be fine," Duffy said. "I'll make sure she's looked after while you're gone."

Sandra didn't like the idea of leaving her daughter here alone with Creek and Teddy, but they were all sleeping, and there were guards posted. Chances were she would be back before the kids woke up.

She followed Colton out to the lobby, where his wife and daughter were waiting.

"Daddy!" Risa shouted, bolting out of her chair.

Kelly had her arms folded across her chest. She hadn't bothered trying to fix the smudged mascara around her eyes.

Colton wrapped his arms around Risa. "Hey, kiddo."

"Anything broken?" Kelly asked.

"Nah, just some scratches." Colton reached out and pulled his wife close in a three-way hug with their daughter.

Sandra stepped outside to give them some privacy. Dale Jackson stood guarding the Volkswagen van in the front drive. He chewed on an unlit cigar and cradled a rifle across his beefy chest.

"Evenin', Nurse Spears," he said.

"Hello, Dale."

She put her back up to the van and watched Colton and his family inside the lobby.

"Nice to see a happy reunion for once," she said.

Dale dipped his hat in assent.

A few minutes later, Colton and his family walked into the parking lot. He was doing his best not to limp, from the looks of it, but Sandra could see when someone was trying to mask pain. Humans were just like animals. There were other tells, like a clenched jaw.

"Drop me and Sandra off at town hall," Colton instructed Dale. "Then give my family a lift home."

"You got it, Chief," Dale said.

By the time they got to the town hall, it was close to midnight. Colton said goodbye to his family and then led Sandra to the conference room, where several folks were huddled around the table listening to a radio. Raven and Lindsey were there, along with Mayor Gail Andrews and the town administrator, Tom Feagen.

100

"Fifty thousand Chinese boots on the ground, and twenty-five thousand soldiers," Raven said. "Plus fighter jets. It's a lot of firepower."

"Chief's back," Lindsey said.

Raven glanced over, seeing Sandra first. "What the heck are you doing here, sis?"

Sandra walked over to give him a quick hug. "Colton asked me to come to the briefing so I can tell the doctors what's going on."

"Have a seat everyone," Colton said. He waited a few minutes, pacing, while several more people joined them in the conference room, including Margaret the dispatcher. Sandra took a seat next to Lindsey. The detective continued listening to the radio while they waited.

After everyone had gathered, Colton cleared his throat and said, "I called this meeting to tell you what's going on out there, and to make some changes in light of the situation with Don Aragon and Sam Hines." He directed his gaze to Mayor Andrews.

"Your tenure as mayor is over," Colton said. His eyes shifted to Feagen. "You're out, too, Tom."

"What?" Gail said, taking off her glasses. "You can't just—"

Colton pounded the table with a fist, the sound echoing through the room and silencing the woman.

"You're out, Gail. You and Tom can clean out your offices, but then you need to get the hell out of this building. I don't want to see you here ever again," Colton snapped.

The raw anger in his voice frightened Sandra. She had never seen the chief act like this before.

"You can't do that," Feagen said. "You don't have the authority. Mayor Andrews is an elected official."

"We're under martial law, Tom, and we have a foreign army on our soil now. Things don't work the way they used to. You're lucky I don't throw you both in jail," Colton said.

"On what charge?" Gail asked.

"How about conspiring to kill Raven and me?" Lindsey said.

Raven bobbed his head. "If it were up to me, we'd kick you both out of town to fend for yourselves."

"You were too close to Don all along, Gail," Colton said. "I don't trust you anymore. And Tom, you're weak. I need strong people running this town."

"Yeah," Raven said again.

Lindsey walked over to Gail and gestured toward the door. "Go and pack up your things," Lindsey said.

"This is crazy," Gail said. "You won't get away with it."

Sandra stepped up next to Lindsey to show her support. She had never been a fan of the mayor, but hearing she might have known something about Don's plot to kill her brother made her blood boil.

Colton jerked his bruised chin toward the door. "Get out," he said firmly.

The former mayor and her second in command both glared at Colton, but then filed out of the room muttering darkly to each other.

"Guess we're going to have to hold another election," Lindsey said.

Colton shook his head. "Right now our focus is on survival."

"You told us to prepare for war," Raven said. "What did you mean?"

"We've got a lot of enemies out there. Not just

Thompson's goons. Men like Fenix and Redford. And winter isn't far off."

"Damn, we just never catch a break, do we?" Lindsey said with a slow head shake.

"We will survive if we're smart," Colton said. "I was stupid to leave Estes Park and try and negotiate with Thompson. He may be dead, but his people have some of our supplies."

"I'm sorry," Raven said.

Colton palmed the table, displaying bloodied knuckles. "I want an updated inventory of the food and supplies after today's charity run. And I want a plan to get back what you guys handed over earlier today."

Raven stared at the Chief's hands and wondered how many lives the chief had taken today with those hands, but he decided it didn't matter. Whatever happened from here on out was justified if it meant saving their families. He and Colton were both prepared to do whatever it took.

"You hear me, Sam?"

Raven nodded. "Loud and clear, Chief."

— 9 —

Fenix opened the breech to make sure the .357 Magnum was fully loaded with six bullets. He snapped it shut with a smile, holstered the gun, and then grabbed his suppressed M4.

The convoy of Sons of Liberty vehicles was stopped on a dirt road at the edge of a dense forest. Sergeant Horton sat in the back seat of a Jeep with Fenix, listening to chatter over a handheld radio.

"Hacker says this is the place," Horton confirmed.

Fenix twisted around to look out the back window at Hacker. The former associate of Nile Redford had provided a map to this place, and while Fenix didn't completely trust him, they didn't have any choice if they wanted to find the boss.

"Let's move out, but tell the men to be cautious. This could be a trap," Fenix said.

Horton gave the order over the radio. Twenty-four SOL soldiers piled out of trucks and Jeeps and fanned out toward the forest with their weapons in combat position, sweeping for contacts. It was two in the morning and freezing, but the temperature wasn't going to deter these patriots from doing what they needed to do.

Splitting off into four teams, the soldiers moved toward their target—Nile Redford's mansion. It hadn't taken much for Hacker—whose real name turned out to be Tony—to give up the location. Fenix had promised him a job, and Hacker had put his finger on the map quicker than a hooker taking a Benjamin for services rendered.

That's what Hacker was now—a prostitute. Fenix would have laughed if he wasn't prepping for battle.

He got out of the truck with Horton and did a quick scan of the area. They were just west of Granby, Colorado, about fourteen miles from Rocky Mountain National Park and eighty-five miles west of Denver.

The last of the fire-teams vanished into the woods, leaving only the drivers and a few sentries with Fenix and Horton. The men had the element of surprise, but some of them would still die tonight. Maybe even Fenix himself. But it was worth the risk.

"Bring Hacker over here," Fenix said.

Horton flashed a hand signal and waited for the prisoner. Hacker kept low, like he was worried about getting hit. That told Fenix they were in the right place.

"You're sure Redford is here?" Fenix asked.

Hacker nodded.

"You wouldn't lie to me, now would you, Tony?" Fenix asked.

"No, sir."

"Good. Now follow me."

Fenix flashed a hand signal and Sergeant Horton took point. He moved toward the forest with his rifle shouldered. Fenix and four other SOL soldiers led Hacker into the woods with rifles at the ready.

These were the same guns his men had given to Theo earlier that day. Funny how that worked, Fenix thought to himself. Now they were going to be used to exterminate the rest of Nile Redford's henchmen, and take everything the bastard owned.

Horton balled his hand into a fist as they entered a clearing. Fenix looked over his shoulder and flashed a shit-eating grin at the man who was going to help the Sons of Liberty enter the Redford compound. Hacker was crouched next to the trunk of a tree, his hands bound and his weapons removed.

"How does it feel to have the tables turned?" Fenix whispered.

"I told you, I never liked Nile much," Hacker replied.

"We'll see about that," Fenix said, pulling out a radio from his vest. He held it up to Hacker's mouth. "Go ahead," he said.

"White Crow, this is Hacker. Reporting in. All is well here, over."

Static crackled from the speaker for several seconds before a voice replied. "Copy that, Hacker. Talk to you in the mornin'."

Fenix pulled the radio back. "How many men did you say are posted here?"

A shrug from Hacker. "Maybe a dozen. Could be less, could be a few more. Just depends."

"Depends on what?" Fenix asked.

"How many Redford decided to post. I don't know, man. It just depends on the night."

"What do you think, Sarge?" Fenix asked.

"I think we can take 'em. We got the cover of darkness and the element of surprise."

"I agree," Fenix replied. "Let's move in."

A messy flood of adrenaline soaked into his nerve endings. It was the calm before the storm, something that always came right before combat.

And Fenix loved it to his core.

Horton crept up to where a man named Geoff Hough

was posted with a sniper rifle. Fenix tucked the radio back in its pouch pocket and then patted Hacker on the shoulder.

"You better hope they bought it, or you're going to be very sorry," Fenix said. He motioned for one of the other men to guard Hacker, and then moved up next to Horton, using the time to scan the mansion on the other side of the fort of trees.

It was an impressive house with a brick and stone façade and a wrap-around porch overlooking a small lake at the center of the property. He counted at least four chimneys sprouting from the roof. Sprawling gardens and fancy metal fences surrounded the ten-acre plot.

"Three contacts," Horton said.

Fenix took up position next to the sergeant. The red glow of a cigarette gave away the position of one of the sentries, but Fenix strained to make out the silhouette of the man in the darkness. He borrowed the night vision goggles. Sure enough, three men were patrolling the porch. He handed the goggles to Hough next.

"Take 'em down," Fenix ordered.

The suppressed crack came a second later, and Fenix watched the lit cigarette fall to the porch floor along with a body. Two more cracks followed, and two more bodies hit the ground.

Horton flashed a hand signal, and the fire-team bolted out of the tree line and toward the drive that twisted up to the massive metal gate.

Two more sentries had been posted here, but both were already on the ground with what looked like massive toothpicks sticking out of their backs.

Indians dead from arrows, Fenix thought, smiling at the irony. The SOL soldier that had fired the crossbow was working on cutting the lock off the gate with bolt cutters.

On the eastern side of the forest, the other fire-teams came striding out, weapons up, moving in combat intervals. They were just shadows in the darkness. As soon as the gate was opened, the teams came together, flooding the property. They had made it halfway through the gardens before gunfire cracked from a third-story window.

"Find cover!" Horton yelled.

He didn't need to tell the men. They were already fanning out and taking up cover behind hedges and brick walls.

"Bring in the trucks!" Fenix shouted.

The engines growled. More shots rang out from the porch as Redford's men figured out what was happening. It wasn't the way Fenix had planned on things going down, but they still had the numbers.

He took up position behind a brick wall, keeping his head low. The pickups and a Jeep pulled onto the road about a quarter mile behind them.

A shout came from his right, and he glanced over to see one of his men take two bullets to the chest. He hit the ground and squirmed for several seconds before going still.

All around Fenix, muzzle flashes lit up the night like drunk fireflies. A round chipped the brick overhead, and he got down to his belly. He crawled to the side of the ledge and peeked around the corner, counting six shooters behind the windows, and five more on the porch.

Another SOL soldier dove for cover next to Fenix before he could fire on any of the targets. It was John Stone, a thirty-year-old staff sergeant who had served under Fenix in Iraq, and he was bleeding bad.

"I'm hit, General," Stone choked, gripping his gut.

Even in the weak light, Fenix could see the man wasn't going to make it. Not without medical support.

"Hang in there, John," Fenix said. Then he shouted, "Get the M240 up here!"

As if in answer, the big gun mounted to the back of the pickup truck barked. Tracer rounds streaked into the mansion, shattering brick and glass.

"Hell yes, that's what I'm talking about," Fenix said. He turned back to Stone. "We're going to get you out of…" His words trailed off when he saw the man was already dead, his eyes staring up at the moon.

"Shit," Fenix muttered. He propped up a leg and aimed his M4 over the wall at the porch. He squeezed off a barrage of automatic fire at one of the enemy shooters.

God, it felt good to fire a gun again.

He held down the trigger, not caring about his ammunition. There was plenty of it, and from what Hacker said, there was a ton of brass and weapons in the basement of the mansion.

Fenix centered the barrel on the other muzzle flash, hitting his target with grim satisfaction. Taking the life of an enemy was one of the greatest feelings in the world. There was no rush of power quite like it.

The 7.62 mm rounds from the big gun on the truck slammed into the side of the house, punching through stone and brick, and shattering glass with cracks and thumps. The man on the big gun was an expert. He raked it back and forth, making the enemy on the porch run for cover while the other SOL soldiers picked them off.

Or, at least, the soldiers *should* have been picking them off. Fenix looked around him to see his men waiting for the M240 to do all the work.

"Fire!" Fenix shouted. "Everyone fucking fire!"

He came up on one knee again to lead by example. The automatic gunfire returned from all directions. The noise rose into a din that made his head hurt, but it was still music to his ears.

Fenix ejected another spent magazine, plucked one from his vest, and then continued firing. The overhang on the porch crashed to the ground, and a gutter fell away from the building. Hunks of broken stone pummeled the dirt and flowerbeds around the house.

A final muzzle flash came from the third-floor window. The man was a brave bastard, but stupid. Fenix aimed his rifle at the last guard—along with every other SOL soldier.

Hundreds of bullets hit the window all at once, shattering the frame and breaking away the brick exterior. The man toppled out, crashing to the porch below.

"Hold your fire!" someone yelled. It took another shouted order before the gunfire finally ceased.

Fenix watched the house for movement, moving his barrel across the façade and broken windows.

"That looks like all of 'em," called a hoarse voice.

"Bring me Hacker," Fenix replied. It took a few minutes, but Horton finally brought the man across the battlefield.

"Twelve to fifteen guards, my ass," Fenix said.

Hacker didn't reply, and Fenix scrutinized him in the dim light. From the look of it, he was shivering. Fenix wasn't sure if it was from fear or the cold. If it wasn't the latter, then he had grossly underestimated the man. He scanned Hacker again, raised a nostril, and then handed the radio to him.

"Tell your boss to get out here," Fenix said, spitting in the dirt.

Hacker relayed the message as the SOL soldiers moved in. Fenix counted twenty soldiers, bringing their losses to just four from the fire-teams.

Not bad at all.

The men stopped beyond the porch, their rifles aimed at the front door. It creaked open a few minutes later, and a man wearing a suit stepped out holding a hat with a red feather. He put it on his head, and then gripped his shoulder.

He thinks I'm going to take him prisoner. That's why he threw on his suit and hat, Fenix thought.

"You got me, General!" Redford shouted. "You won."

Fenix left his position and slowly walked over, cautious but confident.

"Where's my cousin?" Redford asked, looking at Hacker.

Fenix stopped at the bottom of the steps. He reached into his pocket and pulled out a plastic bag containing Theo's eyeballs, which he then tossed onto the porch.

"This is what's left of him," Fenix said with a half shrug.

Redford looked down at the package, and then back at Fenix, his jaw clenched with rage.

"You really thought you could win this?" Fenix asked dryly. "You really thought you could beat the Sons of Liberty?"

He didn't wait for Redford to reply, and gestured for Hacker. The man moved forward and stood at the bottom of the steps. Redford's eyes widened in confusion before realization set in.

Fenix drew the .357 Magnum he'd taken from Theo

and handed it to Hacker.

"Show me you really want to work for the Sons of Liberty, and finish this," Fenix said. Then he turned and walked away. Three beats later, a gunshot cracked behind him.

A smile broke across Fenix's face at the sound of Redford's body hitting the porch. Fenix stopped and walked back to the porch, realizing he had forgotten part of what he'd come to collect.

Walking up the stairs, he then bent down next to Redford's corpse and plucked the hat off his head. Blood splatter had soiled the rim and he wiped it on the front of Redford's fancy suit.

Fenix stood and placed the hat on, smiling at his men. "What do you boys think?"

"I think the Sons of Liberty are back in business, sir," Horton said.

"Damn straight," Fenix said with a dip of his new souvenir.

***

Four days had passed since Charlize returned from Fort Lauderdale. Albert was already making gains in his recovery, and Dave and Ty had taken a real liking to one another. The restoration efforts were moving full steam ahead, with their NATO allies and the Chinese moving up the coasts and inland. Every day seemed to bring another new disaster. One of them was being reported by Captain Harris over the satellite phone.

"Yesterday, a Chinese supply convoy was hit by raiders on a road just west of Jacksonville," he said. "Two Chinese soldiers and a worker were killed. The American forces pushed the raiders back, and the Chinese showed remarkable restraint."

"That's good to hear," Charlize replied.

"Yes, but I'm not sure how much longer that will last. This is the second attack I've seen since the landing, and there are rumors about other attacks."

"I'm well aware," Charlize said. "So far we haven't had any reports of Chinese soldiers firing on civilians, but I'm guessing that will change soon."

"I hope not, but I agree that it's only a matter of time, ma'am. On another note, I've been assigned a liaison that reports directly to General Lin. I'm hoping to get more intel from him, but so far he's been pretty tight-lipped about things."

"Keep working," she said. "Is there anything else to report?"

"Yes, ma'am. As I'm sure you're aware, a Chinese container ship and an American ship collided in the harbor in New York. The Chinese vessel sank with over ten thousand pounds of medical supplies on board."

"I've seen the report," she said dryly. "These are the types of mistakes that costs lives, Captain. We can't afford for things like this to happen."

"I know, especially with the news coming out of SC 115 in New Jersey…"

"What news?"

"Cholera. There are several reported cases."

Charlize cursed under her breath. She would need to give that information to Ellen Price shortly, assuming the Secretary of Health and Human Services didn't already know. It was entirely possible she didn't, though, considering how convoluted the communication network was.

"Is there anything else, Captain?" she asked.

"Negative, ma'am."

"Keep up the good work, and stay safe."

"Will do, and you too."

She hung up the line, returned the phone, and walked back to the conference room for yet another briefing. Inside sat Lundy, Vice President Walter, Price, and General Thor, along with National Security Advisor Duane Ibsen. It looked like President Diego was still running late.

Charlize took her seat next to Price, and looked over to Colonel Raymond, who was standing in front of one of ten maps on moveable stands.

"Sorry about that," Charlize said. "I had to take that call."

"No problem," Raymond said. "As I was saying, in region 1 we are making great strides." He pointed at the orange block of the United States, representing Florida, Georgia, Alabama, and South Carolina. "Most of northern Florida past Orlando should have power restored by this time next month, if all goes to plan. But region 2 won't be so fortunate."

He moved over to the next board, with a map of North Carolina, Tennessee, Kentucky, Virginia, West Virginia, and Maryland.

"The ground burst in Washington, D.C. has caused devastation that we simply aren't prepared to deal with. Between hundreds of miles of destroyed power lines, radiation contamination, and the surge from the EMP, we've got an environmental disaster that will take decades to remedy. And unfortunately, we don't have a solution right now."

"I thought we did have a solution," said Walter.

Charlize looked at the vice president. He was still new to the job, but so was Charlize. Thus far, she wasn't too impressed with the former Fortune 500 executive.

"There's no solution to the environmental disaster, sir," Raymond said.

"That's not what I meant," Walter said, heaving a sigh. He stood and made his way over to the maps. He pulled at his cufflinks before picking up the pointer. Then he traced a circle with the tip around D.C. on the region 2 map.

"This approximate area is to be fenced off and secured for the indefinite future. Signage will be posted warning of the radiation poisoning. All recovery missions will cease. Anyone inside the zone is on their own now."

"We didn't agree to that last part," Charlize said. "I was told recovery missions would continue."

President Diego walked into the room and shut the door behind him. "Sorry I'm late," he said. When no one responded, he ran his fingers through his thick black hair, a nervous tick. "Okay, what did I miss?"

"We're talking about the radiation zone," Charlize said. "Vice President Walter—"

"I just told them we're blocking the area off and canceling recovery missions," Walter said, cutting Charlize off.

Diego looked to his second in command and then over to Charlize, nodding at her in confirmation.

"It's a matter of logistics, Secretary Montgomery," he said.

Charlize knew from experience that he only used her title when he knew she would be pissed. And she was really pissed. Albert had already accepted that his family was likely dead, but how was she supposed to tell him that the government was ceasing all recovery efforts? There had to be other people out there hunkered down and waiting for help.

"Listen, I know how it sounds, but we have to focus on the people we can still save. With that said, I will authorize missions on a case-by-case basis," Diego said.

It was something, but Charlize was still pretty disappointed in the president.

"Shall we continue?" Walter said, handing the pointer back to Raymond.

"By all means, sir," Charlize said.

Raymond waited for Diego and Walter to take seats, and then continued the briefing. They went through the other ten regions, one by one, going over estimated delivery dates for the grid restoration. Some would take months, but many would be much longer than that depending on resistance, weather, and violence.

"These are just estimates," Lundy cut in. "The variables Colonel Raymond just mentioned could lead to…issues beyond our control."

"But *most* of the country will have their lights back in a year," Raymond said.

"How does this change our casualty rate estimates?" Diego asked.

Lundy pulled out a piece of paper from his folder and placed it neatly in front of him. He was a numbers guy, just like the president, which is probably why Diego liked him so much.

"Sir, we estimated about thirty percent of our population would perish in the first month after the blast. That estimate was a bit high, but from the data I've seen coming in from the SCs, it's likely where we are headed. However, if we can continue moving supplies and

TRACKERS 4: THE DAMNED

restoring power, we should be able to bring down the final death count considerably."

"If we can evacuate areas without power into areas with power," Walter said. "That's key."

"Good," Diego said. He grabbed his bottled water with his scarred hand and took a drink. "I've been in constant contact with the Chinese president, and he has promised they will continue supplying LPTs, equipment, workers, et cetera, until the job is done."

He looked to Charlize. "Do you have anything to add about the current recovery efforts?"

"Yes, Mr. President." She stood to address the room. "First off, SC 115 in New Jersey has reported several cases of cholera."

"I'm aware, but I was only informed of that fact a few hours ago," said Price. She didn't ask where Charlize got the information, and Charlize didn't volunteer it.

"The recovery efforts with the Chinese are going well for the most part, but another convoy was attacked yesterday," Charlize said. "What I'm told is that the Chinese soldiers did not return fire despite two of their soldiers and one worker being killed."

"General Lin isn't happy about it, but he also understands this sort of thing is inevitable, especially as we cross into zones where people have had no contact with the government for the past month," Diego said. "When they see Chinese troops, they panic and think we are being invaded."

"Which is why I'm suggesting another air drop of pamphlets explaining what is going on," Charlize said. "The SCs should also be broadcasting this information."

"Make sure it happens," Diego said.

"There's also been a collision in the New York

harbor," Charlize added. "We lost an entire shipment of medical supplies. It's a huge setback."

"We're dealing with that," Diego said. He took another drink. "Is there anything else?"

Charlize shook her head. "No sir, that's all I have for now."

"I do have one more item." Diego twisted in his chair and pointed to region 1. "Since we were on this topic earlier, I thought I would let you know I'm actively seeking a new home for the White House now that we've officially decided to seal off D.C."

He turned back to Charlize.

"And since you are fond of road trips, I'd like you to scout out a few locations for me over the next few weeks. Right now, New York City is looking like one of the most promising places," he said. "Perhaps Officer Randall will be able to accompany you?"

She gave the president a curt nod, but inside she was seething. He wanted her to go check out new locations for the White House when the country was bursting at the seams and barreling toward winter?

"Good, it's settled then," Diego said. "You'll head to New York as soon as your schedule allows to find me a home for the White House."

Charlize flipped her folder shut and stood. "Yes, sir."

— 10 —

Almost a week had passed since Colton had returned from Fort Collins. The chief had warned Raven and everyone else in Estes Park to prepare for war, but the retaliation for Sheriff Thompson's death hadn't come. Fenix, Redford, and their other enemies hadn't shown up either.

Not yet, anyway.

Instead, a traveler named Robbie Cotter from southern Colorado had shown up at one of the roadblocks in Estes Park with other news—news about Nile Redford.

The report had rocked Raven to his core, and he'd raced to the station to talk to the man. Colton was already busy with his own questions.

Raven waited with his back to the wall, arms folded across his chest, trying to get a read on Robbie. The fifty-year-old man sat at a table facing Colton, his baldhead dipped low as he stroked his gray beard. He smelled like a mixture of body odor and grease, which told Raven he wasn't lying when he said he was a mechanic.

"So that's why you came here?" Colton asked. "For work?"

"Heard you guys were offering protection and food to people with skills like mine. I've worked on cars since I was old enough to hold a wrench."

"Okay, but explain to me why you name-dropped Nile

Redford at our roadblock," Raven chimed in.

Robbie looked over. "'Cause I used to work on his cars, man, and he came back to Granby a few weeks ago bragging about how he stole a shit-ton of supplies from Estes Park. I figured you guys might want to know where those supplies are now."

Raven and Colton exchanged a quick glance.

"So you worked for Redford. Why did you leave?" Colton asked.

"I don't like dealing with Nazis."

"What?" Colton asked, leaning forward with his elbows on the table.

"Mr. Redford's teamed up with some Nazis. I left as soon as I heard the news. Started walking north to find a new place to work, and a few refugees told me about Estes Park. I remembered the town from things I overheard Redford talking to his men about, including the raid of your stockpile."

"Wait, back up," Colton said. "Tell me more about the Nazis."

Robbie shrugged. "Nazis, man. That's all I heard."

"Was one of them called General Fenix?" Raven asked.

Robbie shifted his gaze away from Colton to Raven.

"Phoenix?" Robbie said. "Like, Arizona?"

"Just answer the question," Colton replied.

"Never heard of nobody called that. All I know is that Redford had captured some Nazis and then teamed up with the bastards, and that didn't sit real well with me." He reached into a pocket on his overalls and fished out a rolled-up smoke.

"You mind?" he asked.

Colton shook his head. Robbie lit the homemade

cigarette with a match and took in a puff.

"So you got a job for me here or not?" he asked, exhaling through his nose.

"If your story adds up, maybe," Colton said. He gestured for Raven to meet him in the hallway. Raven already knew what the chief was going to say, but he would have volunteered for the mission anyway.

"Let me scope it out, see if Redford is there with any SOL soldiers," Raven said. "If they are, then two birds, one stone. Right, Chief?"

Colton brought a hand up to touch his swollen right eyelid. It had opened partially, but his face was still the color of ripe fruit.

"Look, I know we want those supplies from Fort Collins, but Redford's got our stuff, too. It might make more sense to try and raid his compound than to hit Fort Collins."

"I agree," Colton said, to Raven's surprise. "Take Dale with you."

Raven perked up. "You serious?"

"Yeah. Take Dale and go tonight." Colton held out his hand and gripped Raven's arm, hard. "You see Redford or any Sons of Liberty, you don't kill them, you got it? You're only going on a recon mission to check this lead out. No violence. I need you and Dale alive."

Raven wasn't sure he could hold up his end of the deal. "I mean, if I see a Nazi, I'm not sure I can help pulling the trigger."

"Promise me, or I won't authorize this mission," Colton said.

"Fine. Now, will you let go of my sleeve? It's getting wrinkled."

Colton smiled, or tried to, but his bruised face merely

seemed to distort. Raven returned the smile and jogged out of the station.

That afternoon, Raven spent his time preparing for the road ahead. He and Dale loaded the Swag Wagon with cold weather gear just in case they got stranded. The most important piece of gear was the night vision goggles that would allow Raven to drive in the dark without headlights. On the way out of town, they stopped at the hospital where Raven pitched the mission to Sandra the same way Colton had pitched it to him—recon only.

"It's dangerous to leave Estes Park no matter what, Sam," she said. "Every time you go out there, I worry it'll be the last time I see you."

"I promise I'll be careful."

She gave him a hug, clearly too exhausted to argue. He kissed Creek goodbye and gave Allie a hug, and then drove south to the first roadblock, where Dale motioned for him to stop.

Sarah, the refugee girl, and her caretaker, Jennie, were both posted there with a dozen other people. Dale had taken a real liking to them. They were staying on his property to look after his livestock, but truth be told, Dale seemed happy to have the company regardless of the help. It was yet another reason Raven had changed his mind about the veteran. He'd proven that people could change. Hell, Raven had proved the same about himself. He hadn't taken a sip of alcohol for weeks.

Jennie stepped over to the passenger window with Sarah by her side.

"Can I come?" the young girl asked without so much as a hello.

Dale patted her on the top of her stocking cap. "Not this time, kiddo. You got chickens to look after."

He winked at Jennie.

I see how it is, Raven thought, realization setting in. Dale had a thing for Jennie. Raven relaxed in his seat, giving Dale time to say his goodbyes. To Raven's surprise, Sarah walked over to his side of the van.

"Hey, you never gave me anything," she said.

"Huh?" Raven said.

"Back at the police station, a few weeks ago, you said you had something for me."

"Oh, yeah." Raven sighed, and then fished a butterfly knife out of his rucksack in the back seat.

"Holy shit," she said when he handed it to her.

"Watch your language. And be very careful with that," Dale said. He looked over at Raven and grumbled something about how it was a dumb idea.

"Don't use that until I get back," Dale told Sarah. He turned to Jennie. "Please make sure she doesn't stab herself. Or anyone else."

Jennie laughed. "I'll try, Dale."

"You ready to go?" Raven said.

"I'll be back soon," Dale told Jennie.

"Thanks for the cool knife," Sarah said.

Dale shook his head, but beneath his beard he was smiling. Raven drove the vehicle through the center of the open barriers. Wind whistled through the open window, but no matter what Raven did, he couldn't get the damn thing to roll up. At least it wasn't snowing.

The glow of the sun slowly retreated over the terrain as they drove farther away from the secure borders of Estes Park. It didn't take long before they hit the areas where hundreds of acres of forest had been reduced to ash.

"Holy shit," Dale said. "You guys weren't kidding. It

really looks like the apocalypse out here."

The endless view reminded Raven of the Sioux story about the end of the world, the same story he had shared with Nathan Sardetti. A moment of despair gripped him at the thought of the pilot, and Raven made a mental promise to Nathan that he would capture Shunka Sapa, the monstrous black dog in the Sioux story whom Raven believed was General Dan Fenix.

"I'll find Shunka Sapa, and I'll kill him," Raven whispered to himself.

"What?" Dale asked, glancing over.

"Nothing."

"Who the hell is Shunka Sapa? That one of your Indian gods?"

Raven scowled. He was not in the mood to give a lesson on folklore.

"Sorry, man, not trying to be offensive. Just curious. I don't know much about the, uh, indigenous peoples."

"We're called American Indians. That's the politically correct term, at least."

"Sorry, I meant American Indians."

Raven shrugged. "I don't get my panties in a bunch about it, but it does piss me off when people don't understand why it might be offensive to call us redskins. I don't call you an albino skin, do I?"

Dale pulled off his hat, ran his hand through his hair, and sighed. "I get it, man. I'm sorry." He checked the magazine in his AR-15 and then looked out the window, lapsing into silence.

By the time the sun went down, they had driven fifty miles without seeing a single person. Raven figured the radiation still had people scared, which was good. The less contact they had on this trip, the better.

He waited until the final rays of light receded on the horizon and then pulled to the side of the road to put on the night vision goggles. Once his eyes had adjusted to the green hue, he pulled back onto the road and continued south.

"We're getting close," Dale said. The map was draped over his lap, and he used a flashlight to check it every few minutes.

About five miles north of Granby, Raven finally saw a flicker of movement across the road. He brought the van to a stop behind an abandoned pickup truck and killed the engine. He grabbed his Glock, and Dale readied his rifle.

"What do you see?" Dale asked, leaning forward to look out the windshield.

Raven focused on the shapes moving along the shoulder of the road. "Horses and men."

"They armed?"

"Can't tell."

Dale moved to open the van door, but Raven grabbed his arm.

"Just keep quiet and stay inside. They're heading our way," Raven said. He counted six men, and now he could see they were armed with rifles and shotguns.

Raven caught a glimpse of motion in the rearview mirror, and cursed when he saw more horses a quarter mile behind them.

"Shit, we're trapped," he said.

Dale looked over his shoulder and heaved a breath. "I can't see anything."

"Get down," Raven said. He twisted the key to turn the van back on, but the engine whined, not turning over.

"You got to be fucking kidding me," Dale said.

"Shut up, man."

"Bro, don't tell me to—"

Raven turned the key again, his eyes closed, pleading with the van. "Come on, baby."

The starter clicked again but didn't turn over. When he opened his eyes, the horses ahead were moving faster, and several voices rang out. The men had spotted the van.

"We've been made," Raven said. He considered telling Dale to bail and making a run for it, but he decided to try the key a third time. It finally caught, and the engine growled to life. With no time to waste, he punched the pedal down to the floor. The tires squealed.

"Go, go, go!" Dale shouted.

Raven steered the van around the pickup and into the center of the two-lane highway. The horses were moving into the road to block their escape. Driving on the shoulder wasn't an option; there was no way the tires were going to make it on an off-road trip. Times like these, he really missed his Jeep.

"Dale, roll down your window and shoot over the front of the hood," Raven said. "Aim for the center of the road, at those horses!"

"You serious, man? I—"

The boom of a shotgun cut Dale off. Pellets punched through the windshield and peppered the back seat.

"Son of a bitch!" Dale shouted. He quickly rolled down the window and then leaned outside with the rifle, squeezing off several bursts at the horses.

Raven hated seeing the beasts hurt, but if it came down to his survival, he wasn't going to die out here. He pushed down on the pedal as far as it would go and drove right for the horses. One of them bucked its rider out of the saddle like a rag doll.

At the last second, the other mounted shooters moved the horses away, but not before one of them fired a shotgun blast that punched through the side of the van.

Dale let out a cry, but Raven focused on maneuvering through the gap between the horses. The tires screeched and the rusty chassis clanked as they shot through the narrow pass.

Another shot followed them, taking out the back window and raining glass on the seats. Dale and Raven both ducked as two more booms sounded. Pellets lanced into the back of the truck, penetrating the rusty metal, but within minutes they were out of range.

Raven loosened his grip on the steering wheel, chest heaving. "You okay, Dale?"

Dale managed a nod, but his hand was gripping his shoulder.

"You hit?" Raven said.

"Just a flesh wound."

"You sure?"

"I'm good. Trust me, I've been hit way worse before."

Raven focused on the road, steering around abandoned vehicles, while Dale put a bandage on his shoulder. Several pellets had punctured his skin, but he was right that it was just a flesh wound.

"Who the hell were those guys?" Dale muttered.

"I didn't get a look. Probably just raiders." Raven glimpsed a sign for Granby and jerked his chin at the map on the floor.

Dale finished with the bandage and grabbed the map. "Looks like it's the second exit, then you pull onto a frontage road and head east for a mile."

Raven found the exit a few minutes later and turned

onto a dirt frontage road. He could see the outline of Granby in the distance. The moon had emerged, splitting through the clouds and spreading soft white light over the sleeping city.

"Robbie said the house is somewhere on the other side of those woods," Raven said. He parked the van and jumped out into the cold night, his boots crunching on the frozen dirt. He met Dale around the other side of the van, and they loaded up on gear and ammunition.

"You sure about this?" Raven asked.

Dale looked down at his shoulder. "Brother, I'm fine."

Raven holstered his Glock and then grabbed his AR-15. "Follow me, and keep quiet."

Raven flipped his night vision goggles back over his eyes and led Dale into the forest. The leaf-covered ground crunched under their boots no matter how slowly they moved. It was dead quiet out here, with not even the call of a bird to break the silence. Raven stopped every few minutes to listen, trying to identify any sounds out of the ordinary. He sniffed the air to check for smoke, and picked up the scent of a fire. Someone was definitely out there.

Flashing a hand signal, Raven continued onward with Dale walking cautiously through the forest behind him. The big man was doing a pretty good job of keeping his foot impacts low considering he only had moonlight to guide him.

Although Raven wished Creek was here, he was also anxious about bringing the dog anywhere again. He had taken a bullet for his handler, and seeing the Akita suffer broke Raven's heart. Not that he would be happy if Dale got shot again, but it was different. Creek was his best friend.

"There," Dale whispered, pointing.

Raven saw the mansion a moment later. The building was situated on the shore of a lake, overlooking the sparkling water. At first scan, the property appeared empty. Not a single sentry in sight, but smoke was fingering away from one of the chimneys on the east side of the house. He moved toward the edge of the trees and crouched down. Dale joined him and took up position behind a pine.

"You see anyone?" he asked.

Raven shook his head. He got up and prepared to move, but froze. Flipping up the goggles, he laid eyes on what looked like the burning end of a cigarette.

"One contact," he said quietly.

Lowering the goggles back over his eyes, he focused on the man sitting on the porch. The man got up a few minutes later, after throwing away the cigarette, and walked back inside.

"Come on," Raven said.

He led Dale out into a clearing, and they made their way across the grass to a tall metal fence. About a quarter mile to the east, the front gate was wide open.

Mr. Redford would never leave the front door unlocked.

Raven crushed something under his boot. He reached down and plucked a spent shell casing off the ground. Then he saw the others. There were hundreds of spent rounds littered across the dirt.

A fight had gone down here.

He flipped his NVGs back over his eyes and examined the house. From this new vantage point, he could see it had been hit by thousands of rounds that had shattered windows, chipped the facade, and destroyed the overhang.

Not a fight at all.

A battle.

"What's wrong?" Dale asked.

"We're too late," Raven said.

He did another quick scan of the property. In the gardens, he saw them.

Severed heads. At least a dozen, all mounted on pikes.

"Fucking hell," Raven whispered.

"Dude, what?" Dale asked. "You're freaking me out."

"Stay here, and cover me if someone starts shooting," Raven said. He took off running before Dale could reply. Keeping low, Raven moved into the gardens, using the shrubbery for cover. He made his way over to the front porch and examined the heads. They were a grisly spectacle, but he didn't immediately recognize any of them.

He navigated his way onto the porch, seeing a glow of light coming from one of the rooms on the first floor. After he cleared the area, he moved to the back door, trying the handle.

Raven slung his rifle and slowly picked the lock with his knife. The door creaked open in front of him. He sheathed his knife, pulled both of his hatchets from his back, and moved into a dark kitchen.

Light bled into the room from under the door. He stopped to listen, hearing a rustling noise in the next room. He flipped the NVGs up and then reached for the door. It was ajar, and he slowly pushed it open to see a man warming his hands in front of a fire. A rifle was propped up against the wall.

Raven again stopped to listen, but all he heard was the crackle of burning wood. He moved for a better view, and noticed the swastika on the man's neck. This wasn't one of Redford's men.

As soon as he saw this guy was a Nazi, Raven kicked the door open and then tossed both of the hatchets. One of the blades hit the man in the back with a thump, and the other struck him in the right leg. He grabbed the fireplace mantle, screaming in agony. The sounds didn't draw any other hostiles, but Raven unslung his rifle and raised it just in case the man wasn't alone.

The Nazi thug dropped to the ground. Raven waited for a few seconds, gaze flitting back and forth from the stairs to the man who was trying to crawl away.

Hearing nothing but groans, Raven followed the trail of blood streaking across the expensive carpet. He bent down next to the man, who turned on his side to look at Raven.

"What did you do with Redford?" Raven asked.

The man chuckled up bloody bubbles. His eyes flitted up toward the wall, and Raven pivoted to see a collection of mounted trophies. An elk, an eight-point buck, and several other kills. But there was something else there, something that was out of place.

Raven took a step over just to make sure he was seeing clearly in the faint light of the fire. He swallowed as his brain finally confirmed what his eyes were seeing.

A bloody human head hung among the hunting trophies.

This one, he recognized.

It belonged to Nile Redford.

— 11 —

Albert Randall was doing his best not to eavesdrop on the conversation between Charlize and Colonel Raymond, but he found it hard to ignore.

"Secretary Montgomery, I just got another report of an attack that has SOL written all over it," Raymond said. "Fenix and his men are active, ma'am."

Albert stood outside her office door with Dave and Ty, all of them waiting for Charlize to finish some last-minute work before she left Constellation for another trip.

Albert loosened his flak jacket while he waited. The vest was a better fit than the one from Charlotte. This time it covered his stomach where the bullet had ripped through his abdomen and torn up his insides. After three weeks of recovery, he was finally back on his feet with a new mission. His injuries were still hurting, but he was glad to be out of that hospital bed.

"I really want to come with you, Mr. Big Al," Dave said, pulling on Albert's sleeve. "You promised the Fellowship wasn't over."

Albert put a finger to his lips and strained to listen to the conversation inside the office.

"How do we know it was SOL?" Charlize was asking.

"Swastikas carved at the scene and some very brazen anti-Chinese graffiti," Raymond replied. "It's got to be

SOL, unless there are more Nazi groups in Colorado."

Albert didn't want the kids to hear this. He grabbed the back of Ty's wheelchair and pushed him away. Dave followed them across the hallway, still talking about hobbits.

"I won't be gone long," Albert said. "Then I'll come back, and—"

Dave shook his shaggy hair. "No!" he shouted.

Several personnel walking down the hallway glanced in their direction. Albert let out a sigh and got down on one knee, pain racing up his gut. He gritted his teeth. The doctors had told him certain movements were still going to hurt, and they were right, as usual.

"See, you can't go without me, you're still in pain from the last Orc. This time the Orcs might kill you, Mr. Big Al." Dave blinked rapidly, his eyes shining with frustrated tears. "You need me."

"I'll be fine. You have to be strong and look after the people here while I'm gone. That's your mission now." Albert put a hand on Dave's shoulder.

A single tear fled the boy's eye and streaked down his cheek. He looked down at his tennis shoes, his small potbelly rising up and down with his labored breathing.

"Okay?" Albert asked.

"Yeah, okay," Dave whispered.

"We'll have fun," Ty said.

"And I'll bring you back a DVD of *Lord of the Rings*," Albert said.

Dave looked up with the hint of a smile forming on his lips. "Promise?"

"Promise."

Albert stood and walked over to the office door. Charlize and Raymond were still deep in discussion. He caught her eye, and tapped on his watch to indicate it was time to go. Charlize nodded back. He was already late, and if she didn't hurry, she was going to be as well.

"Every time we send out a team, Fenix and his men are gone before we can get there," Raymond said.

"I don't want to risk another American life until we know for certain that it's SOL," Charlize said. "Let's talk more on the flight."

Albert could hear the frustration rising in her voice, but she held it in check. It had been two months since the North Korean attack, and over a month since her brother had been brought home in a casket from Colorado. Her fuse had been growing shorter as the guilt piled up on her shoulders. But, she had recently changed her approach, saving her anger for the people who had kidnapped Ty and killed her brother instead of venting it at every little frustration.

Two weeks ago, she had confessed to Albert how powerless and angry she felt. "I'd kill every single one of them if I could," she had said.

"With all due respect, ma'am, of course you would. They're Nazis," Albert had replied. "I would give my life to stop them too. This isn't just about your son. It's about stamping out a terrorist organization before the virus spreads."

She had nodded along, but Albert could tell he wasn't really getting through to her. He worried that Charlize was after revenge, not justice.

"Okay, let's go," Charlize said as she stepped out of her office and hugged Ty goodbye. Albert held out a hand to Dave.

"Give me a high-five, buddy," Albert said.

Dave rolled his eyes, then slapped Albert's hand so

hard the smack echoed.

"That hurt," Albert said.

Dave grinned from ear to ear. "Oops."

"You guys done?" Charlize asked, smiling.

Albert stiffened. "Yes, ma'am."

Dave followed his lead, straightening his back and throwing up a salute.

A few minutes later, the kids were sent back to class, and Albert was following Charlize and Raymond toward the elevator. It took them another fifteen minutes to get to the surface through the labyrinth of tunnels, lifts, and trams that made up Constellation.

A dozen Green Berets, led by Sergeant Fugate, were waiting for them outside the blast doors. Breaking up into two groups, they took Zodiacs to the opposite shore. Thirty minutes later, they arrived at an isolated airfield on the mainland.

An armored MATV was idling on the nearby road. Albert took a second to admire it as he walked with the group toward the helicopter landing pad. The mine-resistant vehicle was the American military's answer to the epidemic of roadside IEDs in Iraq and Afghanistan. It had replaced the Humvee in most combat zones, and seeing it in the United States reminded Albert of just how severe it was out on the highways. And he was about to head out there to see it firsthand. Again.

"There's our ride, ma'am," Raymond said. He pointed at the sky, where a tiny black dot was crossing the skyline.

Charlize turned to face Albert. "You're sure about this?" she asked.

"Yes, ma'am." His response was polite, but firm. "I'm sick of lying in that bed or walking those halls. And between you and me, Dave is getting on my nerves."

Charlize smiled. It was odd seeing the sun on her face after so long underground, and he noticed a few new wrinkles. They had both lost so much over the last few months.

Just thinking of his wife and daughters hurt him worse than any bullet. Jane had been the light of his life, and his girls, Kylie and Abigail, had been full of so much potential that would now never be realized. It broke his heart—and, if he was being honest, it made him crave revenge at least as much as Charlize did. His brother, Fred, had also perished in the blast that leveled D.C., so the only family left was his sister. And, once again, he was leaving her behind.

"Don't put yourself in danger on this trip," Charlize said. "I just want you there to make sure Captain Harris is doing his job, and to report back anything I need to know."

"Understood, ma'am," he said.

The chop of the big black bird made it difficult to hear as it descended over the airfield. Charlize waved goodbye, and they parted once again, with Albert hurrying over to the MATV and Charlize heading toward the helicopter. By the time he reached the truck, the chopper was already in the air.

The driver's door to the truck popped open and a friendly face emerged.

"Corporal Van Dyke," Albert said. "It's real good to see you again."

Van Dyke stroked his mustache and grinned. "Officer Randall, you're late. Go figure."

"Sorry. I was saying goodbye to Secretary Montgomery."

Van Dyke brought a hand to shield his eyes as he

looked at the sky. "Damn, that bird has Montgomery on it?"

"That's right."

"Where she headed?"

"D.C., and then New York, for meetings."

Van Dyke lowered his hand and gave Albert an incredulous look. "Shit man, why is she going to D.C.?"

"I'll tell you on the drive. Come on," Albert said. He carried his rucksack and M4 over to the truck and placed them inside. Then he hopped in the passenger seat.

Van Dyke put his seatbelt on with a click and looked over. "I'd much rather be driving the lawless highways than flying to Washington, to be honest. From what I hear, the radiation zone is hell on earth."

Albert watched the helicopter vanish over the horizon. He had heard there were no more recovery efforts inside the radiation zone, and while he was sure his family was gone, he was glad he wasn't going out there with Charlize. He didn't want to see the place where his family had perished.

They were nothing but ashes and memories now.

***

Charlize had dreamt of this moment, but the devastation below was nothing like her nightmares.

It was far worse.

"My God," Raymond said over the comms system.

The six Green Berets in the troop hadn't said a word throughout the flight, but they were all looking out the portholes with awestruck expressions on their hard faces.

Below, the fires had almost all ceased, but fingers of smoke still inched across the heavy sky hanging over the destroyed city. Charlize spotted the Potomac River in the distance, and glimpsed the epicenter of the blast. The nuclear detonation appeared to have changed the course of the river. From there, the fireball had spread in a circle, flattening everything for almost a mile. The destruction continued in all directions, and even at two miles away from the epicenter, buildings were nothing but husks.

The original plan had been to survey the area outside of the city, where the military had constructed fences to keep civilians out of the radiation zone. But Charlize had wanted to see ground zero.

She *needed* to see it.

The chopper continued toward the crater, providing a remarkable view of the blast zone. Buildings, parks, and streets had been completely erased. Everything was charcoaled and melted from the extreme heat.

The pilots circled the epicenter until Charlize had seen enough.

"Okay," she said, waving them onward.

The bird changed course, heading away from ground zero and out toward an area she had once called home. But all the landmarks she remembered were gone. The Washington Monument, Capitol Hill, the White House...

She squinted at what was once 1600 Pennsylvania Avenue.

"Take us lower," Charlize ordered.

The pilots obeyed the order without trepidation, lowering the craft so Charlize could get a better view. The Green Berets continued to watch, but remained silent, not one of them discussing the horrific sight until a young man with freckles and peach fuzz for a mustache pointed and asked, "Is that what I think it is?"

Somehow, despite all odds, the White House had

survived. Although *survive* perhaps wasn't the best way to describe it. The front had collapsed, and the white façade was burned black like an overcooked marshmallow. Twisted metal surrounded the perimeter, and flipped cars littered the streets. She had been pulled out of this place by a chopper the morning after the attack. The area looked very different now. The fires were out, and all she saw was an endless junkyard of roasted metal and ashes. Diego was right about one thing: anyone within the blast zone was long since dead.

"Seen enough?" Raymond asked.

Charlize nodded. "Take us back to the perimeter."

The pilots changed course again, and Charlize closed her eyes, taking in a deep breath of air that tasted like smoke. A few minutes later, her eyes flipped open at the sound of a voice over the comms channel.

"I think I see something moving down there."

The pilot had forgotten to shut off the main channel. Either that, or he wanted Charlize to hear. The Marines scrambled across the troop hold for a look out the windows.

"What do you mean?" she asked.

"Thought I saw something back there," he replied, using a jerk of his thumb behind them. Charlize turned to look out the window, but saw nothing stir in the radioactive wasteland.

"What did you see, Captain?" she asked, curiously.

"I... I think I saw a person."

The reply chilled Charlize to the core. Was that possible? Could the pilot really have seen someone alive down there?

If there were people this far into the blast zone, then it changed everything she had heard about recovery efforts in the area.

"Go back," she said.

Raymond frowned, showing a rare hint of emotion. "Ma'am, I would highly recommend—" he began to say when she cut him off.

"We're going back." The pilots hesitated, and she added, "That's an order."

Turning sharply, the bird curved back toward the White House. She twisted again to look out the window. The Green Berets were all looking out the windows too.

"There," said one of the pilots. "Three o'clock."

Charlize and Raymond both unbuckled their harnesses and moved over for a better view out the windows next to Sergeant Fugate.

"Looks like a person to me," said the other pilot. "Two, actually."

Charlize couldn't believe it when she saw the two figures trekking down the middle of the ash-covered street. They were dressed in white outfits, and for a moment she thought they must be ghosts.

The people crouched behind the heat-warped hull of a vehicle and looked up at the chopper.

"It looks like they are wearing hazard suits," Raymond said.

Charlize studied the two figures as the helicopter circled. "Are they ours? Military, maybe?"

Raymond frowned. "I doubt it. We stopped looking for survivors here a week after the attack."

The figures lifted their arms. Charlize thought they might be signaling for help until one of the pilots yelled, "Hold on!"

The flash of a muzzle came from the street as the two men in suits fired rifles at the bird. Several of the Green

Berets moved over to surround Charlize and protect her with their armored bodies.

"Get us the hell out of here!" Raymond shouted.

The bird rolled hard to the right and then pulled back into the sky, leaving the mysterious men. Charlize tried to look out the windows, but she was surrounded by camouflage uniforms. She listened for the distant crack of gunfire, but couldn't hear anything over the thump of rotors and the blood pulsing in her ears.

Several agonizing seconds later, one of the pilots confirmed they were clear. The Green Berets slowly backed away from Charlize.

"Are you okay, ma'am?" asked the boy with the peach fuzz—Staff Sergeant Thoreau, according to his nametag.

"I'm fine, Staff Sergeant. Thank you," she replied.

"Who the hell were those guys, and what were they doing out there?" Fugate asked.

Raymond shook his head. "No idea."

"They could have been looters," Thoreau said.

"Report this to Command," Raymond told the pilots.

"Roger that, sir."

Charlize settled back into her seat and looked out her window, but there was no sign of other survivors. Only the black landscape. Two weeks after the blast, there had been stories of survivors stumbling out of the radiation zone, suffering from horrific burns and radiation poisoning. She had been one of them, but she was lucky enough to have had the medical support she'd needed to recover.

She closed her eyes and tried to relax for the next leg of the journey. She dozed off, and was awoken sometime later by a hand on her shoulder.

"Ma'am, we're almost here," Raymond said.

Charlize looked out the window at a skyline she had loved her entire life. On the horizon, New York's familiar buildings rose proudly into the sky. The metropolis had mostly been spared from the radioactive fallout, thanks to the winds after the blast. It was one of the few major cities in the entire country that hadn't completely fallen into anarchy. Part of that had to do with the fact that the New York Police Department was a small army in itself with over fifty thousand men and women employees, thirty thousand of them in uniform.

On top of that, the ports had allowed aid from foreign countries to come in and help with the recovery. She glimpsed the piers in the Hudson River and thought back to the North Korean submarine they had stopped from attacking New York. It was hard to imagine what that sub would have done if they hadn't blown it out of the water.

Now, two months after the bombs, New York was starting to recover. But that didn't mean the city was safe. Far from it. Many areas were warzones. That's why she had brought the Green Berets with her again.

Unlike her trips to Charlotte and Fort Lauderdale, though, she wasn't here just to work on the recovery efforts. She was here to meet with the Chinese delegation to discuss the progress of getting the power back on, to listen to a speech at the United Nations, and to help select the new seat of the federal government.

There was a lot to accomplish in a short amount of time, and she was already late. The pilots began the descent and Charlize exhaled, ready for the challenges ahead.

***

Colton rode Obsidian down the center of Main Street, watching as the line of civilians wrapped in heavy coats inched along the sidewalk. Their destination was the Italian restaurant on the river, which the owners had retrofitted into a soup kitchen. The stew there was helping to feed over ten thousand residents, but there were only so many elk and rabbits in Rocky Mountain National Park to hunt. He just hoped the game would sustain his town until the government could finally get the power back on and things started to return to normal.

Normal, he thought. *Yeah, right.*

It was only November. They still had another four months of cold, and at least six months until the power came back on, if Colton had to guess. Every night he listened to the radio about the recovery efforts, and it sounded like the Chinese were helping get the grid back up faster than originally thought.

Until power came back in Estes Park, though, he had no choice but to rule with an iron fist. He couldn't trust Gail Andrews or her staff anymore. Not after what happened with Don Aragon and Sam Hines.

Thinking of the patrol sergeant made him furious, but he still couldn't quite believe Hines had joined Don in the plot to kill Lindsey and Raven.

Colton had thought Hines to be a good man. At one point he had thought the same of Don, but the end of the world had brought out their true natures.

He shook his head and looked over at one of the few people he could trust—Lindsey Plymouth. Colton had just promoted her to captain, filling the role left vacant by the death of Jake Englewood. Colton had even considered making Raven a sergeant, but he wasn't interested in titles, apparently.

Never thought I'd trust Sam. Now I'm trying to give him a badge.

Motion ahead showed Colton even more how much things had changed in Estes Park. A dozen militia soldiers rounded the next corner, all of them carrying rifles and shotguns. Half of these people were refugees, and all of them were working hard to protect the town.

Colton gave Dale Jackson, the leader of the group, a wave. Dale winced as he raised a hand back. He was still recovering from an infection to his shoulder where he had been shot on the mission to find their stolen supplies.

With Nile and Thompson dead, Estes Park had checked off two enemies from the list. But Fenix and other men like him were still out there. The war Colton feared was still a real possibility. They had been lucky the past three weeks to avoid further violence, but the reports of the chaos coming in over the radio had him concerned.

Lindsey was talking to Colton, but he drowned her out, his mind a mess of thoughts. The storm of violence sweeping across the United States—and the presence of the Chinese soldiers—had him on edge. Even with the foreign aid, the country was bordering on collapse, and men like Fenix were doing everything they could to take advantage of the situation.

"Have you been listening to a damn thing I've been saying?" Lindsey asked.

Colton nodded like he'd heard every word.

"Chief? What's the last thing I said?"

"Yup."

She let out a huff.

"I'm sorry, was just thinking," he said.

"You been doing a lot of that lately. Ever since you got back from Fort Collins."

"You sound like my wife," Colton said gruffly.

"Anyways. I was explaining how many people I've got posted out there today. I doubled some of the patrols, and set up a schedule of volunteer spotters so that every point of entry to town is watched."

"Good. We need the additional security on our borders."

"You said to prepare for war."

He was quiet for another moment, and then said, "I'm hoping it doesn't come to that."

Obsidian suddenly halted and let out a snort.

Willow stopped too and shook her head from side to side. Lindsey patted the mare's neck gently. "Easy, girl, easy."

"Something's got them spooked," Colton said.

A rumble sounded in the distance, and Colton and Lindsey both twisted in their saddles to look east, toward Lake Estes.

"What is that?" Lindsey asked.

Colton knew right away. "A plane," he replied.

Everyone on the streets stopped what they were doing to look at the sky as a massive airliner zoomed through the gray clouds. It was low enough that Colton could see it wasn't one of theirs. The white aircraft had Chinese markings on the side.

The raucous sound made people put their hands over their ears. It passed overhead, low enough that some frightened citizens ran for cover. Colton held the reins tight just in case Obsidian tried to bolt. But, aside from pacing, the horse stayed put.

The plane turned sharply, moving southeast toward Denver, and vanished back into the clouds. Colton watched the sky, hoping to see supply crates parachuting toward them, but nothing came.

The rumble faded away, and the citizens all around gathered in groups to talk. Several of them shouted questions.

"What the heck was that about, Chief?" someone asked.

"Was that a Chinese plane?" another person said.

"Are we really being invaded?" came another voice.

"Everything's fine," Colton said.

"What's that?" someone yelled.

Colton followed the woman's finger down the street, to where sheets of white paper were fluttering over the road like oversized snowflakes. He gave Obsidian a nudge, and the horse took off. Willow and Lindsey followed. When they got to the center of the street, Colton dismounted. His boots hit the asphalt, and he plucked a piece of paper off the ground.

To the residents of Loveland, Estes Park, Fort Collins, Greely... the list of towns went on and on. He continued reading past the names.

The United States military and FEMA are working hard with the Chinese government to get the power back on. We estimate that this could take anywhere from one to two years in your area. Until then, please remember to tune in to the emergency broadcast channel for updates and tips on rationing food, water, and medical supplies. Good luck.

"Good luck," Colton said, rolling up the paper into a ball and tossing it onto the ground.

Lindsey stared at the sheet of paper in her own hand. "One to two years?"

Colton kicked the balled-up flyer away and turned to look at the hundreds of people wandering away from the soup kitchen line to see what was going on. The last thing he wanted was for these people to see the timeframe.

"Help me keep 'em back," he said to Lindsey.

"Everyone back to the soup line!" she shouted.

Colton walked toward the crowd, hands up, trying to keep his voice low. He stopped mid-stride when he saw a kid holding up one of the pieces of paper.

"I found something!" he yelled.

A man grabbed it from the kid's hand.

"Read it," someone said.

"What's it say?" another person asked.

Colton cursed as the man read it aloud. Dozens of faces suddenly looked in his direction, and then came the bombardment of questions.

"Guess our luck's run out," Colton said to Lindsey. Two months already seemed like an eternity. He couldn't imagine another two years without power, but, somehow, he would have to convince these people that things weren't as dire as they seemed.

— 12 —

Raven kicked at the frozen dirt. The roar of the plane had scared off his chase—an eight-point buck he'd been tracking for the past hour. Hell, the damn thing had probably frightened every animal within a twenty-mile radius. And while he was pissed, he was also curious about the plane. The craft had vanished into the clouds before he got a good look at what model it was, but it had sounded large.

"Just my damn luck," he whispered.

Raven slung his crossbow over his back and yanked his facemask down. He pulled the walkie-talkie from his vest and whistled for Creek. The dog came bounding around a tree a few minutes later, tail wagging.

This was their first hunt since the unsuccessful execution on Storm Mountain, and the Akita was clearly thrilled to get back on the trail. Raven could hardly keep the dog calm on the ride here earlier. But no matter how happy Creek was to be outside, his energy level was not back to normal. He wasn't the only one; Raven was suffering from a cold, a headache, and a growling stomach.

Every step he took made him consider throwing in the towel for today's hunt. Considering how much he had prepped for this one—the traditional cold water dips, the fasting, the prayers—he didn't want to just give up. But his first priority was the town, and he needed to get back

148

there if something was wrong.

He raised the radio to see what was going on. "Colton, this is Raven. Do you copy? Over."

The crackle of the static echoed through the cold forest.

"Copy," Colton said a few minutes later.

"Yeah...uh, what the hell was that plane doing up here?" Raven asked.

"Dropping info."

Raven stopped mid-stride. "What kind of info?"

"About the power. Sounds like we're pretty low on the totem pole in terms of getting back on."

Raven sneered. He hated the "totem pole" cliché.

"Should I come back?" he asked.

"It can wait. Finish your hunt. Food is the most important thing right now, especially since it's going to take..."

Static crackled from the radio and he held it into the air to get a better signal.

"What was that?" Raven asked. "Chief?"

"I'll talk to you later," Colton said.

"Roger that."

Raven tucked the walkie-talkie back into his vest and filled his lungs with icy air. He had to keep focused and strong. It was the only way he was going to come back with a kill today—and from the sounds of it, that was pretty important.

He signaled for Creek to follow, and continued into the woods. Fasting the previous day hadn't been a good idea, especially being sick, but it was Cherokee tradition to fast before a hunt. Raven reached out to put a glove on the coarse bark of a tree, his headache suddenly beating his skull so hard he squinted from the pain. It felt like someone was hitting him every other second with a mallet. The cold was worse because of another Cherokee tradition—dipping in freezing water the two nights before a hunt.

He had to be careful after everything he had been through, from gunshot and knife wounds to nearly being blown up. The last thing he wanted to take him down was a freaking runny nose. Raven could picture his tombstone now:

Sam "Raven" Spears.
Died of a cold.

Raising his crossbow, he kept pushing through the woods. Snow fluttered down around him, coating the dirt and leaves in a layer of powder. It was heavy enough to cover any recent tracks. The snow didn't just cover tracks—it also disguised traps in the ground, places where Raven could twist an ankle or slip and fall. He picked each step carefully, knowing an injury could take him out of commission.

Creek had his muzzle down toward the ground, sniffing for a scent. Raven picked up the pace to follow. He pushed his stocking cap up above his ears and listened for prey as he moved, trying to pick up the crack of a twig or the rustle of movement. The woods were quiet for mid-afternoon. Aside from the chirp of a few birds and the whistle of the wind, he heard nothing.

Cold air carrying the scent of cedar filled his lungs. He exhaled and flexed his muscles, then relaxed them to keep the blood flowing. He wiggled his toes and fingers every ten minutes. Cramping was also a concern, although he had been drinking plenty of water. It was the one thing Estes Park had in abundance.

He ducked under the branch of an aspen tree and

crouched next to the trunk of a towering ponderosa to scan a clearing. *Light as a feather*, Raven reminded himself. He sure felt like light, having lost over twenty pounds since the bombs.

Creek came back into view, sniffing the ground as he zigzagged up a hill. His back went rigid, and he glanced over his shoulders at Raven. The dog had a scent.

Raven nodded, and Creek took off toward the hill. In seconds, the dog had ascended the slope and vanished over the other side. It took Raven much longer. He trekked up slowly, his muscles straining. Snow fluttered around him, and he stopped to rest and take in the view. To the west, the mountain peaks rose on the horizon like jagged, bleached teeth. A twig crunched behind Raven, and he turned to scan the fence of aspen trees.

Nothing moved in the white landscape.

He tightened his muscles again before relaxing them, willing his legs to continue up the hill. Using his calves, he pushed upward, carefully selecting each step between the trees growing out of the steep incline. Near the top, he one-handed his crossbow and used the other to grab the wide trunk of a Douglas fir. He hefted himself up to the crest and stopped to rest again.

Standing in the open allowed the gusting wind to cut into his body. Even with multiple layers, the cold found its way into his coat. He pulled his stocking cap back down over his ears, making the sounds all around him muffled. Stars floated across his vision from straining his way up the hill. He leaned on the tree and closed his eyes.

When he opened them again, the stars were gone but he was still light-headed. Another twig snapped in the distance, and Raven quickly brought his crossbow up. His eyes flitted left and right over the terrain, searching for whatever was making the sound. A squirrel suddenly raced up the bark of a ponderosa, snow falling off the disturbed branches.

Raven forced air out of his stuffy nose, but that just made his sinuses burn. He got out the binoculars and turned to look over the valley carved through the forest below. A stream meandered through a field on the east side of woods. The elk came here to drink, but today he didn't see a single one of the beasts. Most of them had retreated deeper into Rocky Mountain National Park, and hunting parties were being forced to trek farther and farther to find food. Predatory animals were starving from their food source being killed off, driving them to desperation. Several dogs in town had been dragged off by coyotes. Raven wasn't too worried about Creek, but anyone with one of those yippy little dogs was keeping them inside, just to be safe.

He saw movement along the edge of the forest, where the trees met the meadows, and spotted his Akita. Creek was still following the scent. Now that was a real dog. You shouldn't be able to put a dog in a handbag.

"Good, boy," Raven said. He raised the binos and glassed the valley, dividing it into thirds and scanning the canvas by looking left to right, and then back again.

A flash of white moved near the stream. He held the binos steady. But what he saw wasn't the eight-point buck he was looking for, or even an elk. Instead, a pair of translucent figures was standing at the edge of the trees.

Raven closed his eyes, but when he opened them again, the apparitions were still there. His heart pounded at the sight, even though he knew they weren't real. They couldn't be.

He vividly remembered the dream of Jistu the trickster

rabbit, the Thunderer storm spirit, and the humanoid children with faces of adults called Yunwi Tsunsdi'. But the two men standing below weren't Yunwi Tsunsdi', and Raven wasn't dreaming. He finally recognized them as Nunnehi warriors—spirit hunters. The two men stood there watching Raven, bows at their sides, draped in skins and furs.

You've really lost it now, Sam.

He whistled, and Creek halted in the meadow below, glancing up at Raven with a rabbit in his maw. At least the dog had caught his chase. The Nunnehi warriors were walking along the river now, paying no attention to the dog. Normally the spirit race was invisible, but they showed themselves to humans they liked, and would show up to help during a hunt.

So why the hell were they raising bows at him?

Raven remained frozen, staring. They were just a figment of his imagination, a product of his pounding headache. But he couldn't help but flinch when they fired translucent arrows that curved overhead.

Something slammed into Raven from behind a beat later, knocking his crossbow from his hands. He hit the ground hard, the air bursting from his lungs. As soon as he sucked in a gasp, a blade slashed his leg. The air came right back out in an animalistic holler of pain.

A growl replied.

Raven rolled onto his back and looked up into the majestic face of a mountain lion. The elusive creatures normally avoided humans, but men like Raven had taken so many elk that the beast was starving. Yellow eyes locked onto his neck, and black lips parted to reveal yellow, dagger-like teeth as the beast went for his jugular vein.

Everything seemed to freeze in that moment. He could see the saliva dripping from the creature's maw as it bent down, and watched the fur stretch as the beast flexed its muscles.

He grabbed the creature by the neck and pushed as hard as he could, screaming in a war cry. Hot breath hit Raven's face as the mountain lion fought him, its head just inches from his own.

Raven caught a glimpse of the translucent arrows sticking out of the tree behind the beast. It was then he realized the Nunnehi hadn't been aiming for him. They were warning him of the mountain lion. Raven hadn't been the hunter—he had been the mountain lion's chase all along.

"Creek!" Raven shouted. He pushed harder at the creature's neck, and then used his left hand to hit it in the side of the head. The beast growled, and he screamed back, doing his best to show the mountain lion he wasn't going out without a fight.

Raven bit at the creature's leg and tore out a hunk of flesh and fur. The beast let out a roar of its own and then swiped Raven's stocking cap off with a paw. He reached for his buck knife, pulled it from the sheath, and slashed at the big cat's white muzzle.

The creature let out another roar, hot blood peppering Raven's face. It reared back, giving Raven an opportunity. He went to jam the knife into the exposed chest, but a paw hit him in the face, slicing his cheek.

Barking sounded in the distance. Creek was coming.

The mountain lion looked up, blood dripping from its maw and yellow eyes focusing on the Akita. It leapt off Raven and bolted toward Creek.

You have to get up, Sam.

Red swarmed Raven's vision as he pushed at the ground, bringing himself to his knees just as Creek and the mountain lion slammed into one another.

Creek was badass, but he was no match for the beast, especially with just one eye and wounds that still weren't fully healed. Raven searched the ground for his knife, but saw his crossbow instead. He crawled over and grabbed the crossbow, bringing it up and trying to focus on a target. But all he saw was a mass of white and tawny fur.

"Creek, watch out!" he yelled.

His vision cleared just long enough to see that the mountain lion had Creek on his back. Raven pulled the trigger.

A yelp sounded.

Raven blinked over and over, his heart pounding like an automatic rifle. He dropped the crossbow and scrambled over the ground on all fours, his hand finding his knife as he moved. He picked up the blade and then pushed himself up, stumbling over to see a massive lump of fur and twisted limbs.

An arrow stuck out of the center of the mass.

"Creek!" Raven shouted. He bent down and saw that the arrow was embedded in the mountain lion's back. It had collapsed onto Creek, pinning the dog to the snow.

Raven pushed the beast off his best friend, and Creek slowly got up on all fours. He wagged his tail and licked at Raven's hand.

"Thank God you're okay, boy."

He wiped the blood from his face and then crouched down to examine Creek's wounds. They weren't bad at first glance, just a slash on his back. That was good, but he was afraid to look at his own injuries. His leg hurt, and his back felt numb, which was a very bad sign.

But they were alive, and that was all that mattered. They weren't coming back empty-handed either. Raven looked at the dead mountain lion and the rabbit lying a few feet away, wondering how they would taste in stew.

"What do you think, Creek? Cat-rabbit stew for dinner?" He chuckled, although his words weren't particularly funny. Raven's head swam, and his vision blurred once more.

His legs suddenly felt numb too, and he fell to his knees. A moment later Raven collapsed to the ground, his face hitting the cold snow.

"Oh shit," he muttered when he saw the Nunnehi warriors at the top of the hill. And they were talking now, too.

"My name is Snake, and this is Badger," said the man on the left. "You have to get up, Raven. You can't give up, or you will die here."

Creek whined, clearly concerned for his handler.

"Go get help, boy," Raven managed to whisper before the world started spinning.

***

Fenix pulled the cigar out of his mouth and moved over to the rocky edge of the bluff, where he took a knee next to his second in command. The highway in the valley below was covered in a fresh layer of snow that coated the abandoned cars like vanilla frosting. Nothing stirred in the still landscape.

But that was all about to change.

Two miles to the west, an American and Chinese convoy of highway clearers steamrolled down the road. They were right on time.

Fenix raised his M4 scope to his eye and centered it on a pair of trucks at the front. Mounted blades slammed vehicles into the ditches, clearing a path for a convoy containing industrial equipment and supplies for the survival centers. He counted three tan Humvees behind the lead trucks, and three white Chinese pickups packed full of soldiers following the Humvees. Behind those were four semi-trailers carrying supplies to the survival center outside of Denver. Another two American Humvees followed the trailers.

"Pretty light," Fenix whispered. That was good. It drastically reduced the chance of losing a soldier on this raid.

Over the past month, the Sons of Liberty had rebuilt their small army after losing so many of their brothers, first at the Castle, and then the camp where Fenix had been in hiding. Sergeant Horton's divisions, especially their squads of special ops soldiers, had been key in making this comeback.

Fenix turned to look at those men. They called themselves the Brandenburger Commandos, an homage to the elite Nazi soldiers. There were twelve of them up here on the bluff, all wearing camouflaged clothing and carrying automatic rifles.

"Remember what I told you," Fenix said. "We're the resistance now. Our government has betrayed us. The Sons of Liberty are the only thing standing between the foreign invaders and those of us that are still pure."

A dozen hands went up in the air in a Nazi salute. The men then moved into position to set up their weapons. Fenix turned back to the view of the road. Two more fire teams were dug in with rifles and explosives on either side of the bridge below.

They were well-equipped for this battle, but they didn't have what they needed yet to fight the coming Civil War. That's what made today's raid so important. The semi-trailers at the end of the convoy weren't just carrying boxes of MREs and cans of Dinty Moore beef stew. One of them contained weapons. Heavy weapons he could use to escalate these small raids into very damaging attacks against the traitorous American military and their Chinese allies. Eventually, he would be able to take the fight to the survival centers, and then, after raising a massive army, he could take back the country from President Diego and his bitch, Secretary Montgomery.

Bringing his scope up, Fenix zoomed in and centered his sights on the two trucks at the front of the convoy. The blades slammed into abandoned cars, sending them skidding into the ditch. Snow puffed into the sky, raining down on the vehicles behind the trucks.

He moved his sights to the bridge right below their vantage point. There were dozens of vehicles littering the road between the convoy and the bridge, but it wouldn't take long before the trucks reached it.

Fenix continued scanning the area, pausing where he had seen his men dig in. They had done a hell of a job camouflaging their position. He couldn't see them, but he knew they were there.

"Get ready," Horton said, holding up a balled fist.

The other men were all in position now. A dozen rifle barrels followed the approaching trucks. Fenix centered his sights on the first three Humvees. They were National Guard trucks. The fucking traitors were going to be the first to die. Then he would work on the Chinese, saving them for last. He would show the yellow skins what happened to those that set foot on American soil.

The screech of metal on metal pulled him back to the road, where the two tractors leading the vehicles continued to slam cars aside. They were almost to the bridge, with only about a dozen more vehicles to clear. Horton kept his hand in the air, and Fenix gripped the stock of his weapon tighter, anxious to open fire.

Part of him was hoping for a fight, or at least some resistance, although he had a feeling this was going to be a lot like shooting fish in a barrel. He really wasn't worried about getting hit up here. His only concern was getting out before the Americans or the Chinese sent in reinforcements. Choppers would do a number on his team, but by the time they got here, he would be long gone. Now, if the military sent jets or Chinese fighters, that was another story. It was much harder to hit a fighter jet with an RPG.

The thought sent a tingle through his nerves. His muscles tightened, and adrenaline emptied into his bloodstream. He inched his finger toward the trigger, keeping the Humvees in his sights.

The tractors continued toward the bridge, smoke bursting from their exhaust pipes. The blades crunched into metal, sending another pair of vehicles into the ditch. When they got to the bridge, they did exactly what Fenix was hoping for. The truck on the left slammed into a car that skidded across the icy road. It hit the guardrail while the truck on the right plowed into a pickup. The result was a jam of five vehicles clogging the center of the bridge.

The convoy slowed to a crawl behind the tractors.

A massive explosion suddenly rocked the center Humvee, sending the truck five feet into the air in a fireball. It came crashing back to the ground, tires blowing out when it landed.

"Give 'em, hell!" Fenix shouted as Horton dropped his hand, signaling the Sons of Liberty to fire.

Gunfire lanced away from the cliff, slamming into the other two Humvees. Another explosion blasted the bed of a Chinese pickup truck. The vehicle came crashing down onto the bed of the next truck.

Chinese and American soldiers piled out of the surviving vehicles and ran for cover. But there was nowhere to go. Another fire-team of SOL soldiers was waiting on the opposite side of the road. They were already standing to fire shouldered weapons at the men, riddling bodies with bullets.

Several of the smarter Chinese and American soldiers dove under vehicles. Fenix aimed for one of the Humvees, where two grunts had taken refuge. He emptied his magazine into the side of the vehicle, pushing helmets down.

As he changed his spent mag, he checked the bridge, where his other team was moving in toward the stranded tractors. The one on the right was attempting to back up, but gunfire peppered the windshield, splattering blood on the shattered glass.

Fenix slammed a fresh magazine home and then directed his barrel at the remaining truck. Holding down the trigger, he painted the passenger door with bullets. The driver continued to reverse across the bridge, heading toward the burning Humvees.

"Don't let them escape!" Horton shouted.

"Give me the RPG!" Fenix yelled back.

Horton picked the weapon up out of the snow and handed it to Fenix. Hefting the launcher onto his shoulder, he lined up the sights on the truck. A squeeze of the trigger fired a rocket-propelled grenade that streaked toward the vehicle and hit the road to the right of the driver's door. The explosion slammed into the side of the cab with such force it knocked the entire truck on its side.

"Nice shot, General," Horton said.

He ignored the sergeant and picked his rifle back up, already searching for his next target. This was fun. Another five minutes of gunfire finished off the convoy. Fenix aimed his rifle at the semi-trailers at the end of the line, where the drivers had jumped ship and taken off down the road.

Gunfire cut the four men down before they could get away.

The noise faded, leaving only the sporadic crack.

"That's the last of 'em," Horton said. He stood for a better view of the road, and Fenix moved to the edge of the bluff. Smoke drifted across the winter wasteland, and flames ate at the burned hulls of the destroyed trucks.

Shouting came from the road, and Fenix zoomed in on a trio of his soldiers approaching a pickup truck, where some of the surviving Chinese soldiers were hiding. One of the SOL men lobbed a grenade under the truck, and the three men retreated into the ditch.

A Chinese soldier crawled out when the explosion rammed the truck. The gas tank went up a second later, creating a massive gout of flame and a plume of smoke. Fenix laughed, but then went silent when he saw a burning Chinese soldier running out of the smoke cloud and away from the destruction. Hands waving in the air, he bolted for the ditch.

Horton aimed, but Fenix reached out and pushed his barrel down.

"Let him burn," Fenix said. "Send in the clean-up crew. It's on to phase two."

"You got it, sir." Horton relayed the order over the walkie-talkies, and the fire teams began moving below, weapons aimed at the remaining vehicles. From the looks of it, they hadn't lost a single man.

The crack of gunfire a moment later changed that.

Two SOL soldiers dropped to the road, blood splattering the snow. Fenix brought up his rifle and searched for the shooter. He shouted, "Eyes? Who has—"

Gunfire peppered the side of a truck before he could finish his sentence. He zoomed in on a helmeted head under the truck, the bloody face gone slack in the snow.

Fenix lowered his rifle, grinning. Served the son of a bitch right.

"Move in!" he yelled.

Six of his men jogged toward the trucks. He watched them round up several surviving American soldiers and then surround another truck where two Chinese soldiers surrendered their QBZ-95 rifles. They crawled out from under the back and held their hands in the air.

Fenix eyed their black rifles on the ground, and then scrutinized their blue camo uniforms and matching helmets. This wasn't the first time he had seen them up close, but each time it was still a shock to see the foreign fucks on American soil.

He joined his men on the road and scanned the sky. There was no sign of choppers or fighter jets, but they would have to move quickly to avoid any reinforcements. The distant growl of diesel engines sounded, but those were just the SOL trucks that had been waiting for the ambush to conclude. The pickups stopped near the semi-trailers and men jumped out, preparing to fill them with supplies from the convoy.

Fenix walked toward the two National Guardsmen and two Chinese soldiers. They were on their knees in the center of the road, hands bound behind their backs with zip ties.

Fenix strode past them. He would deal with them soon.

"Jackpot!" someone shouted from the semi-trailers.

Fenix made his way to the back of the truck, grinning from ear to ear at the sight of their biggest score yet. Crates upon crates of ammo were stacked neatly inside. Two soldiers were already going through the crates as Fenix and Horton approached.

"Got M240s, RPGs, and some SAWs, but that's not all," one of the men said.

Looking over his shoulder, Horton flashed a rare smile at Fenix. "Christmas has come early, sir. Looks like we got ourselves mortars!"

Fenix looked inside the truck and examined the weapons with trepidation. The tubes were Chinese-built Type 87 mortars, a battalion-level weapon with a decent range.

"What the hell are they doing with these bad boys?" Fenix muttered to himself.

"More evidence the Chinese are here to conquer and not help. What else would they need mortars for?" Horton said.

Fenix ordered his other men to continue unloading the weapons, and motioned for Horton to follow him. They walked back to the prisoners, and Fenix drew his .357 Magnum.

The two Americans looked up at him, and his gun, their eyes pleading for mercy. Both men were young, maybe in their late twenties. One was a staff sergeant, and the other was a corporal. Both were blond with blue eyes—good Aryan features.

Fenix couldn't tell how old the Chinese men were because they had their heads lowered at the road and hands behind their backs.

That was good. They knew their place.

"It's your lucky day," Fenix said. He wondered if the Chinese soldiers spoke English, but decided he didn't care. He aimed the .357 at their helmets and pulled the trigger twice, blowing their brains onto the pavement.

"As for you two," Fenix said to the American soldiers, "you get to live."

The staff sergeant vomited in the snow, but the corporal just kept staring at Fenix, rage in his eyes. He ignored the man, holstered the pistol, and walked away. He flashed a hand signal to the men at the end of the convoy.

A shout stopped him as he made his way toward getaway vehicles.

"You're that Nazi prick, aren't you?"

Fenix pivoted back to the corporal. He stalked over to the prisoner and bent down to check the man's name. Mark Sussex.

"I'm General Dan Fenix," he said, scowling. "And now that you know who I am, I guess it's not your lucky day after all."

In a swift motion, he drew his pistol, jammed the barrel against Sussex's forehead, and pulled the trigger. Blood splattered over the road and Fenix stood with a sigh. The staff sergeant screamed and rolled away. He began squirming toward the ditch, his hands still bound behind his back.

Fenix shook his head. "Just when I try to be nice, people have to be pricks. Sorry, staff sergeant." He aimed and pulled the trigger three times, shooting the man in the back. Then he opened the cylinder of the revolver and dumped the empty cartridges.

Horton stood glaring at him, and Fenix looked up as he reloaded.

"You got a problem, Sergeant?"

A quick shake of Horton's head. "No sir."

"Then get your ass moving. We have to get out of here before reinforcements come," Fenix said. "And remember, make it look like someone else did this. We can't afford to keep painting swastikas on shit, or the military might decide to send more troops out this way."

He snapped the cylinder shut and watched as his men loaded the pickup trucks with the new weapons and ammunition. War was swiftly approaching, and now they had the tools to fight it. It was time to water the Tree of Liberty with blood.

— 13 —

Teddy's release from the Estes Park hospital should have been a joyous occasion for Sandra. Instead, she was worried sick about her brother. She was trying to keep it together for Teddy and Allie, but Raven had been missing for several hours.

She held the boy's hand as she walked him out of his room and down the hallway. Allie carried Teddy's belongings, including his stuffed animals.

"Where is Creek?" Allie asked.

Sandra couldn't reply. Her heart was beating so hard she couldn't speak. Raven and Creek had failed to show up at the checkpoint where Dale was supposed to pick them up, and Colton didn't have the resources to send out a search party this second. He also didn't think it was necessary—yet.

Still, Sandra's intuition told her something was wrong. Her brother didn't get lost. Plus, he had been under the weather the past few days. She had tried to talk him out of the hunt but he wouldn't listen, which was typical for Raven. Stubborn as always.

Sandra opened the door to the lobby and led the kids out into the waiting area. This was Teddy's first taste of freedom in months. He let out a happy sigh, and Sandra smiled.

Outside the glass windows, the sun was setting over the Rocky Mountains. The temperatures would plummet soon, and she didn't want to think about what would happen if Raven didn't make it back before then. While he could usually take care of himself, if he was injured or worse...no, she couldn't think about that.

Two figures emerged in the parking lot outside, distracting Sandra from her worries. She loosened her grip on Teddy's hand as his parents, Marie and Michael, approached the building.

"Don't forget to come visit," she said. "Not here, of course, but at Raven's house. I'm pretty sure you won't want to come back here for a while, right?"

"No ma'am," he said, looking up at her. Then he glanced over to Allie and raised his stump before lowering it, his cheeks firing red. Sandra had seen him do this a few times as he got used to the phantom feelings from the missing limb. He gave Allie a quick hug with his other arm. She giggled and smiled.

Sandra waved at Marie and Michael Brown as they walked in. "Teddy's all ready to go," she said.

Marie cupped her hands over her face to hide her tears. She lowered her hands and reached out to hug Sandra. "Thank you for everything you've done, Miss Spears."

Michael reached out to shake Sandra's hand after his wife pulled away. "We can't thank you enough," he added.

"You have a very brave son," Sandra said. "He's a fighter."

Allie walked over to the doors, looking at something in the parking lot.

"Mom," she whispered.

"One second, sweetie," Sandra replied.

She continued going over the medicines they were

sending home with Teddy as his parents listened intently. "He needs to take two of these a day, and then one of these before bed. It will help keep any infection from coming back."

"Anything else we should be doing?" Marie asked.

"He still needs plenty of rest and good nutrition to help support his immune system. I've spoken to Raven and the chief about extra vegetable rations for him."

"Mom," Allie said again. Sandra looked over at her daughter and saw Allie pointing out the window.

"Is that Creek?" her daughter asked.

Sandra's heart pounded at the sight of the dog. He was limping across the parking lot, blood staining his fur. She waited for Raven to stumble into view, but the Akita was alone.

***

Charlize looked out the window of her hotel room as the sun crested the horizon, spreading its light over Lower Manhattan. Flakes fluttered from the sky, adding to the foot of snow that already covered New York. Several Chinese snowplows were already clearing the area below, but as for the rest of the city, the residents were out of luck.

Her thirtieth-floor hotel room provided quite the view of the city. A few people were already on the streets, but the only traffic she saw were vehicles shipped in from other countries or old clunkers that had survived the EMP blast.

It looked odd seeing the streets so empty. Although New York was one of the few major cities that hadn't fallen into complete anarchy there were still large pockets of lawlessness and several boroughs that were war zones. Even in the relatively calm areas, like Lower Manhattan, things were far from normal. Most residents hadn't gone to work in two months, and were relying on food and water from the numerous survival centers set up across the city.

Rising above the skyline was a beacon of hope—One World Trade Center. At seventeen hundred seventy-six feet, it was one of the tallest buildings in the world. The number wasn't a coincidence, either. It represented the date of the Declaration of Independence. Seeing the building watching over the city reminded her that Americans never gave up. When terrorists knocked down the Twin Towers, they were rebuilt, bigger and better than before.

Part of her mission today was to find a place to relocate the White House to. Maybe she was looking at it now. The building was a fortress, and housed the FEMA offices. It was in a good strategic location, too, which made it a top choice on her growing list.

She finished getting dressed, putting on a pair of black slacks and a plain button-down shirt. Throwing on a coat, she then headed into the hallway, where two Marines were posted. She followed them down to the lobby. Colonel Raymond was already there, waiting with a cup of steaming coffee.

"Thank you, Colonel," she said with heartfelt gratitude.

"No problem." He handed her the cup carefully, and said, "Did you get some rest last night, ma'am?"

"A little."

She didn't bother saying her room was freezing. Raymond had spent the night in the same hotel, and the rooms were all cold despite the generator that turned on every few hours to power the furnace. They walked outside, where it was even colder. Two green Humvees were waiting, and the Green Berets accompanying her on this trip all piled in. She got into the second vehicle with Sergeant Fugate and Colonel Raymond.

"United Nations building," Raymond told the driver.

The trucks set off, growling toward a roadblock guarded by more soldiers and several police officers. She was anxious to see the rest of the city, and to hear updates on the recovery process.

The first view of that progress came as the convoy set out and rounded the next corner. Several Chinese electrical trucks were installing one of the new large power transformers. The men were all dressed in white coats and wore blue helmets. A small group of Chinese soldiers patrolled the area with machine guns. It was the first time she had seen a crew this close, and something about the Chinese workers and their soldier counterparts gave her the chills. Maybe that was just the freezing temperatures. Either way, she pulled her coat collar up around her neck.

At the next intersection, two NYPD officers stood on the sidewalk. One of them approached the lead vehicle in her convoy and held up a hand. Charlize drank her coffee as the officer spoke to the soldiers in the vehicle. The man quickly waved them onward.

The officers were just two of the hundreds she had seen on the streets so far. An impressive percentage of the men and women in blue had remained on the job after the attacks. While other cities had major problems with desertion, the NYPD had stepped up to the plate.

On the next street, another crew of Chinese workers

came into view. This time they were handing out food and blankets from a truck. They were definitely helping save lives, yet reports were continuing to trickle in about attacks on the supply convoys across the United States. She had just heard about another one from Captain Harris the previous day. She wondered how Harris and Albert were doing.

"We're here," Raymond said.

The trucks pulled up in front of the United Nations building. Flags representing dozens of countries whipped in the wind. Charlize stepped out into the snowy street, and followed her entourage to the entrance of the building. The lobby was surprisingly warm, and a handful of staff were waiting to greet her.

"Welcome to the United Nations, Secretary Montgomery. I'm Linda Watts. If you'd please follow me, I'll take you to the assembly area."

Raised voices speaking in Mandarin rang out in the distance, and Linda looked over her shoulder with a frown. "They have been arguing for a while now," she whispered.

The group stopped outside the assembly room, and Linda opened one of the doors to peek in. She then gestured for Charlize and Raymond to enter. They stepped into a chamber ringed with seats looking over a central platform and podium.

General Lin was already inside, yelling at one of his subordinates. The younger officer threw up a salute and then hurried off, passing Charlize, Linda, and Raymond on the way out.

"Ah, Secretary Montgomery," Lin said. "You're early, but this is good. We have much to speak about before the meeting starts. We just got some very bad news."

Charlize walked down the steps and joined Lin at a table on the bottom floor. He gestured for her to sit, but she declined.

"I'd prefer to stand. Thank you, General."

"Very well." He clasped his hands behind his back and pivoted away to look up at the American flag hanging from the wall. "This morning I was informed that three convoys were hit in the past twenty-four hours. One in Washington, one in Oregon, and one in Colorado."

He continued staring at the flag without turning to face her.

"When President Diego agreed to this deal, he promised me we would not have problems like this, but I have lost two hundred soldiers and over a dozen vehicles. This is unacceptable. I have been forced to give the order for my troops to protect themselves at all costs. They will no longer hold their fire when they are attacked."

Charlize swallowed hard. She had known this moment was coming, but now that it was here, she struggled to find the right words.

"While these attacks are regrettable, I would highly recommend not authorizing any sort of violence against Americans. I cannot agree to allow your fighter jets to engage civilians. While I understand your soldiers on the ground need to protect themselves, I must have your word that you won't drop a single bomb or launch a single missile."

Lin scrutinized Charlize for a moment. "I promised President Diego that I would do everything in my power to prevent bloodshed, but if these attacks continue, I will be forced to use air support on these..." He paused to think, and then added, "*Insurgents*, I believe is the word you call them?"

***

Van Dyke sucked on a cigarette. It was cold, and Albert pulled his coat up around his neck and one-handed his gun so he could flex his other hand. Even with his gloves and heavy boots, his extremities were starting to go numb as they walked alongside a long line of train cars packed with transformers, electrical equipment, and supplies.

Chinese workers dressed in white uniforms and blue helmets jogged past them toward the staging area about a quarter mile away, where heavy-duty trucks were being unloaded. American troops surrounded the zone with several armored trucks, including the MATV Van Dyke had been assigned. Twenty American soldiers stood guard, outnumbered ten to one by the Chinese soldiers.

Albert didn't like the ratio, but so far he had to admit the men had been easy to work with. Those that knew English were courteous and polite. The workers especially seemed happy to be here. It was the American citizens that were causing the problems. The airdrops and information the SCs were handing out hadn't calmed the people, who persisted in regarding the Chinese as invaders, not aid workers.

Charlotte, North Carolina, was especially bad. Albert hadn't wanted to return here after his last visit, but it had been the next stop on their list. He looked toward downtown as smoke rose into the sky. The gangs had completely taken over the city.

"Fuckers are still out there," Van Dyke said, following Albert's gaze.

"I'm sorry?" Albert said, not quite following.

"The assholes that killed Sergeant Flint. I'm still hoping Command sends us back in there with some real firepower. Just need a dozen good men, and we'll show the Latin Kings and MS-13 what we're made of."

Albert understood why Van Dyke wanted revenge, but their job was to be Secretary Montgomery's eyes and ears, not go off on some bloodlust mission to kill the gangs that had attacked them the last time they were here.

As a group of Chinese workers passed by, Van Dyke blew a cloud of smoke at them. One of the men turned and glared.

"Watch it!" he said in perfect English.

"What?" Van Dyke said defensively.

"Corporal, chill," Albert said.

Another worker pulled his friend away while Albert yanked Van Dyke back.

"What's that all about?" Albert asked.

Van Dyke shrugged, took another puff, and watched the men walk away. He had a major chip on his shoulder today, and it was being directed at the aid workers. He flicked his cigarette on the ground and stomped it out below his boot.

"Come on, man, we're late," Van Dyke said.

Captain Harris was at the front of the staging area with his counterpart, a Chinese Captain named Tuan Cao. FEMA was onsite too, along with local and state officials. In a little over an hour, the National Guard had set up an Emergency Operations Center that would help coordinate the movement of these supplies to the people that needed them.

"Van Dyke!" shouted a voice. "Where the hell have you been?"

"Sorry, Captain," Van Dyke said. He jogged toward Harris, who had emerged from the FEMA tent.

"Need your help with something," Harris said. He

gave Albert a once-over and said, "Not you, though, Officer Randall. I promised Secretary Montgomery I'd keep you safe."

"Sir, I'm here to help," Albert protested.

"I know." Harris sighed. "Just follow me, guys."

They ducked below the flaps of the FEMA tent and into a room lit by large lamps. A generator provided the electricity here. Albert took off his gloves to warm his hands as he stood in front of a table that sported a map of Charlotte.

Harris waited for Captain Cao to join them. He walked in a few minutes later and nodded politely. Harris cut right to the chase.

"Since losing the survival center, the city has been in chaos. Our job is to restore order before the crews can move in and begin getting the power back on. We won't be here long, however, as my mission is to continue with General Lin's convoy."

"Is there really a train like this in every major city?" Van Dyke asked.

"Just on the coasts," Cao said. "We will work our way west in a few months to start restoring power to the other regions. FEMA and the military will be evacuating people to the regions with restored power."

"Poor bastards," Van Dyke said.

Cao looked at him quizzically.

"I meant the people in the Midwest," Van Dyke clarified.

"Ah," Cao said. "They will not be completely on their own. We have a fleet of ships heading up the Mississippi river to deliver supplies and generators, but most of our efforts are focused on moving inward from the coasts.

"So what's this mission you got for me and my boys, sir?" Van Dyke asked Harris.

"We need you to accompany the Chinese soldiers to take back the streets from the gangs. General Lin and President Diego have authorized a joint effort to go after enemies of the state."

"Enemies of the state?" Albert asked.

"Gangs, raiders, Nazis," Harris said.

A smile formed on Van Dyke's face. "I thought you'd never ask, sir."

"Careful what you wish for," Harris replied. His gaze flitted to Albert. "Before you say anything, you're not going."

Albert nodded again. He'd been out there once, and that was enough for him. Revenge wasn't his cup of tea, anyway. He just wanted to do a good job and then get back to his sister, Ty, and Charlize.

"You sure?" Van Dyke asked. "Randall is good in a fight."

Harris scratched his chin and glanced at Albert. "Will you give us a second?"

Albert tried to ignore the dressing down Harris handed to Van Dyke. Cao followed him and stood beside Albert outside the tent.

"So you are a police officer?" Cao asked.

Albert nodded. "Capitol police."

"You protect important people." He smiled. "I do that too."

"Yeah?" Albert turned slightly to examine the other man. He was in his mid-thirties, maybe a bit older, with a mustache and short cropped hair under his helmet.

"I was a police officer most of my career," Cao explained. "But a few years ago I got this calling to join the army. I wanted to protect more than just my city. I wanted to protect my country. I am glad I did. Now I get to help protect yours, too."

Albert was slightly taken back at the soldier's story. For the past few weeks, he had doubted the Chinese were really here to help. He still wasn't sure what to think, but hearing things like this made him optimistic that things would get better.

Van Dyke stepped out of the tent a moment later. "You ready, Cao?" he asked.

Cao dipped his helmet at Albert and then followed Van Dyke away from the tent.

"Catch ya' later, Big Al," Van Dyke called over his shoulder.

Albert raised a hand to wave goodbye when a gunshot rang out. At first, everyone froze. But when the next shot came, they all hit the dirt, knowing this wasn't some random potshot. Albert dove for cover behind a bulldozer and brought his gun up to search for the source of the fire.

A Chinese worker dropped to his knees a few feet away, hands clamped around his neck, eyes wide with fear. Blood trickled from between his fingers as he slumped over. It was the same man Van Dyke had exchanged words with fifteen minutes earlier.

Albert crawled next to the edge of the bulldozer blade and saw several riflemen approaching along the tracks to the west, firing at the Chinese workers, who were running for cover. More gunfire came from the east, and Albert twisted to see a Hispanic man with a shotgun running into the staging area. He was close enough to see the Latin Kings symbol tattooed on his arms.

The man fired the shotgun point-blank at an American

soldier, and then let out a scream as he turned the gun at one of the Humvees. Bullets lanced into his body, jerking him back and forth before he finally went down.

More gangbangers ran into the staging area from the buildings at the edge of the tracks, shouting and firing weapons. This wasn't just a few raiders: this was a small army. Van Dyke and company didn't need to go out to find the bastards that had killed Sergeant Flint after all. The gang was already here.

"Not today," Albert said. He got on one knee and aimed his M4 at the men on the tracks. A squeeze of the trigger sent a burst of 5.56 mm rounds downrange. They went wide, and he refocused his aim. This time, the bullets clipped the neck of a man wearing a hoodie. He stumbled away, and Albert roved the barrel to the next target. Someone took cover next to him, and he twisted to see Van Dyke.

"Shit, shit, shit," the corporal muttered as he jammed a new magazine into his rifle. "They're everywhere!"

The mounted M240s barked to life. Albert snuck a glance around the bulldozer blade. The gunners in the Humvees were raking the big guns back and forth at buildings to the south, where more of the thugs were trying to flank the staging area. Chinese soldiers joined the fight, firing at the raiders.

Albert focused his fire on the men running down the train tracks. Several of them had opened one of the cars. He watched as they climbed inside and then began tossing boxes out.

"There," Albert said, pointing.

Van Dyke stood, fearless, holding the trigger down and painting the train car with bullets. Several rounds ricocheted off, but two found a target. A thin man in sweatpants and a matching sweatshirt fell out of the open car door and hit the ground. Three of his friends took off running, one of them holding a box.

The M240s died down in the background, and the automatic gunfire ceased a few minutes later. The fight was already over.

"Hold your fire!" Captain Harris shouted. He stood in the middle of the staging area with his rifle cradled.

That's when Albert saw the bodies. He lowered his rifle in shock. Four workers and several Chinese soldiers, as well as three Americans, lay in the dirt, blood pooling around their corpses.

"Medic!" someone shouted.

Albert turned back to the tracks and raised his rifle at the escaping hostiles, anger raging through his veins. He and Van Dyke stood side by side and aimed at the thugs. A few trigger pulls took down the three men, leaving the box of supplies on the tracks near their dead bodies.

Van Dyke spat on the ground and then yelled, "That's right, you rats!"

Pained screaming came from all directions in the respite of gunfire. Albert moved back into the staging area to see if there was anyone he could help, while Van Dyke stood yelling profanities.

— 14 —

Colton threw the Volkswagen into gear and peeled out of the hospital parking lot. Creek looked up from the floor, shivering from the cold.

"It's okay, boy," Sandra said. She sat in the passenger seat fishing out supplies from a medical bag on her lap to help Creek.

Colton was more worried about her than the dog. Tears welled in her eyes, and her hands were shaking.

"Those teeth marks?" Colton asked.

"Looks like it," Sandra confirmed.

"Probably one of those damn coyotes."

"You think a coyote attacked my brother?"

"I don't know, but we're going to find out," Colton said. He steered onto Highway 34, heading west into Rocky Mountain National Park. The area where Dale had dropped Raven off wasn't far, just a few miles off Trail Ridge Road. There was only one roadblock out this way, and he barely stopped when he got there.

Creek yelped as Sandra put ointment on his wounds.

"He going to be okay?" Colton asked.

"He might need stitches when we get him back to the hospital."

The damn dog has been through a lot, but he's tough. Almost as tough as his handler. He looked to the alluvial fan turnoff and remembered the night of the attack. The memory sent a chill up his spine. He suddenly felt certain

180

something bad had happened to Raven. The man was an expert tracker, so how could a coyote get a drop on him and Creek? That simply didn't make any sense.

Colton spotted the red Chevy pickup on the side of the road. Dale was already here. He pulled over. Sandra finished putting the bandage over Creek's back, and opened the door.

"Show us where Sam is," she said.

Creek jumped out and took off. Flashlight beams flitted through the forest to the east of the road, and Colton set off with his rifle. He took in a breath, picking up the scent of smoke. It could be from one of the cabins out here. They had assigned several refugees to the old Forest Service cabins, but it could also be a fire Raven had built for himself.

"Dale!" Colton shouted. "Dale, can you hear me?"

There was no response.

"Stay close to me," Colton instructed Sandra. He handed her a flashlight.

The lights penetrated the inky black and flitted over the spindly trees making up the winter wasteland.

They hiked for fifteen minutes, keeping quiet and listening for Creek. The dog had long since vanished into the forest, but he barked somewhere up ahead. The scent of burning wood grew stronger as they made their way deeper into the woods. Colton was hesitant to raise his light to the sky to check for smoke. If someone had attacked Raven, he didn't want to draw their attention. He cursed himself for shouting earlier. He wasn't thinking properly.

The bitter cold slowed Colton and Sandra down. She was wearing a coat, gloves, and stocking cap, but didn't have proper gear on to be out here for an extended period of time. Colton wasn't faring much better, if he was honest.

Fifteen more minutes into the hike, Colton saw the glow of a fire. It was faint, nothing more than a dot of orange in the woods. Sandra saw it, too, and she gasped.

"Is that him?" she asked.

A bark sounded, as if in reply.

"Let's go!" Colton said.

Sandra followed him through the woods toward the light. Dale was already there, hunched down to rebuild the fire. Lying curled in a fetal position near his feet was Raven. Creek nudged him with his muzzle, but Raven wasn't moving.

"Raven!" Sandra shouted, running over with her medical pack.

Colton slowed on the approach, raking his light over what looked like a gruesome scene. Crimson crisscrossed the ground in splatter marks. He focused his beam on the source of the blood.

Not a Coyote after all.

A mountain lion was sprawled in the snow, an arrow sticking out of its back.

***

Raven heard distant voices, but he couldn't make them out. He was cold. Freezing. But he was also paralyzed, unable to control his body.

He looked ahead at the two Nunnehi warriors. They were still tracking the eight-point buck. They stalked the beast through the woods, the sun shining on their half-naked bodies.

It was a dream, Raven realized, but he couldn't seem

to wake up.

He followed the two warriors, Snake and Badger, as they moved silently through the forest. A spring breeze rustled the trees around them. Despite the warm weather, his body felt cold, like he was in a snowstorm.

His eyes flitted to the dirt ahead, where he saw deer tracks.

They were fresh.

Snake and Badger both stopped near a clearing ahead. They turned and raised their hands at him, signaling for him to continue.

Raven pulled an arrow from the quiver slung over his back. A meadow of purple and blue wild flowers waited just beyond the warriors. Mountains with snow-painted peaks rose above the majestic land. The soft trickle of a stream sounded over the rustle of the afternoon wind.

Keeping low, Raven walked around the trunk of a ponderosa tree rising toward the sky. He then climbed a small hill, which provided a lookout over the meadow and the creek meandering through the middle.

Standing near the water's edge was the eight-point buck. It lifted its rack of antlers, ears perked.

Raven froze behind the two Nunnehi warriors and held a breath in his chest. Why did his breath feel cold?

This wasn't like most of his dreams. It almost felt real.

The deer went back to drinking from the stream, and Raven made his way up to Snake and Badger. The men simply nodded at him, and although they didn't speak out loud, he could hear their thoughts.

This is your spirit to take, Raven. Do it honorably and swiftly.

Raven took a moment to admire the beautiful creature, recalling the Cherokee story of how deer got their horns. Long ago, it was said, deer did not have antlers. A messenger started a game between a rabbit and a deer to see who could go farther in a race. The deer could run faster, but the rabbit was a better jumper, so they were evenly matched. The winner would get antlers. The rabbit, however, did not play by the rules during this race, and was caught cheating. Thus, the horns went to the deer.

Raven had never seen a beast with such a beautiful rack of antlers. He placed the arrow shaft on the rest of his bow. Then he attached the nock to the string. Making sure his shoulders were perpendicular with the beast, he pulled the string back, closed one eye, and aimed the arrowhead at the buck's heart. After a short mental prayer for a speedy kill, he let the arrow fly.

The animal's ears flicked, and it focused dark eyes on Raven just as the arrow hit its chest. His aim was true, and the arrow struck it in the heart, killing the buck instantly. The creature collapsed on the ground, kicking once with a muscle spasm.

Snake and Badger were on the move before the deer went limp. Raven followed them out into meadow, where the sun hit his skin. But even the radiant glow couldn't take away the freezing chill that seemed to be gripping his bones.

He got down on his knees next to the dead deer, praying again for the gods' forgiveness. The two Nunnehi warriors looked over at him, and he grabbed the bone handle of his sheathed buck knife. He'd use the blade to carve the deer and cut out the tongue to throw into a fire for sacrifice. The Cherokee used all parts of the deer but the sinews and hamstrings, which were left in respect for the spirit.

Raven got right to work, expertly skinning the deer,

while Snake and Badger stood to watch. The sun slipped behind the clouds over their shoulders, and darkness suddenly spread over the land. The purple and blue flowers vanished, and a snowy wasteland took their place. When Raven looked back at the deer, it was nothing but bones.

The Nunnehi warriors both dipped their chiseled jaws.

"The hunt is over," Snake said.

Badger pointed to the east. "You must go now, Raven. An enemy is coming. Only you can stop this evil."

Raven blinked, and the world changed again. In a split second, the warriors disappeared, along with the bones, but the wintery landscape remained. The moon was high in the night sky, and there was a small fire near his body. The wood was burning, but he could hardly feel any warmth. In fact, he could hardly feel anything at all.

Someone was hovering over him, but his vision was too blurred to make out the face. He saw other shapes, and then felt something furry against his cheek.

He snapped alert as he abruptly remembered his fight with the mountain lion. The beast was a few feet away, yellow eyes open and staring at him.

Raven let out a gasp of icy air and reached up, grabbing the arm of the person hovering over him.

"Raven, it's me. It's Sandra," said a voice.

Dale and Colton were there too, both of them looking at Raven with wide eyes.

"He killed a damn mountain lion," Dale said, laughing.

"Raven," Sandra said, snapping her fingers in front of his face to draw his attention.

He focused on her and smiled. "Hey, sis."

She batted a tear away and snorted. "This is the last time I'm coming after you, Sam Spears."

***

Charlize and Colonel Raymond walked along the edge of Central Park with their Green Beret escorts. Aside from the military company, this moment reminded her of the time she had strolled through the gardens with her husband. It seemed like just yesterday that Richard and Charlize had spent the better part of a Sunday walking through the park and eating at a local seafood and chip restaurant. Those had been happy times, and Charlize wished she'd appreciated them more in the moment.

But today she wasn't here for leisure. She was here to check out the final location on the list President Diego had given her of potential places for the White House, and to meet with the Chinese delegation one last time.

"There it is," Raymond said, pointing at the building situated on the corner of Fifth Avenue. Crews had restored power here just days earlier, and most of the windows of the Plaza Hotel were lit up.

Charlize took a moment to appreciate the architecture, which imitated a medieval French château. Hundreds of windows with gold trim provided guests with a panoramic view of Central Park. A green arched roof crested the white building.

"It's big, but that could be a good thing," Charlize said. "We need to house all the branches of government that were lost in D.C., so if we are able to contract with the current owners, we could use this as our central hub during the recovery efforts."

"Let's take a look inside," Raymond said.

The street had been completely cleared of stranded vehicles and snow, and they crossed easily. Several NYPD officers mounted on horses patrolled the area. The sidewalks weren't as busy as they would have been two months ago, but there were still pedestrians. They weren't tourists, though. These people were all on a mission.

Charlize was impressed by the grandeur of the hotel. It would make a beautiful place for the seat of the federal government, but strategically, it would be difficult to defend.

A representative of the Chinese delegation waited in the lobby, which was decorated with ornamented pillars and archways, a marble floor, and gold fixtures. Charlize followed her escorts down a hallway and took the elevator to the tenth floor, where they were led to a meeting room.

Inside sat General Lin and two staffers, an older man with gray hair and glasses, and a woman around Charlize's age. She remembered them from the United Nations building.

"Good to see you again, Secretary Montgomery," Lin said, rising to his feet. "You've already met Wan Shi and Liu Yaping."

"Yes," Charlize said. "Nice to see you."

Wan and Liu both bowed, and Lin gestured for Charlize to take a seat. She and Raymond took up positions across from General Lin.

"I'm connecting us to Constellation," Liu said. She swiveled a laptop screen so everyone in the room could see it. Between the working lights and the internet connection, for a fleeting moment it almost seemed like things were back to normal. President Diego's face emerged on the monitor a moment later, reminding her things were far from normal.

"Good afternoon," he said.

"Good afternoon, Mr. President," Lin said.

"How are you liking the Plaza Hotel?" Diego asked.

"It is a beautiful building," Lin said.

"Not my favorite on your list, sir, for strategic reasons," Charlize said.

"I'm looking forward to talking more when you get back," Diego said. "In the meantime, we have a few other items to discuss. Water supply has become the biggest problem in the survival centers."

That got her attention. Charlize had expected the meeting to start with the attack in Charlotte, where Albert and Captain Harris were currently monitoring a mission to re-take the city.

"Bringing the water treatment centers back online has been one of our main priorities since we landed," Lin said.

"Doctor Price is spearheading the effort, but we're going to need your help, General," Diego said.

"Liu will connect with Doctor Price as soon as possible," Lin said. "We are painfully aware of how important—"

A raucous boom cut the general off before he could finish. The entire room shook, and a piece of gold trim fell to the floor. For a moment, everyone just sat there, rattled and confused.

"Was that an explosion?" Diego asked.

"One moment, sir," Raymond said.

A fire alarm rang out, and then a second boom snapped Charlize into action. The noise was definitely an explosion.

Both of the doors swung open, and Sergeant Fugate entered. "Everyone stay calm, but we need to move."

Two of the Chinese soldiers posted in the hallway moved over to General Lin, speaking in Mandarin. The two groups left together for the hallway and were led to a stairwell opposite to the one where they had come in.

"What the hell is going on?" Raymond asked.

"The building is under attack," Fugate said. He stopped and held up his radio as it squawked.

"Multiple contacts," said the voice on the channel. "Shooters on the west and east sides of the building." There was a pause, with more white noise. Then the speaker came back and said, "Hunker down until we can figure out the safest way to get you out of there."

Faint but rapid gunfire sounded in the distance. This was a multi-stage attack, Charlize realized. First bombs, now shooters. But who would mount such a brazen attack on a relatively secure building?

"This way," Fugate said. He hurried down the hall, rifle shouldered, while the other Green Berets held rear guard. The two Chinese soldiers flanking the officials followed close behind.

The group moved into a stairwell and was instructed to stay put. Fugate pulled out his radio again to listen to the chatter. One of the Chinese soldiers was doing the same thing. The clash of languages made it incredibly difficult to hear anything. From what Charlize could make out, the attack had started when vehicles broke through a barrier a block away.

The gunfire continued below, echoing up the stairwell, getting closer by the minute. General Lin stood next to Charlize. If the man was frightened, he sure didn't show it. He had his fingers wrapped around a pistol. Both of his soldiers were iron-faced, emotionless. Even Liu and Wan appeared undeterred by the violence.

Fugate lowered the radio and jerked his chin up the stairwell. "We're headed to the roof. It's the only way out of here. The building is being overrun."

He looked to Staff Sergeant Thoreau, the kid with peach fuzz on his face, who stood below Charlize.

"Thoreau, you and Sammie cover our escape," Fugate said.

Thoreau nodded at Fugate, and then at Charlize, before moving back down the stairs with the other soldier.

"Good luck," Charlize whispered.

"Let's go," Fugate said.

The climb to the rooftop took five minutes. Fugate opened the roof access door, and then moved out with two of his men to clear the area. He returned a moment later and ushered everyone outside.

The cracks and pops coming from the street below told her the fight was far from over. The sound of a chopper rose over the din of gunfire. To the west, a Black Hawk was coming in fast.

"Come on!" Fugate shouted. He waved them over to the center of the roof. The pilots would have to hover, since there was no place to put down here.

Fugate and his men all raised their rifles and pointed them at the open doorway while Raymond, General Lin, and his staff moved over to where the pilots were lowering the chopper.

Charlize paused to listen. It sounded as if a battle was being waged inside the stairwell where Thoreau and Sammie had remained. The rotor drafts hit her, whipping her jacket violently. The pilots got as close to the roof as possible, and then the crew chief reached down to help Charlize into the bird. General Lin went next, with Liu and Wan following.

The two Chinese soldiers remained below with the

Green Berets, all of them still pointing their weapons at the doorway. It swung open just as Colonel Raymond climbed into the troop hold, and an American soldier stumbled onto the roof, blood soaking his right arm and parts of his neck. It was Sammie, Charlize realized. So where was Thoreau?

The young man yelled something at Fugate before crashing to the ground. The leader of the Green Berets turned and waved the pilots off before turning back to help Sammie and drag him away.

The bird pulled away from the roof, ascending quickly. Charlize watched as the Green Berets and Chinese soldiers took up defensive positions with their rifles aimed at the closed door. The pilots banked to the west, providing a view of the chaos below.

The warped black hull of a vehicle burned in front of the destroyed lobby. The once-white façade had caved in. A black field of debris surrounded the outside of the building, and on the rim of the destruction were dozens of bodies. Most of them seemed to be wearing blue and green uniforms.

"Are you okay, ma'am?" Raymond asked.

Charlize managed to nod, but she was still breathing heavily. She tried to catch her breath as the chopper pulled away, leaving the terror behind. Charlize caught a glimpse of the One World Trade Center as the pilots flew to safety. With the Plaza Hotel in ruins, it would most likely become the new site of the White House.

But she wasn't so sure New York was the best choice for the seat of government after all. Whoever had attacked the Plaza had done so in a coordinated and brutal way. Nowhere was safe anymore.

— 15 —

Fenix took a sip of whiskey. The liquid both warmed and cooled his throat.

"Damn, that's good sauce," he said.

Sergeant Horton raised his glass. "To the general!"

"To the general!" shouted a dozen men.

The twelve Brandenburger Commandos brought their glasses together, the clank echoing through the concrete bunker. The soldiers downed their glasses and then began filing out of the armory, where they were celebrating their newest addition—a dozen crates of weapons, explosives, and fully automatic weapons.

Fenix continued to admire the stacked boxes around him. Every bullet would help him accomplish his goal of taking Colorado back from the bureaucrats and the Chinese invaders.

He downed the rest of his glass and wiped his lips with a sleeve as the footfalls of the men who would help him succeed in this mission faded down the hallway. They were headed back to the central gathering, where a game of poker and more liquor awaited.

Horton, however, remained behind. He flashed a sly grin at Fenix and patted one of the crates.

"We're almost ready to fight our crusade against the insurgents," Horton said. "Just a few more raids like the one today, and we'll have everything we need."

Fenix found his lips cracking into a smile as well. The

thought of the coming fight gave him chills, and the whiskey warming his stomach only helped intensify the feeling.

"We're going to take our country back," Fenix said.

"Damn straight, sir." Horton's smile widened, revealing perfectly white teeth.

Fenix wasn't used to seeing the hardened war hero showing so much emotion. Most of the time, it was difficult to get him to laugh at a joke.

"I couldn't have done any of this without you, Sarge."

It wasn't often he gave praise, but this time it was well deserved. Over the past three weeks, the Brandenburger Commandos had freed Fenix from captivity, taken out Nile Redford and stolen his supplies, and successfully hit three Chinese convoys. On top of that, they had doubled the Sons of Liberty numbers and opened up three new bases in Colorado.

They were now at their new headquarters at Titan Missile Silo, the abandoned Cold War facility Sergeant Horton had taken over just days after the North Korean attack. It was located east of Denver, about an hour drive from the Rocky Mountains.

Tonight, the men were taking a break to celebrate their wins. It was time for the soldiers to sit back, drink, and relax. For Fenix, though, there was never time to relax. He had already lost enough time in Redford's prison cell. Besides, Fenix was expecting company shortly.

He walked into the command center, where his men were starting a game of poker at the metal table. Beer cans littered the area where maps had been earlier. Horton watched with his arms folded across his chest while Fenix poured whiskey from a bottle into his flask.

"Have fun, gentlemen," Fenix said, raising the flask.

"Not staying to lose your money, sir?" asked one of the men.

"Maybe next time." Fenix grinned, took a slug, and retreated to his quarters, deciding he didn't want to be too drunk when his new friends arrived.

When he got to his small room, he propped his feet up and nursed the flask in silence, listening to the hum of the generators. The noise was calming, and he rested his eyes.

Sometime later, he woke up and looked at his watch, cursing when he saw the time. He had to get topside, and fast. He hurried back to the area where his men were still playing cards. Two of them were shouting over a hand. Horton was standing between them to intervene. All three of them stood to attention when they saw Fenix. The room went silent.

"What the hell are you waiting for, Sergeant?" Fenix asked. "Are you ready or what?"

"Yes, sir. Sorry, sir. I lost track of time."

Fenix gestured for the men to return to their game. Normally he would have broken balls, but not tonight. These men deserved a break. They needed it. Even Nazis could get burned out on killing.

Horton hurried into the passage, and they took the first right to the stairs. Fenix went first, and fifteen minutes later he was at the top, his chest heaving and his head spinning from too much liquor. The door opened onto another passage, where a sentry named Miles was guarding the metal hatch that led outside.

Miles stiffened and raised his baldhead when he saw Fenix and Horton approaching.

"Good evening, sir," Miles said. A patch dotted with blood covered the new tattoo on his neck. The tattoo gun was getting passed around at their base a lot these days.

Horton opened a small metal hatch that allowed him to peer outside. After a quick scan, he closed it and opened the door, letting in a gust of cold air. Fenix offered Miles the flask.

"Thank you, sir, but I'm on duty," Miles said.

"It's okay," Fenix said, holding it out again.

Miles hesitated, took a slug, and passed it back to Fenix. The two men drank while they waited. A few minutes later, Horton returned.

"They're here," Horton said.

Fenix put his flask back into his pocket, then pulled out a cap and slapped it over his thick, slicked-back hair. He stepped out into the frigid air, taking in a breath to remind himself what freedom tasted like.

Horton continued down a rocky path leading around a bluff. Three more guards were posted at the end of the trail, crouched behind a rocky wall with their rifles and night vision goggles. They were all focused on the silhouette of a single pickup about a quarter mile away.

"That's them, sir," Horton said.

"They came alone," one of the sentries reported.

"Good, but watch our backs," Fenix said to the other men. He set off around the lookout with Horton following. The moon was out tonight, spreading a soft glow over the white landscape. He wasn't worried about an ambush, but he was always wary. Secretary Montgomery was still on his trail, and wouldn't give up until he was dead or in captivity. That's what made tonight's meeting so important.

It was time for the Sons of Liberty to ally with others fighting for the same cause—to bring down what was left of the federal government, and fight the damn Chinese.

Several flashlights flickered on as he approached the

pickup. Three men, all dressed in black tactical clothes, walked toward Fenix and Horton.

One of the men stepped out in front of the others. "General Fenix?" he asked.

"That's me," Fenix reached out to shake his hand. "Welcome to our humble nuclear missile silo, Sheriff," he said.

***

Albert took the satellite phone from Captain Harris and brought it to his lips.

"Hello, Secretary Montgomery, this is Albert," he said.

"Good to hear your voice. I heard about the attack. Are you doing okay?"

"Yes, ma'am, I'm fine. How is New York?"

"There was an attack here, too. I'm already back at Constellation, and General Lin has been moved to a secure location. He won't be returning to the staging area there for the foreseeable future."

Albert took a deep breath. He hated the idea of Charlize being in danger when he wasn't there to shield her. "Were you hurt, ma'am? What happened?"

"This isn't public yet, but the attack was orchestrated by a group of North Korean sleeper agents. We're still trying to collect more details, but what we know now is that these terrorists were targeting Lin and I."

"Are you hurt?" he repeated.

"I'm fine, but we lost a lot of good people, and so did the Chinese delegation." She paused and then said, "I'm pulling you out of Charlotte. I need you here with me. There's a chopper heading that way tomorrow, and I want you on it. Captain Harris will continue his mission without you."

Albert looked to Harris, who nodded.

"Okay, ma'am," Albert said. "I'll see you tomorrow."

"Stay safe, Big Al."

"You too."

Albert handed the phone back to the captain. Outside the HQ tent, American and Chinese soldiers were preparing for an assault on Charlotte. Van Dyke ducked under the flaps.

"Captain, the teams are ready to move out," he said.

"I'll be right there," Harris said.

Van Dyke shifted his gaze to Albert, and grinned. The corporal didn't look as nervous as the last time they had gone out there. He had excitement written all over his features.

"Be careful, Van Dyke," Albert said. "You may have the numbers this time, but don't underestimate the enemy. Remember what happened to those National Guard soldiers."

"That's part of the reason I'm anxious to go out there, brother. We're going to make these fuckers pay for what they have done."

"Just watch your six, man. I'm headed back to Constellation tomorrow, so if I don't see you before you get back, good luck."

"Thanks." Van Dyke reached out to shake his hand. "Take care of yourself, Big Al."

"I'll do my best."

Van Dyke wiped the smirk off his face and grew serious. "And do me a favor. Tell Secretary Montgomery to keep them Chinese on a short leash. I don't trust 'em."

"I'll pass along your message, but I'd highly

recommend dropping the attitude. So far, they have fought, bled, and died with us."

"Just wait until one of 'em shoots an American soldier. Mark my words, Al, it's going to happen."

Albert didn't know exactly how to respond to that, so he simply held Van Dyke's grip until the corporal let go and walked out of the tent.

Harris and Albert followed him to the staging area between the industrial zone and the train tracks. Dozens of vehicles were lined up outside the warehouses, and hundreds of American soldiers were loading Humvees and trucks with gear and ammunition. Most of the Chinese soldiers were remaining behind to protect the FOB and the supplies still being brought in by train. They patrolled the area, weapons cradled, eyes roving. Everyone was still on edge after the last attack.

Two Apache choppers and a trio of Black Hawks sat on a dirt landing pad about a quarter mile to the west. More American soldiers were preparing outside the aircraft.

"It's the biggest operation on American soil yet," Harris said.

"Two months ago, I would never have believed it was possible," Albert said.

"Makes two of us, Officer Randall."

Harris walked away to talk to one of his subordinates, leaving Albert watching the troops. The convoy and choppers moved out a few minutes later, the growl of diesel engines and chop of helicopter blades filling the afternoon with the din of pre-battle noises.

As the sound faded away, Albert looked around to find that most of the American troops were gone, aside from Captain Harris and his small entourage. Chinese soldiers passed Albert by without muttering a single word.

He suddenly felt completely out of place, but it still beat heading into Charlotte to fight gangs that would happily cut his throat and hang him from a pole.

Captain Cao nodded at Albert as he passed. With twenty-four hours to kill before his ride arrived, Albert decided to make himself useful.

"Captain?" he called.

Cao smiled politely at Albert. "Officer Randall, you didn't go with the other Americans?"

"No sir. I'm supposed to head back home tomorrow, so figured I might pick your brain while I wait for my ride."

Cao looked back with a confused look on his face. "Pick my brain?"

"It's a figure of speech."

"Oh. What you mean is you'd like to talk."

The distant crack of automatic gunfire commanded their attention toward the downtown skyline. The Apaches were circling, and the Black Hawks were dropping troops into the fire zone.

"Good luck to them," Cao said.

Albert said a mental prayer for the soldiers as well as the innocent civilians that could get caught in the crossfire. He stood there for several minutes listening to the thump of what sounded like mortar fire exploding in Charlotte. It didn't take long before the entire area sounded like a war zone.

"Follow me a moment, will you?" Cao asked.

Albert and the Captain walked toward the tents, stopping for a truck filled to the brim with potatoes that had come in on the train. Once the battle was over, the food would be distributed in the city.

Cao held up the flaps to the Chinese HQ tent for Albert. A small heater warmed the space, which was furnished with a desk, table, and two cots.

"Would you like some tea?" Cao said.

Albert nodded. The Captain fired up the burners on a small gas stove set up on the table. A few minutes later, he poured Albert a cup and sat it in front of him. Albert brought it to his lips to take a sip while Cao took a seat behind his makeshift desk. The sound of war continued as they drank their warm tea.

Cao was the first to speak. "I know why you and Captain Harris were assigned to our division," he said bluntly.

Albert lowered the cup.

"You're here to watch us and make sure we don't use unreasonable force against your citizens." He held up a finger to forestall Albert's protest. "And you're here to make sure we have no connection to the North Koreans."

Albert settled back into his seat, waiting for the Captain to continue. He liked the man, especially what he had said about why he joined the military, but he needed to be careful of what he said.

"You don't need to respond," Cao said. "The reason I am telling you all of this is because I received intel this morning about the North Korean attack in New York. It is not going to be the last attack."

Albert raised a brow and broke his silence. "How do you know?"

"Because I know the North Koreans. I was born there. My parents defected when I was five years old. They smuggled me across the border into China."

Cao took another sip of tea, and then continued. "My parents never wanted me to be ashamed of where I came from, as long as I understood what it was like living in North Korea."

The distant sound of an explosion distracted Cao for a moment. The blast faded away.

"As long as there are North Koreans out there, they will continue hating America, and will not give up until your way of life is destroyed. I, like many of my Chinese comrades, may not agree with your form of government, but we still respect it, and will give our lives to help America and China succeed together. But I wanted to warn you that things are going to get worse before they get better... So you can tell your Secretary of Defense when you return home."

Albert sat his cup of tea on the desk, a chill running through his body. The two messages he was returning home with from Van Dyke and Cao were far different. One was a message of division, the other a message of unity.

But Cao also had another message, if Albert was understanding the Captain.

"Are you saying the war with North Korea isn't over?"

"Yes." Cao stood and pulled down on his uniform. "We are fighting two enemies now, Officer Randall. The Americans that don't want us here, and the North Korean sleeper agents that were activated after the attack."

Cao grimaced at the sound of another distant explosion, and then said, "I can assure you, we are not the enemy. The North Koreans are, and they always will be until they are all dead."

Outside, the sound of raised voices and engines filled

the staging area, effectively distracting both men. Albert left his tea and went to look.

Chinese soldiers had surrounded the American Humvee and were helping unload the wounded. The first American soldier was conscious, and reached up toward a Chinese medic with a blood-soaked hand. They rushed him to the medical tent, then pulled out a second soldier, who had severe burns on the right side of his face.

It took Albert a long moment to realize the man was Van Dyke. He rushed over to help. The corporal's left eye flipped open and blinked several times, but the right was swollen completely shut. He tried to speak, mumbling something that Albert couldn't make out.

"You're going to be okay, man. Just hang in there," Albert said, but it was a lie. It would be a miracle if the man survived, and even if he did, it would be a long recovery with those burns.

Van Dyke's gaze flitted from Albert to the Chinese soldiers carrying him. For a moment, there was a look of confusion on his burned face, then fear. His eye slowly closed, and his breathing became raspy.

Albert watched the medics carry Van Dyke off to the medical tent. The corporal might not trust their Chinese counterparts, but those soldiers and medics were doing everything they could to save him.

— 16 —

Sandra was sitting next to Raven's bedside a week after the mountain lion attack. He appeared to be sleeping peacefully, but his body was covered in a slick sheen of sweat.

Across the room, Allie slept in a chair with Creek at her feet. The dog had his remaining eye on his handler. Every now and again Creek would close the eyelid, only to snap it back open a moment later. Sandra wasn't the only one worried about her brother; the dog could also sense how close Raven was to death.

After surviving gunshots, knife wounds, and multiple beatings, a bacterial infection had finally taken him to the edge of life and death. He was fading right in front of her, and there was nothing she could do about it but try and ease his suffering. He wasn't going to survive more than a few days if they didn't get him some powerful antibiotics.

The only hope for her brother was standing in the hallway. Marcus Colton, Dale Jackson, and Lindsey Plymouth waited outside the room, discussing a mission that could save her brother's life.

"I'll be right back," Sandra whispered to Raven, although he probably couldn't hear her. He stirred, and his eyelids fluttered, but he didn't wake up. She gently shut the door behind her.

"What's the plan?" Sandra asked.

Lindsey stepped closer to Sandra and, keeping her voice low, said, "This is confidential, so keep it quiet, okay?"

Sandra felt her heart skip, knowing she was about to get some very bad news. It was no secret that the government wasn't going to make it this way for a year or even longer. The pamphlets had stated as much, and everyone in the town had heard the news.

"We don't have enough food to get everyone through the winter. Especially if we can't count on any help from the Feds. There are simply too many mouths to feed, and the elk and other game have moved deeper into the park, making them more difficult to track and bring back. We're low on gas, low on food, and low on meds," Lindsey said.

"We're not even going to make it through the winter?" Sandra asked.

"Not so loud," Colton said, bringing up a finger to his lips.

Sandra checked the hallway behind her. No one was nearby, but she dropped her voice anyway. "What are we going to do?"

"This winter will be a struggle unless we make something happen, and that's exactly what I'm going to do," Colton said. "I'm taking the special squad Raven and Lindsey put together for a raid on Fort Collins. We're going to take our supplies back, plus some."

His tone was confident, but Colton massaged the grip of his pistol nervously. After what Sheriff Thompson had done to him, Sandra didn't blame him for being anxious about returning to Fort Collins, even though the sheriff was dead.

"If all goes to plan, we will be back before tomorrow

morning with the meds to save Raven's life," Colton said.

"How do you know where to go?" Sandra asked.

"I just got back from scouting out the warehouses Colton marked on a map from his time in captivity there," Dale said. "Going back to find medicine is the least we can do for him after all he's done for Estes Park."

Sandra couldn't believe her ears. Dale, of all people, was risking his life to save her brother.

"Thank you," she said. "Thank you so—"

A voice cut her off. "Chief, that you?"

Everyone turned to see Nurse Jen walking side by side with John Palmer. Colton's face went white at the sight of the bandaged stumps where the firefighter's arms had been.

"John! Hey buddy, how are you doing?" Colton said.

Palmer raised his stumps to give everyone a better view of what was left of his arms. "I'm bored as hell and want to get back to work, but can't do much without hands."

"Looks like you're making a great recovery. You'll be back to work in no time," Lindsey said. "You can help at the station."

Palmer's eyes lit up at the suggestion. "Help with what?" he asked.

Lindsey looked to Colton. "I was thinking you could be the watchman out at the Crow's Nest."

"Yeah...yeah I could do that," Palmer said. His lips curled with a slight smile, the first Sandra had seen in weeks. He looked over at her and asked, "How's your brother?"

"Not so good."

"Keep this to yourself, John, but we're headed to Fort

Collins tonight to get medicine and supplies," Colton said.

Palmer's smile vanished. "If you see Jason Cole, put a bullet in his head for me."

"He's a dead man. I can assure you of that," Colton said darkly.

"Good luck, Chief, and stay safe out there," Palmer said. He and the nurse continued down the hallway.

"We really going after Jason Cole tonight?" Dale asked quietly.

"If we see him, hell yes," Colton said.

"You're the boss, Chief."

The door to Raven's room creaked open, and Allie looked out. "Mom, Uncle Raven is awake."

Creek poked his head into the hallway, sniffed, and then retreated into the room.

"I'll be right back," Sandra said to the officers.

She moved back to Raven's bedside. He reached for her hand, eyes alert and wide.

"The Nunnehi said... They said the evil is coming," Raven mumbled. He licked his lips. "They said I have to stop it. They said..."

Sandra grabbed the bowl of cold water and dipped a rag inside. Then she dabbed his forehead. "Calm down, Sam. You're okay. Everything is just fine."

But everything wasn't fine, and he wasn't okay. This was the second time he had spoken of the Nunnehi warriors, which told her he was continuing to hallucinate. Raven's dark brown eyes flitted back and forth. He wasn't truly awake, and he wasn't sleeping; he was somewhere in the middle, a mixture of reality and fantasy.

As she went to dab the rag back into the water he grabbed her arm, and squeezed her wrist, hard.

"Ouch," Sandra said.

"Adsila," he whispered.

The word took Sandra's breath. She locked eyes with her brother, but he seemed to be looking through her, not at her.

"Adsila," he repeated.

"No," Sandra said. "It's me, Sandra. Your sister."

Allie hugged Creek. "You're scaring me, Uncle Raven."

Raven kept his gaze on Sandra, and again called her by their deceased mother's name.

"Adsila, I'm sorry for lying. I'm sorry for not taking care of you. I'm sorry..." Raven's eyes rolled up into his head as he once again slipped back into a dream state, his hand falling limply away from Sandra's. She took in a deep breath, trying to understand what had just happened. Raven had never spoken of their mother like that.

"What the hell was that all about?" Colton said.

Sandra twisted to see the chief and Lindsey standing in the open doorway.

"Go get those meds, Marcus," Sandra said. "My brother doesn't have much time left."

***

Colton flicked the safety off on his suppressed AR-15 and took point as they moved into position around the warehouse. The hard part was over. They had safely snuck into Fort Collins using the moonlight and their single pair of night vision goggles. Both of their trucks were stashed about a mile away.

Dale hunched down next to Colton, wearing a

rucksack and also carrying an AR-15. The intel he had gathered was going to save Raven's life and help Estes Park survive the winter.

But not without a fight.

They had come prepared, with ballistic vests and plenty of ammunition, and Colton had a feeling they were going to need every bullet. He did another scan of the area with his night vision goggles. To the west, a junkyard provided plenty of cover. Their sniper, Susan Sanders, had taken up position there behind a rusted-out Chevy Nova with her bow and a high-powered rifle at the ready. He couldn't see her, but he knew she was there.

To the east and south were two roads leading back to the city. If anyone was headed their way, they would see them long in advance. Captain Plymouth, Detective Ryburn, and Todd Sanders were a mile back with the two trucks, ready to move in at a moment's notice. John Kirkus had provided a dozen of his own people to help with the escape, in exchange for a percentage of the supplies they were able to retrieve.

The plan from here on out was simple. Neutralize the guards. Steal the medicine, food, and supplies. Then book it back to Estes Park, sealing the road behind them. If any of Thompson's crew gave chase, they would be stopped at one of four checkpoints. If one of the barriers fell, everyone would retreat.

Colton focused on the two grunt sentries outside the warehouse. He flipped the night vision optics up to scan the area with his naked eyes. The two men were dressed in camouflage and wearing baseball caps. They had smoked three cigarettes so far, which told Colton these guys had plenty more inside. He was going to replenish his own supply, if they had room, although Kelly would not be happy about that.

For another fifteen minutes, Colton watched and waited to make sure they hadn't missed any patrols earlier. He balled his hands, flexed his forearms, and wiggled his toes to keep his circulation moving while they waited.

When the guard on the right lowered his rifle and moved out of the wind to light another cigarette, Colton finally gave the order. An arrow streaked away and hit the man holding the cigarette in his neck, pinning him to the side of the metal wall. By the time the second man realized what had happened, he had an arrow sticking out of his chest, just above his heart. The near miss gave him just enough time to let out a muffled cry and look down at the shaft. Susan let another arrow fly a beat later, hitting him in the heart this time.

Colton and Dale were moving before the corpse hit the ground. They ran at a hunch, rifles shouldered and aimed at the entrance of the warehouse. When they got there, Dale took up position to the right, and Colton took up a stance to the left.

He nodded at Dale, and the veteran kicked the door open.

Colton moved in first, sweeping the barrel around the interior of the warehouse. It was lit by lanterns on the first and second floors. Another guard sat with his feet propped up on a desk in front of a row of metal shelves. The man scrambled for his pistol, but Colton put two bullets into his chest before he could draw the gun. The guard fell backward in his chair, hitting the ground with a thud.

A shotgun blast punched the wall near Colton, and he dove for cover behind a shelf, peering up at a contact on the second floor. The man was searching for Colton with the barrel of his shotgun, but Dale found him first, squeezing off three shots into the man's chest. He let out a cry and tumbled over a railing. His body hit one of the shelves, knocking it into the next one and creating a domino effect. In seconds, all ten shelves had slammed into one another, spilling their contents on the ground.

"Clear," Dale said.

Colton already had his walkie-talkie in hand. "Lindsey, we're good to go," he said.

"On my way, Chief."

Colton and Dale quickly made sure the hostiles were dead. Then began the search for medicine. That was priority one; the food and other supplies would come next.

"Over here," Dale said a few minutes into the search.

Colton hurried over to find Dale looking through a box of pill containers. "This is the one on the list, right?"

Colton examined the bottle and nodded. "Bring 'em all, just in case."

"This shit was easier than I expected." Dale tossed the bottles into his rucksack.

"We still have to get out of here, and we need to hurry."

"Don't worry. Susan's got our back, Chief."

The two men spent the next five minutes stacking up the medicine and crates of MREs near the garage door. He flung the garage door open and shielded his eyes from bright headlight beams. When they dimmed, he saw a Jeep Cherokee parked outside. Not just any Jeep. It was Raven's baby. The sons of bitches had stolen her the last time Colton visited Fort Collins.

Before he could raise his rifle, a voice called out, "Drop your guns or she's dead."

Susan Sanders was on her knees in the dirt with a pistol pointed at the back of her head. Two men stood behind her, the second holding an AK-47 angled at Colton.

For a moment Colton considered his options. He could tell Dale to open fire and risk getting Susan killed, or they could surrender and hope the men didn't kill them before Lindsey got here with reinforcements.

"Easy," Colton said, slowly lowering his gun to the ground to buy time. He instructed Dale to do the same thing, but Dale shook his head, which was exactly what Colton thought he would do.

"No way. These men will kill us," Dale said.

The man with the AK-47 angled it at Dale. "Drop your gun, or my buddy spills her brains," he said. "And don't think about trying anything funny. The sheriff is on his way."

"Do it, Dale," Colton said. He wasn't sure who had taken over for Thompson, but maybe the man would listen to reason, maybe he would...

Colton's faint hopes died when the moonlight illuminated the face of the man with the machine gun.

It was Jason Cole.

Colton resisted the urge to pull his holstered pistol and blast the bastard in the face. Jason would definitely kill them both, especially after what Colton and Raven had done to him in the Estes Park jail.

Dale slowly set his rifle to the ground, and Jason grinned. He nodded at his friend, who pulled the hammer back on the revolver pressed to Susan's head.

"NO!" Colton shouted.

His words were shattered by the crack of gunfire.

But the sound wasn't from the pistol or the AK-47.

A muzzle flash came from the connecting road, where two pickup trucks suddenly flashed their lights, blinding Jason and his comrade. Susan hit the dirt, and Colton scooped his rifle off the ground.

"Ambush!" Jason yelled.

Colton fired off a burst as Jason dove for cover under the Jeep. The other man took several rounds to the chest from Dale's rifle, jerking back and forth before hitting the dirt and going still.

Jason crawled away while Colton fired bullets that pinged off the undercarriage of Raven's Jeep. He got down to his belly and prepared to fire, but Jason was already running into the junkyard, his AK-47 lying in the dirt.

Lindsey and Todd pulled the trucks in front of the building and Colton got back onto his feet.

"Load 'em up!" he shouted. "I'll deal with this prick."

Colton ran around the Jeep and into the junkyard, cautious even though Jason had dropped his rifle. Slowing down likely saved Colton's life. Two bullets zipped past his face. One hit the window of a car right behind him, shattering the glass.

Crouching down, Colton looked for his target. He saw the man, now holding a pistol, duck behind a truck.

I got you now, you piece of shit...

Slowly rising, Colton fired off a volley with his AR-15. The bullets hit the rusted pickup truck Jason was hiding behind. He took off running, and Colton followed him deeper into the junkyard.

A cloud crossed over the moon, and Colton slowed his pace. He scanned the darkness for shadows and shapes, his rifle up and ready. His boot caught the edge of a tire and he almost lost his balance, but righted himself and fired off a shot at a shadow that moved behind an old tractor.

Another flash of motion came from the left, and Colton sent a burst in that direction. He crouched down to listen and watch for movement.

"Hurry up!" Dale shouted. "We're about to have company!"

Colton waited there another few moments, his heart pounding. He hated to leave without Jason. Turning his back on a man like that was a big mistake, but they were running out of time.

Just as he got up to move, a crunch sounded behind Colton's back. A rush of fear raced through his body. He stood and whirled, to find Jason had gotten the drop on him.

"Hey there, Chief," he said. His lips twisted into a satisfied smile as he raised a pistol at Colton's head.

A razor-sharp arrowhead suddenly burst through his open mouth. Colton flinched as a bullet whizzed past his ear with a deafening crack. An instant later, Jason crashed to the ground face first, feet jerking. The back of the arrow protruded from the base of his skull. Susan bent down to snatch it out, placing her boot on his back, and then giving the bolt a good tug.

"Thanks," Colton said, unable to hear his own words.

She nodded, and they hurried back to the trucks, where Dale, Lindsey, and Ryburn were finishing loading the crates into them. Raven's Jeep was packed too. Colton moved his fingers through the air in a circle, signaling it was time to move out. He jumped into the Jeep with Lindsey, while Susan and Todd took one of the trucks. Dale and Ryburn got into the other truck.

The convoy sped off, heading west at breakneck speed. Colton watched the warehouse in the rearview mirror. Part of him had been conflicted about taking supplies from people who might need them, but not these men. All he felt was satisfaction. The best part was that they hadn't left any witnesses behind to point in the direction of Estes Park.

Lindsey pounded the steering wheel and whistled. "We did it, Chief. We really did it!"

"We're not out of the woods yet," Colton said. He ducked down for a better view out the windshield, scanning the road for vehicles or ambushes. Then he shifted his gaze to the rearview mirror to check on the two trucks packed full of supplies. Seeing them brought a rare smile to his face—a smile that faded when he saw three pairs of headlights moving on a road to the west that would intersect with their own road soon.

"More company," Colton said, cursing. "Gun it, Lindsey."

She pushed the pedal to the floor.

Colton alternated his gaze between the vehicles to the west and the rearview mirror, cursing again when he realized their trucks were falling behind. He pulled his walkie-talkie out and said, "Todd, Dale, we got three hostiles at nine o'clock."

"We see 'em," Dale said.

Colton changed the magazine in his AR-15, and then climbed into the back seat. He rolled down the window and jammed the barrel out.

"This is going to be loud," he said to Lindsey.

She nodded without taking her eyes off the road. He pressed the rifle butt against his shoulder, and aimed for the headlights of the front vehicle. The gunfire rattled the windows from the staccato of semi-automatic bursts.

The convoy continued flying down the road, the drivers undeterred. They were quickly coming up on the intersection, and while Colton was pretty sure Lindsey and Dale would make it through, he wasn't sure about Todd's truck. It was falling even farther behind.

Colton focused on the incoming convoy and continued firing. The lead vehicle finally swerved off the road and into a ditch, the beams flitting skyward, but the second two kept coming.

"They aren't going to make it!" Lindsey shouted in the respite of gunfire.

Colton slapped in another magazine and held in a breath. He could see the details of both vehicles now. The lead appeared to be a pickup truck, and the second was an old-school muscle car.

He squeezed off burst after burst at the truck. One of the headlights blew out, draping the left side of the road in darkness, but the driver kept speeding onward.

"Colton, they aren't stopping!" Lindsey shouted.

She let off the gas and swerved around an abandoned van, then pushed the pedal back down. Colton squeezed off another volley at the approaching vehicles as they neared the intersection.

He moved away from the window at the last second as gunfire flashed from the passenger window of the pickup truck. Bullets hit the back of the Jeep, punching through the metal and into the seats next to Colton. He turned to watch Dale's truck power across the intersection, but Todd's vehicle was t-boned. The truck tipped over onto its side, and then flipped several times.

"No!" Lindsey shouted.

Colton felt his heart climbing into his throat. The headlights of the enemy vehicles remained back at the intersection. Men with rifles jumped out and moved toward the wreckage. A wheel continued spinning.

"Todd, do you copy?" Colton said into his walkie-talkie.

"We have to go back," Lindsey said.

Muzzle flashes lit up the road, and Colton slowly lowered his radio. It was too late to save Todd and his wife. Even if they had survived the crash, they were dead now.

It was a hard pill to swallow, considering Susan had just saved his life in the junkyard, but he couldn't put everyone else in jeopardy to bring them home.

"Keep driving, Lindsey," he said.

"But Marcus..."

"That's an order, Captain."

Colton climbed back into the front seat and tried to keep his eyes off the mirrors. Looking back wouldn't do them any good now. They sped away from muzzle flashes and crack of gunfire. Lindsey sobbed, and Colton worked on managing his breathing. Neither of them said a word for several moments.

The road curved, and Colton focused on the mountains in the distance. They would cross over into friendly territory soon, but the trip had come at a dire cost.

Squawking from the radio made him flinch, and he looked down at the device as a voice crackled over.

"Marcus, you listenin'?" came a very familiar voice.

Lindsey looked over, confused, as Colton pushed the radio up to his mouth.

"Who is this?"

"I'm hurt you don't know," said the same deep voice. "It's your favorite neighborhood sheriff."

Colton blinked, trying to make sense of what he was hearing. He knew who it sounded like, but there was no way it was Sheriff Thompson. He'd watched him die.

"Next time, aim for the face, Marcus," Thompson said. "Or at least make sure your man isn't wearing a vest."

Colton thought back to the day he'd gunned Thompson down on the side of the road. He'd shot him in the chest, but had never checked his pulse or ensured he was dead.

"Shit," Colton whispered.

"I've been waiting for this day a long time," Thompson said. "You messed my plan up tonight, but I promise you that you're dead, and so is everyone you love. Enjoy your present when you get home."

The radio shut off, and Colton looked to Lindsey.

"What does he mean?" she asked, fear gripping her features.

"Drive, Lindsey. Drive like the lives of everyone you love depend on it."

Colton had a feeling they did.

— 17 —

Fenix sat in the shotgun seat of a Humvee on Highway 7, just three miles south of Estes Park. The heat from the vents warmed his face as they waited. He reached up and adjusted his helmet, then patted his ballistic vest.

Armed with a brand new M4 and "four eyes" night vision goggles, he was fully prepared for battle, and so were the Brandenburger Commandos. They were positioned on the side of the road, waiting for a radio update from his scouts.

"You sure about this, sir?" Horton asked from the driver's seat. "Why the hell are we the ones attacking tonight? Why isn't Thompson sending men?"

"Goddammit, Horton, we've been through this. You just don't get politics, do you?"

Horton looked over, his jaw set.

"Don't get your panties in a wad," Fenix said. "We're softening the defenses, and getting the intel Thompson will need for his attack tomorrow. Think of this as just a recon mission. A very fun recon mission that will net us that damn Indian and his family."

The new radio they had plucked from a Chinese vehicle barked to life.

"Sir, looks like the town militia has mostly been moved to beef up their defenses on Highway 34. The vehicles that left earlier were heading to Fort Collins."

Fenix raised a brow at that. "What the hell are they doing in Fort Collins?"

"Raiding a warehouse owned by Sheriff Thompson. I just got off the horn with him. He's fucking pissed, sir, but he said to proceed with your mission. He needs that intel for his attack tomorrow."

"Roger that."

"Good luck, sir."

Fenix tucked the radio back in his vest and dipped his helmet at Horton. "Let's roll, Sergeant."

Horton put the vehicle in gear and pulled back onto the road. Fenix shouted up to the soldier manning the turret. "Miles, trade me spots."

As soon as the young commando came down from the turret, Fenix took his spot on the big gun. Grabbing the M240, he roved the pintle mount into position. Fenix blinked at the green hue of his night vision goggles and waited for his eyes to adjust.

The other two vehicles were following them at combat intervals, just in case Chief Colton had ambushes set up out here. Fenix doubted the man was that cunning. He might actually be dumber than Fenix thought, trying to raid a warehouse owned by Thompson.

The sheriff owned everything east of Estes Park now. After taking down the FEMA camp, he had also taken over Loveland. In just two months, Thompson had built quite the empire for himself. That's part of the reason Fenix had decided to join forces. They needed each other.

He turned to look at the pickups following the Humvee. Both of them had once belonged to the Chinese, but now sported fresh black paint. He smiled proudly at the Sons of Liberty logo on the hoods. Then he swiveled the mount back to the front of the vehicle, the wind blasting his exposed face as Horton picked up speed. They weren't far now.

Around the next turn, two trucks and a minivan had been pushed up against one another to block the road. Concrete barriers were set up in front of them, with a barbwire gate serving as a makeshift doorway. Framing the road was a ditch, blocked with more vehicles and debris. There was no way to pass on the shoulder. He counted five figures standing behind the barriers, but only one of them was pointing a weapon at the road.

He'd already been warned that there would be women here, but when he saw that one of the five people was much smaller than the others, he held his fire. Even in Iraq, he'd done his best to avoid killing children.

The hesitation lasted only a moment. War was war.

He squeezed the trigger while they still had the element of surprise, sending tracer rounds lancing through the night. They slammed into the concrete barriers and clipped one of the men standing guard. A geyser of blood shot into the air, and he dropped like a tree.

Return fire was almost instant, and Fenix roved the barrel of the big gun toward the muzzle flashes coming from behind the barriers. Two more guards had come into view. Both of them were firing from behind a pickup truck.

Horton stayed the course, driving full steam ahead even as bullets pecked at the hood and windshield. One of them pinged off the armor surrounding the M240, but Fenix too remained steady. He fired bursts that slammed into the bed of the pickup truck and punched through the metal and into the flesh of the guards. Both men spun away.

Fenix quickly roved the barrel back to the concrete barriers, where three of the four remaining hostiles were firing rifles. A bullet whizzed close enough to his head that he flinched. Then he fired a burst that took down two of the men just as they popped up to fire again, leaving two remaining hostiles.

Horton slowed the vehicle when they were a few hundred feet away, and coasted to a stop while Fenix unloaded on the blocks. Rounds pockmarked the sides, breaking away chunks of concrete.

The small figure darted away to the side of the road, and a woman raised an arm to reach after the child. Fenix took her arm off with several rounds, and then finished her off with one to the torso.

He eased off the trigger and scanned the roadblock, his heart pounding with excitement. Another gunshot cracked from under the mini-van and pinged off the armor surrounding his gun. Fenix ducked down as more shots hit the armor. When they stopped, he grabbed the gun and unloaded on the mini-van, taking out the tires and pinning the shooter underneath.

The echo of the gunshots faded away, leaving only the whistle of the wind. Steam rose off the dead at the barriers, their blood pooling on the frozen road.

Fenix ordered the teams out of the vehicles. The men approached slowly, rifles shouldered, scanning for movement while he slowly raked the barrel back and forth.

He could see most of the dead sentries from his vantage in the turret. Two men and a woman lay on the concrete near the barriers. One of the men was missing most of his head, and the other had taken three rounds to the chest, opening up gaping holes. The other bodies were all back near the vehicles, and none of them were moving, except for the man pinned under the van. The chassis had crushed his back, but he still moaned and tried to get away as the SOL soldiers approached.

Miles aimed a pistol point blank at the man's forehead, firing a round that shattered the silence. Fenix continued searching for other hostiles. The kid was long gone, from what he could tell.

"Move the barriers," Fenix ordered.

Working together, the SOL soldiers pushed the concrete barriers out of the way, opening a gap for the Humvee and the trucks to pass through. Horton would do the rest by slamming into the mini-van and pushing it off the road.

Fenix suddenly glimpsed motion in the ditch to the right of the roadblock. A girl was hiding in the bushes, a knife held in one hand and a pistol aimed at Miles.

"No you don't, kid," Fenix whispered. He fired a blast of rounds into the dirt at her feet, kicking up debris.

"Drop it!" Fenix yelled.

His men whipped around and centered their weapons on the bush. The girl remained there, apparently thinking she was invisible. His next shots were closer this time, tearing over the top of the foliage.

She finally tossed the gun over the bush and onto the concrete.

"The knife too!" Fenix shouted.

The knife came next.

"Put that kid in one of the trucks," Fenix ordered.

His men grabbed her, and then dragged her kicking and screaming to one of the black pickups.

"Horton, let's go," Fenix said.

The Humvee rolled forward, and the cow guard

crunched into the mini-van, metal scraping metal. It took a few minutes, but Horton managed to push the vehicle perpendicular to the others, opening a gap for the convoy to continue.

Horton gunned the engine, leaving the dead behind without a second thought. Reaching up, Fenix flipped his NVGs off and stared up at the dazzling, star-filled sky. He took in a deep breath of fresh, freezing air. Prospect Mountain rose into the sky. They weren't far now, and in an hour or less, he would have what he came here for.

A flare suddenly streaked away from the crest of the mountain. Fenix watched it climb toward the moon before exploding and spreading a red glow over the town. They had been spotted, but it didn't matter. The Brandenburger Commandos were ready for a fight.

He plucked the radio out of his vest and gave orders for the three vehicles to split off to their destinations. Then he opened the private channel to Sheriff Thompson.

"Crow 1, this is Eagle 1. Do you copy? Over."

A few seconds later, an enraged voice came over the channel. "Roger, Eagle 1, this is Crow 1. What's your fucking status? Over."

"We just took out the first roadblock and are heading toward Prospect Mountain."

"You see Colton, you don't touch him. Got it?"

Fenix didn't like Thompson's tone, but he held his tongue. After all, Colton had shot Thompson and his men, leaving them for dead on the side of the road. That'd make anybody touchy.

"Roger that, Crow 1. Proceeding with the mission. In a few hours, I'll have that Indian's head on a pike, and you'll have the intel you need to add Estes Park to our expanding territory," Fenix replied.

***

Raven stopped at the edge of the river, his bare feet sinking into the mud. Teepees lined the riverbank to his right. Smoke fingered out of the pointed tops. The scent of sizzling meat hit his nostrils, and he walked toward the river camp. Hissing wind and chirping crickets filled the warm night.

He knew it was another dream, but this one was peaceful, unlike the nightmares. Raven continued walking next to the river, calmed by the sound of rushing water.

The peace was shattered by a high-pitched scream.

And then he saw them.

The figures emerged from the water on the riverbank below the camp. They were naked men, six of them, their pallid flesh dripping in the moonlight. Sinewy muscles glistened across their bare flesh as they climbed the steep slope on all fours, like animals.

At the top, they stood, then moved at a crouch toward the teepees. One of the men remained behind, his shiny skull tilted up at the moon. He suddenly twisted and looked in Raven's direction. His face was not the face of a man. Jagged teeth rimmed his carmine gums, and eyes as black as obsidian fixated on Raven's location.

These were Water Cannibals, and they were here to kidnap children and bring them back to their underwater lairs, where they would feast on the tender flesh.

Raven felt the paralyzing fear that always came with dreaming about the monsters. He remained behind the bush, staring through the spindly foliage as the Water Cannibals snuck into the village.

Another scream finally snapped him from the dream, and his mind reverted back to reality. His eyes focused on a dimly-lit space, with only a small lantern illuminating the sheets covering his body. Across the room was a medical chart.

He remembered, then. He was in the Estes Park Medical Center.

But had the last scream come from his dream, or had it been real?

Raven squirmed in his bed, trying to wake up and focus on the room. The chair Allie had been curled up in earlier was empty. In her place was Creek. The dog was by his side, tail wagging, whining at him as if to say, "Get up."

Raven's gut knotted. He knew something was wrong. But he could hardly move or think. His entire body felt numb, like it didn't belong to him, and his mind was in a muddled fog.

A scream came from outside his door, and a gunshot followed. He knew the sounds were real from the way Creek reacted. The dog's back went rigid, and he bared his teeth at the door.

The hospital was under some sort of an attack, and his family was missing.

Raven tried to move again, and this time managed to roll onto his side and throw a leg over the side of the bed. Creek nudged up against it, his way of trying to help.

Another scream, and a flurry of gunshots. Raven swung his other leg over the bed. He stood on bare feet and reached out for the wall, palming it to keep his balance.

Breathing heavily, he held there for a few seconds, trying to get his breath and focus. He was dressed only in green pants. Shoeless and shirtless, he stumbled over to the door. He grabbed the handle and slowly opened it to peer out into the dim hallway. A lantern set up halfway down provided just enough light to see the passage was empty. Creek wedged his body next to Raven to look out.

"Back," Raven whispered.

A wave of light-headedness passed over him, and he forced his eyes closed to prevent himself from passing out. Then he opened his eyes and stumbled out into the hallway.

The gunfire had ceased and the screams had faded, but Raven could make out the sound of crying somewhere in the distance.

He grabbed the railing attached to the wall. He had no weapon to defend himself, but there was no time to look for one. He had to find Sandra and Allie.

Creek trotted ahead, sniffing the tile floor. His nose stopped at the edge of a red streak. Raven's heart thumped at the sight of blood.

He stopped to look in the nearest room. This was where John Palmer had been staying, and Raven could see the bed was empty. Martha Kohler, the doctor refugee, wasn't in her room either.

Raven continued slugging along, using the railing and the lantern light to guide him. His body tingled, numb and distant. For the first time in his entire life, he truly felt as light as a feather.

That's a good thing, Sam, he tried to tell himself. *Just keep moving. One step at a time.*

Creek followed the trail of blood to an intersection, where his tail dropped behind his legs. A figure backpedaled around the left corner, nearly bumping into the dog. The man slowly turned, revealing black eyes and a mouth full of jagged teeth in the dim light. Raven knew what he was seeing couldn't be real. He blinked, and the man's face changed from that of a Water Cannibal into something worse...

A swastika and other black tattoos in the shapes of Nazi symbols covered his neck. The dark mustache hanging over his lips curled into a grin when he saw Raven and Creek. He quickly raised an M4 rifle, but Creek was faster.

"Attack!" Raven said, his voice nearly a shout.

Creek leapt onto the unsuspecting man. The dog tore a chunk of flesh away from his neck, pulling a vein with it and silencing the man before he could scream for help. The rifle clattered to the ground, and blood painted Creek's fur red.

Raven staggered forward and leaned down to pry a knife from the man's belt as Creek continued tearing strings of flesh away from the man's neck. An awful gurgling sound came from the Nazi's lips as he tried to scream. Somehow, he continued squirming as his neck gushed blood.

"You piece of shit," Raven whispered. He got down on his knees and rammed the blade deep in the man's gut. He jerked and focused wide eyes on Raven.

That's right, Raven thought. He continued jabbing the knife into the man's side, holding his gaze the entire time until the man went limp.

Raven stopped to look at his handiwork, but stars floating before his vision blurred his view. When they cleared, he saw Creek's muzzle was dripping red onto the tile, and strands of gristle were hanging from his teeth.

"Back," Raven muttered.

The dog retreated. Raven went to stand, but slipped in

the puddle. He reached over to grab the railing, and hoisted himself up with one hand, the knife in the other.

A muffled scream sounded in the distance.

Raven scooped the rifle off the ground and rounded the corner with the blade in his left hand, the gun in his right. As soon as he stepped around the corner, he saw bodies. Doctor Newton was sprawled on the ground, his white uniform splashed with red and his eyes staring at the ceiling panels. Two patients were face down, their backs bloody messes from what looked like knife wounds.

The man Raven had just killed must have done this, and Raven had a feeling he wasn't alone. He set off through the scene of carnage, his naked feet leaving tracks in the blood.

This hallway was darker. The lantern lay on its side, its glow partially obstructed by the floor. Raven stopped when he heard a stifled scream. It had come from behind him. Laughter followed, and then a voice Raven recognized.

"Let her go!"

Was that Allie?

Hearing his niece in distress made Raven's blood boil. He didn't need the railing to keep moving now; adrenaline fueled his actions. He turned around and strode down the hallway, gun shouldered, with the knife pressed up against the grip of the handle. When he got to the operating room doors, he waited.

"My brother is going to come for me!" Sandra shouted.

More laughter followed. Then a deep voice. "Your brother is passed out like a drunk. He ain't coming for you, bitch! We already made sure of it, but don't worry. I already sent Greg back to kill his dog. When we're done with you, we'll bring your unconscious brother to the General."

"NO!" Sandra screeched.

Raven clenched his jaw, and Creek moved into position, his single eye focused on the door as if he could understand what was happening on the other side. Raven adjusted his grip on the rifle and the knife, then slowly shouldered the door open and brought the barrel up, freezing at the sight that greeted him.

Sandra was on the floor in the middle of the room with two Nazis holding her down. A third stood watching, with arms folded across his chest. Her features were swollen and bloody.

In the corner, Allie was curled up with a nurse who also had cuts on her face. All three men looked at Raven, eyes widening when they saw he was holding a rifle.

"You just made the biggest mistake of your lives," Raven said. He pulled the trigger before they could respond, hitting the bald man on the left in the chest with two rounds. The man with folded arms took four rounds before the magazine went dry.

The third thug got up and barreled toward Raven, screaming, a vein bulging across his forehead right above a swastika symbol. Sandra raised a foot, tripping him before he could get to Raven. He crashed to the floor and slid toward Raven and Creek. They both descended on him like Water Cannibals.

Creek clamped down onto his neck while Raven jammed his blade into the man's back so hard the blade penetrated the other side and clicked on the tile floor. Raven yanked the knife out and continued stabbing him, over and over.

Raven went to work on his chest and stomach, carving him up like a Thanksgiving turkey. After he was finished with the torso, he stuck the sharp edge into the cheek and jaw, and finally the eyes. By the time Raven and Creek were done, the man was gushing from a dozen puncture wounds.

A voice finally stopped him.

"Sam!"

It was Sandra, and she had crawled over to grab him by the arm.

Blood pulsating in his ears and lungs wheezing, Raven pushed himself back up and tried to blink away the stars crossing his vision. He crashed to the floor with exhaustion, dropping the blood-streaked blade. His vision went in and out again as the adrenaline began to fade.

There were other voices, and then blurred shapes appeared all around him. He blinked to the sight of someone crouched by his side. At some point he lost consciousness, only to be snapped back to reality by a smack to his face.

He felt that, and saw a second smack coming, but he reached up to grab the hand.

"Don't," Raven grumbled.

Hands gripped him under his armpits and helped him to a sitting position on the floor. He blinked rapidly, trying to focus on the figures surrounding him. There were voices in the distance, cries for help and frightened shouts.

He let go of the arm and focused on the person it was attached to. It was Chief Colton, and his face was also streaked with blood. Dale moved in behind him and helped Allie to her feet.

"You're okay, Sam, but don't close your eyes," Colton said. "We need you for the coming battle."

— 18 —

"The battle for Charlotte is over," Captain Harris said. "We won the day, but took heavy losses."

Charlize stood at her desk in Constellation with the satellite phone clutched to her ear. She had been waiting for this call all morning.

"One hundred American soldiers are KIA. The surviving gang members have scattered, and we're planning to retake the SC in a few hours. I've already got the convoy of equipment and food ready to move to get distributed to the people who need it."

"Good work, Captain," Charlize said.

"It's not over yet. Hold on just a moment, ma'am."

Charlize looked over to Albert, who stood in the corner, his arms folded across his chest and eyes downward, although he was clearly listening to the call. He had just returned back to Constellation an hour earlier, and still had blood on his clothes. Chinese and American, according to him. He had been there when Corporal Van Dyke died in the medical tent.

"Sorry, ma'am, I just got word the Chinese are preparing to move out," Harris said. "I don't have any updates for you besides what you already know. Captain Cao and his team have been a great help here, as I'm sure Officer Randall will attest."

"I'm about to speak to him now," she said. "Stay safe out there, Captain."

"You too, Madame Secretary."

Charlize set the phone down on the desk and smiled at Albert. "Are you glad to be home?"

"Not sure I'd call this place home, but I'm glad to be back."

She gestured at the chair in front of her desk, and he took a seat.

"How are you?"

"I'm okay."

"Big Al, you can talk to me. Tell me how you're really doing."

He shrugged his linebacker shoulders. "Things were pretty bad on the road, especially in Charlotte, but I'm optimistic about the partnership with the Chinese. Captain Cao seems to be an honorable man. He told me the real enemy to worry about is North Korea."

"After the attack in New York, I'm going to have to agree with the Captain." She sighed and took a seat.

"Is that how many we have lost?" Albert asked, pointing at something behind her.

"Lost?"

Albert got out of his chair and walked over to a chart hanging on the wall, which showed the estimated death toll across the United States.

"Yes," she said.

"How is that possible?" He turned away from the wall to look her in the eye. "Seventy-five million people dead?"

"That was a few days ago," Charlize said. "That number will continue to rise, especially in the Midwest. It's projected to be closer to one hundred million."

Albert grimaced. "I've seen how ugly it is out there, but it's still hard to imagine that many people gone."

"I know, and that's why I'm relieved to hear things are going relatively smoothly with the Chinese so far. With their help, we will have the power back on for most of the country in a year. The aid we're getting from our NATO allies, combined with theirs, will save over a hundred million lives."

"That's if the North Koreans don't have another trick up their sleeve. What if they have a backpack nuke or—"

"I've already put a plan in motion to protect the country from further attacks. Every functional law enforcement agency is being warned to be on the lookout for terrorists. And we're going after domestic terrorists too, like we did in Charlotte. Fenix is next. Mark my words, we're going to find his weasel ass soon."

Albert nodded. "I'm glad you're in charge, ma'am, and I'm glad to be back with you."

"Thanks, Big Al, it means a lot to hear you say that." She stood and gestured toward the door. "Let's go see the boys and get something to eat for lunch, shall we?"

"Sounds good to me, I'm starving."

An hour later, they were in the cafeteria with Ty and Dave. The kids both peppered Albert with questions.

"What's it like beyond the walls?" Dave asked around a mouthful of green beans.

"The walls?" Albert asked.

Charlize smiled at Dave. "I think he means Constellation."

"No, this is Helm's Deep." Dave stopped chewing and stared back at her with a very serious look.

"Just play along," Ty whispered.

Dave's gaze flitted to Ty, and they both laughed. The sight warmed her heart.

"Big Al, I have a question," Ty said.

"What's up?"

"Are the Chinese good people?" Ty asked, tilting his head.

Albert responded quickly. "Yes, I think they are."

"Will they help us find Fenix?" Ty replied.

Charlize and Albert exchanged a look.

"The Chinese are helping us turn the power back on and get our country up and running again," Charlize said. "And yes, they are helping us track down men like Fenix."

Dave shoveled another forkful of vegetables in his mouth, chewing and listening intently to the conversation. "Are the Chinese like the Elves?" he asked.

"They are our allies, if that's what you mean," Charlize said.

After swallowing his food, Dave asked another question. "Then who are the Dwarves?"

"You just don't give up, do you, kid?" Albert said with a chuckle. He wiped his mouth politely with a napkin. "I'm going to go check on my sister, ma'am."

Charlize nodded. "I hope she's doing okay today."

"She's much better, thank you."

Footfalls tapped on the cafeteria floor, and Charlize twisted in her chair to see Colonel Raymond walking through the mostly empty room. She sighed. Of course she couldn't have a single meal without an interruption.

"Secretary Montgomery, I'm sorry to bother you, but there's something I think you're going to want to hear," Raymond said.

"Excuse me, I'll be right back."

"I'll stay here with them," Albert said.

The kids continued talking to the officer as she followed Raymond out of the cafeteria. She heard Dave ask if Albert had brought him back the DVDs he'd promised. She stepped into the hallway before Albert gave an answer.

They stopped at a small room manned by two military officers listening to radio equipment. One of the officers handed Charlize a headset. She put it over her ears and waited for the message.

"This is Police Chief Marcus Colton of Estes Park, Colorado."

Charlize raised a brow.

"We have been attacked by soldiers from the Sons of Liberty and need assistance. When you get this, please contact me immediately."

The message ended, and she plucked the headphones from her head. "When did this come in?"

"We just discovered it a few minutes ago, but sounds like it came in last night," Thor said.

"Christ," she replied. "Do we have confirmation?"

"Working on that," Raymond said from another station.

Charlize glanced at the Colonel. "Tell our pilots to get ready. If this is real, I want to be on the first flight to Estes Park."

***

Colton wiped the tears from his face as he looked out over Bond Park. Snipers were setting up shop on the rooftops of buildings around town square, and civilians were building defensive positions on balconies and porches overlooking the mountains.

It was late morning the day after the raid on Fort Collins and the attack by the Sons of Liberty soldiers.

Smoke still drifted across the sky. Colton stood in front of town hall, one of the buildings targeted in the attack. His boots crunched over the skirt of glass around the front entrance. He couldn't bear to go back inside, where Margaret and several members of the militia lay dead.

It was his fault. He had pulled most of the defenses away from town and placed them on Highway 34 to back him up on the raid.

Outside, civilians were milling around the square. Some of them were looking for loved ones, and others just wanted news. Some of these people didn't even know what had happened. Truthfully, Colton was still trying to put together the pieces himself.

What he did know was this: Sheriff Thompson was still alive, and had teamed up with General Fenix. They were each dangerous enough on their own, but put them together, and the two sociopaths would leave behind a trail of devastation.

The violence that had hit Estes Park the previous night was just the beginning.

The broken front door to town hall opened behind him, shards of glass raining to the concrete.

"Chief, I've got the most recently updated numbers," said Lindsey.

He didn't want her to see him with wet eyes. His people needed to know he was strong, that he could still lead them. "Go ahead," he said, trying to steel himself.

"Seventy-seven dead, and one hundred and five wounded," she said, choking up. "Doctor Newton is dead, and Doctor Duffy and the nurses are overwhelmed with patients. We have a few med students helping with the worst of the trauma, but they are overwhelmed."

"God help us," Colton whispered. Another tear fell

from his eyes. Part of him felt like this was his doing—that he had caused this. But the attack last night from General Fenix had clearly been in the works before he'd decided to raid Fort Collins.

He walked back toward the building, stopping to stare at the blood-splattered lobby, and thinking of the horror that had occurred here when the SOL soldiers barged in. Margaret had gone down firing her Glock, giving the other civilians in the station enough time to escape out the back while the militia battled the Nazis.

Lindsey patted him on the back.

"It's okay," she said. "Everything is going to be okay."

"Yeah." It was the only thing he could say. He walked inside, to where several men were standing and talking in low voices. Dale Jackson, Detective Ryburn, Officer Matthew, and John Kirkus turned to face him.

"We've moved the deceased out of the station, and have taken a tally on the weapons that are left," Ryburn said.

"It's not good, Chief," Dale cut in. A ring of sweat surrounded his collar, and blood coated the front of his sweatshirt. "Those Nazis took most of our weapons in the safe room."

Colton grimaced. "Fenix didn't just come on a shooting spree last night," he said. "He came for intel and to take our weapons, opening the door to a major attack from Thompson."

There was a moment of raw silence in the lobby, leaving only the chatter of civilians outside. Lindsey was the first to speak.

"What do we do, Chief?"

Colton put his hand on the grip of his Colt .45. He was all out of tricks, and exhausted emotionally and physically. There was only one thing they could do.

"We fight," he said. "I told you to prepare for war when I got back from Fort Collins. I made the mistake of not making sure Thompson was dead. That's on me. These deaths, are on..." he choked before the final word, and then added, "*me.*"

"No, they're not, sir," Lindsey said firmly.

"She's right, Chief," Dale said. "This isn't your fault."

"It doesn't matter right now. All that matters is keeping these people safe and figuring out a way to survive the winter." Colton pointed to the crowd outside.

There were several nods.

"So here's what we're going to do. Lindsey, get out the bullhorn and drive through the streets, telling everyone to go to the high school where we sheltered after the North Korean attacks."

Colton shifted his gaze to Dale. "Dale, I'd like you and John to handle security on Highway 36. That's where Thompson will likely try to bring his vehicles."

"What about 34?" Kirkus asked.

"I'm going to flood it and destroy the road," Colton said. "That will cut off a major artery and force Thompson to either use Highway 36 or come in from the south, on Highway 7. We will concentrate our forces there, and put snipers along the road. If he wants to add Estes Park to his territory, we're going to make him pay dearly for it."

Kirkus inclined his white cowboy hat. "Same goes with Storm Mountain. Thompson's going to bleed if he wants our land."

"Do we know how many men he has? How many weapons? How many working vehicles?" Ryburn asked.

The soft-spoken detective looked at Colton with fear

in his gaze. Officer Matthew was also clearly rattled, his right hand shaking by his side.

"Dale, can you answer that?" Colton asked.

"He's got about a dozen vehicles, and soldiers in the hundreds as best I could tell. Not sure on weapons, but my guess is he's got us outgunned."

"That's close to what I saw when I was in captivity, but this new alliance with Fenix could change things. There's no telling how many soldiers Fenix might add to the cause," Colton said.

Shouting came from outside as citizens flooded over the lawn and streets. Colton's family would be joining them soon. He had told Kelly to gather the neighbors and head to the station in Jake's Chevy pickup.

"You better say something, Chief," Lindsey said.

"Get me the bullhorn."

She retreated into the station to grab the loudspeaker while Colton stepped back outside. He scanned the crowd of hundreds that was making its way toward the building. Some of them were crying, while others were shivering from the cold. Most of them were women, children, and the elderly. Those that could fight had already been deployed to the roadblocks.

Lindsey returned with the bullhorn.

"Any word from Secretary Montgomery?" Colton asked.

She shook her head.

"Ryburn, back inside and try getting another message through," Colton said.

"You got it, Chief."

Colton stepped outside with Lindsey to address the civilians. There were hundreds here, maybe even a thousand. He lifted the bullhorn to his lips as he saw his wife and daughter emerge from the crowd.

He waved them over, but then realized they'd see the gore-stained floor inside the building. Kelly wrapped her arms around Risa, who looked at Colton with wide eyes.

"It's okay, sweetie," he said although he knew it wasn't okay. What else could he say? He could no longer shield his daughter from the horrors of this world. Kelly took his hand, showing her support, and he stepped out to address the growing crowd.

"Everyone, I know you're scared. What happened last night was an act of terror. But today we must come together as one. Neighbors, friends, family, and above all, Americans." Colton paused as more people joined the crowd on the streets.

"The attack last night won't be the last. Soon, the men that perpetrated it will come back, and this time they will come for everything we have," he said.

Almost everyone in the crowd seemed to begin talking all at once, hundreds of voices ringing out.

"Please listen," Colton said over the murmurings. "We must band together and fight. Our very future depends on it."

The civilians quieted in the park and streets, hundreds of eyes fixated on him. "Everyone that's able to fight, please come forward. The rest of you will be taken to shelter at the high school," Colton said.

"What if we surrender?" someone shouted.

"Yeah, why can't we just lay down our weapons?" another person yelled. "Surely the Sheriff of Fort Collins won't slaughter us if we act reasonably."

"Like last night?" Colton said, his response was firm and quick. "Surrendering is not an option against this enemy. We must fight and defend our town. If they want it, we must make them pay dearly."

He lowered his bullhorn and looked back at Kelly, his rock. They had been through some tough times, but she had always stood by his side. She smiled, and he raised his bullhorn back to his mouth. Everyone was focused on him, hoping to hear something reassuring or hopeful, but they needed to hear the truth.

"Some of us will die protecting Estes Park in the coming days, and I may be one of them. If I fall, I will die proudly to protect the people and the town I love."

***

Twelve hours after taking the first of the antibiotics, Raven was finally starting to feel better. His back still hurt, but his fever had broken and he didn't look like a ghost anymore. But even better, he had plenty of energy to interrogate the one surviving member of the Sons of Liberty raiding party.

"You up for this?" Colton asked.

Raven answered by grabbing the door handle and walking inside. Colton followed and closed the door behind them. They were inside the utility room in the Estes Park Medical Center where they had Miles, a member of the Sons of Liberty, handcuffed to a metal pipe. They had found him hiding in a ditch a few hours earlier with a broken leg.

"I'm going to make this really easy," Colton said. "You're going to tell us where General Fenix is hiding, and I will allow our remaining doctor to set your leg."

"If you don't tell us where Fenix is, then things are going to be...interesting." Raven used his boot to push down on the young man's left leg, where the bone had split through the skin.

Miles let out a scream as Raven applied pressure. He eased off a moment later, and bent down next to the soldier. His shaved head glistened with sweat that streamed down his pale forehead and youthful features.

"How old are you?" Raven asked.

Miles whimpered. "I just turned seventeen."

Raven looked up at Colton, who shook his head. Miles was just a kid. But he was still the enemy.

"I'm sorry, I really am. I only shot at people that were armed. I promise. I could have killed the girl we took on the road, but I didn't."

Raven leaned down. "What girl?"

"Sarah, I think." Miles adjusted his cuffed hands so he could look at Raven. "Please, please don't kill me."

They already knew Jennie, Sarah's caretaker, had been killed on the road, but learning Fenix had taken the girl was a shock. When Dale Jackson found out, he would be furious.

"Tell us where Fenix is," Colton said.

Raven knew the chief already had his mind made up about the fate of the young man in front of them. It didn't matter how old Miles was. He was a Nazi, and he had made his choice. Any conflict Raven felt about his age ended when he remembered the three men who had beaten, and were preparing to rape, his sister in front of Allie the night before.

"Tell us," Raven said. He stood and prepared to push his boot against the wound again.

Miles stared up at Raven. "He'll kill me if I tell you."

"We will kill you if you don't," Colton replied.

Wincing, Miles straightened his back against the wall.

"He's got an FOB not far from here. He's preparing to

use it when Thompson attacks Estes Park."

Miles's eyes flitted toward Raven. "He will come back, I promise you that. He wants you."

Raven swallowed hard. Once again, his actions had put his family at risk. He knew then that he couldn't wait for an attack. He had to go to Fenix before his men could attack.

Colton pulled out a folded-up map and placed it on the floor in front of Miles.

"Show us where," Colton said.

"Promise you'll let me live?" Miles asked.

Colton unlocked the handcuffs so Miles could point out the location. He winced in pain and rubbed at his wrists as he studied the map.

"You help us, and we will help you," Colton said. He drew his Colt .45 and pointed it at Miles and added, "You lie to us, you die."

Miles swallowed. "This is where Fenix is," he said, pointing.

Raven looked down to the spot. "Lily Lake? That's only a couple miles south of town."

"How many soldiers are up there?" Colton asked.

Miles squinted in pain. "Only about thirty. But he did bring the big guns. M240s and some mortars we picked off a Chinese convoy."

"Jesus," Colton said.

Raven stood and scratched at the stubble on his face as he thought of the implications. Thompson and Fenix were preparing to launch a full-scale attack on Estes Park, and they were going to do it from two different directions.

Miles slowly wagged his head. He sighed when Colton lowered his gun and motioned for Raven to meet him back at the door. When they got there, Colton aimed his pistol at Miles.

"No!" the teenager shouted.

The shot hit him in the center of the forehead, slamming his head back and painting the ceiling with blood and brains. Colton holstered his gun like nothing had happened, and stepped outside with Raven.

"We have to get this message to Secretary Montgomery," Colton said.

Raven closed the door so he didn't have to see the dead boy's destroyed head.

"There might not be time for that," he said. "We have to stop Fenix on our own."

"No, we need to stay here and man our defenses."

Raven shook his head. "Chief, we do that and we die. He's got fucking mortars. I'm going out there to stop him."

"You're going to fight thirty men?"

"I know someone that will help. You heard Miles— they have Sarah. Dale will get her back."

"I really need you both here," Colton said, frowning. He gave Raven a side glance. "You're right, but you two aren't going alone."

Raven shook his head. "Let us go. You need everybody on the barriers. I'll take one of the working radios and report back. It's close enough you can deploy some militia if needed."

Colton thought on it, and then nodded. "I'll keep trying to reach Secretary Montgomery with this new intel. In the meantime, you two go see if Miles was telling the truth. I'll hold the fort down here."

Raven reached out with his fist, and Colton bumped it back.

"Keep my family safe, Chief."

"Keep mine safe, too," Colton replied.

— 19 —

The front door to the Estes Park Medical Center opened, and a young woman with freckles and crystal blue eyes stepped inside the lobby, taking off her scarf and hat.

"Who's in charge here?" she asked.

Sandra waved a hand. "You're Rea?"

"Yup."

She directed the young med student toward the doors to the hospital. She would join the other five already working inside.

"Doctor Duffy will get you started. I'll be right there to help," Sandra said.

Rea nodded, swallowed, and headed for the doors. Sandra couldn't help but wonder if this was the first time the student had actually seen a patient. But right now, they needed all the help they could get.

Sandra turned back to her family. Raven's dark skin had regained some color, and he was walking unaided, but he still looked like death warmed over. Allie stood to his right, stroking Creek's coat. She hadn't said much at all since the attack, and it broke Sandra's heart to see her daughter once again terrified. She brushed a strand of brown hair from her bruised face with a shaking hand.

"I know you have to fight, Sam, but you need to rest at least another day," Sandra said.

"I'm almost back to normal," Raven said, revealing his snow-white teeth in a half grin.

"Bullshit. Those antibiotics may have kicked in, but you're weak. You need—"

"So give me something to make me strong," he said. "You guys got new meds last night from the raid on Fort Collins, right? Let's put 'em to good use. Don't you got some stimulants or something I can have?"

Sandra sucked in a deep breath and looked out over the families sitting in the lobby. They were clustered in the small room like animals, the scent of sweat filling the stuffy space. Many of them were sobbing and clutching one another as they waited for word on their loved ones.

"I have to get back in there, Sam," she said.

"I know, and I have to get out there to make sure more people don't end up here."

Sandra let out her breath in a sigh. She was doing everything possible to hold it together, but after the attack, she was a nervous wreck. They had several volunteers working in the operating area, including Doctor Meyers, who had helped save Creek at Storm Mountain, and Doctor Martha Kohler, who was nearly fully recovered from her own wounds. But even with Rea and the other med students that had shown up, it wasn't enough. It would never be enough.

She looked back to her brother, and then Allie and Creek. Her heart longed to stay with them, but she knew her duty was to help here with the injured and dying. She also knew Allie would be safer at the designated shelter—and that Raven had to go out there to fight.

"Sandra, you with me?" he asked.

She nodded. "I'm sorry. I was just thinking."

"We're alive, and that's all that matters. But in order to make sure we stay alive, I need to fight. I think you know that."

"I don't want you to fight anymore," Allie said, speaking for the first time in hours.

Creek let out a whine.

"Uncle Raven has to fight," Sandra said, crouching in front of Allie. "And you have to go to the shelter with Teddy and the other kids."

"No, Mom, I want to stay with you."

Sandra wiped a fleck of dried blood off Allie's face that the tears hadn't washed away.

"I will join you when I can, sweetie. But for now, you have to go."

Allie looked up at Raven. "You're taking me to the shelter?"

"Yes, *Agaliga.*"

Sandra almost smiled at the Cherokee word for "sunshine." Even now, when all seemed lost, her brother's love for Allie warmed her.

"I love you, Sam. Please, please be careful out there," she whispered.

"I love you too, sis." He put his hand on Allie's head, ruffling her hair. Allie giggled at that.

A flash of red and the clank of an ancient metal truck came from outside. Jake's 1952 Chevy pickup pulled up in front of the doors with Lindsey behind the wheel. She had several families in the back that were heading to the shelter.

"See, there's Teddy and his parents," Sandra said, pointing. A dog's head poked up in the pickup bed.

Allie smiled. "Hey, that's Teddy's dog!"

"Yup, and that truck's our ride, kiddo," Raven said.

Sandra gave him another hug, holding him an extra few seconds and praying this wasn't the last time they would embrace. When they let go, she told him to wait for a minute. She hurried back into the hospital, the sounds of moaning patients and the scent of bleach overwhelming her. She forced her way past the overflowing beds. Some of the patients reached out for help.

"I'll be right back," she said. "I promise."

She raided the pill cabinet, found the stimulants she was looking for, and then raced back out to the lobby. She handed the bottle to Raven.

"If you get drowsy, take these. They will help with the pain and help keep you alert."

"Thanks," Raven said. He turned to Allie. "Time to go, kiddo."

"I love you, Mom," Allie said.

"I love you too, baby," Sandra said. Normally, she would have shed tears as she left her family. But today she didn't have any tears left to shed.

***

The sun was high in the sky by the time Charlize made her way to the tarmac. A V-22 Osprey was waiting in the shimmering heat. Sergeant Fugate and his team were finishing their final gear checks and loading crates into the back of the tiltrotor military aircraft.

She counted ten of the Green Berets. Thoreau and Sammie, the two men who had helped hold the stairwell in New York, had both been killed during the North Korean terror attack.

"This better be worth the trip across the country," Colonel Raymond said as they took seats in the Osprey. Albert sat next to Charlize and strapped in.

"Colton is a good man," she replied. "My brother

trusted him, so I trust him."

"I'm not doubting that, ma'am. I'm just concerned about this standoff he's reporting with the Sheriff of Fort Collins. We can't get caught in conflicts between communities like this." There was anger in his voice, the first time Charlize had heard him ever speak with anything but respect.

"I understand that, Colonel, but if what he says is true—if this Sheriff Thompson has teamed up with Fenix—then I'm inclined to step in."

Raymond still wasn't backing down. "But do you have to go there personally? This could end up being a disaster if we don't catch Fenix."

"We *will* catch him this time."

"I'm certainly going to do everything to ensure that happens, ma'am. I've already got several military assets on their way."

"What assets?" she asked.

"A Black Hawk out of Denver, plus a Marine fire-team that's been guarding a Chinese crew," he replied. "Chinese and American air support is also standing by."

"Good, but I don't want a single weapon fired until we're positive it's Fenix."

"Understood."

"We got your back, Secretary Montgomery," Fugate said from his seat.

"I know you do, Sergeant. Thank you."

The ring of her satellite phone sounded, and she fished it from her pack as the lift gate of the Osprey began to close.

"This is Charlize Montgomery," she said.

"Secretary Montgomery, this is Captain Harris. How are you?"

"I'm good. How are things in Charlotte?"

"Good, ma'am. We're setting up shop at the SC again, and then I'm moving out with the convoy to the next location. I wanted to let you know that things have improved greatly since you were here last, thanks to our Chinese counterparts."

"Excellent news, Captain."

"There is some bad news, though."

Her heart fluttered. The overhead and bulkheads hummed as the pilots flipped on the engines of the Osprey.

"I'm getting word of several white supremacy groups popping up on the east coast, attacking the Chinese and American convoys. They are killing workers, too. Apparently they are being told to rise up by a man they call The General."

Charlize cursed under her breath. If that was true, then Fenix was extending his reach beyond Colorado. She wasn't sure how that was possible, but she couldn't let his racist tendrils spread through the platform he was using to convey his message of hate.

"Don't worry about that, Captain Harris. You just keep doing your job, and I'll take care of this General," she said.

"Roger that, ma'am. I'll talk to you soon."

The Osprey pilots took off vertically from the small tarmac, and pulled the bird into the air as she hung up the phone. She patted Albert on his forearm and then looked over at Colonel Raymond.

"Hope you're ready for this, because I'm not coming home without Fenix this time," she said.

***

Colton had done everything he could to prepare for battle, including reaching out to the Secretary of Defense. But while her people had promised to check out the location Miles had given, she hadn't agreed to send any support to Estes Park to fight Sheriff Thompson. He guessed the federal government didn't want to get involved in skirmishes like this.

He took a slug of water and tried to focus through the exhaustion. He hadn't been this tired since the time he and Jake had spent thirty-six hours on patrol in Afghanistan—the same night Colton shot and killed his first Taliban soldier.

I wish you were here with me, buddy, Colton thought. He stood on the cliffs above Highway 34 with Lindsey. Like Jake would have done, she was standing by his side, ready to fight anyone that would threaten Estes Park or the United States of America.

The war in Afghanistan no longer seemed much different than the one they were fighting now. In both cases, innocent people were going to die at the hands of evil men, and good people would die defending them. All Colton could do was keep fighting and hoping the bloodshed would end soon. He centered his binoculars on the road to watch the refugees fleeing the canyon below.

"Why haven't they attacked yet?" Lindsey asked.

"Waiting for night is my guess."

The mountains were preparing to swallow the sun, and when the light was gone, Colton had a feeling Thompson would make his move. It was a fatal error on the Sheriff's part, giving Colton time to prepare. Everyone living along the highway had been evacuated over the course of the day, and with night falling, Colton was preparing for the first part of the battle for his city.

"That's the last of them," Lindsey said.

Colton moved his scopes to the south, where a caravan of armed civilians conscripted into soldiers were heading down Highway 36 to man the new barriers at the intersection with Mall Road. That's where he would be going next.

He pivoted to look over the town. His family and most of the other civilians were holed up at the high school, where Detective Ryburn had organized over one hundred fighters to protect the building at all costs. To the south, another two hundred people were set up along various places along Highway 7.

"We've done all we can," Lindsey said.

"If Miles was telling the truth, it won't matter," Colton replied. He lowered the binoculars to look at the captain. "Do you know what mortar fire and an M240 will do to our defenses? What it does to a human body?"

"John Palmer," Lindsey said quietly.

Colton dipped his head. "Let's hope Raven and Dale find Fenix before they can do any damage."

Lindsey looked to the south, where Raven and Dale were heading out on horseback. She didn't say a word, but Colton could tell she was worried. Over the past two months, she and Raven had become close—close enough that Colton wondered if they might have developed into something more than friends under different circumstances.

"Raven can look out for himself," Colton said.

"Yeah, but he's still not one hundred percent better. He was just on his death bed a few days ago."

"He's been near death before."

"Yeah, but…"

A flare suddenly streaked to the east over Big Thompson River. Colton followed it into the sky. The flare bloomed over Storm Mountain.

"It's begun," he whispered.

Colton brought the walkie-talkie up to his lips and counted silently. In his mind's eye, he could picture Thompson's vehicles racing up Highway 34 along the river. They were about to get one hell of a greeting.

He centered the binos back on the canyon. John Kirkus and his men were camped out on Storm Mountain, hoping that Thompson's attack would pass them by, but if that didn't happen, they would escape out the back route and meet up with Colton's forces along Mall Road.

Headlights confirmed the enemy vehicles had indeed passed by Storm Mountain. Thompson's eyes were on the prize—Estes Park. Colton centered his binos on the first of the vehicles, a truck with metal plates welded over the windows and the back bed to protect the soldiers. Another three trucks were moving up the canyon behind the lead vehicle.

"Matthews, blow the dam," Colton ordered into the radio.

He lowered his binos and hunched down with Lindsey. They both looked over at the Estes Park Lake, where hundreds of millions of gallons of water were about to come gushing into the canyon.

One by one, the blocks of explosives went off across the dam wall, moving left to right until they reached the center. Water gushed out of the gaping holes. Spider-web cracks raced across the concrete wall as more water burst through gaps. In a minute, the entire wall collapsed, letting out the frigid water.

Colton stood and watched in awe as the flood raced down the road, churning toward the convoy of vehicles. The trucks had all stopped on the road while the drivers tried to figure out what was going on. The lead truck attempted to turn around, but it was too late. The wall of water slammed into the side with such force it knocked the entire convoy away like toys.

"Hell yes!" Lindsey shouted.

Colton simply watched and waited, knowing this was just the beginning. He wanted to believe Thompson had been in one of the first vehicles, but he knew the man was smarter than that. This was just the first wave. Colton knew, because it's what he would have done.

"Come on, Captain, let's get into position," he said.

***

The explosions had startled the horses. Both of them paced on the narrow path, snorting the cold air.

"Easy, girl, easy," Raven said to Willow.

Dale looked over from his mount, Rhino. "Was that the dam?"

Raven pulled out his radio. "Hawk 1, this is Akita 1. Do you copy? Over."

"Roger, Akita 1, this is Hawk 1. We just blew the dam. What's your status?"

"On our way to the coordinates. Will report in shortly."

"Good luck, Akita 1."

Raven gave Willow a gentle kick to the ribs and gripped the reins tighter, urging her down the windy path carved through the thick forest. Branches reached out across the path, scratching at his coat and the ballistic vest stuffed with extra magazines. They were about a mile away from Lily Lake, and a soft snow was fluttering from the dark sky.

It was the first time Raven had been outside since the mountain lion attack, and he had finally accepted his body wasn't ready for this. His head pounded, and his back burned. For the past hour, he had held off on taking any of the pills, but as they neared the potential location of Fenix and his men, Raven decided to take one.

Dale nudged his large horse next to Willow as the path widened.

"You feeling good, boss?" Dale asked. He watched Raven down the pill with a slug of water.

"Boss?" Raven said with a raised brow. "I'm fine, just got a headache."

"Good. I need you frosty. When I find the fuckers that killed Jennie and took Sarah…" His angry words trailed off.

"We're going to find Sarah. Don't worry, brother." Raven adjusted the strap of the crossbow slung over his shoulders. It had caught on one of the hatchets sheathed behind his back. His AR-15 was hanging over his chest, and he grabbed the grip once he'd finished with his crossbow strap.

Creek bolted through the woods ahead, tail up. The dog had picked up a scent.

"Let's go, girl," Raven said, giving Willow another nudge.

The two horses took off after the dog. Raven scanned the terrain for movement in the green hue of his NVGs. Colton had given them the precious optics for this mission.

They were coming up the back way to get a better

view of the lake and the highway on the other side of the water, which was where Raven suspected Fenix and his men were camped out with their heavy weapons. But so far, he didn't see any fresh tracks from man or machine.

Spindly pines lined the bluff on the right side of the path. Raven directed Willow up the slope, her hooves crunching the snow. At the crest, Dale and Raven dismounted and followed Creek to a ridgeline that looked over the lake. The rocky terrain stretched about a quarter mile around the lake.

Raven checked the ridgeline, and then got down on his belly to crawl to the edge, where they propped their rifles up and scanned the lake below.

"See anything?" Dale whispered.

Raven did a quick scan without his scope, looking for movement or anything out of the ordinary. All he saw were some abandoned cars covered in snow on the highway, and another few parked near the lake. That was it. No trucks or Humvees. Nothing to indicate the presence of SOL.

"The fucker lied to us," Raven mumbled.

What if this was a trap? What if Miles was trying to get Colton to send men south of town?

"We have to get back," Raven said, pushing himself to his feet with a grimace. His head was still acting up, and he felt light-headed.

Dale cursed. "Maybe he wasn't lying after all. Look at the highway again."

Raven brought his scope up and zoomed in on the highway one last time, where he saw something he'd missed earlier due to his damn head. The tire tracks on the road were fresh enough that the snow hadn't covered them yet.

Creek growled, but Raven kept his eyes on the tracks. They were heading north, directly toward Estes Park.

He took his right hand off the rifle stock to reach for his radio, but then he saw another set of tracks. These were boot prints leading away from the lake, up the slope, and into the trees about a tenth of a mile from their position.

Creek growled again.

"What the…" Dale begin to say.

Raven was already bringing his rifle up. He moved it to the right and held it on a figure in white camouflage, holding a shotgun and moving at a hunch along the rocky ridge.

"Dale, get down!" Raven shouted.

The boom of the shotgun sounded before Dale could move, peppering the ground with pellets. He rolled away, and Raven stood with his rifle shouldered. A trigger pull sent three rounds punching through the center of the shooter's white coat, splattering it with carmine. He crumpled to the ground, bleeding out onto the snow.

Muzzle flashes came from the trees a hundred feet away from the fallen man. Raven hunched down behind a rock with Creek while Dale found cover. Bullets cracked off the rocks all around them.

"Two hostiles in those trees," Raven said. "I'll draw them out, and you take them down."

"No, you're the better shot. I'll go."

Raven agreed, and raised his gun over the rock, firing a three-round blast to give cover. Dale took off running, drawing fire instantly.

Holding in a breath, Raven aimed for the trees. His first shot lanced into bark, but the second clipped the arm of a shooter. The man stumbled away from cover, and

Raven put a bullet in his neck. He then trained the barrel on the final hostile and put a three-round burst into the right side of his chest. The man spun away from the tree, hitting the dirt on his side.

"Clear," Raven said. He did a final scan, and then looked for Dale. The big man was panting behind a rock and gave a thumbs up.

The gunshots faded away, leaving the two men in silence. The cold wind rustled their clothing as they waited to make sure there weren't any other snipers on the ridgeline. But every second they held position was a second closer to Fenix storming Estes Park with those M240s and mortar rounds.

Dale moved over at a crouch. "That all of 'em?"

"I think so," Raven said, looking over at Creek. The dog sat on his haunches, relaxed.

Raven pulled out his radio. "Hawk 1, this is Akita 1. We took down three wolves, but the rest of the pack is on the way to the pasture."

"We're about to have company here, too, Akita 1. Get your ass back here and find the pack."

"Roger that."

"Let's check those dead guys. Then we get to the horses and hightail it back to town," Raven said.

Rifles shouldered, Dale and Raven made their way across to the ridgeline at a cautious trot. The first man lay sprawled in the snow on his back, eyes open and staring at the moon. Raven bent down to pull his stocking cap off, revealing a shaved head.

"Definitely a Nazi."

Dale was already on his way to the trees. "Got a live one," he said.

Raven hurried over.

The man was squirming on the ground, holding his guts where Raven had shot him with a 5.56 mm round. Dale had picked up his dropped M4. Raven picked up the other M4 from the third shooter, who was already cold to the touch.

"Hurry. Police up their ammo," Raven said to Dale. Then he bent down next to the dying man to look him in the eyes.

"Where is Fenix?"

The man's eyes flitted to Raven. He winced in pain and tried to speak, but all that came out was a bloody bubble that popped on his blue lips.

"Tell you what. I'll give you a few of these if you tell me. It's going to ease your pain." Raven reached into his pocket and pulled out the bottle of pills Sandra had given him.

The SOL soldier reached up with a gloved hand, but Raven pulled the pills back. "Not until you tell me where Fenix is."

A distant chopping noise sounded to the south, drawing the man's attention. Raven and Dale both turned to look at the sky.

"You hear that?" Dale asked. He hurried back over holding two grenades he had taken from the corpse.

Raven slowly stood and put a boot on the man's arm so he couldn't move. Creek trotted over and sat next to Raven. The sound grew louder into a *whoop, whoop, whoop* that left no doubt in Raven's mind. He knew that noise like a gunshot. The black bird came into focus a few seconds later, the helicopter carving through the clear sky like a boat in calm waters.

"It's a Black Hawk," Dale said.

"Yeah, but is it one of ours, or is this more SOL backup?"

Dale and Raven hunched down, just in case.

The man reached out for the pills again. "Please," he muttered. "It hurts..."

"Tell me where they are," Raven said.

"Mo..." Blood bubbled from his mouth again, coating his lips in red.

Raven pulled out his water bottle and brought it to the man's lips, earning a frown from Dale. He coughed and tried again to speak, but the Black Hawk drowned out his voice. Looking over his shoulder, Raven saw it had veered toward the lake. The bird did a quick circle and then flew northeast, toward Fort Collins.

"That was one of ours," Dale said. "Must have been Secretary Montgomery's people checking out the coordinates."

Raven snorted. Charlize had sent the pilots to this location to see if Fenix was really here, but the man had already bugged out to a new location.

Smart son of a bitch.

Raven looked back down at the SOL soldier and put his finger into the stomach wound, expecting a scream. But the man didn't make a single sound. His eyes stared at the sky, cold and dead.

"Fucking hell," Raven said.

Dale handed out one of the grenades. "Take this. I have a feeling we're going to need them."

— 20 —

The cold wind stung Colton's eyes. They had adjusted to the darkness, and the vibrant moon provided just enough light to make out the terrain beyond the roadblock. He crouched behind a concrete block with his AR-15 aimed down Highway 36.

The barriers were set up at the intersection with Mall Road. There were a dozen vehicles blocking the road ahead, and then a wall of concrete blocks covered with barbed wire as a second barrier. Mall Road was clear, giving John Kirkus and his men from Storm Mountain passage to come from the north when the battle started.

Sporadic coughing and whispers came from all around him, and he took a moment to look at the silhouetted shapes. There were thirty civilians-turned-warriors positioned here, and another twenty at the roadblock a half mile behind them. There were snipers posted on every street, just in case Thompson's men made it past the barriers.

All throughout Estes Park, men, women, and teenaged boys and girls pointed weapons. Colton imagined many of them were praying it wouldn't come to violence. But he knew it would. After seeing the Black Hawk, he too had hoped it wouldn't come to war, but the bird had kept flying, and hadn't returned.

Now that the military had decided not to intervene, Thompson would roll right into town, sacrificing his own people for a shot at expanding his territory.

This was where the heart of the battle for Estes Park would occur, now that Highway 34 was washed away.

"Shit, it's cold out here, but at least the snow stopped," Lindsey said. She was crouched behind the barrier to Colton's right, looking up at the spotter that had climbed the transmission line. "Jack's got to be freezing up there."

Colton snuck a glance at the high school baseball star perched high in the tower that had once distributed power to Estes Park. The boy had volunteered to climb it and watch for hostiles. His friends Alex and Gordon, both track stars, had also volunteered as scouts on Highway 36.

"Any word from Gordon?" Colton asked Lindsey.

She shook her head. "He's still not answering."

"Try him again."

Lindsey spoke into the radio, but a different voice came over the channel. It was Alex this time.

"I see light," he said at a whisper. "Looks like about twenty vehicles. Maybe fifty...no, seventy men."

"Give that to me," Colton said, heart racing at the news. Seventy men? That was a small army. How could his people stop so many with their shotguns and pistols?

"Alex, you hide until those vehicles pass," Colton ordered. "When it's safe, you get back here, got it?"

"Yes, sir."

Colton contacted Raven next.

"Akita 1, this is Hawk 1. What's your status?"

It took several moments for Raven to respond, and Colton used the time to check the roadblock to the east. He was already considering pulling people off that one, but he needed them there just in case Thompson had ground troops moving toward town.

"I read you, Hawk 1," Raven said over the radio. "We're following those tracks. Looks like they took a detour around the roadblock here on Highway 7. Must have Humvees or something heavy duty."

Colton cursed. They were already being flanked. "How many vehicles?" he asked.

"Four."

Colton gritted his teeth. "Find 'em, Raven. Find 'em before it's too late."

"On it, Chief."

Colton put the radio back in the pouch and rose very slowly to take in the faces of those around him. They came from all walks of life. There was the owner of the Stanley Hotel, Jim Meyers, next to Rex Stone. Even Tom Feagen was here, holding a shotgun to his chest.

Missing were all of those who had perished in the past two months. Colton took a moment to think of everyone from Captain Jake Englewood and Major Nathan Sardetti, to refugees like Susan and Todd Sanders.

Colton would not allow their sacrifices to be in vain. He would not allow his town or country to fall into anarchy.

"Listen up, everyone," he said.

Every set of eyes focused on him in the low light. Cold breaths puffed out of mouths as the civilians waited for him to say something reassuring or profound— something that would encourage them to stand their ground when the bullets started flying.

"We are the town's first defense," he said. "What happens here could very well determine the fates of our loved ones in the high school. Make no mistake, the men that are coming will not show mercy. I saw what they did to residents of the FEMA camp. We must hold them here at all costs. We must make them pay for every foot of asphalt."

"Every foot," Rex Stone growled. There was anger in his voice, and pain. Colton could tell he was ready to die to protect the only thing he had left in this world: his wife.

"When they come, we must stand our ground. We are stronger together," Lindsey added.

Colton imagined the terror of the gunfire that would be on them shortly. Some of these people, like Tom Feagen, had never even fired a gun, let alone been shot at. Truthfully, Colton was more worried people like Feagen would accidentally shoot him in the chaos.

But he needed boots on the ground here. Numbers meant everything.

"Remember to conserve your ammo and fire on the vehicles. We can't let any of them get past these roadblocks," Colton said.

A crack sounded, and the black cowboy hat Jim Meyers was wearing flew up into the air, part of his head flying off with it. There were screams, but Colton's mind was still trying to process what had happened.

Jim slumped to his knees, and then fell face first into the ground, gore spilling from his broken skull.

"Sniper!" Colton finally yelled. "Everyone down!"

Lindsey and Colton hunched behind the barrier. Return fire came from the roadblock. That was good; at least his people were fighting back. But the noise made it impossible to hear where the next shot came from.

"Hold your fire!" he shouted.

Most of the firing ceased.

"Does anyone have eyes?" Lindsey yelled.

Several cries rang out as another gunshot cracked, pinging off the barrier Lindsey was hiding behind. Colton gestured for her to crawl over to his position. Another flurry of gunfire came from the blockade, but it quickly ceased.

Silence claimed the night.

"Did anyone see where it came from?" Colton asked. His radio crackled with a message from Officer Matthew, but Colton ignored it.

Another shot broke the momentary quiet, and a cry of pain followed. Judging by the noise, Colton put this weapon at a high caliber, and judging by the gaping hole where Jim's hairline had been it, was probably a 30.06.

"Who has eyes?" Colton said, louder this time.

"Came from the trees at three o'clock," someone yelled back. Colton looked to the right of the road. Someone had snuck into the timber without them seeing.

"Covering fire," he said to Lindsey.

She nodded and got to one knee, preparing to fire at the pine trees, while Colton moved into position. As soon as she fired off a burst, he came up at a crouch and fired a blast into the woods. Rex fired with him, and they painted the trees with enough rounds that branches fluttered to the ground.

Colton went to crouch back down when he saw something streak toward the barrier of vehicles blocking the road in front of their barricade. The projectile hit the center of the junked vehicles, exploding in a brilliant flash of light.

"Down!" he yelled.

Shrapnel and shards of glass whizzed through the air, slicing into several of the sentries that hadn't gotten down in time.

Someone had fired an RPG at their first line of defense, blowing a gaping hole in the wall of cars they had pushed together. He heard engines a beat later, and then saw the small armada of vehicles rounding the corner of Highway 36.

"Open fire!" he shouted.

The gunner in the bed of the lead vehicle fired first, filling the night with the bark of an M240. Gunfire lanced into the concrete blocks and cut down several people in front of Colton, splattering him with fresh blood.

He hunched down and looked up at the distribution tower behind them.

"Jack, get down!" Colton yelled up to the boy. Then he rose to scan the road. The man with the RPG was standing behind a ditch, attempting to reload. A muzzle cracked from the tower, and the man dropped with his launcher.

"I got him!" Jack yelled.

The boy's bravery attracted tracer rounds from the vehicle barreling toward the roadblock. Several bullets cut into Jack and slammed into the tower. He dropped limply to the ground like a fried bird.

Colton closed his eyes, gripped by a messy combination of fear, anger, and despair. When he opened them, he saw people staring at him on both sides. Terrified people with wide eyes, shaky hands, and sweat dripping down their cold skin as 7.62 mm rounds slammed into their defenses.

You have to lead these people.

"Aim for that truck!" he shouted, standing to set the example.

He let out a war cry, and aimed at the muzzle flash of the mounted gun on the first truck. All around him, the militia stood and opened fire, sending a stream of rounds into the convoy. Someone to his right dropped, screaming in pain. Lindsey shouted an order, and someone else moved to take the fallen person's place.

The gun on the pickup went silent, and the truck skidded to a stop just in front of the smoldering hole where their roadblock had been. Colton finished off his magazine and reached for another when he saw another flash from the woods. There was more than one sniper.

He palmed a new mag home and aimed at the trees, waiting for the next flash. It came a second later, and he squeezed the trigger. Something stung his shoulder, jerking him to the right, as he fired off a shot. He grunted in pain, then found his target again and fired two bursts into the bushes where the sniper lay.

Pain ripped up his arm and neck. The bullet had missed his ballistic vest and cut right through his flesh. He could feel the blood flowing. His first thought was of Kelly and Risa, but he didn't have time to worry about what they would do without him. His priority was saving them.

Pushing the butt back into position, he squeezed off another barrage of shots at the incoming convoy. An old tow truck with a cow guard was screeching toward what was left of their blockade of vehicles. It hit the flaming mini-van and pickup truck with such force they skidded into the ditch, providing a window for Thompson's trucks to drive through.

"Fire," Colton yelled. "Keep firing!"

He waited several seconds, and then nodded at Lindsey. She pulled out her flare gun and aimed it at the ditch to the right of the destroyed vehicle wall, and Colton aimed his flare gun at the left.

The trucks squeezed through the smoldering gap in the vehicles, and then stopped to let their soldiers out. This was it; if they made it through the barrier Colton was holding, then they would be able to drive right into town.

He squeezed off his flare, sending it streaking into the ditch, where it caught fire on the pool of gasoline. The men jumping out of the trucks screamed in horror, several of them going up in flames as the fire spread across the road.

"Don't let up!" Colton yelled. He tossed the flare gun aside and brought his AR-15 back up to fire. The flames provided plenty of light to find his targets by, and he took down hostiles with quick squeezes.

All around him, his people killed to protect their loved ones. War brought out the rawest emotions, and Colton saw it happening all around him. The screaming, the distorted faces, the rage-filled eyes of people who had never harmed a fly.

It was then he realized he was screaming too as he cut down the burning men trying to take his town.

He changed his magazine and raised the gun again when a raucous blast sounded from the east. The ground rumbled under his boots. For the third time in as many minutes, his heart skipped a beat. He bent down behind the barrier and caught Lindsey's gaze. Then he turned back to Estes Park, where a massive explosion had erupted in the center of town. A second blast quickly followed, sending flames catapulting into the air.

The mortar barrage had started.

Colton pulled out his radio. "Raven, where the fuck are you?" he shouted over the din. Gunfire drowned out the response, and he pushed the radio up to his ringing ear, grimacing in pain from his shoulder.

"We're almost back to town, Chief," came Raven's reply. "I'm tracking Fenix and his men right now. That mortar fire is coming from somewhere on Prospect Mountain."

"Hurry and find them!" Colton yelled into the receiver. Then he opened a channel to Ryburn. "Make sure everyone is hunkered down and hold the line there at all costs."

"I will, Chief."

Colton transmitted a final message to Officer Matthew, who was in charge of the two roadblocks at Highway 7, telling him to abandon the posts and head for Prospect Mountain. Then he looked back at the next roadblock a half mile away. Several figures were already running toward his position.

He snorted when he saw them. They were supposed to stay put. And where the hell was John Kirkus and his men? Colton looked down Mall Road and saw nothing.

He came back up on one knee to continue firing at the survivors holding position behind the first wave of parked vehicles. Another set of lights flipped on around the corner up Highway 36, as Thompson deployed another wave.

Shit, shit, shit. We're going to be overrun.

"No," Colton said. "Hold them here!"

Empty shell casings rained down on the pavement, and more civilians fell to the ground as the second wave of vehicles drove toward their position. Tom Feagen raised his shotgun to fire and took a bullet to the leg. He screamed in pain and fell to the ground, gripping his thigh and screeching in agony.

As more of his fellow townsfolk dropped, Colton pulled out his radio and turned to the channel he'd been using to communicate with Charlize Montgomery's people.

"Secretary Montgomery, this is Chief of Police Marcus Colton. If you're listening, the Sons of Liberty and Sheriff Thompson are slaughtering civilians in Estes Park, Colorado. We need help!"

Colton nearly dropped the radio as he went to put it back in the pouch. Once it was secure, he placed a hand on his wounded shoulder and scanned the battlefield.

Lindsey was still firing, raking the barrel back and forth and taking hostiles down like a veteran combat soldier. Colton did his best to ignore the explosions coming from the town, and aimed for the metal armor covering the turret on one of the new pickup trucks driving toward their flaming wall of bodies and vehicles.

He took his time to line up the sights and finished off his magazine. The gunner slumped out of the bed and hit the pavement. A second man jumped up to take his place, but Lindsey took him down with a shot to the head.

After ten minutes of fighting, Colton and his captain found themselves side by side. He looked over, trying to focus past the stars in his vision. Rex Stone was still in action, as were three other men to his right, but their numbers were thinning by the minute, and Kirkus and his men still weren't here yet.

"Fall back," Colton said. "I'll hold them here."

"Hell no," Lindsey said.

"Get these people out of here!" Colton shouted.

She looked at him, her face distorting into a mask of fear and sadness. Gunfire suddenly came from Mall Road, and Colton turned to see a group of men on horseback and an old black Chevy car clanking along the road. Four old-school snowmobiles followed the hillbilly convoy.

Two dirt bikes also sped over the snowy asphalt.

"Kirkus!" she shouted.

Colton almost smiled, but a round zipped over his head and he grimaced instead. He rose to his feet, aimed at Thompson's vehicles, and squeezed the trigger again. More rounds narrowly missed his face, but he remained standing, undeterred.

Another bark of an M240 came from the timber to the left of the road, far behind the dying flames. The sight seized the air from Colton's lungs.

Tracer rounds spat out of the trees and cut into Kirkus's men, knocking them down like bowling balls. The spray hit the Chevy next, punching through the old metal. The snowmobiles swerved to avoid the gunfire, and both drivers on the bikes lost control.

Colton watched as a man with a white cowboy hat climbed off his fallen horse and stood to fire a long rifle at the M240 in the trees. It was Kirkus, and his aim was true. He killed the gunners and limped over to the roadblock with several of his surviving fighters right behind him.

"Sorry we're late," Kirkus said, wincing in pain.

"You're hurt," Colton said.

Kirkus glanced over at Colton. "You're hit too, Chief."

"I'll be fine."

"You got a plan?" Kirkus asked.

Colton was trying to devise one in his mind, but all he could focus on was the mortar rounds raining down into his town. Buildings burned around town hall, and several houses in the residential areas were flickering plumes of orange.

He could only hope Raven found Fenix and stopped him before the Nazi bastards took out the high school.

Thompson's second wave of trucks made it through the barrier, and Colton did the only thing he could do.

"Retreat to the next barrier!" he shouted. "Everyone, fall back!"

Feagen yelled out for help as the militia soldiers began to run. Colton, Rex, and Lindsey provided a wave of covering fire as the first group escaped down the road.

She looked over at him between bursts. "We can't leave Feagen."

Colton agreed with a nod. "Cover me."

"Go!" she shouted.

Colton ran over to Feagen's position and bent down to help him up. Rounds zipped all around them, but somehow Colton managed to escape with the man leaning on his left side as a crutch.

"Thank you," Feagen panted.

***

Fenix brought his binoculars up to watch a mortar shell explode in the middle of the intersection at Elkhorn Avenue and Riverside Drive. Several civilians cartwheeled through the air like miniature rag dolls.

He let the binos hang around his neck, and clapped at the sight of burning buildings below. From his vantage point on the tramway station cresting Prospect Mountain, he had a gorgeous view of the battlefield.

So far, everything was going as planned.

The military had passed the town by after checking out the fake location Miles had given his captors. He could still remember the young man's leg snapping.

"It's your duty as a soldier of the Sons of Liberty," Fenix had said right before stomping on Miles's leg and then leaving him behind.

He wasn't sure what had happened to Miles, but the kid had done his duty. Now that bitch Charlize Montgomery wouldn't have any idea what SOL was doing, and by the time she did, Fenix would be long gone.

Until then, he was going to have some more fun. His field mortar crew wasn't far. They were using the Chinese-built Type 87 mortars. He didn't like Chinese built products, but these were going to go to a good use.

A shell thumped away from the field on the western slope of the mountain and into the town, at targets his spotters had identified with their scopes. Most of the targets were high value targets, like snipers, or nests where militia soldiers were hunkered down. After all, Fenix had promised Thompson he wouldn't destroy the town.

But that didn't mean all the rounds hit their targets.

Fenix laughed as a house exploded south of Elkhorn Avenue. Another shell took out the top of a building, eliminating another potential hostile for Thompson to deal with once he broke through the barriers on Highway 36. It wouldn't be long now. The sheriff was using the weapons Fenix had loaned him from raids on the Chinese convoys: twin M240s, an RPG launcher, and grenades. But Fenix and his men still had plenty of toys to play with.

"Horton, you got a SITREP?" he shouted.

Another shell curved overhead and into town, destroying a building on Big Horn Drive in a spray of metal, glass, and wood.

Fenix clapped again. "Nice shot!"

Sergeant Horton jogged over from the railing, where he was supervising the mortar crew. He made his way past the corpses of the dead Estes Park militia soldiers that had been posted on the tramway lookout. The bodies were riddled with bullets.

"Big mistake on their part," Fenix muttered to himself. Leaving only two men as lookouts had been a devastating error by the chief that would cost him the town. The two spotters could have warned Colton, but Fenix and his men had cut them down before they could get off a flare.

Fenix turned back to the railing to look out over Lake Estes, which was now more of a puddle, the majority of the water having flowed down Highway 34. The ambush had cost Thompson his first wave of vehicles and bought the Estes Park militia extra time to fortify their defenses on Highway 36—and apparently lay another trap.

The gas-soaked ditches framing the highway were still burning below, having already taken out the second wave of Thompson's trucks. The third wave was slowly making their way toward the barrier that was being abandoned by the militia soldiers.

"Colton's not as dumb as I thought," Fenix said to Horton.

Horton shrugged. "Thompson's not going to like taking this many losses, but we will take this town."

"Bring up the M240s, Sergeant."

"Yes, sir."

Two teams of Brandenburger Commandos lugged crates out of the trucks parked behind the tramway shops, and moved them over to the railings overlooking the eastern side of the town. Fenix instructed them where to put the big guns after scanning the battlefield a third time. He brought his pocket watch up as the men worked.

It was going on nine o'clock, and he wanted to be out of here in an hour. After they finished with the mortar and M240 fire, his mission would be complete. He could then return to his silo for a good night's sleep. At this rate, he'd be there shortly after midnight.

"Hurry that shit up!" he growled.

He gripped the railing with his gloved hands and studied the fight on Highway 36. The Estes Park militia had retreated to a second roadblock, and Thompson's vehicles were preparing to maneuver out of the flames to pursue them. Mortar fire continued to pound the town square, destroying buildings and blowing hunks of concrete out of the street.

"We've got contacts on the northern slope!" someone suddenly shouted.

Fenix leaned over the railing to see a dozen silhouettes making their way up the mountain.

"Take them out," Fenix said, pointing.

The M240 gunners moved the guns, and Fenix clamped his hands over his ears. The cry of the gun rattled his body as the men unleashed a volley of 7.62 mm rounds into the trees below. Adjusting the spray, the soldiers found human targets, coating the slope with steaming blood.

Fenix raised his M4 and picked off several of the stragglers, the gunfire ringing in his ears. When it ceased, the gunners moved the M240s back into position and waited for his order to fire again.

Bringing up his binoculars, Fenix checked the roadblock on Highway 36 again, using the moonlight and glow of the flames for light. He had wanted to wait for the team to abandon the second barrier, but Colton's forces were still holding their ground and looked pretty well dug in.

"Fuck it," Fenix snarled. "Open fire."

"That's too far, sir," Horton said.

"I gave you an order."

"Sir, yes, sir."

Fenix clamped his hands back over his ears and scanned the sky for any sign of the military, but the cloudless sky was still void of any blinking craft. A mortar round arched overhead like a shooting star moving in slow motion. It slammed into a house on the north side of town, blowing the roof into splinters.

He let his binoculars hang from his neck and looked out over the landscape with grim satisfaction. The snow-brushed town almost looked like something from a Christmas card—aside from the burning buildings, of course.

But they could pass for Christmas lights, he thought with a smile.

— 21 —

Raven could feel his pulse beating in his neck. The mortar barrage coupled with the explosions from RPGs and the bark of M240 gunfire brought him back to the chaotic mission behind enemy lines in North Korea, where a raid to save two American girls had ended in a bloodbath.

But this was America, home of democracy, and the brave. It wasn't some foreign authoritarian regime.

How could any of this be real?

He focused on the patrols and troops holding sentry around the mortar crew launching rounds into Estes Park. He and Dale had abandoned their horses and were hiding behind the thick trunk of a ponderosa, their night vision goggles allowing them to see without being spotted. There were ten soldiers on patrol, another ten in the mortar firing area, and more on the platform above.

"Where's our backup?" Dale asked quietly.

"I don't think they made it," Raven said. He looked up at the area where the M240s had been positioned a few minutes earlier. The guns were now out of sight and firing somewhere to the east.

"It's just us," Raven said.

"Us against twenty heavily-armed Nazi soldiers?"

"We have Creek," Raven said. That didn't seem to inspire confidence in Dale, who looked over at the dog sitting calmly on his haunches.

"We have no choice, brother," Raven said. "Sarah is

probably up here."

Dale swallowed so hard his Adam's apple bobbed. "I had a good run in this life. Let's go kill us some Nazi pig-fuckers."

"That's the spirit," Raven replied. "It ain't over until the fat lady sings…or something like that."

The line got a grin from Dale, but Raven remained stone-faced. He too was prepared to die for those he loved.

"You go north and I'll go south. Creek will hunt with me. We'll meet back in the middle and then work our way up to the tram to take out those guns. Use your blade until we're spotted," Raven said.

Dale reached out with a gloved hand. "Good luck, Raven. It's been an honor."

Something about the other man's words seemed so final, and as Raven looked back out at the enemy they were facing, he realized it was likely this would be the last time the two men would shake hands.

"Honor is mine, brother," Raven said, gripping Dale's hand firmly.

Dale let go and began to creep around the base of the tree. Raven drew in a breath, thinking of Sandra and Allie, and then of Lindsey and Colton. Their lives all depended on his actions.

Light as a feather, he thought. The stimulant he had taken a few minutes earlier was starting to kick in, and he indeed felt light. But more importantly, his brain was clear. He was in tune with nature. He motioned for Creek and rose into a hunch. Adrenaline warmed his veins as Raven moved away from the tree, separating from Dale.

There were four Nazi commandos patrolling under the tramway concrete platforms to the south. They were setting off again to comb the area. Those were his targets. Each wore black tactical gear with facemasks, and carried M4 rifles.

Raven had his own M4 slung over his back, looted from the dead Nazi back at Lily Lake. He moved cautiously through the fence of aspen trees jutting out of the slope. He brushed against snow-covered boulders as he passed, and he stayed close to them just in case he needed to duck for cover. Creek had already vanished, hunting solo in the frozen terrain.

The group of soldiers began to move into a thick area of ponderosas, and Raven stopped to aim his crossbow at the Nazi holding rear guard, and squeezed off an arrow that thumped through his neck. The man dropped his rifle in the snow and fell to his knees while the other three men continued walking in the opposite direction.

Raven placed another bolt in the weapon and followed them, waiting for his next opportunity. When he got to the fallen Nazi, he used his knife to finish the job, jamming it into the squirming man's temple.

One down, twenty to go.

He started for the fence of trees, seeing two of his chases had vanished from view. The third man stopped behind a tree, his body partially hidden by the bark. Raven aimed at the exposed part of the soldier's head and fired an arrow into it. The commando stumbled a few feet. By the time he hit the ground, Raven had already dropped the crossbow and pulled out both hatchets.

He stalked the next two Nazis, moving in the shadows while they walked unknowingly down a path. The amateurs didn't look over their shoulders, and neither of the men had stopped to see where their buddies were.

Big mistake, buckos.

In just over two minutes, Raven made it within throwing range of the final pair of chases. But then he made his own mistake—crunching a stick under his boot. The sound gave away his position, but by the time the first Nazi turned, a hatchet was in the air.

The blade planted itself in the man's forehead with a crack. As he slumped, Raven ran toward the fourth soldier, holding his other hatchet in his knife hand. He got all the way behind him without being seen, and brought the edge down on the back of the commando's skull with a dull ringing noise that echoed through the night.

Creek had taken down a fifth soldier on patrol that Raven hadn't seen earlier, and Raven ran over to help finish the man off. The dog's jaws were latched on to the man's throat, and Creek had already torn out his vocal cords. Raven brought the hatchet down on the soldier's nose so hard it got stuck.

Grunting, Raven pulled it out and fell on his back. He quickly got back up. Covered in steaming blood, he gestured for Creek to follow. They hurried back to the mortar crew, stopping only to pluck his other hatchet out of the corpse and grab his crossbow.

He loaded a bolt when he saw the edge of the mortar firing area. The men were continuing to load rounds in an organized manner, listening to the spotters who were yelling down from the concrete tramway platform.

The chatter of the M240s continued in the distance, the sound drowning out the crunch Raven's boots made over the snow. The guns were firing from the same platform where Raven had killed Brown Feather nearly two months prior. His decayed corpse actually wasn't far from here.

The irony wasn't lost on Raven. Prospect Mountain was cursed with evil by Nazis, Water Cannibals, and a half-Cherokee, half-Sioux Indian that had committed more sins than he could count. Raven shook away the chilling thoughts and continued toward the field area, where six soldiers manned the mortar tubes. Another four stood sentry. The other soldiers they had seen earlier were out of sight, aside from one spotter.

Raven still didn't like the odds, but they were better than before. But that was assuming Dale took down five of the other men.

Where the hell are you, Dale?

Creek nudged up next to Raven, keeping watch while Raven searched for his partner. The gunfire and explosions in the distance rose into a crescendo, and Raven grew more impatient by the second, knowing each one that passed meant another dead civilian. He aimed his bow at the closest Nazi. He couldn't hold here much longer—he had to stop them.

Raven finally spotted Dale moving between two trees. In his right hand he gripped a long, saw-toothed bowie knife glistening with blood, and in his left hand he held the butterfly knife Raven had given Sarah. They had found it on the roadblock earlier when they were looking for the girl.

Dale waved the bowie knife at Raven and then pointed toward the pickup trucks on the road. Raven brought up his crossbow scope and zoomed in on a small figure in the front seat. It had to be Sarah. He confirmed it by zooming in with the scope on his bow. Then he changed weapons, unslinging his M4. Dale did the same thing, but Raven changed his mind when he saw the pile of mortar rounds next to the firing area.

Maybe there's a better way...

Raven balled his hand at Dale and then lowered his rifle. Instead, he grabbed the grenade they had taken off the dead soldier back at Lily Lake. He pointed with his bow at the pile of munitions. Dale nodded back and pulled out his own grenade.

They both pulled the pins and lobbed them like baseballs toward the mortar rounds. The grenades rolled right between the launchers and the soldiers manning them.

Only one of the sentries seemed to notice. He walked over and tilted his head like a curious dog. Raven reached back for his own dog, and shielded Creek with his body, pushing the Akita against the snow.

A moment later, the explosions boomed through the night. The ground rumbled beneath Raven as the mortar rounds went off in a massive blast. He could feel hunks of trees sailing overhead. Dirt and small chunks of shrapnel rained down on his body as the explosions rocked the field.

Creek squirmed under Raven, but he held the dog down, waiting until the final blasts. The boisterous noise faded into an echo, and Raven slowly got up, his ears ringing. He picked up his M4 and directed it at the smoke swirling across the devastation.

A crater was all that remained in the center of the mortar firing area. The soldiers were gone, their body parts littering the snow all around Raven. Two boots remained where a soldier had stood moments earlier, the ankles still sticking out, but the legs and rest of the body were missing.

The smoke cleared, and the ringing subsided in Raven's ears. That's when he heard Creek's growl. Four commandos had moved onto the platform above, looking over at what was left of their comrades. Dale fired his M4 at the men, and Raven brought his barrel up, but froze when he saw more soldiers move up to the railing.

Not just four.

There were a dozen men.

The squad trained their fire on Dale and painted the area with bullets, several of which hit the big man. He moved behind a tree, fell to his butt, then pushed himself back up against the bark.

Raven sprayed the platform with rounds, hitting three men. One of them fell over the ledge. Then Raven dove for cover and crawled behind a tree.

Dale peered around his tree and squeezed off several shots, killing another two soldiers and bringing their numbers down to six or seven. But the survivors were fanning out and firing at both Raven and Dale.

They were pinned down on the slope, and the SOL commandos had the perfect vantage point.

We have to flank them.

Raven knew that was going to be next to impossible for Dale. The big man was hurt, and hurt bad. He shouted over at Raven, "You have to take out the big guns and then get Sarah!"

Raven held his position against the tree.

"Go, Sam. I'll distract them!"

Dale stared back with his NVGs still over his features. Raven closed his eyes for a moment, exhaled, and then did what any soldier would do. He took off to finish his mission.

***

The mortar fire had stopped after a massive explosion, but Colton's people were being cut down by the M240s on the aerial tramway. Unless someone pulled off a miracle shot, they didn't have much of a chance of taking the gunners down.

He cursed himself again for leaving the Crow's Nest undefended. The two sentries must not have seen the attack coming.

It didn't matter now. The mistake was his, and it had cost them dearly.

Every team he had pulled off the other roadblocks had been cut down on their way up the mountain. And he wasn't going to risk pulling anyone away from the high school. There were just twenty survivors of the original sixty militia soldiers on Highway 36 now. Most everyone had some sort of injury, from sprained ankles to gunshot wounds. And the enemy was closing in from all sides.

To the east was Thompson's small army, all of them hellbent on getting to the roadblock to kill those responsible for burning and shooting their comrades. To the west, the Sons of Liberty were using M240s to spit rounds from the top of Prospect Mountain.

One of them streaked by Colton's head and slammed into the door of the van he was crouched behind. The pickup truck to his left had been taking the brunt of the gunfire, but a few rounds punched through the truck and hit the van he was up against.

He got down to his belly and snuck a glance under the vehicle to see that Thompson's trucks were now free of the flaming first barrier. Several veered off into the town.

He'd lost control of the situation.

You never had control!

An explosion suddenly rocked the barriers about

twenty feet from the van, blowing the three militia people stationed there into chunks of gore. Colton shielded his face from the heat with his arm, and Lindsey screamed out in pain. He pulled his hand away to see her gripping her wrist, a shard of metal sticking out like an arrow.

"I'm okay," she said, tears welling up in her eyes.

Colton gritted his teeth, trying to keep his rage in check. He wanted to get up and squeeze off his magazine, but instead, he pulled out his radio and reported the vehicles to Officer Matthew, who was now the last hope at stopping them.

"On it, sir," Matthew replied. "I've got another team moving into position to take out those M240s. We've got a few snipers left."

"Hurry, and do *not* let them get to the high school," Colton said, his voice cracking. He tried to contact Raven again, but he didn't answer. Finally, he decided to try the channel to the Secretary of Defense. Gunfire continued around the barrier, his people still putting up a fight while he tried to save them with a final plea.

"Secretary Montgomery, this is Police Chief Marcus Colton. We're being slaughtered by the Sons of Liberty and Sheriff Thompson. Please, if you get this, send help!"

He put the radio away and then pressed the gauze back onto the gunshot wound. The blood loss was starting to make him feel queasy. Kirkus scrambled over and put his back next to the van. He was in bad shape too, after taking two rounds, one to his right bicep and the other to his hip. Feagen was still alive, somehow; he was resting with his back to the van a few feet away. Rex was to his left, firing shots off to the east.

"Can you fight?" Colton asked, looking at Kirkus and then over to Lindsey. They both nodded grimly.

The torrential downpour of 7.62 mm rounds from the aerial tramway suddenly ceased. Colton slowly rose to look over the pickup truck riddled with bullet holes to see that the muzzle flashes had stopped. It was too dark and too far away to see movement, but the M240 had stopped. Now he could hear the sound of rifles on the other side of the mountain. Finally, his people had made it to the top.

"Everyone up!" Colton shouted. He pushed the barrel of his AR-15 through the broken van window to fire, but what he saw took his breath.

The trucks and cars had all made it through the barrier, and had moved into position. Over forty men were standing behind the parked vehicles, their rifles aimed at the roadblock.

"Drop your weapons!" someone shouted.

Colton looked for the source of the voice, and saw Sheriff Thompson standing behind one of the trucks, his muscular arms folded across his chest.

"I just want Chief Colton," Thompson said. "The rest of you, lay your weapons down and I'll let you live."

"Don't do it," Lindsey said. "He will kill us all."

"That you, Plymouth?" Thompson said. "I've got special plans for you."

"Fuck you!" Lindsey looked like she wanted to charge the barrier, but Colton grabbed her by the arm. He looked over at Kirkus, who was struggling to stand.

Kirkus said, "Let me handle this. Bastard killed my brother and my son."

Colton could tell by the sad resignation in his eyes that Kirkus had given up on life. And, judging by his condition, he didn't have much time unless they got him to a doctor.

"We're all ready to die here, Thompson," Colton shouted. "If you want to take this town you are going to have to take—"

"What are you doing!" Lindsey shouted, silencing Colton.

He looked to his left to see she was talking to Feagen, who was pointing a pistol at Colton.

"Do us all a favor and turn yourself in." Feagen wagged the barrel of the revolver. "Go, or I'll shoot you myself."

"You don't know what you're doing," Lindsey said. "Thompson will not let the rest of us go."

Colton stared at the heavy-set former town administrator in shock, but then he realized he shouldn't be shocked at all. Even after Colton had saved Feagen's ass earlier, the man was only thinking about himself.

"You got one minute before we open fire," Thompson yelled.

Feagen pulled back the hammer on the revolver, and Colton could see by the crazed look in his eyes he was ready to kill him right here and right now.

"Don't, Chief," Lindsey said.

Colton locked eyes with her. In that moment, they came to an understanding on what had to happen next.

"Time's almost up!" Thompson yelled.

Feagen followed him with the barrel as Colton began to walk around the van. He halted at the bumper to pull his Colt .45 out and slip it into the wide sleeve of his coat. He crossed his arm over his chest and put his hand on his bloody shoulder to hide the lump in his sleeve and appear he was gripping his wound.

Then he walked around the van and set off through the barriers, his stomach churning at the sight of his people. Colin and Tim, both insurance agents, were slumped over their concrete barrier, orange-sized holes in their backs from the 7.62 mm rounds. Sally and her brother, Jeff, were face down next to a sedan, their bodies torn apart by the weapons. Then there was the area where Mike and Thomas had been hunkered down. There wasn't much left of either of them but limbs after the RPG had ripped them to charred pieces.

Colton focused on the man responsible. The fire still blazing in the ditches behind the parked vehicles illuminated the crazed smile on Sheriff Thompson's face.

"There he is!" Thompson yelled. He moved from behind the truck and looked over Colton's shoulder.

"I said put down your weapons," Thompson shouted. His eyes flitted to Colton. "Tell your people."

"You said you'd let them go," Colton said.

Thompson shrugged.

"I'm not telling them to do that until you give me a guarantee."

The grin on Thompson's face widened. "Remember what I told you?" he asked.

Colton snorted, and Thompson let out a laugh. He turned to look over his shoulder, and Colton seized the opportunity.

"NOW, Lindsey!" he yelled as he pulled the Colt .45 from his sleeve. By the time Thompson turned, Colton had the barrel pointed at the sheriff's head.

"You said to make sure I shot you in the face next time," Colton said.

He waited a split second for Thompson to take in his words, and then pulled the trigger. The bullet slammed into the sheriff's broken nose, and exited out the back of his head in a spray of blood, bone, and brain matter.

The gunfire that followed came so fast Colton didn't even have a chance to dive for cover. A round hit him in the left arm. The impact jerked his entire body and threw off his next shot. Another round hit him in the right leg, bringing him to one knee, and a third hit him in the upper right of his ballistic vest, knocking him on his back.

He rolled over to his stomach and searched for cover. The first thing he saw was Feagen's dead body under the van they had been hiding behind. Lindsey must have shot him in the head before turning her rifle on Thompson's men.

"Colton, stay down!" she screamed.

Next, he saw Kirkus limping toward him, but the man was quickly cut down with three rounds to the chest. The leader of the prepper community fell to both knees. He pushed himself up using his rifle as a crutch, and locked eyes with Colton just as a bullet hit him in the head.

Colton let out a shout of rage and aimed his Colt .45 at the men behind the vehicles. There were dozens of them, all firing at his people. He picked a bearded man with glasses and shot him in the neck.

Another bullet hit Colton in the shoulder, and a second shot him in the left leg. He screamed out in agony and tried to raise his gun at the shooter. The man lowered his rifle to change the magazine, giving Colton a moment to take aim.

He squeezed off a shot that went wide. The second shot also missed. The gun clicked. He reached for more rounds, his entire body numb and on fire at the same time.

The man with the ski mask brought his rifle back up to shoot Colton, but went down from a headshot before he could pull the trigger.

"Hold on!" Lindsey shouted again.

Colton fumbled for more bullets, dropping several onto the ground in the process. He bent down to grab them, and caught sight of his ruined body in the process. His legs were both bleeding out, and he could feel the heat from the blood gushing on his shoulder and arm.

There was no coming back from this. Even if they could get him off the road, he was losing too much blood.

I'm sorry, Kelly. I'm sorry, Risa. God, I love you both so much.

He flipped the break open and put in several more rounds.

"You won't hurt my family. You won't take this town!" he shouted as he squeezed off more shots. In the respite of gunfire came the squawk of the radio in his vest.

"Chief Colton, this is Colonel Raymond. Do you copy? We have fighter jets on their way to Estes Park. ETA five minutes. Please advise as to where SOL is located, over."

Colton lowered his pistol and reached for the radio. Another shot hit him in the left leg. He screamed in pain and dropped the radio. Gritting his teeth, he reached over and grabbed it again.

"Colton!" Lindsey shouted. "Colton, hang on. I'm coming!"

Gunfire lanced all around him.

"Stay put, Captain!" he managed to yell.

He lay there bleeding out, gasping for air, knowing he only had a few more seconds of consciousness. But he couldn't die yet. He still had one final mission. Bringing the radio up to his lips, he choked out his response.

"Prospect," he croaked. He licked his lips and tried

again. "Prospect Mountain. They're on the tramway."

"Copy that, we're on our way. Get your people out of there if you have any on the mountain." Raymond hesitated and then added, "Are you all right, Chief Colton?"

Colton felt the darkness sweeping him. He changed the channel to the one he used with Raven, struggling for air. He used his last breath to relay his final message.

"Raven, get off the mountain. If you make it, tell my family I love them."

— 22 —

Fenix couldn't hear anything aside from a dull ringing in his ears. Over the years, his hearing had been damaged from being too close to explosions, but this was the worst it had ever been.

I'm deaf. I'm fucking deaf!

Although he couldn't hear the gunshots, he could see his men on the platform overlooking the area where his mortar crew had been just moments before, firing at hostiles. Smoke swirled into the sky, obstructing his view to the west. The smell of burned flesh was overwhelming.

He was still trying to piece together what was happening. His first thought was one of the shitty Chinese mortar tubes had blown up, causing a chain reaction. But seeing his soldiers at the railing, this was no accident.

Some of Colton's people had made it up the slope and past his commandos. As he waited with Horton next to the aerial tramway shops, he had a feeling he knew exactly who it was—the same man who had ambushed the Sons of Liberty at the Castle a month earlier.

Damn that fucking Injun!

His soldiers were supposed to have taken care of Raven Spears the night before, and Thompson had promised Fenix the Indian's head after today's battle, but sometimes you just had to do things yourself.

Fenix crouch-walked around the corner of the

concrete ledge with his M4 at the ready. The gunfire from the platform, where his remaining men were in prone positions near the edge overlooking the western slope of the mountain, continued. Smoke shifted away from the firing zone, revealing the crater where his mortar crew had been.

He looked over at Horton. The sergeant's lips were moving, but Fenix still couldn't hear anything.

"What?" Fenix shouted, unable to hear his own voice. Horton pulled Fenix back behind the wall and then used his hands to tell the story. There were two hostiles over the slope. Horton pointed at the sky, which told Fenix they were going to have more company soon.

"Get to the trucks," Fenix said.

Horton nodded with understanding, and motioned for Fenix to follow him. They began to move along the concrete walkway curving away from the platform and toward the area where tourists had once boarded the red tramway cars. To his right, a staircase led to a coffeehouse, a gift shop, and the second lookout.

They took a path around the building to the south side, where multiple walkways had provided tourists with gorgeous views of the town, lake, and mountains. The trucks were on the other side of the building, disguised with camouflage tarps.

Both of the M240 guns remained in position overlooking the eastern side of the town, but Fenix didn't stop to grab either of them. The tides had changed on the Sons of Liberty, and he was once again feeling the vise clamping down.

He did pause to sneak a glance over the railing to see the battle on Highway 36. From what he could see, the fight was starting to die down. Fires still burned at the first barrier along the highway, and sporadic muzzles flashed from the second barrier. Return fire came from a cluster of vehicles where Colton's militia was making its last stand, but most everyone was dead or injured, from what he could see. Bodies littered the road.

His hearing began to return as he followed Horton around the building and onto a dirt path. Fenix glimpsed the outlines of their camouflaged trucks at the end of the path. The silence gave way to a ringing sound, and then the muffled noise of gunfire.

Fenix looked to the west, where his men were still firing at the two hostiles. Judging by the rapid fire, he had a feeling there were more Estes Park militia soldiers out there. No way could a single Indian and his friend keep his men so busy.

Horton suddenly stopped in the path and balled his hand.

Raising his rifle, Fenix searched for whatever had spooked the sergeant. He scanned the trees framing the path, looking for any movement. Horton did the same thing, sweeping the left while Fenix swept the right.

A flash of white darted between two ponderosas, and Fenix squeezed off a burst that slammed into the bark of the second tree. He followed the direction of the movement and fired again.

Shadows darted back and forth around the two men, and Fenix followed them with the barrel, moving from left to right and then back again. He exhaled an icy breath and tightened his grip on his rifle. His fingers were freezing, and he could hardly feel the stock.

Horton bumped into Fenix as he backpedaled and fired off his own shots into the forest on the other side of the road. The bullets pinged off rocks and slammed into the base of a tree.

Over the gunfire, Fenix caught the sound of a growling animal. He saw the dog a moment later, stalking them from behind a row of rocks.

"I got you now," Fenix said. He lined up his sights on the animal. He had never really liked dogs, and had no problem killing this one.

The animal walked slowly, giving Fenix a chance to line up a shot on its head. Before he could pull the trigger, Horton bumped into him again, sending the shot off target.

"You dumbass!" Fenix yelled.

Horton suddenly dropped to his knees, his hands behind his back as his fingers fished for the grip of a hatchet buried between his shoulder blades. Fenix quickly whirled to fire on the man that had thrown the blade.

The bullets lanced into the sky, narrowly missing the enraged face of Sam 'Raven' Spears, the Indian Fenix had been tracking for months.

Raven plowed into him with such force it knocked Fenix off his feet. On his way to the ground, he saw the dark eyes of the former Marine that wouldn't die.

The snow padded their landing, but Fenix still hit dirt hard enough that the wind escaped his lungs. He managed to wrap his arms around Raven's back and hold him down before the Indian could hit him in the face.

"I'm going to enjoy killing you," Raven growled.

"Good luck," Fenix snarled back, bringing his head up to hit Raven in the nose. The Indian reared back and brought one hand up to his face. He kept his other hand on Fenix's chest.

"Help!" Fenix shouted, hoping some of his men would hear. He craned his neck to look at the timber, searching the upside-down terrain for his soldiers, but all he saw was the growling Akita with a muzzle crusted in frozen blood icicles.

Something hot slid into Fenix's side, and his eyes widened as a sharp wave of pain rushed through his body. He screeched in agony. His eyes flitted to his stomach where Raven had jabbed him with a knife.

"He's mine, Creek," Raven said to the dog snarling at Fenix. The Akita slowly backed away, and Raven bent back down so his lips were next to Fenix's left ear.

"Guess a *redskin* got you after all," Raven hissed.

Fenix blinked and tilted his head so he could look Raven in the eyes. "You're nothing but a mongrel son of a—"

Gunfire silenced Fenix, and Raven looked over his shoulder as three Brandenburger Commandos fired at Creek. Bullets punched into the dirt, and the dog scrambled away.

Fenix groaned in pain as Raven rolled off his body, leaving the knife in his gut. The Indian tackled his dog and dove into the underbrush off the side of the path. Bullets ripped into the bushes a moment later, but Fenix couldn't see if the commandos had hit anything. He focused on the knife sticking out of his side, reaching for it with shaky hands.

"Sir, are you okay?" one of his men asked.

Fenix managed to point to where Raven and his dog had escaped. "Go...go find them."

Two of the men took off with their rifles, sweeping for Raven and Creek, while the third soldier bent down to help Fenix up.

"Best to leave that in for now," the man said.

Fenix saw it was Brian Sanderson, a forty-year-old

former corporal that had served under Fenix in Iraq. He was one of the best fighters left in the Sons of Liberty.

"Get me to the truck," Fenix said, his voice crackling.

Sanderson helped him down the path toward the vehicles. More gunshots rang out in the distance, but it was the sound of a helicopter that made Fenix freeze. His blood boiled as he looked up at the sky and saw the Black Hawk. This was the end of the road for the Sons of Liberty unless he got the hell out of here soon.

The bitch Secretary of Defense was coming for them.

***

Raven rested with his back against a ponderosa, panting. Creek was looking up at him. He could tell his dog was scared. Raven was scared too. But they were alive, and neither of them had been shot.

Yet.

He peered around the tree to check for the two Nazis hunting them. This would never have happened if he hadn't taken his time trying to kill Fenix. Now the man was about to escape.

Raven's mind shifted from thoughts of Sandra and Allie back to his friends on the road. The message from Colton had crossed into his muddled mind when he heard the faint but unmistakable sound of a helicopter on the horizon. The clock was ticking.

Shit, we have to get out of here.

If the military was on the way—if they knew Fenix was here—they would likely carpet-bomb the entire mountain. Raven checked the magazine in his Glock. There was one round left, but two men stalking them. His crossbow and M4 were both empty, and he'd left them behind to travel lighter. Both hatchets were buried in SOL soldiers, and his knife was stuck in the gut of their general.

One bullet, his bare hands, and a very pissed-off Akita.

It would have to do.

Raven looked to Creek. The dog knew what to do. He took off into the woods, leaping over a fallen log and vanishing behind a cluster of snow-covered rocks.

Drawing in a breath, Raven snuck a glance at the closest of the SOL men. They were moving slowly, their rifles sweeping with calculated precision. These men were trained killers. Probably former soldiers.

But they weren't Marines.

Raven moved out from behind the tree and aimed at the closest of the men, pulling the trigger. As soon as the bullet left the barrel, he was running for cover.

Gunfire riddled the snow where he had been a second earlier, and he leapt through the air into a ravine, sliding down the side. His boots hit the bottom, and he quickly climbed up the steep embankment on the other side. At the top, the remaining soldier was striding toward the area Raven had just abandoned.

Taking off at a hunch, Raven flanked the man. The sound of the approaching helicopter disguised the crunch of his boots in the snow. The man looked toward the sky, and Raven slipped behind a tree. He waited, and then moved back into the shadows. His advantage was the night vision goggles he still wore. The SOL soldier had nothing but moonlight.

Raven saw his opportunity a second later, the same moment Creek emerged from his hiding spot. Together, they slammed into the unsuspecting soldier. The dog tore into the man's leg while Raven climbed on top. He pulled a knife from the Nazi's belt, looked him in the eyes, and then traced the blade deeply across his neck.

"Let's go, Creek," Raven said. He traded the knife for the M4 on the ground and took off toward the trail where the vehicles were located. An engine growled nearby, and he ran faster, leaping over rocks and fallen logs until he got to the road.

The camouflage tarps had already been removed from the three Humvees, and Fenix and the man that had helped him were driving toward a curve in the road ahead.

Raven aimed the rifle and fired at the truck, bullets pinging off the back before it rounded the corner. He ran after them, his rifle clutched across his chest, sucking in cold air and doing his best to will his body forward. His muscles and mind were exhausted, and the pills were starting to wear off. Even worse, he kept thinking of Sandra and Allie. Not knowing their fate was eating him alive.

But this was his duty. He had stopped the mortar and M240 fire, and now he had to stop Fenix.

The sound of the helicopter grew louder, and he saw the big black bird to the west. It was a Black Hawk, and while he wasn't sure if it was the same one that had flown over Lily Lake, he was certain this was just a recon party. The real threat was coming from the south.

Raven froze at the low rumble of fighter jets. It had been ten minutes since he had talked to Colton, and it appeared the clock had finally run out.

Oh shit.

"On me, Creek!"

Raven looked to the path that curved off to his right, away from the other two Humvees. If Dale was still alive, he would be down there with Sarah. Fenix was already long gone. Raven would let the military deal with the bastard. He had to get off this mountain with Dale and the girl.

He made his way back to the smoking crater in the middle of the field. The scent of burned flesh and death filled his nostrils. Creek took off as Raven searched the gore-peppered area for Dale and Sarah.

A few minutes later, barking came from near a truck across the debris zone. Raven ran over to find Creek had located Dale and Sarah. The big man was on the ground behind the truck with the girl by his side.

Sarah said something to Raven, but he was too busy staring at the pickup. The explosion had speared the tires with shrapnel and peppered the hood. There was no way they were driving it out of here, and he didn't want to risk going back to the Humvees without having a key in hand.

"Raven, you have to help Dale," Sarah said.

Dale moaned. "Get her out of here, man."

"Not leaving you," Raven said. He pointed down the hill. "Sarah, go get the horses. They're tied up about a quarter mile down there. Creek, you go with her!"

She didn't hesitate, and took off with Creek while Raven bent down to help Dale up. The big retired soldier had taken at least three rounds, from what Raven could see, and couldn't stand on his own.

"Are those fighter jets?" he rasped.

Raven nodded. "We have to get off the mountain."

Dale leaned on him as a crutch, and they set off down the slope.

"You shouldn't have come back for me."

"Like you wouldn't have done the same for me," Raven said.

They navigated the rocky terrain like they had each been trained decades ago in boot camp, moving together as one. Brothers. Raven's head ached from a migraine, but adrenaline kept him going.

The roar of the fighter jets closed in. Raven had heard that sound many times, and knew what was coming. He moved faster, a mistake that cost him his footing. They went down together, rolling until they came to a stop against a fallen tree. Raven pushed himself up and reached back down to help Dale.

"No, man, I'm too far gone—" Dale protested.

Raven could barely hear past the raucous sound of the approaching jets. He bent down and yelled over the noise, "Get on!"

He picked Dale up and set off with the man over his shoulders. This wasn't the first time Raven had carried another man. Back in the Corps, he had carried his fair share, but that was years ago, and he was now hurt and out of shape. And Dale was heavy as a horse.

Raven focused on each step, trying to ignore the sound of incoming death. The jets were closing in. There were three of them, and they were heading right for Prospect Mountain. Several missiles slammed into the aerial tramway far above them. The explosions rocked the mountain, and Raven lost his balance again.

"We have to get up. They will be back," Raven said, crawling over to where Dale had fallen.

"Leave me," Dale said.

"Get your butt up, Dale!" shouted another voice. "That's an order!"

Dale and Raven both looked to their right to see Creek and then Sarah, who was standing with the reins of both horses clutched in her hands. The little firebrand had come through for them.

Creek barked at them as if to say, *move!*

Raven helped Dale over the back of Rhino, and then climbed on to Willow, with Sarah clinging to his back. Raven gave the horse a good nudge and then whistled at Rhino.

The horses took off down the steep path as the fighter jets were preparing to make their second pass. Raven looked up to see two of them were Chinese L-15/JL-10 and one was an American F-22 Raptor.

"Go, go, go!" he shouted.

Sarah wrapped her arms around his waist. The horses loped down the slope, hooves crunching over snow and fallen branches. The rumble of the jets was so loud Raven had to resist the urge to clamp his hands over his ears. Another salvo of missiles lanced away from the Chinese jets, and the F-22 Raptor dropped a bomb that tumbled away toward the top of the mountain.

"Hold on, Sarah!" Raven shouted.

The concussion seemed to shake the entire slope. Rocks and snow rained down, and shards of broken trees torpedoed through the air. A sharp piece of bark stuck into Raven's arm, and Sarah screamed in pain as she was also hit.

A wave of heat followed, and Raven looked over his shoulder at a tsunami of fire racing down the mountain. Creek was right behind them, running between trees and jumping over rocks.

Raven turned and focused on a bluff just ahead. If they could jump over the edge, they might just have a chance of not being barbequed.

"Jump, boy!" Raven shouted at Creek.

Willow protested when he kicked her, but a second

kick pushed her forward. Raven grabbed the reins on Rhino and pulled the beast after them. Creek didn't need to be told twice. The dog darted past them and leapt over the edge. The horses both jumped a moment later.

Sarah screamed again, and Raven looked up just as an avalanche of snow, fire, and debris rushed overhead.

— 23 —

The top of Prospect Mountain had vanished in a blast like a volcanic eruption. To Charlize, it seemed like a fitting end to the Nazi bastard that had terrorized Colorado and killed her brother.

Normally she would have felt the messy adrenaline rush that came with flying into battle. But this time she wasn't in the cockpit; she was in the troop hold of a Black Hawk, and right now there was nothing but anger coursing through her veins. She had waited a long time for a chance to get Dan Fenix, and that moment had finally arrived.

The bulkheads vibrated from the rumble of the squadron of fighter jets. The F-22 Raptor led them this time, and the two Chinese L-15/JL-10 tailed close behind. A second bomb dropped from the F-22, and another torrent of missiles hit the peak of the mountain, sending rock and flame toward the heavens.

"I hope there aren't any civilians up there. You think Colton's people got out in time?" said a voice.

Charlize pulled her gaze away from the view to look at Sergeant Fugate. The ten Green Berets were all watching the fighter jets pounding the aerial tramway. They were armed with a variety of weapons from M4s to M249 SAWs. All of them wore ballistic gear and helmets topped with "four eyes" night vision goggles.

They weren't the only ones that had come prepared

306

for a battle. Charlize also wore a ballistic vest and carried an M9. Flanking her were Colonel Raymond and Albert, both of them armed and ready for combat.

The Chinese jets veered away, screaming as they curved across the Estes Park valley. Charlize turned back to the windows with conflicted feelings. This was the first time she had authorized the Chinese pilots to use deadly force, and by doing so, she had not only dealt with Fenix and the Sons of Liberty—she had allowed General Lin a win for his Chinese troops. Hearing it had been missiles from the Chinese fighters that had helped take the Sons of Liberty down would be a great morale boost to the Chinese soldiers that had been ambushed by domestic terrorists in multiple locations throughout the United States.

Hopefully there is enough left to identify Fenix's remains, she thought. They would need to prove he was dead. The last thing she wanted was to make him a martyr and a ghost.

"Secretary Montgomery, there's still gunfire on Highway 36," said Captain Howey. "Looks like quite the fight down there. Some of the vehicles retreated when the jets showed up, but a group has remained behind."

Charlize looked toward the cockpit, where new pilots Captain Mayberry and Captain Howey were manning the controls.

"Looked like a bloodbath to me, and it's not stopping," Mayberry said.

Albert stirred in his seat and grimaced, apparently thinking the same thing as her. They had all hoped the military presence would stop the violence.

"What do you think we should do, Big Al?" she asked.

The question took him off guard. But that was the point. She wanted his honest opinion.

"Those may not be Latin Kings down there, like in Charlotte, but anyone that kills civilians is evil in my books. If they aren't scattering from the threat of a bomb and missiles, then they don't respect the government."

The explosions continued in the distance, the floor vibrating beneath her boots. For the past twenty minutes, they had stayed out of sight for fear of being snagged by an RPG or gunfire, but they couldn't wait any longer while the citizens of Estes Park were slaughtered.

Raymond must have known the order was coming. "I highly recommend not getting involved in a situation like this, ma'am. Stopping Fenix is one thing, but Estes Park and Fort Collins have warred over resources and—"

"Your dissent is noted, Colonel, but this isn't 'warring over resources.' This is a bloodbath with innocent civilians dying. We need to stop it."

Raymond sighed, but the Green Berets were ready for action. There was an approving gleam in Fugate's eye that made her sit up a little straighter.

"Take us down at a safe distance," Charlize said.

The bird quickly changed course, curving in a long arc around Prospect Mountain and over the town. They passed over a park outside town hall, the place where she had dropped off supplies after her brother's death.

Several buildings were burning around the town square. One of them collapsed as they passed over. Bodies littered the roads below, and even from this height she could tell they weren't all soldiers.

"My God," she said. Seeing the devastation and loss of life in the once-quaint tourist town nearly took her breath away. Houses burned in the residential areas. To the east, Estes Park Lake was nothing but a shallow puddle, the dam destroyed.

"Two o'clock," said one of the pilots.

She stood and made her way to the cockpit at a hunch to get a better view. The battle was still raging at the roadblock. A cluster of trucks had surrounded the Estes Park militia, and Sheriff Thompson's men were still firing.

"Sergeant Fugate, take out the hostiles at that barrier and save as many people as you can. This ends now," she ordered.

"Yes ma'am," Fugate said without hesitation.

"I really think you should reconsider, Secretary Montgomery," Raymond said. "It's not safe down there, as you can see."

"Colonel, I gave you an order."

Raymond pulled his M9 from his holster, and for a moment she thought he might be preparing to point it at her, but he checked the magazine and said, "I'm with you, ma'am."

The Black Hawk lowered to the street, and Fugate opened the door. The Green Berets piled out, fanning across the street toward the barrier. Charlize started to get out, but Albert put a hand on her sleeve.

"Stay behind me, ma'am," he said.

Before they could all exit, Captain Howey craned his helmet out of the cockpit. "Ma'am, I just got a report from our Raptor pilot that a Humvee escaped Prospect Mountain and is heading south on Highway 7. They are asking for permission to fire."

Albert looked back at Charlize. "You think it could be Fenix?" he asked.

"Shit," she said, her eyes flitting back to the road. The Green Berets were running toward the burning vehicles and gunfire. Raymond had paused on the street, his pistol still in his grip.

"Tell those fighters to hold their fire and stand by. We'll check it out," she said. "If it's Fenix, I want to be the one to end him."

Albert nodded, and Raymond jumped back inside the chopper, leaving the Green Berets to fight with the Estes Park militia. The bird lifted back into the sky, and the pilots veered south.

Smoke choked the skyline, rising off the burning structures and the smoldering top of Prospect Mountain. She pulled the M9 out of her holster and palmed a magazine into the gun. She pulled the slide back on her pistol to chamber a round. Raymond straightened his flak jacket, and Albert checked the magazine in his M4. They both looked at her as the bird continued over the town toward Highway 7.

"I've got eyes," said Captain Howey a moment later. "One o'clock."

She looked through the cockpit windshield at a pair of headlights on the road. The beams flicked off when the driver realized they were being tailed, but it was already too late.

"Open the door," she instructed Albert.

He moved over and pulled it open, letting in a rush of frigid air. She grabbed a handhold as the pilots moved into position over the highway.

"I'll take out the tires," Albert said. He shouldered his rifle and waited for Charlize to give him the okay. She waited a few more seconds until they were about a hundred feet behind the Humvee, then dipped her head.

Albert squeezed off an automatic burst, hitting the back of the vehicle and then painting the side with rounds. The driver swerved but leveled out and continued speeding down the highway.

"Get back!" Raymond yelled as the front passenger window rolled down. A rifle barrel stuck out of it, but the pilots were already moving. They banked hard to the left, out of the line of fire, giving Albert another angle. He fired at the driver's side, taking out the window and hitting the door with several rounds.

This time the Humvee veered into the ditch, where it slammed into an embankment and came to a violent stop.

"Nice shot, Big Al," she said. She motioned for the pilots to put them down on the road.

"Hold on," Captain Howey said.

Charlize made sure she had a good grip on the overhead handle as the Black Hawk descended to the road. The bird set down gently, with only a slight jolt as the wheels hit the snow-covered highway.

"Stay here, and kill those rotors," she instructed the pilots.

Albert jumped out first, his M4 trained on the smoking Humvee. Charlize and Raymond went next with their pistols up. The rotor drafts hit them in the back as they moved low under the blades, which were already beginning to slow.

Albert moved in front of her to shield her just in case anyone had survived the crash. Smoke whipped away from the hood of the truck and into the night. When they got to the edge of the road, the passenger door suddenly burst open and a man slumped out into the ditch. Albert aimed his rifle at the potential hostile, and Raymond walked to the right for a better firing field on the left side of the truck.

"Don't shoot!" the man yelled, one of his hands in the air. The other was clutched around something protruding from his side.

Raymond gave the all clear a moment later. "Driver's dead," he said.

The rotors waned behind them, the final blasts of cold air rustling her clothing as she stared at the man in the ditch. His face was covered in cuts, and his nose was bleeding. Long, dark hair hung over his face. He flicked it away, revealing two hate-filled eyes.

Was this him? Was this the man she had been hunting for so long?

"Stay here, ma'am," Albert said.

"Like hell," she replied, moving past him with her pistol up. They walked to the ditch where the man was lying on his back, a knife handle sticking out of his gut. He winced in pain and squinted up at Charlize.

"That you, bitch?" he asked.

Albert moved forward, but she put a hand on his back to stop him before he could do anything rash.

"I've got this," she said.

The look Albert gave her was one of deep concern, but there was understanding too. He knew how important it was that she be the one to bring Fenix down.

"I've got your back, ma'am," Albert said.

"I know, Big Al."

She walked closer, with Albert by her side. The scent of diesel filled the night as it leaked from the tank of the Humvee. The injured man watched her like a bird studying its prey, dark eyes following her every move.

"Dan Fenix, I presume?" she asked.

The man grinned. "You finally got me, Charlize," he said.

"Secretary Montgomery," she corrected.

"Not to me you're not. You're just a traitor bitch that let the damned Chinamen overrun my country."

Charlize wiped the smirk off his face with a pistol whip. He cried out in pain, and then spat two teeth into the snow. He glared up at her with stone-cold eyes. There was a hatred there that she had only seen in a few people before.

"You can take me in, but my cause will live on while I await trial," Fenix said, spitting more blood. "I've created a movement that you can't stop."

"Wrong," she said.

"You think you can stop it?" Fenix asked. He smiled again, a wide, shit-eating grin that exposed his broken front teeth.

Charlize looked over at Albert. He was a lawman and had always followed the rules, but she could tell by the look on his face that he condoned what she was about to do.

"Your movement will die with you," she said. Bending down, she yanked the chain with his dog tags off his neck.

The grin on Fenix's bloodied face vanished and his brows furrowed as she backed away. He held up a hand. "Now let's not be hasty, Secretary Montgomery," he said, the tone of his voice changing to something almost respectful. "I may be guilty of a few crimes, but I still have rights. I'm a citizen of this country."

"No. You're a domestic terrorist. Nobody will care if I burn you at the stake."

Fenix seemed to relax at that statement, apparently not taking her literally. She jerked her chin at Albert, and they moved back up the ditch to the shoulder of the road, where Raymond watched with his pistol aimed at Fenix.

"What are you doing?" Fenix asked.

She grabbed a flare from Albert's tactical vest. Fenix's

eyes widened when he saw what she was holding.

"No," he said, raising both hands. "Please, you can't...you can't do this. I have rights."

She pulled off the top and hit the flare's tip against the striker surface. A flame burst out, and she held it there for a moment while Fenix pleaded for his life.

"You bitch!" Fenix screamed as she tossed the flare into the ditch. The gas instantly caught fire, raging around the Humvee. Albert led Charlize to a safe distance, where they stopped to watch with Raymond.

Fenix had made it to his stomach, and crawled several feet before the flames engulfed his legs and then his back and neck. He let out an agonized scream as it consumed his body. He flopped and squirmed to try and put the flames out. She had wanted to leave behind an easily-identifiable body, but watching him burn was too satisfying. Besides, she had his dog tags to prove he was dead.

Charlize stood there for a good ten minutes, even after Fenix had stopped moving. Sometimes justice was a very violent thing, especially at the end of the world.

***

Sandra wiped the sweat and tears from her face with a sleeve, and focused on the doors of the emergency room, trying to see through her suddenly blurred vision. After Chief Colton had arrived with five bullet holes in him, she didn't know how much more she could take. He had died long before he made it to the hospital, but Lindsey had insisted on bringing his body here anyways.

More Green Berets were streaming into the room. They had pushed Thompson's men back, and were now bringing in more injured. Sergeant Fugate, the leader of the team, was helping Lindsey Plymouth. She had a shard of metal sticking through her forearm, but she looked just as fierce and determined as ever.

"It's over!" Lindsey yelled. "The battle for Estes Park is over."

For a moment, everyone stopped what they were doing to look at Lindsey. Sandra finished the bandage she was putting on a patient and took in the makeshift emergency room in a quick scan. Lanterns lit the open space, illuminating what looked more like a field hospital from the Civil War than a modern medical facility. Beds with severely wounded patients surrounded her in all directions. There were buckets collecting blood. Hacksaws and knives glistening red on metal tables. Over the cries and moans, Lindsey continued her announcement.

"We won," Lindsey said. There wasn't enthusiasm in her words, and Sandra had a feeling it had to do with the fact they had lost so many people in the attack. "Thompson's forces have retreated. What's left of them, that is." She continued talking, but Sandra ignored the words when she saw two new patients moving toward the open doors.

"Sam!" Sandra shouted.

Raven limped into the open space with Sarah by his side. Just behind them, two soldiers were helping carry Dale inside. Sandra let out a sigh when she saw her brother looked mostly okay. He raised a hand at her and forced a smile. Then he saw Colton's body and his hand fell limply to his side.

She hurried toward Raven and wrapped her arms around him when they met. Behind them, more people piled into the lobby outside the hospital. She didn't recognize three of them. Wait…hadn't she seen the woman with short-cropped hair walking through the lobby before? The doors to the operating room shut, blocking Sandra's view.

"You okay, sis?" Raven asked.

She managed a nod. "Is Allie okay?"

"The high school was untouched," Raven said. "Everyone is fine there."

"Where's Creek?"

"Sitting outside."

Sarah tried to dart away from them, but Sandra bent down to check her for injuries.

"I'm fine," the girl said. "I'm going to sit by Dale."

Sandra nodded and looked back to her brother.

"Is it really over?" she asked.

"I think so." He turned to look at Colton again, a tear flowing freely down his filthy cheek.

"He was hit seven times before he finally went down," Lindsey said, stepping over with her hand still gripping her wound.

"I should have been there," Raven said quietly.

"You saved lives, Sam. If it weren't for you, we would have all died on that road, and those mortars would have destroyed the high school. You and Dale are heroes."

"No," Raven said. "Chief Colton is the hero."

"Sandra, we need you!" Doctor Duffy yelled. He was standing next to a table where Dale was stretched out. Sarah held the big man's hand.

"Go help him," Raven said.

Sandra nodded and left Raven and Lindsey to speak privately. The macabre sounds of the battle's aftermath took over, but Sandra was able to drown out the screams and cries to focus on Dale.

"You're going to be okay," she said.

Dale looked at her, his face pale from the blood loss, but his eyes alert.

"Your brother saved us," he said. "He saved us all."

Sandra wanted to smile, but all she could do was nod. Chief Colton had died a hero's death in the battle for Estes Park, but apparently a new hero had also emerged—someone she'd never thought would be a leader. The fight was over for now, and for the first time since the North Korean attack, she trusted they would be okay. Her brother and Lindsey would watch out for Estes Park in Colton's stead.

— Epilogue —

Three months after the North Korean attack

Raven Spears fidgeted with his tie. He hated ties, and he hated wearing a suit, but today he was an honored guest at the unveiling of the new White House, along with his sister and niece. Creek trotted along next to them. The dog hated being on a leash about as much as Raven hated being in a suit.

"Don't worry, boy. We'll be free again in a few days," Raven said with a grin.

Creek stopped to lift a leg on a fire hydrant. Allie gripped Raven's other hand, gawking at the skyscrapers towering above them. It was fairly warm for December, but not warm enough to keep away the snow. Light flakes fluttered from the sky, and a snowplow idled at the next intersection. The driver smoked a cigarette while he waited to see if the snow would materialize into anything heavier.

It was a long time since Raven had last been in New York City, and the metropolis had changed dramatically. Lower Manhattan looked relatively normal, but although the lights were on, it wasn't the bustling zone of fancy boutiques, high-end restaurants, and twenty-dollar girly drink bars that he remembered from his last visit. Most of the shops were still closed, and plywood covered windows and doors.

The sidewalks and intersections were no longer bustling. Instead, small knots of civilians rushed from one place to another. There weren't people talking on cell phones or listening to music either. In their place Raven saw groups of Chinese and American soldiers patrolling, rifles cradled, but eyes flitting like hawks.

The streets weren't filled with bumper-to-bumper traffic or cabs honking at daring bicyclists trying to squeeze between traffic. The few vehicles that were running were stopped at roadblocks manned by NYPD officers.

Security was tight, but while the city appeared safe, Raven knew there was danger outside—and possibly inside—the island of Manhattan.

Smoke fingered away from fires on the horizon, and the military flight in had shown a city that looked like a war zone. Brooklyn had fallen into anarchy after the North Korean attack, and hundreds of buildings had been burned to the ground. He had heard rumors of mass graves.

"What are they doing here?" Allie asked.

Raven looked down to see her pointing at the Chinese soldiers. Sandra gave him a look that said *You explain this one, Uncle Raven.*

"Those men are here to help us get things back to normal, *Agaliga.* They are here to help."

"Why don't they have them in Estes Park then?" she asked.

"Because we're not a big enough town," Sandra replied.

The answers seemed to satisfy the girl's curiosity, but she continued to examine the foreign soldiers in white uniforms walking along the sidewalk and in the streets. Raven did his best to ignore them. At first he hadn't trusted the Chinese, but Lindsey had told him the word coming in over the airways was mostly positive. If they were here to finish what North Korea had started, they would have done so a long time ago.

"This way," Raven said, shepherding his family down Church Street. At the next intersection, FEMA workers were handing out meals from the back of a semi-trailer to a crowd of civilians. Raven recalled the food vendors that used to have carts on the corners, and wondered if the smell of hotdogs, pretzels, and ethnic cuisine would ever return to these streets.

"I'm hungry," Allie said.

"We're going to eat in a bit," Sandra replied. "We're almost there, see?"

Allie followed her mother's finger toward the One World Trade Center. The new location of the White House had seemed odd at first, but now Raven understood the significance. The tower represented the strength and resolve of the American people to rebuild and keep fighting.

Creek pulled on the leash to paint another hydrant, but this time Raven scolded him. The dog did as ordered and fell into line next to Raven. Security increased as they approached the One World Trade Center, and Raven didn't want his best friend mistaken for a stray.

"Keep moving," an NYPD officer said, gesturing toward Greenwich Street. Dozens of people in civilian clothing were streaming toward a gated entrance with military sentries just outside the 9/11 Memorial.

It took them a while to get to the front of the line, where a stern-looking American soldier that reminded Raven of Jake Englewood asked for their badges. Raven handed over their credentials. The man looked at each one, checking Raven, Allie, and Sandra. Then he looked down at the dog and raised a brow.

"He's the guest of honor today," Raven said with a grin. He reached into his pocket and pulled out a slip that had been non-negotiable—the military approval for Raven to bring Creek to the event.

"He's a service dog," Sandra said.

The soldier looked back to Raven and smiled. "I heard about you guys. Welcome to New York City."

"Thank you…" Raven looked at the man's tag. "Sergeant Maddow."

"Sorry, but I have to ask," Maddow replied, "are you carrying any weapons?"

"Yes," Raven said.

Maddow jerked his chin toward another soldier next to him. "Cunningham will have to take them for now, but you can pick them up on your way out."

Raven hesitated. He didn't like going anywhere unarmed, but he also didn't have a choice. He reached into his suit and pulled the Glock out from the holster. Then he bent down and pulled a .45 revolver from his right boot. He handed the guns to Cunningham.

"That it?" the soldier asked.

Raven just looked at him.

"You got a knife or anything?" Maddow asked.

Raven shrugged and then bent down to pull out a knife from his left boot. He handed that over too.

"We good?" Raven asked.

Cunningham chuckled, and Maddow handed Raven a

slip of paper with a number on it.

"Don't lose this," he said.

Raven took the slip and led his family through the open gates down Fulton Street toward the north memorial pools.

"You're famous, Uncle Raven," Allie said.

Raven shook his head. "No, I'm not. Creek is."

She chuckled and Raven directed them toward a group of people gathering in the open space between the pools and the front of the One World Trade Center building.

Hundreds of people.

From all walks of life.

Raven had always felt out of place in crowds, and the thought of being recognized in front of so many people, especially while dressed in this silly suit, really made him nervous. Sandra reached over and squeezed his wrist.

"You should be excited," she said. "This is a huge honor, and we're very proud of you."

"Yeah," Allie said with a smile. "You're a hero!"

Raven took in a deep breath as they made their way through the crowd. No matter how hard he tried to sell it in his own mind, he couldn't bring himself to believe he deserved any sort of recognition. He had stewed about even coming here after receiving the invite. But they were here now, and he needed to make the best of it.

"Sam Spears," came a booming voice.

"That's me," Raven said, holding up a hand. A large African American man dressed in slacks, a navy pea coat covering a blue button-down shirt, and a black tie, walked toward Raven.

"I'm Officer Albert Randall, the head of Secretary Montgomery's security detail. Welcome to New York City. Thank you for coming." He nodded politely at the others. "You must be Sandra and Allie Spears."

"I like your shoes, mister," Allie said.

Raven looked at Albert's new Air Jordans and grinned.

"Thank you," Albert said.

They followed the officer through the growing crowd to two rows of white chairs facing a ribbon stretched across the entrance to the One World Trade Center. Several Marines stood stiffly on both sides of a podium set up behind the ribbon. Raven swelled with pride at the sight of his brothers.

"Please have a seat," Albert said, gesturing toward the front row. The chairs were already filling with people dressed in fancy clothes. He hesitated for several seconds. Never in his life had he sat in a front row. He could tell by their expensive suits and fur coats that the other people sitting here were some of the most powerful people left in the country. Politicians, the one-percenters, and military officers with chests full of medals.

Some things don't ever change.

Several faces turned in his direction as he finally moved down the row to find a seat. Scrutinizing eyes swept over his ponytail and dark skin, his sister and niece in their simple dresses and coats, and finally on Creek.

"Is there a problem?" he said to a middle-aged woman wearing a fur coat.

"Not at all," she said, focusing back on the podium.

Creek growled at her.

"Sorry, lady, my dog doesn't like your coat," Raven said.

Sandra smiled politely at the woman as she pulled her collar closer together.

"It's okay, Sam," Sandra whispered. She took a seat with Allie and patted for Raven to sit next to them. He did as ordered, and stroked Creek's fur to calm himself. His heart was beating like an automatic rifle. It was worse than the pre-combat jitters. He was more nervous now than when he was squaring off with SOL soldiers.

A crowd gathered behind the white chairs. Albert made his way to the front of the building, where he pulled out his radio and spoke into it. The glass doors of the front entrance finally opened, disgorging two more security guards and Colonel Raymond. It was Raymond who had convinced Raven to come here.

Behind the colonel stood Secretary of Defense Charlize Montgomery. She looked stately in a white coat. Albert and another officer in plain clothes led her toward the podium, their eyes scanning the crowd.

Raven continued to pat Creek's head. The dog looked back with his one eye and then licked Raven's hand. His loyal friend always knew how to calm him down.

Secretary Montgomery stepped up to the podium. Ty wheeled his chair up next to her.

"Good afternoon, everyone. For those of you that don't know me, I'm Secretary of Defense Charlize Montgomery, and this is my son Ty," she said.

Ty raised a hand in a shy wave. The crowd quieted, and Creek's ears perked to listen.

"I'd like to welcome you to the One World Trade Center, and new home of the White House. President Diego wished he could be here with us all today, but he is working on important matters in California." She smiled. "It's my great pleasure to be here in his absence and recognize a few of our honored guests in the audience. When I finish, I'll talk a little bit about the future of our country. After that, we will head inside and begin tours of the new White House that is now located on floors five through ten."

Raven looked up at the building towering above them. He had been a young Marine the day the Twin Towers came crashing down. So much had happened since then, but he was proud of the man he had become through the chaos, and for the first time he was excited to stand up in front of these people, to represent all those that had died so this day could happen.

"Today, we're here for the ribbon-cutting of the White House, but we're also here for much more than that. We're here to remember everyone we've lost over the past three months, and we're here to celebrate our country." Her words reflected what Raven was thinking. "This, *this* is what America represents. Resilience. Strength. Freedom."

She paused and smiled sadly at her son. "Many of our heroes aren't here today. Today we bow our heads to remember them, and to thank them for their sacrifice."

Raven lowered his head with those around him, thinking of the heroes they'd lost: Captain Jake Englewood, Major Nathan Sardetti, and Chief Marcus Colton. But he wasn't thinking about how they had died—he was thinking about how they had lived: Honorable, brave, and selfless.

"Thank you," said Secretary Montgomery, looking up at the crowd. Her eyes scanned the crowd, and then the rows of seated people, stopping on Raven. His heart thumped.

"We're also here to recognize several people that are still with us. These men and women have shown extreme acts of bravery in the face of pure evil since the North

Korean attacks. To start, I'd like to call Officer Libby Hawks up to the podium."

Raven twisted in his chair to see a young woman dressed in an NYPD uniform. Her red hair, freckled features, and confident gait reminded him of Captain Lindsey Plymouth. He held back a smile as he remembered Lindsey's final words before he got on the chopper. She'd not only agreed to that drink he had been hounding her about, but also a meal when he got back from his trip.

"Thank you again, Officer Hawks, for your service to the citizens of New York City," Secretary Montgomery said once she'd presented the woman with her medal. The crowd clapped while Hawks walked back to her seat. Secretary Montgomery directed a smile at Raven and motioned for him to stand.

"I'm also honored to have Marine Staff Sergeant Sam Spears from Estes Park, Colorado and his Akita, Creek, here with us today," she said. "Come on up here, you two."

"That's you, Uncle Raven," Allie said with a huge grin.

"Come on, boy," Raven said. The dog stood and followed Raven down the row. Several people moved their legs to let him and Creek through.

"Sorry...excuse us...sorry...thank you," Raven said politely. He could feel the eyes on his back, but he ignored them. He wasn't here to impress these people; he was here to remember his friends.

"I appreciate you making the long journey here, Staff Sergeant," said Secretary Montgomery. She shook his hand. "Thank you for everything you have done for our country. And thank you, too, Creek."

She bent down to pet Creek on his head. His tail

whipped back and forth. Raven moved next to the podium as Secretary Montgomery stepped back up to the mic.

"Staff Sergeant Sam Spears, better known by his friends as Raven, helped bring down the leader of the Sons of Liberty." She looked over at him. "Actually, Raven helped bring down the entire organization. He and his wonder dog put their lives in harm's way more times than I can count."

"Thank you for what you did at the Castle, sir," Ty said. He held up a medal, and Raven bent down so the boy could put it around his neck.

"My pleasure, buddy," Raven said.

Ty pulled a second medal off his lap and said, "Come here, boy."

Creek looked up to Raven, who gave his dog permission with a nod. Trotting over, Creek sat on his hind legs and let Ty put the medal around his neck.

Colonel Raymond gave Raven a firm handshake. "Good job, Marine," he said.

Secretary Montgomery nodded firmly. "Good job, indeed. Would you like to say a few words?" she asked.

Raven swallowed hard and looked toward the crowd. The woman wearing a fur coat was still glaring at him like he didn't belong here.

"Yes, I think I would, Secretary Montgomery," he finally said, moving over to the mic. He adjusted it and then grabbed the side of the podium, focusing on his sister and Allie in the front row.

"I am not a hero," Raven said. "I have never been a hero. In fact, I have done some very bad things in my life. Some of them I did to protect my family, my town, and my country, and I would do it again. There are far better men that should be standing where I am today."

Raven paused and carefully pulled the medal from his head, careful not to get it snagged on his ponytail. He held it in his hand and said, "Today I'm dedicating this to those men, and to Ty Montgomery."

He looked over at the boy, who had a surprised look dawning on his face. Raven stepped away from the podium. Charlize took his place there and said, "You are a hero whether you want to be or not."

"Thank you, ma'am." Raven grabbed Creek's leash to lead him back to his seat. For the first two seconds, they walked in silence, everyone staring at the American Indian man and his dog. And then, to his surprise, the audience broke into applause and stood. Even the woman with the fur coat rose to her feet and clapped.

Raven returned to his seat, heart pounding with pride.

"Good job, brother," Sandra said. She placed a hand on his thigh and he couldn't help but smile. The grin lasted for the rest of the award ceremony. When Secretary Montgomery finished handing out medals, her words took on a more serious tone as she spoke about the state of the country.

"It will take a long time for our country to recover, but one thing is certain. People like the heroes we have recognized today will help us get there. We have already had great success in bringing the power back on in several states. Our supply lines and distribution efforts are running smoother than ever. Our Survival Centers are operating at full capacity, but with the help of our NATO allies and the Chinese, our citizens are staying alive in desperate times. However, there are still threats out there." She paused to look again at Raven.

"Domestic terrorists, gangs, and outlaws have taken

advantage of suffering Americans, and while we have brought down Dan Fenix, there are more like him out there. On top of that, the North Korean threat persists. We have already taken out two terrorist cells in Chicago and Los Angeles."

The Secretary of Defense stopped again to let the words sink in. Raven appreciated her candor with the crowd. They needed to hear this.

"I'm dedicated to preventing evil from planting roots and growing in our country. I will eliminate every Dan Fenix out there, with the help of men and women like Staff Sergeant Spears and Officer Hawks." Secretary Montgomery looked over her shoulder to Albert, who walked forward with a pair of scissors.

"What does she mean?" Sandra asked Raven.

"I think she has something planned for me and Creek."

Secretary Montgomery gestured toward the crowd. "If our honored guests would please join me."

Raven led Creek back up to the ribbon, where everyone crowded behind Ty's wheelchair. The boy held up the scissors and cut through the ribbon to the sound of applause.

"Today marks a new beginning for our country," Secretary Montgomery said. "Today, our government has a home again."

The clapping continued for several minutes. The glass doors to the One World Trade Center whisked open, and tour guides began instructing people to follow them into the building. While Sandra and Allie made their way toward Raven, the Secretary of Defense pulled him to the side.

"So, Staff Sergeant, how would you and Creek feel about hunting some Nazis and North Koreans?" she asked.

Creek looked up, his tail wagging.

Raven patted the dog's head. "We thought you'd never ask, ma'am."

—End of Book 4—

About the Author

Nicholas Sansbury Smith is the New York Times and USA Today bestselling author of the Hell Divers series, the Orbs series, the Trackers series, the Extinction Cycle series, and the new Sons of War series. He worked for Iowa Homeland Security and Emergency Management in disaster mitigation before switching careers to focus on storytelling. When he isn't writing or daydreaming about the apocalypse, he enjoys running, biking, spending time with his family, and traveling the world. He is an Ironman triathlete and lives in Iowa with his wife, their dogs, and a house full of books.

Printed in Great Britain
by Amazon